emerge 19

ABOUT *emerge*

In its nineteenth year, *emerge* is an annual publication produced by students, alumni, faculty, and industry guests of the Writer's Studio. Students are assigned to teams and, over a four-month period, work with the publisher, editors, designers, our printer, and local booksellers to produce, market, and sell this anthology.

ABOUT THE WRITER'S STUDIO

The Writer's Studio is an award-winning creative writing program at Simon Fraser University that provides writers with mentorship, instruction, and hands-on book publishing experience. Over the course of a year, students work alongside a community of writers with a mentor, developing their writing through regular manuscript workshops and readings. Many of our alumni have become successful authors, and have gone on to careers in the publishing industry.

The Writer's Studio 2019 mentors:
Carrie Mac—*Speculative Fiction and Writing for Young Adults*
Kevin Chong—*Fiction*
Joanne Arnott—*Poetry and Lyric Prose*
JJ Lee—*Narrative Non-Fiction*

The Writer's Studio Online 2018–2019 mentors:
Eileen Cook—*Speculative Fiction and Writing for Young Adults*
Jen Sookfong Lee—*Fiction*
Kayla Czaga—*Poetry and Lyric Prose*
Claudia Cornwall—*Narrative Non-Fiction*
Stella Harvey—*Fiction and Personal Narrative*

sfu.ca/write

emerge 19

THE WRITER'S STUDIO ANTHOLOGY

Chelene Knight
Foreword

CREATIVE WRITING
AT SFU CONTINUING STUDIES

SFU SFU PUBLICATIONS

Simon Fraser University, Vancouver, B.C.

Cover Design: Solo Corps Creative
Cover Illustration: Karen Poirier
Typesetting and Interior Design: Solo Corps Creative
Printing: Friesens Corporation

Printed in Canada

LIBRARY AND ARCHIVES CANADA CATALOGUING IN PUBLICATION

emerge 19: The Writer's Studio anthology /
Foreword by Chelene Knight

ISSN 1925-8267
ISBN 978-1-77287-064-0 (paperback)
ISBN 978-1-77287-065-7 (ebook)

A cataloging record for this publication is available
from Library and Archives Canada.

Creative Writing | SFU Continuing Studies
Simon Fraser University
515 West Hastings Street
Vancouver, B.C., Canada, V6B 5K3
sfu.ca/write

SFU Publications
1300 West Mall Centre
8888 University Drive
Burnaby, B.C., Canada, V5A 1S6

To the families and friends who
fanned the flames of our urgent wish
to write these stories—thank you
for your support, generosity, and belief.

Water, stories, the body,
all the things we do, are mediums
that hide and show what's hidden.

Study them,
and enjoy this being washed
with a secret we sometimes know,
and then not.

—*Rumi*

Contents

NON-FICTION

FICTION

Foreword

Home. This is the word I've always had tucked in my pocket even before I started writing. Every day I ask myself: what does it truly mean to be at home? Whether home is a community of writers, or whether it is infused into the core of the writing itself, having a literal and metaphorical place to share, exist, and grow, is integral to thriving in the publishing world. Early on in my writing career, I learned that establishing a community of my peers would make or break the possibility of seeing any success as a writer. Writing alone is just the beginning. It's phase one. In order to write good stories, I had to begin building. I knew this from day one. I had to bring all my pieces into the room with me.

As writers, with our fragments spread out before us, it's important that we learn to embrace the mess that is a first draft. We have to feel at home in the mess. We acknowledge the building, the glueing, and we hold close the beauty of the patchwork. Then, we sit alone stitching together puzzle pieces until we have something that resembles semi-completeness. This is the solitary act of the writer.

When I first walked into the Writer's Studio orientation almost seven years ago and saw the chairs positioned to form a tight circle, I knew I was no longer writing in solitude. I felt safe knowing that this circle of writers would help me rip the loose threads from my work. They would help me pull the fabric taut, and iron out the wrinkles. They would be my second pair of eyes and hands. *This* is the job of community. This is what makes writing good writing, and it's what enables writers to keep going.

As you read through these stories, essays, and poems, you will see and feel community. You will be pushed into the notion of strength, hold in your hands the ties to time and place, and the importance of putting down roots. The students anthologized in this book are resilient. Their stories are time capsules. With each turn of the page you will be taken away to unknown worlds built from broken pieces. Every story, poem, and essay has earned its space, and offers you much more than a peek through a dusty window, or a partially open door. With this book you are offered a seat at their table.

We need community when we write and when we don't write. An anthology is a community made of stories. Like community, stories are created through hope and a glimmer of a dream.

And it is from a dream that sparks the desire to enter into a contract with the page. No single piece of writing is created without a spark or without that *one remaining brick wall*. You will see the flickering ignite an idea and watch it bloom into fantastical colours, sounds, and tastes— this is the evolution of the written word; this is *emerge 19*.

—*Chelene Knight*, Vancouver, 2019

Poetry

Ashley Hynd
Aki

once before I was a song unsung
in my own throat I knew you
before you even knew yourself

a shipyard scattered with broken
bits of wood, a forest lot abandoned
with one remaining brick wall

I dreamt you

head cradled to my breast, lips soft
pressed against your scalp, the scent
of your unwashed hair in my nose

dearest lover

oldest friend

all this nothing that is to become of you

Blinking my way into heaven

I was the Sahara Desert before monsoon
licking cracked lips when I saw my first
glimpse of God he was holding back tears
at the sight of a dove pecking a dead
dog's eyes out   I cleared your blood
from my beak — tasted lies — decided
it was best that the dog get up walk away
past bookstores past bakeries past parks
with uncomfortable swings — the kind
that squeeze your hips tighter than a
night at the bar and cause you to get surgery
in your eighties   the kind that
make your legs forget how to walk away
from angry gods who teach like everyone
is listening — still, you hear nothing
but the crinkling of paper label it coconut
sweat and marijuana   waver
on the horizon bent and blurry sipping tea
steeped in the tears of children   green
as the day you went drinking to drown
cultural appropriation with the repulsive
tongue of serendipity hung slack
from your mouth   when you got home
there were three flowers in a vase
on the kitchen table — you asked God

what it meant he said *just enjoy being
loved my child* — so you never bought me
flowers instead turned me into a mouthful
of forevers a dialect clenched between
teeth — you will answer all my questions
speak in tongues of melted snow remain
grounded in this military innocence
call back because the clocks were wrong
*ayaa   nibwaakaawininiwag   gaa   wiikaa
getenanda-gikendan*—water   r   u   n   s
through   the   cracks   in   the   mud

Rebellion is on her way

Resistance   Resilience

trust is a shaking
in your   bones
before stepping,

a vibration just   the vibration held
out of ear drum,   by your heart beat
a rhythm you know   drummed rhythm
but can't seem to follow,   you know to follow,
you're offbeat   step in kind

all these skeletons   past these skeletons

of glass stretched
towards sky,

under street car   despite street car

rumbled history

we were here,   *we are here,*

we were meeting here   *we are still living*
long before they were   *truth shaking*
trust shaking   *in their bones*

we were here   *we are here*

we are still here

Anishinaabeg

my people are the bones
beneath this earth that know
better

than oil and consumption
and always burning

my people are soft sweat
after love making
laughter

in a field of sisters singing
one-another into safety

my people are fresh dew
on morning ground that
remembers

my people are history
praying to repeat itself

Yong Nan Kim
My Year Without Books

1976 Busan, Korea
Mosquitos 1

waves of mosquitos rise from the wet pools by the creek
when the sun sets there is a place between light and dark

fewer and fainter the mothers' calls of *come eat dinner!*
you can see quiet grey between gold and silver

you can hold your breath and wait   finally sigh
when evening comes looking for innocents

the dark air thickening with waves of mosquitos
an oncoming choir getting louder and louder

they surge through closed doors and windows
leaving us to retreat into mosquito tents

spiral-shaped incense burns toward its centre
as each millimetre glows   white-grey ashes land

on the dish a funeral procession on my favourite windowsill
my hiding place between metal and ricepaper

i travel the world in hundreds of novels
there must be unknown endless stories like mosquitos

1979 Santos Beach, São Paulo, Brasil
Mosquitos 2

we are walking in a wet field of tall grass at night
noisy brush teems with creeping and crawling undertow
a brand-new house sleeps in the middle of the field
lonely nights stream out of the windows with dim TV light

a pale young woman peeps out while nursing her baby
she doesn't smile when she sees us
your father's not here then shuts the door
i'm not sure why we can't stay

retracing our steps we walk through the dark field
the mosquitos escorting us
my friend's mother is a wild woman in strappy dress
i have questions i don't know how to ask

at the beach a voluptuous blonde in a *tanguinha* bikini
clings to rugged dark blue Fausto
that night there is a new twosome
whispering moaning giggling in our hotel room

mosquitos whine   they needle into my dreams

1979 Rua Guaiaúna, Penha, São Paulo, Brasil
Dona Paraíba

on Guaiaúna Street in my new home
at the edge of the dunes of urban dirt
Dona Paraíba lives in the basement of her store
a chandelier of dried pig's ears and *linguiça*
the long departed in pickle jars
convivially lined on shelves
rice and black beans stacked in front
an apothecary dark but alive
sword woman Dona Paraíba
flings open the door
swings her shiny machete
sparks fly in a piercing screech
i'll show those boys!
she wins us the battle
inspires us to wage war
us little girls
with water to dump and rocks to throw

1981 Rua Três Rios, Bom Retiro, SP, Brasil
Don't Open the Door

1

my little brother's violin teacher
Mr Suzuki is knocking
my brother comes running
mouthing *don't open the door*
i play along and get a big smile
Mr Suzuki quits after our prank
maybe i should've opened the door
maybe i wanted my brother to stop playing
twinkle twinkle little star out of tune

2

late at night my sister the sleepwalker
is playing piano in bed
she's getting up
concert's over
she's heading to the door
don't let her open the door
she's probably going down the staircase
walking the dark hallways of a nightmare
where days ago
a stranger waited for her at the top of the stairs
he told her that she was very pretty
he was going to give her a kiss goodbye
but instead he bit her face so hard it bled
i want my sister to play piano tonight
dream about the songs she would love to play well

3
my drunk father is going after my mother
as she opens the door to flee
father tries to grab her
he says he's not finished
mother slips through the door
there is just no reasoning with the drunk
we can hide in closets and under the bed
but she has nowhere to go

we wait for father to come looking for us
he's shouting
where's everybody
come out already
he's not going to play hide-and-seek this time
we come out and see him about to open the door
don't let him open the door

something comes over me
i step in front of him
yell *aren't you ashamed of yourself*
it is dark for a moment before lightning hits my mouth
i can't think i can't feel any pain
i don't remember what happens next
does he open the door
does mother come home safely
father doesn't remember a thing the next day
mother doesn't look at me
she has nothing to say

Jacqueline Willcocks

Epigenetic memory

When a microscopic invader, such as a grain of sand or parasite, breaches the dense protective shell of an oyster, it buries itself in the soft-bellied mollusk. Unable to be rid of it, the creature covers it over and over again with a substance harder and lighter than concrete, thousands upon thousands of microcrystals bonded together to catch the light. When something intrudes an oyster, a pearl is created.

Remember when you were intruded, were shocked by your own fragility? (Yes, life is that serious, and no, there is no getting out of it.) You are marked forever; the baby skin you came in with is wearing proof of your actions. Life will touch you, however sturdy your shell may be, showing you your soft underbelly. You are naked and ill-equipped for such handling. You have fallen from grace.

I was taught that healing meant to purify and detox my humanity away, so that my clean and clear soul could shine through and, when it did, everything would be better. I've been told my sins are too heavy and burdensome to carry, that it would be much better to get rid of them. I have agreed, spent years peeling away the crusted masks I have worn. I've sweated in studios, chanted, prayed, and forgiven; I've walked through fire. But, naked as I have become, light as I have aimed to be, I am as heavy as ever.

The intruder—the irritant grain of sand—is still there, grating on me. It's the unforgivable. Everyone has one I think.

It's fireproof and unmoved by chanting. It sticks in your pores regardless of how much you sweat. It's embedded into your very fingerprints. The oysters would say, "Fantastic! You are here, and I am here; now let me pour the best of myself around you." This kind of radical acceptance offends me.

I want to know exactly what happens to the thing inside. Does it want to come out? And when it does, will it seek revenge? Is it frozen in time, waiting for me to let my guard down? If it cannot transform, will it stay preserved, like a mummy monstrous in its rage?

Does the grain of sand hurt the oyster, like the intruder hurts me? Maybe the mollusk accepts that it's just different now, unable to go back to a time when there was no irritant invading pure flesh. But, instead of dissolving into despair, it sends out the best of itself. Creates lemonade out of lemons and voila! the threat is contained in shimmering light which becomes even more valuable than the oyster itself. Finds itself on white bridalwear and the crowns of kings.

What does this mean for our unforgivable? Will it be the truth that stands long after the soft parts of our body have worn away? We'll say, "This is what happened to her," or "This is where he fell." Generations later. Gazing into the luminescent face of the pearl our struggle has left behind.

Absent Fathers

1/ Mine was home
after work
on weekends sometimes
He wore his underwear
and socks   watching TV

His body was pale
like mine, he was there
    to tell me not to
gulp my milk
show me his belt when
I was bad

He drove the car sometimes
on the straight prairie
highway. When I lost
my virginity
I wondered if he could tell
I was different

I remember shouting
my abortion, one night
where were you? I cried

He was there
sitting   standing but not really

2/ My children ask
when is dad coming home?
every day
        and everyday
they use my phone
call him

He says
soon
or
not til later

He tells them

clean their rooms
do the dishes

they hand me back the phone
satisfied
turn back to their games
books
snacks

and I

look around

3/ One summer
he took off his hat   brought it
quickly to the ground
so the butterfly
couldn't escape
showed me how to hold it
so the dust didn't
brush off their wings

One summer
it rained
drops falling into the lake
like pebbles. He said
the water is warm
the sky lit like an opera
    and together
we swam   in the storm

One summer
we went walking
on a trail that ribboned
up to   a mountain lake
I dipped my hat into a passing
stream
to cool my head
like he did

We saw a moose that day
she turned, looked at
me legs still
as her baby
leapt into
the waiting trees

4/ I'm in the bathroom and
can't move
I say
cradling the phone
before panic makes
me drop it
to the floor
where I long to
run fingertips over cool
tiles   soothe
the fire in my brain
I'll be there
he says
I nod
forgetting he can't see me
shuffle stiff limbed
out   into
the sea of parents
alone
I'm outside
under the shade of a tree
hiding
when my breath
lets all
the way
out
We stand
together
watch our son with
a microphone sing
Ch-ch-ch-ch changes.

5/ I wonder if I write
long enough
could words bring
him back
into my life?
My father would know
the underside of my heart
hold it in his hands
recognize
himself
in me
We would laugh
maybe   with tears
I would bask in
his presence
holding me
In the kind of light
   I shine
on my children

6/ My husband
is downstairs
he says
I will make the kids
breakfast
pick them up from school
he does
a better job
than me
asks for my attention
I pivot
   turn
towards
myself
touchy as
the princess and the pea
bruised
from a long night
of feeling
the spaces
between us

7/ So what do I know about absent fathers? When they were
sitting
standing
there
but not really

Catherine Lewis

Red Shoes

fitting to buy my first Valentino shoes on Valentine's Day
two thousand miles from home
by Newport Beach's flaming orange sunset
as one stage in my fertility journey ends
today the tenth and final time ova are surgically plucked
    from my body
without anesthetic
    at this California new-age last-ditch fertility clinic
I don't plan to care about ovulation again
no matter how this motherhood story ends
and Mama needs a new pair of shoes
    to commemorate this day
shiny red 4-inch stilettos
    trimmed with spiky gold pyramid studs
for several days' take-home pay
which is insane
but one pair of shoes is more than I've ever had to show
for all I've spent on fertility drugs

girls' night out
with new dance class friends
all unencumbered by motherhood
I walk five minutes in sleek maroon dress, red heels
binge on high-end steak, cocktails at sparkling Yaletown boîte
before we hop to next nightspot

watch friends fend off men who try to dance with us

as the girls pass around coveted cigarette on bus stop bench
they stare down at my feet
Cat, I can't believe you wore those shoes all night, they gasp
I swear, I'm fine, I insist
though big toenail throbs for weeks before falling off
it still hurts less than if I'd stayed in touch
with old friends who became soccer moms
and left me behind

stumble home from my birthday dinner
last selfie of red shoes capping off red skintight dress
right stiletto now missing rubber tip, only raw metal left
for I had felt my stiletto catch between the cobblestones
that get me every time
cobbler refreshes both heel tips for a mere fifteen bucks
small price to pay to preserve
last faint hope I once had of motherhood

123456

on Mom's phone, WhatsApp group chat named "123456"
cryptic to a stranger
except Mom is one of six siblings and this chat holds them all

Mom, second-oldest of five girls
it took six tries to get a boy

so rare all six are assembled
ocean and Rocky Mountains divide us eleven cousins
transpacific trip a hefty expense for middle-class worker bees

(1) YYZ – HKG – YYZ
in grade school we fly back twice to summer at Grandma's

on final trip, Mom takes sis and me out for lunch with her dad
suave Grandpa who left decades back
he pops down from corporate office in crisp suit
for dim sum at swanky Landmark Mall
flips through the novels we kids are reading
so proud of his granddaughters' native English proficiency
he makes no mention of our broken Cantonese

that day I learn shoes aren't returnable in Hong Kong
should have triple-checked whether they pinched my feet
before Mom paid that morning
for black patent leather adorned with single sparkling jewel
love isn't enough to make things fit

two years later, phone rings
Mom sits on my duvet, says her father has passed
she doesn't fly back for the funeral
she's just come back from visiting his deathbed—
the only thing that could draw all six siblings together again
they posed for formal studio portrait with their mother
　　to mark the occasion
no one wore black
except in their shattered expressions

(2) HKG – YYZ –SFO – HKG
in childhood, we summer with both grandmas around

Mom's mom flutters in
she teaches me to knit and crochet
makes us milk custard pudding
sews quilted blanket for my Cabbage Patch Kid

with both grandmas and sis and me
we even have the requisite four players for mah-jongg
before Mom's mom flutters off again
to make camp with some other grandkids
in San Francisco, maybe Hong Kong

YVR –HKG –YVR
sis tells me, *you need to fly back and visit Grandma soon, even if just for a week, she's not doing well*

hubby and I fly back
hour-long train-and-taxi treks
to bring Grandma bakery desserts and takeout chicken wings
before we fly home, rush back to work

days later she enters palliative care
all six of her children nestle together in hospital
keep vigil, sleep on waiting room couches
whisper farewells when doctor tells them, *it's time*
at least this is what my mother said
I'll never really know, I wasn't there

I couldn't have known
I would be the last grandchild to feed Grandma solid food

(3) *Mom, what? they're getting married after all these years?*
    yes, your cousin's setting a date—we'll let you know when

YVR — HKG —YVR
fourteen-hour flight to my first Hong Kong wedding

hubby and I stand across from my cousin and his bride
in her gold bangles, her red traditional embroidered dress
they serve us steaming hot tea from red and white paper cups
everyone laughs as bride and groom switch to English
        to tell my white husband, *drink tea*

my mother and most of her siblings sit and natter on couch
        under 'double happiness' red velvet sign
the siblings grab aunt number three as she finally arrives
in her mother-of-the-groom black and red dress
covered in gold and silver phoenix embroidery

they pose for photos of all six together
smiling, complete

Steffi Tad-y
Flickering

I have an uncle / whose name always comes up / every time I am asked about my family's medical history. / In the story my father told me, / my uncle would rouse from his sleep past midnight / and whisper to his siblings, / "I have the perfect plan / on how to get to the moon."

In the morning that followed / he landed / his fist on the neighbour's cheek / in a secluded parking lot / where young brown boys / brandished their Bruce Lee moves. / There / in The Devil's Island as it's called / he would sustain / an orbital fracture.

Sometimes / I picture this uncle / death-defying / dreaming deeply of a fighter's path that begins with a lunar rover /stationed / with me and our family at the *punong* / gorging on bellies of milk-fish after a day of flexing and waiting / throwing our lightweight rods into the pond./

I picture us / under the night sky / one eye closed and the other squinting / impatient with the telescope / yet eager to point to the Big Dipper / Orion / / Cassiopeia. /

With a swig of San Miguel / I would tell him about *Harry Potter* and he'd remind me of J. K. Rowling writing / that just because it's in our heads / why should it mean / that it's not real /

But we'd break into laughter this time / knowing / as our patient records reveal / that some things are just not real. /

We would move on / talk about the Thrilla in Manila / and for the thousandth time / after the most heated argument with the rest of the clan / resolve / that Muhammad Ali is pound-for-pound the greatest and in the quiet thereafter /

we'd breathe. /

We'd look up at the vast / phosphorescence above us / and break the silence / in a race to quote Bruce telling us to be like water. / "Be like water, my friend." /

Though I also imagine him also telling me not to be afraid of fire / but to tend to it / to not be afraid of what is furious / within us and them and we /

telling me / to not be afraid of regrets / and what we believe we have torched with our words. /

I imagine him / alive / and telling me / not to resent my darkened parts / and to never resent / the big bang in our lives. /

In the cadence of Ilonggo that raised me in my childhood / he'd tell me / that having our brains on fire / doesn't mean / we were only made / to burn things down. /

I hyper focus on the silvery tips / of his black moustache / to distract myself from the heave in my chest / the grief stored in my lungs. /

As we throw more wood into the heating pile / we arrive at "okay, / should we ever burst / we'll strive to burst / into something useful."

Cruel Strokes

REMEMBERING THE NEGROS 14

When I found out that my tongue

could be a scythe
on a shearing spree

I decided I would only eat
what would make my mouth bloom.

Later on I learned
that to speak only in flowers

in a field like this
is the sharpest blade of all.

Tara Borin

Pit Kid

When your dad owns
the bar, it becomes

your second home
and his first.

As a baby, you play with pool balls
at the staff parties,

sip shot glasses of water
and get passed around for photos.

Up for days,
Dad likes to slur on

about his perfect child
to anyone who'll listen.

Drunks call your house
at night, looking for a loan,

and you learn your mom's
furious whisper in the dark.

When you're ten, you
and your friends

play *Super Mario*
in the tobacco'd office upstairs.

You're sent down
on occasion for supplies,

stand in the doorway
to the tavern

while your dad
fills an empty beer box

with cans of pop and
small bags of Lays potato chips.

Your mom, her make-up done,
your friends' parents

around a table
with pitchers of beer,

singing *Wagon Wheel* as someone
abuses an acoustic guitar.

By the time you're twelve,
you switch to soft ciders,

steal smokes from packs
left unattended around the house.

Mom talks about taking you to stay
at her sister's in Ontario.

Dad sleeps on the chintz sofa
whenever he comes home.

He gets sober,
takes you fishing for grayling

is drunk,
falls down the stairs.

You learn that nothing lasts.

He wants you to take over
the business some day

but you know better.

You dream
of lighting a match,

and not even staying
to watch it burn.

Cecil Hershler

Athens, Greece

I remember the last time I danced like crazy
like life would never end
and the world would keep on spinning forever
I was twenty and touring Europe with a backpack
and a few dollars a day

At a youth hostel I met Y,
an American girl from Minnesota
and we walked around Athens
beautiful, stinking Athens
with its curving narrow alleys and
ancient broken stones

Somewhere that afternoon we were joined by X,
an older Greek artist,
selling black-and-white paintings
of body parts and sex
The three of us drank beer on Ermou Street

In Stamatopoulos Tavern, I saw Y slap X's face
She grabbed me
and said "let's dance, you are my fiancé"
and we danced for hours
in a tavern
in Athens, Greece

I was twenty
whirling like Zorba
with plates on my head
spinning in the air
until my clothes soaked
and the plates smashed

X sat watching us, drinking beer
then he spat on the ground
and left
Later, Y and I walked back to the hostel
laughing
under starry skies
and went our separate ways

Harare, Zimbabwe

Have you ever seen

rows of women
standing erectly alongside a road
holding baskets of tomatoes
begging for buyers

rows of cars
parked silently alongside a road
waiting days for petrol stations to open
to fill their empty tanks

rows of shops
built brickly alongside a road
shuttered   empty   locked
blankly vacant

rows of men
sitting patiently alongside a road
hoping some lorry will stop
and give them work

I have seen this last week
in a country called Zimbabwe
whose cries are not heard
whose blood is being spent

On a dusty country road
I met a young barefoot girl
Magadini—How are you—I greeted her
Moshi—I am fine—she smiled

Cupping her hands
she softly clapped
a message of hope
into the sun-drenched air

Writing

Take a pen
between thumb, index
and middle finger

the point of the pen
carves an undulating line
through the white night

Your mind treads
tentatively
along this path

like a deer
marking her tracks
in fresh snow

at her own pace
at peace with the trees
and the wind

looking for her mother
and a place to rest

Barbara Carter

Tamarindo Concerto

(Allegro moderato)

like planes on a runway

like thirsty kids after recess

like yoga moms at Starbucks

lizard lineup

lids lowered long blinks

lizards   all sizes

waiting their turn on hot tiles

poolside in early sun

camouflage green-grey

they're old their skin is cold

they're true to their own natures

mesozoic metaphysics

through coral toes I spy on them

the perennial tourist

here or there

true to my own nature

prehistoric shuffle

all heartbeat rhythm

ta-da ta-da ta-da

one at a time

waiting a-waiting

mandarino manna

blue bus revelation

break on through

when the music's over

emerge 2019

bask

dressed to kill

hiding in plain sight

baroque cloak finery

grey-white slate

vogue-ing in a tree vee

of dreadlock vinery

hooded eyes   lazy blink

like a pimp in the club

barstool predator

canny canopy smarts

hot intent   languid pose

leashed fury   packed muscle

are you gonna come my way

across the pool

gorgeous creatures sway

to the reggaeton beat

emerald dance floor flickers

palm frond maracas

sun flashes on crimson, coral, chrysoberyl

organza skirts swirl

soft wild promises

hooded eyes   lazy blink

flicker and flash   birds startle

jaws sink into fleshy petal

luscious colour drools and pools

bask

(*Rondo*)

the tamarindo sun

sinks in tangerine marine

a ring of fire erupts in the sand

firedancer rises

dreads like a banyan

silhouette limbs akimbo

batons swirl against a citrine sky

mandarino lace trailing

warp and weft

weaving a promise

conjuring pura vida

the tico tease

B. D. Neufeld

creature

the house was cold
empty and lonely
it stood like a solitary sentinel
on the outskirts of town
she asked around
if anyone knew the
owner but nobody
could quite remember
and the story changed
from person to person
perhaps, she thought
this place would serve
as the perfect penance

suitcase in tow she pried
open the front door
a musty smell
overwhelmed her nostrils
there stood a small table,
two chairs, and a rusty wood stove
a narrow staircase led up
to the loft, the bedroom
a light layer of dust coated every
surface like the ash after Vesuvius

she quickly got to work
making the house her own
soon it felt like home
she bought a gallon of
bright yellow paint
bringing life to the
grey worn-out walls
with wire wool she
scraped the rust-covered stove
and made it like new

one night, sitting at the table
reading by candlelight
a sound came from
somewhere inside the house
a mixture of toad and
some other creature
a faint green glow emanated
from beneath the floorboards

she ripped out a board
and the creature emerged
a glowing reptilian canine of sorts
how long had it been there?
perhaps this was the reason
the house was abandoned

they stared at each other
it tilted its furry, scaly head
trying to decipher if
its rescuer was friend or foe
the floorboard had been nailed
into place, obviously someone
had trapped it down there

she put out a shallow bowl
of water and a slice of bread
the creature was still unsure
but slowly waddled over
lapped up the water and
nibbled on the bread
what are you? she whispered
croaking and purring all at once
it looked up at her with
its wide-set eyes
as if to say
I don't really know what I am
and that's okay

S. Sloan MacLeod
Reciprocity

to each other we explain

philosophies
  —some mud, while unpleasant, is crucial

or lessons learned
  —disallow anything that makes your petals wilt

or vital needs
  —not merely to grow, but to prosper

or tides that turned
  —the rain still comes, but, too, the sun

never, however:
ourselves.

a flower blooms without explanation
rightfully entrusting the world around it
to understand its presence

what is love, really
if not to be understood
without explanation?

to be watered and shone upon
to be someone else's water and sun

Insomniac's Lullaby

nothing shatters quite like glass, except for maybe nightmares in the witching hours, the sound of stirring into a bed that feels empty despite my being in it is quite a lot like bottles kissing floors—it is hard, at these times, to remember: i am whole, despite how much i feel that there are holes inside me.

close your eyes

there was, i'm sure, there must have been, a time when i could sleep, but things change, i got older, shyer, more ashamed; people hurt me, i pulled inward; clown car, contortionist; but i'm grown now, so shouldn't i be better—i'm not, the pain evolved; got meaner, misery followed, just, became numbness, which is still a misery, only, quieter.

rest your heart

i moisturize my hands at least twice each day and still they crack, bleed, dry; that's how it feels, when my mind collapses in on itself for the billionth time, when still you haunt me every; single; night; and yeah, i spend less time now, wide awake at midnight, sliced up by my glass-fragile panic, though it's still there, it's there still, though, it merely scrapes now; i'd like it if loneliness would stop being my loudest emotion, but it always screams within me, has always screamed within me, will always scream within me—eventually you just get used to the ringing; tinnitus.

close your eyes, rest your heart

A Garden, After Fire

in a way i'm almost happy that i burnt down our house.
not that you were choking on smoke, never happy about that.
but now: wisdom.

The house was beautiful.

it was. it scared me.
so i set it ablaze. and i ran away so i couldn't get burnt.

And now, in its place?

a field. and i'm standing in it.
and the soles of my feet are blackened by soot—
that's all that's left of it—its shadow.
and memory.
and feeling.

Are you alone?

well, yes. and no.
you're there, still i'm alone.
you look not at me, but i, at you.
it burnt me anyway,
after everything. it burnt me anyway.
we're both scorch marks on skin now.
before us there's … something.
time. caring. mess.

The mess is yours.

well, now i know what i had—
and what i lost.

And what then?

i do the only thing i can:
start collecting the debris.
i can't rebuild it, not alone at least,
but i can wash the grime right off its shadow
and plant flowers in all its saddest parts
watch them bloom
yellow,
orange,
red.
new flame.

Are you seen?

you notice lush unfolding,
and wonder why, then,
did i light and throw the match before?
you ask me what i'm doing.
i can only say *atoning*.

Impressive, Really, a Bird Becoming a Scapegoat

first i entrapped you: seduction being effortless
manïpulation—which must have come from outside myself,
as i am both clumsy and extemporaneous—though certainly
you were blind to the paradox, since you, in the end, loved me
without knowing me

then i entrapped myself: the construction not of walls so much
as cage—something i'd always lamented not having,
something i'd begged to be put into, boundless bird in
incessant migration—but that was the compromise, in
keeping you out, i kept me in

first i entrapped, then i entangled, ensnared, enmeshed
according to you: always suggesting a dastardliness, a cunning
of which i am incapable, canary made into vulture by
increasingly distorted whisperings, whisperings. i am not a
villain. and you. no innocent. i do not entrap. and you. you do
not liberate.

Zofia Rose Musiej

#20 Victoria

to the brim full / with raucous merrymakers / college kids
coming from downtown / and drunk / and red faced / and now
a noisy row of young men sing Kiss From A Rose / with nary
a note out of tune / off key / in fact sound so lovely / I
harmonize / in the chorus / the only words I know / with some
confidence / not that it matters / to these troubadours /
serenading us across Hastings / up Commercial Drive / I sit
adjacent to this group / warming myself on the small trickle /
of relief that is / light of humanity seeping in / song ends and
up / they start again but / now aided by some other guy and
his guitar / this is when I wonder / was that there / was I here
all along / bus claps / applaud the rowdy crew who lap it up /
offer smiles / beams / grins and now standing / move away
from where I sit / to all but gallop / bounce / bound out the
doors / waving back to their adorers / those who sung / and
sang and us / those of us left behind are flushed / with
remnants of that spark of joy / the almost tangible liquid gold /
combination of compassion and connection / these things I
witness / these moments I cherish / take home with me to lay
with / as I lay next to him / he who happens to be / the reason
I never see these things / the reason I rarely go out /

disimprison

needed you to make it real
shut the door   lock it
need to find an even keel
one   without you in it

from one
forty-something guy who fucked me
to you   another
forty-something guy who fucked me
                         "you're no good for her"

not you for I   nor he for me
but if not for the other
of the two of you
I might not have found
my way out   from either

survival skills

my instinct is to manipulate men
my ex will read this
and say   *I told you so*

but wait
I don't mean it like that
I mean men offer protection
resources   fuel for my desire
body heat   courage
I mean men offer safety nets
I don't mean it to sound
like greed

my instinct is to survive on my wits
my ex might read this
and say   *she's lying*

it takes two to undo

compassion floods chest cavity
eyes well as well
streaming out
through double ducts
subtle chucks
under chin
let me see your face
look me in the eye
growth takes time
I choose to believe again
this body drowns
in hope

nice

It's ok / and this won't hurt / but it will / it definitely will /
luck be found in holding hands / hands held when I lose my
grip / twist an ankle / snap at Satan / walk away / need rest /
need to take a break from others needing rest / communicate
desire to do well / alter habits to be more human / more loving
and attentive / less afraid / less fearful of the words "I choose
you" / because if I don't know what to do with nice then what
can nice hope to do with me / besides shine a light on my
value / besides listen to my stress without it adding to his own
/ besides offer me oasis and decompression / without a price
tag / with no requirements / with no regard to how much
chaos I feel I buzz with / it hurts / it's already hurting / but
nice and I still choose each other / and nice has quickly
become safe and worth getting to know / might I walk a while
alongside him / I don't have any expectations but I desire /
him / decide I like auditioning to be his teammate / decide to
be grateful and lean into him / lean on purpose on purpose /

Janna Walsh

Banshee

i.
Connemara, long associated with the old traditions.
Burial mounds dot the countryside among glacially scoured loughs.
Gaeltacht locals speak in Irish, of sheepshearing and groceries and
folktales. Ancient Croagh Patrick rules over drumlins in the bay. Pilgrims have climbed this cone for 5000 years, long before the Church
claimed it for St. Patrick.

ii.
Across the road, a bronze sculpture of a Coffin Ship recalls the terror
of The Famine. Tatters hang from skeletons slung from masts and
beams. A million souls fled, another million starved. The phantom
vessel summons the mind toward all famines, cataclysms, slaughters—
around the world, then and now.

iii.
Bean Sidhe, the banshee, crouches beneath yews. Flies in moonlight,
wailing over an imminent bereavement. She is of the air, shadowy,
shapeshifting: beautiful red-haired girl, pale silvery woman, veiled
crone, all with ever-streaming hair. In the mist, her howling strikes fear,
but she does not bring death itself, only a warning.

Croagh Patrick has always been sacred for believers,
coffin ships endlessly echoed the haunting cries of banshees

Oculus

Arriving, sweating, in Piazza della Rotunda, I encounter
porticoed columns and fountain sun-blasted by the white light
of midday Rome. Black-clothed nonnas, some bent nearly double, beg
in the square. This is a church, after all, and the church feeds
its own one way or another.

Respite from the city's maddening hectic streets,
what pleasure to arrive here, at this fountain with its obelisk
and quartet of dolphins. Massive doors twinned in bronze open to a
cool and coffered vault, and I am soothed.

The monumental dome, unwindowed—a single
shaft of light amidst the patience of textured stone, the aperture forty
metres above the wandering mortals below: god's own eye.

Luminous, ineffable, a reverse sundial, the sun circles
the foramen as the day revolves: genius loci.

Gabbling tourists fade away, sneakered Americans ticking off
one more famous "sight" vanish. A private hush drifts down on me, the
hot sky traded for a single lacuna of blue.

Smoothing my scraped and raw crust from the city,
the delicate beam cascades to geometric marble.
I am in the finest company here, alone with Rafael, kings,
and a tiny bird, black as the nonnas' dresses,
swooping joyously around the reaches of its own heaven.

Monument Valley

AN EXCERPT

Spending time here in the Valley, if you open yourself, is to experience stones as alive as anything that breathes. Everything in this place—sun, wind, and water, together with the beings that creep, run, fly, and grow—is integral to life as the Navajo understand it. The valley's size whittles you down to a whisper of humanity, so trivial on its own, but so connected.

Not long ago, I stood alone here, contemplating a carmine archway with an almost perfectly round hole at its apex. My two companions were some way off, our tour guide out of sight with our jeep. I stood for a long time in silence, listening, the rugged formation seeming to stretch a canopy over me, although I had not moved closer. A raven soared in long lazy arcs, pitch black against blue so bright it was almost painful.

I saw a speck in the corner of my eye and turned to see two men, one on horseback, one on foot, approaching me from what seemed miles away. When they came near, I could see their sun-burnished skin was creased and finely netted with wrinkles, but their age impossible to tell. Between forty and seventy? I could peg it no closer. The mounted one left his horse, not bothering to tie it, and it sauntered off to nibble some scrabbly weeds. Both wore faded dirty jeans, dusty boots, and worn flannel shirts. One wore his hair in a long braid down his back, gleaming as black as the raven's wing. The other was crowned with a sweat-stained and well-used cowboy hat.

They came closer to me, a solitary elderly white woman quietly listening to their land and watching the raven fly. I don't recall any greeting, but we all smiled to each other, and they came closer still. Then their arms were around me, and we three just hugged each other and smiled.

The one with the shining braid asked me softly if I admired their land—not liked, not loved, did I admire it? The other squeezed my shoulder and bade me to look up—the raven was far distant now, but replaced by an eagle with white head and tail feathers coming nearer to us. Then, still bound together by our group hug, they urged me further toward the wide-mouthed cave formed by the mighty arch. The arms of these short sturdy men felt like a cradle of love and generosity. The crisp wind had died, or at least I could no longer feel it. The mineral smell of sunbaked rock mingled with the slight scent of sweat soothed and reassured me. I was held by their embrace so as not to stumble on the raw scree underfoot. Held by their embrace as if in a spell.

Who were these warm and rugged men who came from nowhere to acknowledge me? Were they tribal elders protecting their gorgeous, dangerous, heavenly territory? I was unaware of the meaning of our circled arms and their obvious satisfaction in encountering me. Old enough myself to represent the folkloric crone, I could not possibly fulfill any expectations in my ignorance of their myths and traditions. Why did they choose me? Did they recognize me as spiritual nomad, or the rare visitor who was simply joyful in that place?

We never broke our embrace. They smiled at me again, then sweetly touched my light, wind-jumbled hair and walked away to find the horse, grazing in the scrub a few yards away. I remained, speechless and still and suffused with happiness, watching them leave and my friends approach. Blessed by this magnificent desert.

Kamakura Daibutsu

*I was so moved that I started welling up. It wasn't just Buddha's
majesty and dignity, it was the sheer weight of history and generations of
people's hopes, prayers, and thoughts that broke over me.*
—*Naoki Higashida, age 13,* The Reason I Jump

Take the train from Tokyo Station, the Yokosuka Line.
Switch to the Enoden electric train at Kakamura.
Get off at the third stop. Walk to the modest wooden temple of
Kotoku-in and pass through the temple gate.

A punch of awe. Everything shifts: the sweet air,
the exquisitely verdant gardens, the sense of being.
Daibutsu, the Great Buddha of Kakamura.
It stuns with size, rarity, reverence.

The monumental statue meditates with hands in lap,
lotus position, eyes half-closed, serene yet aware.
Old bronze weathered to verdigris. An aura of tenderness,
mudra of perfect repose, passionless calm.

Icon of Japan, subject of millions of postcards,
Daibutsu, unmoving, transports a visitor to bliss.

Martha Warren

Berengaria

1. Apologies to Daphne du Maurier, but *Last night I dreamt I went to …*
Cyprus … *again*. (*Rebecca*, Chapter 1.)

I dreamt of Queen Berengaria,
a storm in the Gulf of Adalia,
her dromond foundering off the Cypriot coast.
She was held captive until Richard the Lionheart turned up,
rescuing her on his way to Jerusalem.

Their marriage was a political alliance of kingdoms,
leaving her in the shadow of a powerful mother-in-law.
And then Richard moved on to face Saladin
and pursue other lovers.

How gothic.

To escape the heat and humidity of Limassol,
Berengaria went up to the village of Platres
in the Troodos mountains,
where the air was cool, and scented with pine and cypress.

She saw the soutzoukos, the strings of almonds
dipped in grape jelly,
hanging in the market square,
sold by the old woman with the black headscarf,
who used her hand to wave away the flies.

11. *If only there could be an invention that bottled up a memory, like scent. And it never faded, and it never got stale. And then, when one wanted it, the bottle could be uncorked, and it would be like living the moment all over again. (Rebecca, Chapter 5.)*

Then I might remember better.
And I would think of the other women who came before me.
Like the one who tapped her pen on the writing table,
sipping her demitasse of coffee.

Her husband, a commanding officer in the Grenadier Guards,
that is how they came to Alexandria,
and then to stay in the Forest Hills Hotel
in the Troodos Mountains of Cyprus,
for refuge from the dust and noise and heat.

Here, among the pine and cypress, she could think in peace.
Here, she could write.
She tapped her pen some more, thinking about her novel,
about how the ghost of the first wife could haunt the second,

she, herself, being haunted by a ghost,
her husband's former fiancée,
who threw herself under a train.
It doesn't matter whether you're in Cornwall or Alexandria,
those ghosts travel with you.

She had found the bundle of love letters in his desk,
and knew about the female staff officer,
and the mistress in Fowey.

How gothic.

At the market in Platres,
the old woman with the black headscarf gestured her closer,
waving her hand at the strings of soutzoukos for sale,
the flies lifting from the grape candy
like a black lace tablecloth.

III. *I am glad it cannot happen twice, the fever of first love. For it is a fever, and a burden, too, whatever the poets may say.* (*Rebecca*, Chapter 5.)

I think of another woman who comes to Cyprus with her first love
to pursue his ambition to take over the family business,
despite the mother-in-law for whom nothing is right,
despite the Bulgarian in his office
seated on the corner of his desk in a short black skirt.

On weekends, they drive high into mountains west of Nicosia,
past olive groves shimmering silver in the heat,
past fields of citrus,
where asparagus and capers grow wild at the side of the road.

She wanders through the market in Platres,
where the old woman with the black headscarf beckons,
whose eyes have seen foreign wives like this before,
shipwrecked on the island, marriages in tatters,
that same haunted look.
The shroud of flies lifts
as she waves her arm over the soutzoukos for sale.

Ignoring the signs to keep out,
the couple stop to explore derelict remains of the hotel,
gardens overgrown,
building almost hidden in the pine and cypress.

She steps carefully over pieces of broken mirror and debris.

A construction worker finds her inside,
running her index finger across a desk, wondering.
You should not be here, he tells her. It's dangerous.
He nods at the desk,
This is where Daphne du Maurier wrote *Rebecca*, you know.

How gothic, she mutters.

She hears her husband's voice calling outside,
and she would have gone to him,
but for the icy, ethereal hand that grasps hers
out of nowhere,
gently, but firmly, pulling her away,
away from his voice,
away to the open window looking west.

IV. *We can never go back, that much is certain. The past is still too close to us.*
(*Rebecca*, Chapter 2.)

Here I sit at my desk in cool winter light
far from that Mediterranean forest,
and I wonder,
Was there ever a relationship without a Rebecca in it?
Former and current lovers, ex-wives, mothers-in-law,
each capable of burning Manderley to the ground,
reducing love to ashes
with a passion and determination so fierce,
it lights up the sky.

df parizeau

A Moment, in a Day, in the Life of Данкан Гидонович[1]

AFTER ALEXANDR SOLZHENITSYN

Today,
I found cartilage
in a mouthful
of soup—
a stray nugget,
probably
a piece of knee
that evaded the
colander.
Instead of spitting
it out in disgust,
I thought
of Иван Денисович[2]

How
cap upon knee,
packed

---

1 Dankan Guydanovich
2 Ivan Denisovich: The protagonist of Solzhenitsyn's seminal work, *One Day in the Life of Ivan Denisovich.*

like sunflower
seed
in shell, a sly
sickle would have
crept up Иван's[3] face.
Pleased
that this lost
gristle
found his bowl
and not that
of a fellow зэк.[4]
How
Ваня[5]
would have rolled
the avian joint
around, a жемчуг[6]
in his mouth—
fished
from the depths
of his barren, mildewed,
dishwater баланда.[7]

Slowly,
sucking & savouring
every liquid scrap
that had found

---

3 Due to incompatibilities between the English and Russian possessive forms, the English possessive "s" was used here for clarity, despite it not appearing in Russian.

4 Zek: Russian slang for "prisoner."

5 Vanya: A diminutive form for Ivan, which denotes a sense of familiarity and attachment to the person.

6 Zhemchug: Russian for "pearl."

7 Balanda: Russian for "skilly" or "gruel."

its way
into the pores
of this special сокровище.[8]

Sucking
& savouring,
hoping
this stray nugget
would return стойкость[9]
to his own
destitute joints. Sucking

& savouring,
cap upon
his knee,
knowing he may never
have this much везение[10]
from this very
moment, until the final
bell
of his sentence.

And so
I sat there, cap
upon my head, more
walnut than seed,
pondering
my ravaged
knees.

---

8 Sokrovishche: Russian for "treasure."
9 Stoykost': Russian for "stamina."
10 Vezeniye: Russian for "luck."

Sucking & savouring,
the part of the animal
we are taught
to discard. Sucking
& savouring,
a telling smile
waxing across
my face,
as I come to terms
with the knowledge
that I will never
find the same радость[11]
as Ivan
would in such
a moment.

---

11 Radocst': Russian for "joy."

Deborah Vieyra

Glitter Smashed

The crash embedded a crystal in her face—
bloodied diamond.
The window glitter smashed;
the crystal lodged.

Out they pulled the crystal—
excavated, mined—
the crystal now in tweezers—
marinated in blood—
thrown like a universe
into medical waste.

here, inside the glass crystal is a glass teacup, and next to the
glass teacup is the LOL doll that grownups think are too
expensive, if they even know what they are, but kids know,
just know how wow they are, so whatever.

the earth outside makes noises like grumbles in a heaven
tummy, if heaven was so sick it couldn't even go to Heaven
School that day because it would make other heavens sick,
and the explosion she knows is coming, because that's what
the grownups say.

even Gloria the babysitter, the one who comes and sleeps
almost the whole time, even Gloria was scared this evening,
and said that not even the superhero shield from the Dollar

Store can protect you this time, because when the Rupchore
comes, it will even tear apart the houses and crack the rooms
like an unboiled egg, and all will be Red, like a blood flood.
like this unboiled egg had a yolk made of blood and now it is
going to crack like someone was having the world for
breakfast.

and the water would be Red, even feel like air. And there
would be no breathing because the water would be
everywhere, and taste like when you lick your finger with a
cut on it and it's metal tasting like having a silver spoon in
your mouth. blood tastes like having a silver spoon in your mouth.

she heard on The News that people are already speeding out
of town because The Great Rupchore is coming, but what's
the point, because it's coming everywhere, the Rupchore, so
there's nowhere to run. and she can hear right now it's already
started, like the wind is making itself into sticks, playing the
trees like xylophones, but not pretty. just banging and making
noise so people will want to leave, because when the
explosion comes and it's all split apart, the world will turn
Red.

The Rupchore. she doesn't know what that is, but they always
say it, she knows it's coming because that's what the
grownups always say

it is, and it's coming, so they're going, the people,

but they're not even sure where, because every direction they
go is nowhere

everywhere is the possibility of disaster, every corner takes your breath away, and not in the way when things are too pretty, but in the way when things are DEAD, so all you have to do is hope, and clasp onto something with your hands, in HOPE that you too can find yourself somewhere that is not a crack, because now we know it's not

WHETHER, or IF

it's WHEN

is what the grownups say

and they don't know the answer to that question of when, except soon, and so she looks at her glass teacup and she wonders how many rounds it would take to use it as a bucket to get rid of The Red, because right now Mommy has not come home, which is normal because it's Saturday nighttime and work, and Gloria drank that clear wine again while watching her shows that are not for kids, and now she's sleeping again.

again Gloria is unwakeupable, because that's what the wine does to some people. after they can't remember how to make sense. Gloria is waiting for a tomorrow to wake her up so she can make more promises to herself of how she is going to be better. but that tomorrow is not here yet, and if that tomorrow comes and is Great Rupchore Day, then, well maybe Gloria won't have more days to try and be Better Gloria, without all the wine,

but if The Great Rupchore comes tonight, and Gloria is
asleep, and Mommy is not there, it's her that will have to fix it
somehow.

so she looks down to the teacup, and then at the LOL doll and
asks them out loud: Will You Please Help. and then prays a bit
like she saw on that show, she is on her knees like that show,
with her hands kissing each other, like that show. but she's not
sure if the prayer is going to get where it's supposed to be
going.

and if the prayer goes nowhere, all there is here is the teacup
that's glass and fragile, and the LOL doll that she stole
okay from the kid who dropped it on the bus, okay
but that's not a problem now because she doesn't even know
that kid

and here in her room, she hears the Rupchore clanging louder,
and all out of tune, and she knows what that must mean. it
means it's coming.

so she picks up the LOL doll and tapes it firmly with stickers
to the wall so that when the explosion comes, at least the doll
will be saved, because the LOL doll is what she always
wanted, well at least this year, so she better save it from being
exploded, because who knows how well a LOL can survive an
explosion even if it's stuck to a wall.

so she peeps through, and sees the earth is starting to redden,
and the house is getting swooshed

and she can't remember if bricks are meant to hold up
anything, or where her Mommy is again? or if she must wake
up Gloria to tell her that the time must be coming, or if Gloria
can even wake up if she tries.

and so she does, she tries, she gallops

out of her room, and down the hall, and there she is by Gloria now,
snoring and dribbling like she's crying out of her mouth, and
so she shakes her to get her awake

but Gloria might as well not be here at all, she's gone, the
Inside Gloria gone, and only Outside Gloria here, she's gone
to somewhere that is nowhere even close to here in this house,
even though she's still breathing. so there's no hope of Inside
Gloria coming back in time for anything, so she better go back
to her room, just close the door and make a fort that will save
her from whatever is coming, and pray again to nowhere.

the noise grows and grows, and she covers her ears in the
hope that it's going to go, but it doesn't, it bangs louder than
an ear can take, and the world goes red around her all red and
metal and her room turns upside-down, and the right way
round and back and forth until it stops

and the Red comes in gentle gentle like watercolours. the Red is
not scary, just here.

she looks up at the wall. there's the LOL doll not even cut in
pieces. it's whole. lit up in red but whole. she's whole.

Elizabeth Armerding

Don't Let the Bedbugs

*i. sleep tight / don't let the bedbugs bite / if they do, take your
shoe / and beat them til they're black and blue*

YOU are hosting a dinner party!

Actually, a breakfast, lunch, and dinner party
enjoyed in three bites
one
after
the other.
Against your will, you have actually

Become
breakfast, lunch, and dinner, and you feel that it is

Excessive
to eat breakfast, lunch and dinner all in one sitting, and

Disappointing
to have been eaten out of house and home, not to mention

Brave
to have assumed everything would turn out fine, as well as

Unhinging
to have lost control of your own party, and furthermore

Graceless
to be wrapping your guests in plastic for six to eight months.

ii. sleep tight / don't let the ------- bite

snug as a bug in a rug
your thousand count fortress
a mighty keep for majestic dreams

until

stealthy in exoskeleton
a bloodthirsty army marches out of outlets
and abandoned telephone jacks

they nestle neatly between books
behind picture frames
and await your snore

netflix wonders if you're watching
as they station beneath sweet slumber

tiny, they slide between satiny sheets
fall into formation and tuck in
to you, juicy banquet

napkins around necks, a toast
is proposed to breakfast, lunch and dinner

satisfied, the troops fall back
settle between sturdy seams
and curl up; just another dormant day

iii. if they do, take your shoe

You do not do,
leathery house shoe
sported by my mother,
yanked off to spank
the dog's and my
behind.

A sturdy peep-toe, her
rough heels exposed
like white cliffs of Dover.

From bed I picture the slipper
slamming at bugs who blend in
with warm florals,
disguised as thorns
on yellow roses.

Her bathrobe matches
the wallpaper.

Saffron and brown,
era-cusping colours
before neons, and hot pinks.

Bought
the year of my birth,
it hangs in my closet,
pilled.

I play dress up
and make believe.

The sturdy peep-toe,
white heels exposed
like a clear moon.

But still
you do not do,
you leathery house shoe,
sported by me now,
slamming at nothing.

You do not do
for Ledetta, from Sylvia Plath's "Daddy"

iv. beat them til they're black and blue

In grade three I beat up Andrew Kirkham because of his stupid temper. It's always out of control, like last week he threw a whole jar of paintbrushes at Stacey Pinkson's head. His freckles are this really dark red instead of brown, and they look mad, like blood vessels. Anyway we were at the monkey bars and he was having one of those tempers for no reason, and I got him down so fast he couldn't even run. Then I saw his freckles up close on his white skin and they looked even more mad, like paintballs. His arms were weird and cold when I had him down, and I saw this one really big freckle. The woodchip got in my socks, it gets everywhere and makes everything itchy. I hope it got in his shorts. I bet it did because I kept him down and he was trying to get away forever.

I never get in trouble, they just ignore it. I think it's because they don't think girls can beat up boys.

Speculative and
Young Adult Fiction

Maggie Derrick

The Witch's Patron

AN EXCERPT

There was a shadow emerging on the horizon—just a hint of the thing, like a spectre haunting the edge of the sky. Most wouldn't have noticed it, perhaps mistaking it for a low rain-bearing cloud or a waft of smoke. But Noori Owusua knew better.

Most people—even more-experienced seafarers who had been sailing three times as long as Noori had been alive—weren't as keen-eyed as she was when it came to catching the first signs of a ship on the horizon. Noori always knew. It was as though she felt an approach like a tremor in her bones, a tugging that drew her spyglass to what was usually still only a suggestion of a ship's silhouette creeping across the water.

"We have a mark," she announced with a grin, her eye still pressed to the lens. "Are you ready, Toddrick?"

"Aye aye!" her best friend and first mate called in reply. Seated in the stern, he gripped the tiller with chapped and steady hands.

Mystic Sal, Noori's small but formidable cutter, sliced through the choppy morning ocean like a dream. They were coasting in open water, and here the sea played no games. Beneath the hull the western sea churned, dark and deep and murky. Soon the sun would break over the horizon and burn off the low ceiling of gloom that smothered the mouth of the harbour. If the previous evening's red sunset was any indication, the city of Fernweh had a stunning sky waiting for it on the other side of the morning's clouds. But for now there was only this: the dark sea, the heavy cover from above, *Mystic Sal*, and a shadow.

"Eyes to starboard," Toddrick shouted over the slosh of sea spray leaping off the bow and the bellow of cold wind that slapped their faces raw. "We're not alone."

Noori glanced to the right and saw it—a small schooner creeping in from a wall of grey to the north. She recognized the sails in an instant.

Lady Bethel was sailed by an unruly crew of local coastal shippers, known for being perpetually broke and dangerously bored. For these hobblers, piloting was a way to make some extra money between jobs; the often perilous open-water racing that came with the job was a happy bonus as far as they were concerned. Captained by a man named Cort, *Lady Bethel*'s crew sailed their employer's schooner with all the sophistication of schoolboys on a stolen dinghy. This wasn't the first time they had tailed *Mystic Sal* in hopes of beating her to a fare.

"I suppose the boys are looking for a race." Noori laughed loudly, knowing it would be heard across the water on Bethel's deck. "Let's show them how it's done!"

Noori tightened the jib sheet with a mighty heave as Toddrick pointed the tiller. *Mystic Sal* picked up speed the way a stallion charges across an open expanse, breathtaking and powerful. She tacked starboard at a sharp angle over the water's surface. By now the shadow on the horizon had taken shape: a massive galleon seeking berth in the port of Fernweh. If she squinted, Noori could see a flag of white and red snapping in the wind; they were calling for a pilot.

Out here the waters were deeper and more alive than in the relative calm of the sheltered harbour. Waves rose higher, pitching the *Mystic Sal* up and down. But Noori and Toddrick were old hands at this, and they steadied their vessel with skill. Cutting through the water, they navigated cleanly through the restless waves and closed the distance with ease.

The hiss and slosh of *Lady Bethel*'s progress registered in Noori's ear. They were giving them a good run, but Noori wasn't concerned. She thrilled at the chase; she loved the challenge.

"We're nearly there," Noori called to Toddrick. Her normally buoyant hair was matted down with the slick of salt water, her cheeks glowing with the effort and the excitement of the race. "Shall we put them out of their misery?"

Toddrick grinned up at her, delighted. "It would be the courteous thing to do."

They craned *Sal* to port, whooping as the deck dipped low. Noori took a deep breath, revelling in the sharp scent of briny air that filled her lungs and fanned the smouldering embers in her heart. How, she wondered at times like this, could anyone feel alive anywhere else but out at sea?

Their cutter sailed clear across *Lady Bethel*'s path, not so close that they risked colliding but close enough that any decent sailor would err on the side of caution.

Cort and crew may not have been smart, but at least they knew when to cut their losses.

"Go on and gloat," Noori heard Cort bark as *Mystic Sal* sailed by. "Easy to win fares with Daddy's schedules in your pockets."

Noori smiled and rolled her eyes. She was long used to the bitterness of other pilots—the ones who assumed the only reason she could ever be the first to greet approaching ships was by virtue of her father's role as harbour master and not her own skill. "Good morning to you too!" she called back with a jovial wave of her hand.

Turning her back on the crew's grumbling and tasteless gestures, Noori darted aft and raised the flag that signalled they were there to help. Together, she and Toddrick tucked the cutter in close, and within moments a ladder of rope and board was cast down to them.

Noori turned to Toddrick. His eyes were sparkling and his smile broad, an expression that looked as triumphant as she felt. "I'll see you back on the docks?" she said.

He nodded. "See you there, Owusua."

Noori pulled herself onto the ladder, suspended above the crashing waters below, and began her climb. Halfway to the deck, she paused for a moment and looked back over her shoulder. The stern of *Lady Bethel* slipped back into the mist, no doubt returning to a less volatile anchorage to await another fare. On the other side of the eerie grey void was the harbour, with its wharfs and dry land. It was now Noori's job to get this ship, her crew, and her cargo there safely.

A beaming man with a red face and a neatly trimmed beard met Noori at deck level. He extended a hand to help her aboard, and she accepted with a bright smile of her own.

"I believe you're in need of a pilot?" she asked, standing straight to look taller than she was. Already she could see the curious faces of the crew taking her in and sizing her up. She didn't hold their disbelief against them—pilots were rarely as young as she was.

If her age was a problem, it didn't seem to concern the man who had helped her aboard. He grinned at her, deep crow's feet pinching at the corners of his eyes.

"Captain Cunningham," he said, introducing himself. "You must be the notorious Noori Owusua I've heard tales of."

"Only good things, I hope."

He guffawed. "I assure you, your reputation is sterling. I was hoping you'd be the one to sail us in."

And so, after a brief negotiation of fare, Noori did exactly that. Around her the galleon's crew busied themselves with the tasks of coming to port, while she focused on getting them there. It was a lifetime in these waters that made her an excellent pilot. She had quite literally been born at sea, arriving two weeks early to the great surprise of her father and mother, who were out enjoying what they believed would be one of their last good sails before parenthood. This, Noori believed, was the reason she knew the harbour's waters better than she knew herself. She had topography tattooed on her brain. Her veins mapped the currents.

By the time the ship rounded the final outcropping of land and forest that sheltered the harbour from the open ocean, the sun had lifted its head and chased away the fog. Noori smiled without thinking as the city of Fernweh came into view. She liked this view of her home best—the skyline as viewed from the water. In some ways, it was the only view of the city she recognized.

A sailor raised a flag indicating that the ship was seeking berth. Noori raised a spyglass to her eyes and searched the docks for a response. When it came—another flag, raised this time by her father's crew—Noori turned to Captain Cunningham and handed his glass back to him.

"They've got a mooring clear for you, sir," she said. "Welcome to Fernweh."

Purnima Bala

The Circle of Silence

An excerpt from a novel

I was intensely aware of, and yet disconnected from, my walk down the passage, my footsteps a soft whisper around me, fingertips tracing the names and dates carved along the stone walls. There were more than I'd last seen—more names on these walls, names once familiar, shadows dancing around them as the torches flickered, a smattering of dust caught in the dappled yellow glow. There were only ghosts in the tunnels that night.

My pace was steady as I navigated the twists and bends, following a pattern ingrained into my muscles—left at the fork, second left, down the path, then right, past the headstones lying in caverns here and there—until I reached a row of hollowed-out rooms. Block-printed curtains, edges tattered and dirty, covered their entrances. A dryness settled over my tongue, my eyes fixed on the farthest room on the right.

Last chance to turn back.

Doubt only leads to more doubt, and that doesn't help anyone: hadn't I learned that the hard way over the years, spending too long enveloped in my thoughts instead of taking action? And yet I hesitated, buried feelings clawing their way forth while my heartbeat echoed in my mind. Gritting my teeth, I stepped forward, and again, until I found myself standing in front of the room, hand on the curtain, the coarseness of the fabric grounding me, making it all real.

I stepped inside.

She was standing in the middle of the room, hands clasped behind her back. Her eyes pierced mine, reflecting a weariness I felt in my bones, and I stood stiff, surrounded by silence, tenseness throbbing in the air around us.

"It's good to see you, Lin," I said, my voice raspy and low.

Lin loosened her stance, smiling gently, and gestured to the chairs off to the side. "You never replied to my message," she said, taking a seat. "I wasn't sure if you'd come."

"But you were waiting here anyway."

"Of course."

I gulped, swallowing a lump in my throat, and looked away, examining the room while I composed myself. It was just as I remembered it— bare and practical, with rugged walls and chunks of loose stone fallen around. A faint smell of damp earth hung in the air, no doubt drifting over from the stream behind the outer rockface. It was as I remembered it, but not quite. Time hadn't left this place unattended. Nor had death.

Lin was different, too. More lines creased her forehead, heavily etched in, and streaks of silver ran through her pinned-up hair. A jagged scar ran down the side of her neck, stark against her waxy complexion.

Three years. Had I really been gone that long?

"When I heard you were back, I wasn't sure whether to believe it," Lin said, gazing at the opposite wall. "A part of me was sure it was a trick, that the Wardens had somehow found out about our network, sent out this rumour to mislead us, get us vulnerable and hit us hard. But I had to be certain."

"For the record, I got your letter," I replied with a shaky laugh. "Took me by surprise, if I'm being honest. I didn't expect to hear from you. Not after ... well."

"Ah, so it was just a good old case of overblown guilt. And there I was worrying you'd forgotten how to read the code." Lin nudged me in the side with her elbow.

"Never," I replied. "I think I'd sooner forget my own name."

"At least I know the training plan works."

"Works? It's bloody insane is what it is. I still have the scars from that combat day when I understood the instructions wrong."

"A small price to pay to stay alive." Lin smirked.

"That it is."

I remembered the long hours we spent drenched in sweat, straining our muscles and our minds continuously, pushing forward even when we felt like we couldn't go on. Lin put us through our paces, testing us at the end of every month with mock assignments, giving us our combat- and rescue-operation orders in the form of innocuous office memos— *Mal, please get tea and index the attendee files. Kaylee*—which got more and more bizarre as we progressed.

At first I didn't understand the seriousness of what we were doing, the laws we were breaking, what we were fighting for; my young teen-age mind was more focused on the thrill, the secretiveness, and I threw myself into training with knee-throbbing excitement. Four consecutive fails in the monthly assignments—born out of nothing but ignorance, I now knew—helped temper my energy, but everything changed for good the first time we came here, to these Tunnels of the Dead, or as I later dubbed them, the Crypt-ic Maze.

There'd been seven in each group, the higher levels having fewer. (I once asked Lin if that was because smaller teams work better together, to which she only said, "It wasn't planned.") We'd slip into the tunnels after nightfall, mingle around and drink to the dead, scratching their names into the walls with our daggers. Afterwards, we'd separate into our respective groups and go into each of the curtained rooms to commiserate.

How many of us were left?

"I ... I saw the walls," I said to Lin. "Ken, Janie, and Malaya?"

"Among others." She sighed, rubbing her eyes with the tips of her fingers. "We lost Ken after a raid, about two years ago, now. He ... things didn't go as planned, and a couple of Protectors spotted us leaving the building. Ken decided to stay behind and distract them, managed to hold them off long enough for the team to get away. At least he passed easy. Took a black pill before the Procs could haul him off."

"He always said he wanted to go down in style."

Lin nodded. "Malaya's situation wasn't so clear-cut. She got an assignment to go undercover. Managed to pass on invaluable information about who the Protectors were targeting and also some of the new laws they wanted to pass. But we stopped hearing from her about a year ago, and our spies told us her identity was blown. We can only hope that she died before going through whatever the Wardens had in store for her."

I touched two fingers to my forehead in respect, Lin's words repeating over and over in my mind. The Wardens. Nothing about them boded well. A shiver crept over my skin.

The Wardens were normal people—outwardly. With full families, they dutifully followed the Protector norm, spread out through every sector like a network of ants, lurking in the shadows until called upon. People taken to the Wardens were never the same, turned into blank slates and reprogrammed to lose all sense of self.

Could it be called torture when no one remembered what happened?

I had never found out how they did it. I'd never even found out who they were. And there was nothing scarier than seeing enemies in strangers every day—the grocer around the corner, the mechanic, that middle-aged beer-bellied man who loved his flowery shirts. It made finding friends that much harder.

"What about Janie?" I asked, despite the bitterness in my throat, my stomach panging in protest. "Did the Wardens get her too?"

"Janelle ... no." Lin gave me a look of deep despair, brow furrowed and lips turned down. "Not the Wardens. Sometimes I wonder which is worse ... not that any good comes out of it."

She cleared her throat. "It was four months ago. When she didn't come for our scheduled meeting or get in touch, we didn't think much of it at first. It wasn't new, you know? She had to manage her responsibilities at home, and sometimes she couldn't sneak away. But things were bad ... really bad. And I don't know why she never told us. Did she think it was nothing, that she could handle him? How could we have missed the signs?"

I reached out to grip Lin's arm, for my comfort as much as hers, and felt her tremble. My heart twisted in dread as she took a deep, shuddering breath, blinking rapidly.

"We didn't find out until it was too late," she said. "I … I saw her body later, saw everything he did to her, Rekh. It'd been going on for a long time. A long, long time. There were bruises everywhere, and cuts. She was finally strangled to death. In bed."

My eyes grew misty, the room around me blurring, colours merging into one another, and a heavy weight settled over my limbs. "And the husband?" I whispered.

"Inducted into the Protectors."

Danielle Boyd

Niall

*An excerpt from "Assassins By Night," a young adult fantasy novel
set in a world where if you die in your dreams, you never awake*

Niall....

The name had been on my mind all day, the ghost impression of a
figure at the edges of my consciousness that I couldn't quite compre-
hend. It was a bit concerning; I didn't know anyone named Niall. Still,
the name and vivid images from last night's dream kept replaying over
and over in my mind. My thoughts had been clouding my judgment all
day, confusing me. I'd dumped three tablespoons, instead of teaspoons,
of baking soda into the bread dough. My distracted mindset at the bakery had frustrated Ma so much, she'd sent me to the market instead.

It had rained the night before and the dirt roads were reduced to
mud. I did my best to avoid the worst of it, but my black boots still
turned brown as I walked, along with the hem of my green wool cloak.
Hopefully, the brisk autumn air and cloudy skies would dry out the mud
quickly. Maybe even in time for my return trip.

Typically, Ma and I visited the market on Saturdays, when the farmers from the surrounding lands travelled into town. The Wednesday
market could be just as plentiful. My adoptive mother, Zoe, owned the
only bakery in town. Veen was a small village, so the market was only a
short walk from our home. Today, Ma had given me a list of spices for
some of our more popular buns and pastries. It felt like an empty errand,
but I was happy to get out of the kitchen and ease my distracted mind.

I quickly found myself at Flora's spice stand, near the centre of the market square. It was my favourite stand in the whole market. The table was covered with the best smells and colours. I wasn't sure where Flora got all her exotic spices. Being so far removed from any real royal oversight, there was no one around to question her. We just accepted the delicacies, and the old woman was always gracious and flashed us a quick wink, like we'd taken part in something surreptitious together.

Today the fresh rosemary nearly jumped off the table into my hand, its aroma overtaking my senses. I picked up a sprig and held it to my nose, relaxing.

Flora smiled knowingly. "Rosemary aromas have healing properties," she said, with a crook in her brow, "for the mind and body."

"I'll take some." I wrapped the sprigs in a new cloth before placing them into my basket next to the cinnamon sticks and currants.

I passed her three bronze coins, feeling instantly at ease as I inhaled the calming scents. Reluctantly, I turned away—and collided with my best friend.

Celia was shorter than me, with thin strawberry-blonde hair, the opposite of my own thick black locks, which I'd barely contained in today's braid. She wrapped her arms around my waist and laughed. "Morning, Nova." Her light and happy voice brought a smile to my face. Her eyes darted across the stand. "More spices already?"

"Always." I linked my arm through hers and let her guide me away through the market.

A craftsman was selling practical furniture with unique designs carved throughout, twisting and turning with the wood. Another woman sold beautifully woven fabrics that caught Celia's attention, but she was distracted. The added bounce in her step and her darting gaze was enough to know.

"Any news?" I asked, searching her face as she regained her focus, her bright eyes meeting mine.

"You will never guess what we've got coming to the inn tonight!" She was always one to jump straight into a story. I couldn't believe she'd waited for me to ask her. Her excitement was infectious, and I couldn't help but beam back.

Celia's family ran the Veen inn. It was the only one within a two-day ride, unless you went north into Mias. The village used to have a constant flow of merchants, tradesmen, and travellers heading back and forth between the kingdom of Mias and our country, Odin. That was until twelve years ago, when our King inexplicably closed the border. Now the inn was quiet; in fact, the whole town was quiet, except for the odd border guard coming off six weeks of duty. Celia and I had gotten to know some of the guards well enough over the years, and they told us of the bleak conditions in Mias without our trade. While it was definitely difficult to digest, truth be told, all of us were suffering.

"I can't guess, you'll have to tell me." I squeezed Celia's hand.

"A legion. One of the King's!" Celia squealed and bounced on her toes with excitement.

I gaped. A royal legion of Odin's soldiers could easily fill the inn for the first time in years. The commerce they would bring in one night would help local families stock up for the impending winter.

I understood her excitement, but I hesitated to join in. "What is a King's legion doing so far north?" I asked, catching my lower lip in my teeth.

"Who cares! That's Zoe speaking." Celia swatted at me playfully and winked. "Think of all the new people! Exotic men of the South. Aren't you excited? Plus, I hear legions tip well."

I laughed. Celia was right. Ma's distrust of everything always put my nerves on edge.

I wondered if Veen would remember how to cope with the number of people a full legion would bring. Our streets would be packed and the night would be loud. "So is your father planning a big feast?"

"I think so." Celia sighed and held up empty cloth bags. "He's just sent me to fill these with cabbage, carrots, and onions."

"Well, let's get you some!"

Celia and I walked to Pry's farm stand. Pry was a local merchant who helped at the market on the days the farmers were working. Each morning he would ride out, buy fresh goods from the closest farms, and bring what he could to town. As usual, it wasn't much, and we scoured the crates for the ripest selection. I was elbow deep in cabbage when I received a sharp poke to the gut. I scowled at Celia, who had been the culprit.

"Don't look now," she whispered, "but that man over there is staring at you."

She nodded to the left, and I immediately looked, ignoring her growl. Over by the blacksmith's, a tall young man leaned against the fence. He wore a dark cloak around his shoulders and a brown cap that shadowed his face. Dirt and mud stained his pants, and I could tell he'd been travelling for days.

From under the shadow of his cap, piercing blue eyes stared at me. I turned away sharply, fear bubbling in my veins.

Niall…. The name came back to the forefront of my thoughts. The dark field, the Ravens, the sickle. Was this him, the murderer from my dreams? No. It was impossible. That had been a dream. But he'd killed that poor old man, and now he would never wake up. My hands started shaking and I dropped a cabbage. I ripped my gaze away from the blue eyes.

Stop it! I screamed at myself. It had been a dream, my dream. So no one had died, right? I couldn't quite convince myself. The same goosebumps from the morning rose on my forearms, sending chills down my limbs as I tried to shake the panic from my mind.

"I think I should get back." My voice came out in a weak whisper, and Celia had to lean closer to hear. "Ma will be expecting me."

"What? So soon?" Celia frowned. "But—"

"The evening rush starts soon; Ma will need my help."

"Fine," she sighed heavily.

I looked back toward the blacksmith's, but the mysterious figure was no longer there. I turned and made for home, wrapping my cloak tightly around my shoulders.

"I expect you at the inn tonight!" Celia called after me, and I waved as I scurried away from the market.

Elisabeth de Grandpré

The Empress

An excerpt from "Briar,"
a young adult sci-fi fairy-tale novel

Isadora stared out at the pure and perfect wash of white in front of her. The snow had fallen in flakes the size of fists. She remembered the first time she had experienced the sensation of fresh snow turning to water on her warm hands. The crisp bright scent had assailed her nostrils with a frozen burn.

She caught her reflection in the glass that protected the palace from the harsh winds that swirled the snow into a thick haze down below. Her crown glinted, her features blurred. She closed her eyes and still felt the ice tearing bits of flesh off her cheeks, even after so many years. Everyone knew if you stood outside without the proper armour for longer than a few minutes, the force of the wind and surrounding ice would skin you alive.

Her beloved brother, Charles, had dared her to go out for a full minute, and she hadn't been able to refuse the heir. Wanting to impress him, she had gone out in the windstorm but kept a close eye on her timepiece. The wind wasn't at full strength yet, so she was safe watching the seconds flash. Her bare hands had just started to tingle as it reached the full minute. When she went to open the castle door, it didn't budge.

Charles had locked her out. She beat on the door for at least two minutes, as the wind whipped around her. Her big brother had betrayed her. She covered her face, palms on her eyes, as the wind shredded her hands and cheeks. Hope drained out of her as the wind struck harder. The ice-wind reduced her thick clothing to tatters and covered her in millions of deep gashes across her body before her maid could pull her inside. She had lost most of the skin on her face and hands.

Isadora observed her now flawless face in her reflection and wiped away the solitary tear that fell. It had taken one year in the healing waters of the subterranean ice baths to restore her. She had missed her own sixteenth birthday party. At first she had screamed as the servants pushed her in and held her down. Near the end, she came to prefer the soothing frost of the baths to the warmth of the castle.

Mother and Father never punished *him*, but it left her forever changed. She was far more comfortable in the icy cold now and kept the castle as chilled as she liked. It was inconvenient that they lost at least one servant each year to hypothermia, as good help was scarce in the northern lands.

Isadora sensed Cassie waiting at the door. "Enter," she commanded.

"Your Imperial Majesty." Cassie bowed before her.

She enjoyed looking at Cassie. Her trusted scientist had an impeccably symmetrical face. Her jet-black plaits were pulled back precisely, not a single stray hair out of place. Cassie wore the white woollen tunic Isadora had ordered for her. It created a sharp contrast with her dark brown skin.

"Is it done?" asked Isadora.

Cassie nodded. "I have disposed of the prime subject."

It was done. Isadora wouldn't have that spoiled child haunting her any longer. Relief swelled in her chest. The prime subject had been useful for a time, but that time was over. "Excellent. We will move forward with the expansion into the House of White's territory." She smiled, left the window, and sat on her crystal throne.

Frigg burst into the room. "Excuse me, Your Imperial Mighty and Distinguished Majest—"

"What, Frigg?" snapped Isadora. "What do you want?"

Admiral Frigg was not enjoyable to look at. His face looked like a misshapen rock with an unsettling overbite. His clothes, while clean, were simply too tight for his broad and large frame. Isadora often contemplated having him removed, but he was the most loyal commander of her forces. She sighed.

"The prisoner has refused to eat until you visit him. I've only now gotten word from the dungeons, but he's gone a week without food."

Isadora froze, holding up her hand. She did not have time for *him* today.

Frigg puffed out his chest. "If you would just let me dispose of him once and for all—"

Isadora stood and looked fixedly at the much shorter man. "I am the Empress of the New Galilean Empire. I do not provide leniency without reason. You will not question *my* judgments. Now you have brought this to my attention, you will leave and attend to moving my forces south."

Frigg was motionless.

"Now!"

He bowed and exited the chamber quickly. Isadora sat back down on her throne and tapped her long nails against the side.

Cassie kneeled at her feet. "Pardon my impertinence. Perhaps you might consider transferring the prisoner into my care at the Perception and Correction Institute. We can keep his mind active, yet he will no longer disturb you."

Isadora delicately placed her hand under Cassie's chin and tilted her head upwards. "I will keep you in mind when I am done with him. If I give him to you, you can play with his mind any way you like." She grinned.

Cassie presented the smile back to her. *Perfection.*

⁓

Isadora took her private elevator down to sub-level six to visit the prisoner's solitary cell. She smiled at herself in the mirrored walls. The silver tone of her dress hugged both her wide hips and slight chest. The purple shift in the fabric brought out the green in her eyes.

As the door opened, her breath came out in puffs of ephemeral mist. The luxurious feeling of frost was a treat. She stepped out onto the stone flooring and kicked away a mound of dirt directly in her path. No matter how many servants she sent down here to polish the stones, they never got them clean enough. She pressed on until his cage came into view.

"Brother," she said, "I have come to you as the dutiful sister I am. I'm concerned you haven't been eating."

"Where is she?" He rattled the bars. He looked dreadful with his signature long locks shaved off and a threadbare blanket wrapped around his shoulders, tied like a cape. *Pathetic.*

"She?" Isadora smiled sweetly.

"You know damn well who I'm talking about."

"Oh yes, Kai. She's well. She is bouncing around the palace somewhere. It is so hard to keep track of that girl—"

"You will not harm her!"

"Because King Charles Yu says so?" she said. "No, sad fallen man, I will not harm my beloved niece, because I am her Celestial guardian. I promised the Gods and Goddesses I would protect her, and I shall not go back on my word. It remains up to you whether she is protected in a cell like yours or remains free in the palace as the Lady of the House of Ice."

"I've given up everything. My throne, my lands, my life. I want to see my daughter. Why must you torment me?" Charles crumbled to the floor.

She laughed. "Because I can. Because you are weak, and you've always been weak. When your precious Paisley died, you became unbearably pathetic. Kai is better off believing you are dead."

"What?" His mouth fell open.

"Dead in the same southern raid that killed your entire court. Didn't I mention that?" She smirked.

"Why keep me alive? Why not just kill me?" He reached out and grabbed the bars, his hands trembling.

"As tempting as that is, knowing you are here withering is too delicious to give up. I want you to suffer for a long time. But for that, you must live. Now, I want you to eat." She clapped her hands twice and the silent guards came out with feeding tubes. They were so outdated, but too fun not to use.

"Do you *hate* me that much?"

"I *love* you, brother. I can't have you go hungry." Isadora hummed brightly and went back to her pristine throne room, as coughing and gagging resonated behind her.

Brynn Morgan

Niernen Docks

AN EXCERPT

I lift my hand from my face, eyes adjusting to pale blue light that is streaming in from the window. The leftover haze from my sleep starts to clear, and my mind begins to piece together why I woke up in the first place. A soft click, the sound of a lock sliding into place, echoes in the back of my mind.

My eyes flutter open, just to squint themselves at the closed door. Everything is in place, just as I saw it before. *I probably dreamt it,* I think, shifting around under the covers. Before I attempt to fall back asleep, my eyes dart to Cheribu's sleeping body. It is now a pile of blankets on an empty bed.

I fall out of my bed in a jolt of terror and adrenaline. My head zips to Sapphire's bed, in hopes that I haven't woken her with the noise. Tossed sheets and an empty space meet me.

My rapidly accelerating heartbeat pounds in my ears. I just sit in the middle of the floor, eyes darting between the still empty beds of Sapphire and Cheribu. My face burns with the stress, my hands shaking on the floor.

The leaders will keep you safe. SJ's words echo in my head, over and over. *Failing that, Cheribu will be by your side!*

I can't move. *But what if they're both gone? SJ! SJ?*

My limbs return to me, and with new inspiration I slide over to Sapphire's side table. *I'll call SJ,* I reason, *and she'll get me out of this!* But as much as I look, Sapphire's phone is nowhere to be found.

I rake my hand down my face as I stand over the empty side table. It's the dead of night. The only sound outside is the quiet slosh of water and the rare croak from a sleepy toad. *If I can't get to SJ*, I think, the pit in my stomach deepening, *I'll have to find a phone somewhere else.*

Taking a few deep breaths, I try to prepare myself for the outside world. My backpack seems to have fallen along with me, its contents strewn on the floor. My favourite hoodie, a thick maroon wool mess, is lying on top. With some struggle, I push my head through the neck hole and grab the spare set of keys. *At least those aren't gone*, I think, pushing open the door.

The docks move with me, bobbing with every footstep. My nose begins to sting from the cold air as I secure the lock behind me. I start to shake again; I'm not sure if it's from nerves or the temperature. The shadows seem to creep from their corners, non-existent threats becoming a reality. Empty doorways now seem occupied by still figures using the darkness to conceal their devious plans. The dock, still unsturdy, is the only thing shielding me from the black glass below, disturbed only by the faintest of ripples. I shift over to a wooden pillar and wrap an arm around it while grasping the key with my other hand. A soft glow emerges from the dark buildings, a yellow light I can see only from this angle. It's only a few streets away.

I throw caution to the wind. With a shaky step, I plunge into the darkness of the streets in search of the glow. My back is rigid. I can't help but cradle myself in my own arms as I shuffle down the dock. I try to keep my eyes toward the light, but buildings are blocking my view.

A creak, probably from a rickety plank, cries into the night sky. I abandon all hope. Breaking into a full sprint, I turn corners and duck down unfamiliar streets, until finally I can fully see the source of the light.

Unlike the rest of town, which is covered in a sheet of darkness, the entire square is revealed by this glow. The giant tree, the one I saw earlier, has grown giant, glowing fruit on the tips of its branches. Their milky contents shift around, as if the light is trying to burst out. A larger orb, nestled between two branches, slowly tears itself apart, its cloudy glow dripping down. The nectar falls onto the grass below; the tall blades are covered with the odd substance. It seems that has happened in other areas, since other glowing spots cover the grass and parts of the small wooden fence surrounding the property.

The tree is lit enough that I can see its every detail. The surrounding shops are noticeably less illuminated, but they still retain their colours from that morning. Past them lies the path out of town, a stretch of boardwalk that eventually leads into pure darkness. There are other paths leading off to different districts, but this one is larger and reaches into the abyss of the forest. I can see the tips of branches reaching out, eating anyone who dares to enter at night.

I shiver and turn away.

The gate that was latched before has been left ajar. *I wonder if this 'Soul' is back*, I think, glancing at the painted name on the mailbox. Before I can push the gate open, a shrill creak from the boardwalk grabs my attention. Soon after, another creak rings out, louder than the one before.

My adrenaline skyrockets as my eyes zip around, searching for a place to hide. Without thought, I vault over the fence and lie still in the tall grass. I clamp my eyes shut in fear.

This is a horrible idea, I rail at myself, quickly repenting my choice of hiding spot. *I could have just run, but no!*

The creaks continue, a shrill squeak every few seconds. Forcing my eyes open, I see I've landed very close to the fence, in such a way that part of my face can be seen. I try to re-manoeuvre myself, but a final creak, right outside the square, shrieks into the night.

Two figures, both sporting thick cloaks, enter the square. The taller of the two has a dark green cloak that shimmers in the tree's light, while the other, shorter and leaner than the first, is draped in a thick midnight-blue cloak. The kind that royal guards wear.

"It's nice to walk around at night, don't you think?" one notes, their sing-song voice only barely reaching me. The other figure doesn't respond.

"Gah," the first continues, clearly annoyed, "you're no fun today."

The two pass through the clearing, leaving it empty like before. I sit up from the damp grass, unsuccessfully trying to brush dirt off my hoodie. When I look up after vigorously rubbing at an annoying patch of dirt, I meet the eyes of a familiar figure standing in the entrance to the square, looking as confused as I am.

Sapphire and I are both frozen, lost for any kind of reaction. In a fit of anxiety, I wave at her.

"Sor!" she hisses, speed-walking toward me. "What are you doing outside? Why are you here?"

"Both of you were gone!" I hiss back. "I tried to call someone, but your phone was gone! I had no choice!"

"You could have stayed inside! Well, it's too late now." She reaches her arm out and pulls me over the fence. "Did you see the people who walked through here?" she asks, motioning me to follow her. I nod. "Those are the people we're after." Peeking around a corner, she whispers, "Those are the Flip-Siders."

Melissa Garcia

Liliana

*An excerpt from a young adult novel; Liliana is forced
into a world she never knew existed when her
lifelong captor—her mother—disappears*

Something's not right. Get up!

Coughing heavily, I woke feeling groggy and confused. Will I never get a peaceful sleep again? Hands were on me, dragging me out of bed. I forced my eyes open. Smoke limited my vision, but I could vaguely see Oren's shape. He was picking me up, dragging me out of my room.

"What is happening?" I shouted through a coughing fit that shook my body.

"They've set fire to the house! I tried to put it out, but it spread too quickly," he said, setting me down in the hall.

I tried to get past him, back into my room. "My things!" I couldn't let all my memories and belongings burn. Dread hit as I realized I hadn't packed anything to go.

"There's no time! We have to get out now!"

Oren began dragging me down the hall to the stairs. He was stronger than I'd imagined he would be. I tried to fight back, beating my hands against his chest, but coughing got the better of me.

Tossing me over his shoulder, he rushed down the stairs. Hot flames licked at my face as we descended. The entire outer wall of the house was going up in flames. My mind still felt foggy, and I didn't know if I would cry. All I really wanted was to go back through my mother's belongings again.

Oren dropped me on the floor; clearly he'd expected me to land on my feet. I looked up at him, my eyes watering from the smoke, though I couldn't be sure it was only the smoke.

He grabbed me roughly under the arms and hauled me to my feet. "Listen very carefully," he said, bringing his face way too close to mine. I tried to lean back, but his fingers dug into my shoulders. The serious look on his face terrified me. "We go outside, and as soon as we move past the door, you put a protective orb around us. I'll open a portal while you protect us. You have to do this, Lili."

He shook me once, hard, as I tried to process what he was saying. "I don't know if I can," I said. Fear began to choke me just as much as the smoke was. *I can't do this.*

You have to, or we die.

I nodded my head. I knew she was right. I tried to find courage inside, but all I could feel was panic.

Oren spun me toward the door, his hands still on me, forcing me closer to the wall. I turned my face to avoid the flames. "I'll break the door open," he said, "but I know they're waiting out there. As soon as we step through, put the orb over us." He moved to stand in front of me. "Don't hesitate! You need to protect us, or we're not getting out of here." He moved closer to the flames, pausing to see if I would follow.

I have to do it. I can't die yet. I still had too many questions. I moved to stand against Oren's back so I could feel when he moved to break open the door. *I've got this. I can protect us.* I wanted to take a deep breath to calm my nerves, but I didn't want to inhale any more smoke. We needed to get out now, before my nerves—or lack of oxygen—caused me to black out. Pushing against Oren's back, I envisioned my energy within to prepare the orb.

Oren kicked the door open in one quick motion. I followed him, my body still pressed against his. The orb surrounded us.

As soon as we were through, Oren dropped to his knees in the dirt. "Keep this orb up while I open the portal." He gave me a stern look and began moving his hands across the ground.

My eyes burned as the sweat slowly trickled its way down my forehead. I wasn't sure how much longer I could send out this much power. I wanted to wipe away the drenched locks of hair that clung to my face, but I was afraid if I moved my arms, the orb surrounding us would shift, or worse, fall. I wasn't ready for this complex magic, but I knew I needed to give Oren at least a few minutes to prepare the portal for our escape.

"How much longer can you hold them off?" he shouted over his shoulder.

I was momentarily distracted by the way he etched symbols into the ground and then moved his arms above them in some sort of magical dance.

A loud crack rang out through the orb.

Carly Daelli

The Soul of Dessia

AN EXCERPT

The first night I saw the cat on my windowsill, I dismissed it.

No way a cat, standing upright on its back legs, was outside my bedroom window. It was impossible for it to get up here. And really, when was the last time I even saw a cat? It had been four or five years, at least. I was sure it was the spotlight from the police helicopter, scanning the city to unsuccessfully prevent the crime that had been going on for years.

The next night, I woke up about the same time, and there the cat was again. I noticed there was a gold glow around it. It jumped off the ledge when we locked eyes.

By night four, the cat was becoming brave. It would watch me until it caught my eye, then seem to have a staring contest with me. I examined the cat while it scrutinized me. I may not have seen a cat in a long time, but there was no way this was the way I remembered them. It was about five feet tall, wearing a long dress of purple silk with a bright pink tutu over it. The colours were intense; I hadn't seen colours like that since I was a little kid.

The weirdest thing about it was the glow. The cat shimmered even though there was no light. The glow seemed to come from within, like it was incandescent.

Each night, the cat stayed at my window longer. I was getting tired of it bothering me. It had some way of waking me up when it came. But all it did was study me.

After a week, I finally said something. "Please leave. I need my sleep for school." If I fell asleep in class, not only would I be taken to the head teacher again, but my parents would be punished with more hours at work. Again.

"I'm here to make sure you are the right one," the cat said in our city's old language.

I pulled back, shocked to hear words I hadn't heard in many years. Before the Takeover, our city had had a beautiful, complex language. I understood it because my parents and grandparents had spoken it, against the Bureau's orders. I, however, couldn't speak it, because it was banned in school and in public, and my parents didn't do anything against the Bureau now. "What? Right for what?"

"You will see," the cat said and jumped off the window.

The next day at school, I could barely concentrate. Had I been having a recurring dream for the past week? There was no such thing as a five-foot-tall glowing cat, right?

Wynne noticed my exhaustion. "Adira, girl, if you don't start getting more sleep, you are gonna get yourself into trouble," she said at lunch.

"I know," I said, completely drained. Wynne definitely wouldn't believe me if I told her there had been a cat at my window. "I haven't been sleeping well. Every time I go to the depot, someone gets tasered. I'm so sick of seeing it."

"Yeah, I'm glad my dad picks up our food."

She shook off the gloom, her big earrings swaying. "Hey, look over there. I think Booker is looking at you." She bumped her shoulder against mine. All Wynne thought about was being in love.

I glanced across the room, and Booker looked away. "I'm sure he was looking at you," I said, feeling quite ordinary next to my beautiful friend. Her very short, dark curly hair was always styled perfectly and looked amazing next to my long, messy waves. Even though she was wearing the exact same ugly outfit I was, she rocked it. Wynne's mom had died in the Takeover, and Wynne had kept everything of hers. From her old knee-high socks to her big, dangly earrings, Wynne always found a way to wear something of her mom's, despite the fact that we always had to wear our uniforms.

"Naw, I've caught him looking at you before," she said. "But I've been looking at Laz." She glanced across the room and nodded her head, and I realized that Laz was looking straight at her. She smiled at him. "See? He's cute, isn't he?" She smiled again.

"Wynne, why do you bother? We can't date, and we have no choice about who we'll marry next year. So what's the point?" I asked, a little bit irked at her ability to flirt and at the attention she got from both guys and girls. I looked around to see if any adults were within earshot. "If we get caught talking about this, we'll be dragged off to see the head teacher. Or worse." The thought of going to the Bureau made me shudder.

Wynne moved her head closer to mine and whispered, "Oh, Adira, someday it will be different. I believe by the time we're at 'marrying age,' all this shit will be over, and we'll get to make our own decisions on who we marry, or even if we get married."

"Well, I've only got three months." I pushed my waves out of my face. "And you don't have much longer than that." It was six months until Wynne turned fifteen.

She looked across the room again. "I'm hoping by then no one will care if we marry a boy or a girl," she said, giving a flirty smile to some girl I didn't know.

I rolled my eyes. Nothing was going to change that drastically in less than a year. Probably not even in our lifetime. Wynne was so optimistic that sometimes I couldn't be near her.

The bell rang, and she kissed my cheek. "Don't fall asleep in class," she reminded me.

☞

Walking home from school, I dared to ask Ozias about my unusual night sightings. "Has anything been outside your window this week?"

He scrunched his face up in confusion. "What? How would anything get up to our windows?" He pulled his jacket closer to his cheeks, against the mist from the grey sky that was spraying straight into our faces.

"I don't know. I guess it's just the police spotlights. There must be a lot more crime lately," I replied, thinking that I might be going crazy. I shivered, not sure if it was the cold weather or the uneasiness I felt from my nighttime visitor.

"Well, whatever it is, if you don't start getting more sleep, you are going to get our whole family in trouble," Ozias said, kicking at a puddle on the sidewalk.

He had noticed my exhaustion too. The rest of the walk home, I thought about what I could do to help myself stay asleep. But all I could think about was my glowing guest.

After two weeks, I finally caught the cat. Well, I grabbed its pink tutu as it jumped from my window, but the fabric slipped between my fingers, sliding away. I looked out the window but didn't see anything. I leaned further out.

"Are you looking for me?" said a musical voice behind me.

I jumped, startled, but luckily the bars outside my window kept me from falling.

I turned around slowly, and there was the cat. Inside my room!

"Yes, I am!" I almost shouted.

"I have decided you are who I am looking for. So let me introduce myself. I am Shiny." The cat stuck out her paw. She spoke in the old language, as she had the other day.

I cautiously walked toward her, mostly because I'd never shaken hands with a cat before.

"Hi. I'm Adira," I said.

"Yes, I know. I know all about you," the cat said in her magical voice. She moved across the room, fleeting streaks of light following her, like she was a meteor.

Shiny's gentle movements and voice kept me reassured, although I could feel something rising up from my gut. It was something like panic, but I couldn't quite figure out why. The cat's calm demeanour piqued my curiosity and also gave me reason to trust her. "How do you know who I am? Why have you been watching me?" I asked.

"I know you because you are the right one. The person I have been sent here to find," Shiny replied.

My mind raced. Besides the fact that I'd never had a conversation with a cat before, I didn't understand what she was talking about. "The only thing I'm right for is …" I trailed off. I wasn't right for anything; I never had been. My grades were so-so, my looks were average, I was clumsy, and I definitely was not popular.

"To save us," Shiny finished.

"Save? Us? Save who? From what?" I usually wasn't this inarticulate, but Shiny wasn't making sense.

Shiny sighed. "Come, Adira. I can explain everything while we are on our way." She gently led me to the window, holding out her paw. A mist of gold floated over me.

"Ready?" When Shiny looked at me, her glow became brighter and she somehow became even more peaceful and familiar.

I shook my head, trying to get this cat out of it. I had to be dreaming.

"I will be back tomorrow," she sang. "It will be your last chance to come with me, as time is running out. I hope you make the right decision." And with that, Shiny bounced out the window.

R. D. Hughes
The Mage of Thunder
AN EXCERPT

Clive Rezno has been accepted to The College Arcana, the only
school of magic on the continent. He has been there for a month,
and has only just begun his magical instruction

Clive settled into his seat in the back row, his arms crossed on the table, holding up his head. A sudden impact on his back made his blood rush and snapped his heavy eyelids open. Cursing under his breath, he shot upright in his chair. "Oi, what was that for, Walshy?" The centre of his back burned as he looked up.

There, leaning against the desk, a wide smile plastered across his tanned face—Walsh O'Cally. Clive didn't mind the guy, but he was a bit weird. Especially that crazy mess he called a hairstyle. Walsh stood there, comb in hand, running it through his grease-slicked hair. The back and sides swept back and the rest had been slicked up in a sort of cone that protruded past his face but held still, like gravity had no hold on it.

"Ain't no time to be sleeping!" said Walsh. "You need some fresh sea air in your lungs." His bottomless pit of energy was astounding. Clive had never seen someone so energized all the time.

Magnar Kelm entered the room, his giant figure barely fitting through the doorframe, and made his way to the desk at the front of the classroom, next to the giant green chalkboard with gold ornate flourishes around the edges. The students all rushed to their seats, their conversations put on hold.

"Now then, class," Magnar's high-pitched voice rang out. "Today is an important day for each and every one of you." Clive waited expectantly to hear what Magnar would say.

"Today is the day you learn your first elemental spell," Magnar announced, a smile on his face. Clive, along with the rest of the class, let out a cheer. He had become brain-dead from the constant theory work they had been doing so far.

Magnar pulled out an ornate box from one of the desk's drawers. "These here"—he opened up the box, revealing different-sized stones, gems, and crystals—"are similar to the stones used to test mana affinity. The difference is, these represent multiple elements and will only react to a mage who is aligned to that element. So, one after another, I will present the box to you, and you will fill the stone with mana, just like you were taught in the affinity test. You will try this with each one in the box."

Clive watched nervously as the people ahead of him went through each stone, letting some of their mana flow through it. If they didn't have affinity for the element, the stone didn't react. If they did, the stone lit up. Some shone more brightly than others; some flashed instead of a steady glow. Magnar would then decide what their best way forward would be and gave them a book.

When the box came around to Mila, two of the stones reacted very brightly to her mana, which led Magnar to let out a high-pitched whelp of what Clive could only assume was joy. "Well now, Miss Zhurick. You are a rare thing indeed," Magnar said, as he ran back to his desk. He began opening drawers and shuffling through them.

"What does this mean, Mr. Kelm?" said Mila, with everyone's eyes on her. Clive was curious too. Up till Mila, nobody had been able to light more than one stone. Yet she'd been able to light two.

"Well, in basic terms, you are a dual elemental user. Let's see, now. You lit up a water stone and an earth gem." Magnar shuffled through drawers for a bit longer, then pulled out a few books. "I should apologize though. Dual elemental users are rare, and until we find out what your true element is.... Well, we will just have to keep experimenting until we find what works. That's what I had to do."

"You're a dual elemental user too, Mr. Kelm?" said Mila, staring at the bunch of books Magnar had just placed in front of her.

"Yes, well, when I was in this class, I was able to light up a fire stone and an earth gem. I'm embarrassed to admit it, but it took me a whole six months before I figured it out."

"And? What element do you wield?" one of the students interrupted.

Magnar smiled and made his way back to the front of the room. Rolling his sleeves up, he held his hands slightly apart, like he was gripping a ball. Clive could see his lips move but couldn't hear what he was saying.

In the empty space between his hands, a liquid ball of orange and red started to form. The front-row students all leaned back, trying to get further away from the ball. The heat in the room began to spike. Clive could feel sweat start to form on his forehead.

Magnar stretched his hands apart and the ball stretched with them. With a flick of his hand, the ball formed into a sort of pillar sitting in his palm. He moved his free hand around it, his fingers bending and pulling like he was trying to sculpt it. Eventually the pillar twisted and formed into the shape of a dragon. Then the hot liquid faded away into the air.

"I can wield lava, and there hadn't been a recorded user until I came along. So imagine how much of a struggle that must have been." Magnar chuckled as he resumed the testing.

As the stones reached Walsh, Clive could feel his heart beat in his neck, the blood pounding. Was he nervous or excited? He couldn't tell at this point.

Walsh stood up, hands rubbing against his pants, like he was about to make a running jump into a lake. "Which one is the water one, sir?"

Magnar pulled out the smooth, pearl-like stone and handed it to him. Walsh held it in his hands. His shoulders dropped as he stared into the pearl. Within a few seconds, a blue light pulsated from the pearl, a firm sphere in the centre with streams of light flickering in and out of sight randomly.

"I knew it!" said Walsh. "No way a man of the sea such as myself would ever be related to anything other than water." His ever-energetic smile radiated even more than usual. He refused to test any other stones, on the grounds that he would be cheating on his love the ocean if he even tried. Magnar tried to convince him otherwise, but Walsh stuck to his guns on this one.

The box was slid under Clive's face. In it sat five stones: a jagged gemstone with charred outsides, the fire stone; a crystal with salt rock encrusted around it, the earth stone; a smooth, disk-like stone that looked like it had been cut over and over to make it so smooth, the air stone; and the stone Walsh had just held, the obvious water stone.

A sudden sense of dread began to sink into Clive. What if nothing lit up? What if he wasn't an Elementalist? His palms began to sweat, and he rubbed the tips of his fingers against the bottom of his palm.

A dull bluish light caught his eye, a jagged gemstone with a yellow-tinted centre. He picked it up. The gem was cold to the touch, and all the sweat he had felt seemed to evaporate. He tried to empty his mind of the doubts that had set up camp inside him. He felt a slight pressure on his torso, and a tingling sensation moved from his chest to his shoulder and down his arm, culminating at his fingertips.

Clive, Walsh, and Magnar squinted as a bright light filled the area. With his eyes barely open, Clive could feel his eardrums rattling as a sharp wailing sound assaulted his senses. The sound of smashed glass was followed by an intense sting in his hand.

When he opened his eyes, the gemstone was just shards scattered across his desk, along with drops of red. His hand began to throb as a warmth rushed to his palm. Little cuts were all around his hand where shards of gemstone had caught or embedded themselves in his skin.

"Mr. O'Cally. Can you please escort Mr. Rezno to the healer's wing?" Magnar instructed Walsh.

"Wait. What does that mean, though?" Clive couldn't think straight. His ears rang, his head pounded, and his hand throbbed and bled.

"You are a lightning Elementalist, Mr. Rezno. I will come by after class. Go get that looked at."

Clive couldn't help but feel like there was something Magnar wasn't telling him.

Michael Aaron Mayes
Not the First Incident

*The first chapter of a novel about a fifteen-year-old kid who
can physically combine with things by ramming into them*

It's not easy staying calm when the face of the cutest girl you know is
screaming at you underwater because she thinks you're trying to drown
her.

Not that I blame her. If that had been the first time I looked down and
saw the lower half of my body completely jammed into someone else's,
I would have been freaking out too. But that wasn't the first incident for
me. Hardly.

I realize this is going to take some explaining.

Here's what happened.

It was June. The fourth-last day of school. Everyone was at Kaploosh!
water park for *Summer Fun Daze*. The teachers spelled *Daze* like that
in an attempt to show us they weren't always serious. And then a few
of them couldn't help but talk about the debate that went into spelling
it wrong on purpose, and whether or not it actually looked more fun
or simply promoted poor spelling, which we were horrible at already. I
know. Ridiculous.

Anyway, smack in the middle of the afternoon, the very cute and
somewhat fussy Leela Pawar had just slid down the Shoot-the-Chutes
slide and splash-landed into the pool at the bottom. Maybe she got water in her nose. Maybe she couldn't figure out which way was up. Maybe
she wanted to make sure her hair was out of her face before she came out
of the water. Whatever it was, she was still in the "impact zone," directly
beneath the slide, when I came shooting down and landed on top of her.

I should let you know that I try very carefully to avoid incidents like this. Sometimes they happen anyway.

Me landing on top of Leela was awkward enough. What made it much worse, and why she was trying to scream even though she was completely underwater, was that she was looking at the same thing I was looking at. From our hips down, we were stuck into each other like conjoined twins. Attached at the waist. Four legs kicking around beneath us. It wasn't pretty.

I knew from experience that looking at her wasn't going to help me any. The only way to undo these things is to try to stay calm and relax my way out of it. I also knew that I had to fix it before we floated back up to the surface, or things were going to get way more complicated.

The whole Grade 9 class of King George Junior High was there, plus loads of other kids from other schools. People were probably already rubbernecking from the yelp Leela let out when I landed on her. And all the flailing. If anyone saw us stumbling out of the pool stuck together like that, I can't even imagine what would have happened next.

I had to untangle her from me.

Leela continued to scream mostly bubbles. I closed my eyes, held my breath, and tried to focus on anything but her. The sound of my heartbeat pounding in my ears. The warmth from the sunlight through the water. The liquid swirling between us. Thankfully, a few seconds later, Leela kicked her way free and swam frantically up for air.

At that point, I just wanted to stay down there floating around underwater as long as possible. The only thing I could hope for was that Leela didn't fully understand what had just happened. Things look weird underwater, so I could probably try to explain it one way or another. Our legs got tangled up. My bathing suit snagged in hers. I swallowed a bunch of water, couldn't see clearly, thought someone else had landed on me too and panicked. I don't know. Any of those are more likely stories.

I swam to the stairs at the end of the landing pool as quietly as possible, hoping everyone was looking somewhere else when I dragged myself out of the water. By the time I made it over to my towel on the grass, Leela was already surrounded by a cluster of her friends, two teachers, and a lifeguard, making sure she was okay. Nobody looked too concerned about me. Brutal, right? I mean, I could have been drowning for all they knew.

Eventually, one of the teachers did come over. Mr. Wells was a slow-moving guy who seemed to be constantly contemplating the state of the universe. Even in the middle of all this, he strolled over with his hands in his pockets, studying the ground in front of his feet as they made their way in my direction and stopped on the grass in front of me.

"Milton. You okay?" he said, looking at me with both eyebrows raised.

"Yup," I said quietly.

"Leela's pretty upset. She says you were holding her underwater. Had her in some sort of leg lock. Is that true?"

I shook my head.

"No? Okay then, want to tell me what happened?"

Here's the problem. How do you explain to someone that your body sometimes combines with things and you have no idea why? Not the kind of thing you can just blurt out in the middle of a sunny afternoon to a teacher who doesn't know much about you.

"We just got tangled up, that's all." I said. "I didn't *mean* to land on her."

"Tangled up, hey?" Mr. Wells said, not looking convinced. "Regardless, I think you'd better apologize to her." He turned around to see where Leela was. She had a towel draped around her shoulders, and her friends were walking her to the change room. Mr. Wells turned back to me. "Right now's probably not the best time, though."

Then he gave me a look that meant who-knows-what and made his way back to where the other teachers were standing, with his hands still stuck in his pockets the whole time. And that was that.

For the rest of the afternoon, I stayed off the slides, stayed out of the water, and waited for the day to hurry up and be done with. After a good fifteen minutes, Leela came out from the change room dressed in her regular clothes and sat on the grass hugging her knees. She didn't go anywhere near the water either.

I was trying to figure out how to walk over and say something casual, like "Hey, Leela. Sorry about landing on you," mainly to make myself feel better. But then what? What would she say? What would she accuse me of? Which fake story could I tell her that seemed more likely?

It didn't end up mattering. Before I could figure out what to say, we were both back on the bus with every other sun-baked, chlorine-soaked, half-dizzy kid in my grade. Which was probably better anyway, given how awesome I am at talking to people.

I was just glad I had my noise-cancelling headphones with me so I didn't have to listen to anything ridiculous on the trip back. I was even more glad there were only a few days left of school.

Unfortunately, in those last few days I already started hearing a few different versions of the story flying around.

Version One: I tried to hold Leela underwater on purpose to mess with her, because everyone knew I liked her but she wasn't really into me, and I am therefore a sexist bully.

Version Two: I intentionally raced down the slide and tried to land on Leela so I could pretend it was an accident and feel her up underwater without her realizing it, and I am therefore a juvenile sexual predator.

Version Three: I accidentally landed on Leela, thought I was drowning, panicked, and clung to her for life, dragging her underwater with me, and I am therefore an anxiety-riddled wimp who would drown a girl to save himself.

And those were just the stories I heard about.

Don't get me wrong. Those things are all bad. It just left me wondering if there were any *other* stories going around that I didn't hear about. Ones that might be closer to the truth. The truth is a whole lot harder to explain.

Before I get into all that, I should probably tell you the basics first. Just in case something horrible happens to me. And by horrible, I mean something *more* horrible than the stuff that's already happened.

Here goes. My name is Milton Mitsuo Ash. I'm fifteen. I live at 2 Canyon Hills Drive with my sister Misha and my parents. I go to Eagle Ridge High School. Or at least, I did go there briefly, until a few months ago when I was forced to leave for reasons beyond my control.

The rest is complicated.

I'm just going to try and explain things the way they happened to me, because there's all sorts of stuff I'm not supposed to know and tons I still need to figure out if I can.

They don't tell you this when you're a kid growing up, but there's no way of knowing much without figuring out how things work for yourself. Plain and simple. You can watch what goes on in the world. You can look stuff up. You can have someone explain to you how to do almost anything. But until you're right in the middle of it, doing things yourself, you can't really know what's going on.

And even then, you might not know for sure.

Isobel McDonald

A Modern Witches' Congress

AN EXCERPT

Most witches live hidden in plain view of the human world. I've lived in Victoria's Chinatown since the 1940s. The shop was much the same then as it is now and almost always overlooked. It has crystals embedded in the doorframe, with powers of non-visibility. The building is built over one of Victoria's famous ley lines, a crack in the earth's surface that emits powerful magnetic energy, which magnifies the power of the crystals and other forms of natural energy. I was at the height of my power and popularity when this magical spot was offered to me as recognition for my service and leadership in our community. I share this charmed location with my friend Li, who was also honoured. She is an extraordinary scholar and a witch historian. Li and I may no longer be popular, but we are still powerful, and with a few powerful friends. I hope I can still make myself into an influencer. I have to.

The arrangement to take students came when I was asked, not all that nicely, to accept three alchemy students for their final practicum before they sat for their novice witch exams. I couldn't really say no, not without questions being asked. Normally I wouldn't care, but now that I was up for election at council, I didn't want the cold gaze of the Registrar pulled my way. And I was pretty sure my nemesis, Breye of the Ruby Ravens, had sent the students my way, hoping I'd refuse and self-identify as uncooperative in a time we all needed to pull together. Or better yet, take the students and be kept busy at a time I should be organizing the research I was presenting to council when the moon waxed next. Either way, Breye had won, for the moment.

When I entered the room, I got my first look at the three. They stood back to back like they were taught, a defensive posture. They were wisely disguised in the most popular brand of athletic clothing, famously unsuited for large bodies. Witches hate misogyny, and this was something we wouldn't be caught dead in. I relaxed a bit. Imposters wouldn't be so adroit. It was hard to tell their ages, but they were young. I wondered what they had heard about me.

I thanked Li in Mandarin, and I could see by their faces that only the dark-skinned student understood. I looked at them more closely and saw one was a slender man. Good. We'd become less inclusive in this millennium, and I was glad to have the diversity. I greeted them in conventional witch speak. "The air whispers."

"The fire leaps," they responded in unison.

"The earth asks."

"The water answers," they said.

"Who are you?" I said.

"We are the wind, the waves, the blossoms, and the sun," they answered correctly.

"Okay," I said. "Welcome. We'll do introductions later. You are here to work, so we start now. I want you to go out and have a conversation with the plant members of our family living in ditches and the cracks of sidewalks and back alleys in this neighbourhood. When you meet them, record the conversation and see if they will tell you what they are thinking about today, their hopes and fears. Write down this list: morning glory, kinnikinnick, lavender, buttercup, horsetail, broom, nettle, violet, burdock, dandelion, and chickweed. Be back by sunset, not earlier, and come together." With that, Li gently herded them out the door.

Li stood up, moved her shoulders around, and stretched her neck. Dropping the disguise she had assumed just to be on the side of caution, she became a tall, fit woman. Her eyes, which had seemed small and dim, were now large and sparkling. "I see you couldn't get rid of them fast enough. That was a PhD thesis you gave them to do." This was one of Li's favourite expressions for too much work—a PhD thesis. She thought it was hilarious. So ridiculously non-witch.

"I know. I'm too busy for them now. I've got a Skype call this afternoon that I'm not prepared for. They want the key points of my election campaign, but I'm afraid if I tell the wrong people I'll be shut down before I can even get my nomination documents completed. I don't know who is part of the Ruby Ravens and I don't know how far the Ruby Ravens have already gone."

"I can keep the students busy," Li said. "I'll tell them you're at a meeting. We'll go to my cousin's for some wonton soup. Special wontons in special soup."

"You don't have to tell me that," I said, smiling. "Save some for me. And thanks. I'll try to have my act together to meet with them tomorrow morning."

Our campaign slogan is Magical Thinking Is Not Magical Thinking. I overruled my support team, who wanted Magic for Balance, Magic for All. But I was trying to make the point that only stupid witches would believe we could survive alone. And only stupid witches don't believe in science. The human world doesn't know about the old virus coming back yet. The Ruby Ravens are denying the virus exists and are accusing me and my supporters of trying to inflame and manipulate witch public opinion to convince witchkind we need to share what we know with humans. I know very well their leadership fully realizes the threat of the virus is real, and I know their sinister intent. Their numbers are growing, and they have recruited many Indigenous leaders too, the Shamans we have always worked with. This new development worried me deeply. Without the Shamans' help it is almost impossible to find and prepare the herbs we need. Our green allies are harder to locate all the time, due to loss of habitat.

My team keeps reminding me to be careful not to insult my opposition. Under no circumstances am I ever to refer to the witches I don't respect as "deplorable." I really have a hard time believing just how popular the Ruby Ravens are getting.

My research shows, through historical records, that once a body is infected, the natural immune response to the virus will kill most of the affected. It's bad. Our ancestors discovered the impact of the illness can be lessened by herbal formulas that quell the lethal inflammatory response. Taking herbs, the right herbs in the right dosage prepared the right way at the right time, is the difference between life and death.

I strongly suspect—no, I know—the leadership of the Ruby Ravens want to "cleanse" the world by letting the human population die off, as many as possible. But I need to show how our world will also be destroyed if we let the human world perish from the viral plague. I have to make the council understand we need to share our protected scientific knowledge, our magic, and pull away the veil between our coexisting civilizations. Otherwise we are as doomed as the humans we blame for wrecking the planet.

I needed to clear my head. Another advantage to living in these times is that so many humans here in Victoria are training for the Ironman or some other marathon that no one gives me a second look when I go for a run. I'd been on my own so much, focused on my research and now my campaign, that I was missing our Connectedness Gatherings. Nothing replaces the group chanting and dancing, but at least I could run on my own. The saying "My body is my temple" came from the witches originally. We live it. I needed to move.

Leaving through the back door, I ran along the ley line through downtown Victoria, past Munro's Books on Government Street, where another Sister lived, through Beacon Hill Park, and down to Dallas Road, where I could breathe in the powerful energy from the great Pacific Ocean. The sky was overcast and the air was cold. I concentrated on feeling the rush of air in and out of my lungs, chanting the simplest of mantras—in and out and in and out—to clear my mind.

The wind picked up. I had been running along the sea wall for about twenty minutes when I heard quick clicking steps coming up behind me. I sped up. Dark clouds filled the sky. The sound of rhythmical clicking behind me was getting louder. I turned around and screamed as a four-point buck reared up and drove his hoofs into me. I threw out my arm to break my fall. The impact savagely wrenched back my wrist but saved my face from hitting the ground. I felt crushing pain as hoofs trampled on my back.

Robert Jay Groves

The Ghosts of Christmas Past

I opened my eyes and found myself standing over a dead body. The only illumination came from a flashing neon sign. I stared down at the corpse without emotion. The amount of blood was overwhelming. My jacket was saturated. Fluid dripped off my right gloved hand, making a faint splashing sound like a distant but annoying faucet. An enormous kitchen knife lay at rest on the bed beside the recently departed. Neurons were starting to fire, but none of what I was seeing made any sense. Looking again into his lifeless eyes, I hadn't the faintest glimmer of recognition. Who was this man and why was I here?

With each pulse of light, I attempted to gain my bearings, searching for any clue that might indicate my location. Blocked by the bed, most of the floor was in total darkness, but I could make out some old furniture along the back wall. The type you'd find in seedy hotels, marred from use and darkened in spots from burnt cigarettes. There were no personal items on display in this cramped, shabby space. All I could smell was death.

My senses heightened, I heard the first hint of a siren. It was just audible over the Christmas bells rising up from the street below. How I'd got here or what part I'd played was a complete mystery, but staying here any longer would be a huge mistake. I needed to get going.

Tentative in the darkness, I took a small step but lost my balance anyway. I had tripped over something. It was a rather large something. I wondered if it was too much to hope that I was there to buy a Persian rug. It took only one flash of neon to confirm my worst fear: I was face to face with a second unrecognizable body, who was just as dead and bloody as the first. I righted myself and continued with caution toward the door. Grateful that I didn't encounter any more obstacles along my path, I switched on the light. It was then I got my first glimpse of the carnage. A total of eight people were in the room, and I was the only one alive.

As the wailing continued to get louder, I discerned that multiple emergency vehicles were en route. I doused the light, hoping that the cops had only a general description of the disturbance. This action of course plunged the room back into darkness. I was about to depart when a cellphone went off.

By habit I reached for mine, but it wasn't there. In fact my pockets were empty—no wallet, no keys, and no phone. The sound appeared to be emanating from one of the dead men. Slightly panicked by this new development, I clambered over the bodies in an attempt to silence the device. My only guide was its repeating ringtone, a catchy little holiday favourite, Brenda Lee's "Jingle Bell Rock." I answered it with as calm a demeanor as I could muster, trying to create an illusion of normalcy amongst the chaos. The deceased had just won a trip to Jamaica. I started to laugh at the absurdity of my situation and found it difficult to stop.

What seemed only seconds later, the police arrived. Multiple vehicles screeched to a halt, sirens ceased, and doors slammed. Escape seemed impossible, so I sat down amongst the bodies and waited for my fate to arrive.

Soon a herd of thundering boots reached my floor. There was the sound of splintering wood and many voices shouting, "Police!" Then silence. To my surprise, they weren't coming for me: the commotion was concentrated across the hall.

Reprieved, I listened intently for a while but heard nary a sound. (Apparently I start to talk like a Scot when I'm under pressure.) My door was fitted with a peephole, common for this type of establishment, and I soon plucked up enough courage to look out into the hallway. It was illuminated by a low-wattage bulb that cast a strange shadow on the opposite wall. My breathing was still rather ragged from the ordeal, and I managed to fog up the convex glass quite quickly. I can't be sure, but I believe I saw some movement, just a glimpse of motion and then nothing. I waited another five minutes, but there was no further evidence of life.

Having no means of transport and fearing the police may return, I grabbed Mr. Jamaica's keys. Under the circumstances I didn't suspect he would mind. I took one last look into the hall, confirming the coast was clear, and exited. What remained of the door across the hall was hanging by one hinge and had been left wide open. With caution, I peered inside and was amazed to find the room entirely empty.

Descending the stairs, I met no one. The lobby too was devoid of people, as was the street. I pressed the fob, which alerted me to a late-model Jaguar parked halfway down the block. Attempting to appear casual, I sauntered over. A fresh dusting of snow crunched underfoot. The dash clock read 2:14 a.m. From this vantage point, I found the source of the room's illumination: a twenty-foot-high neon sign bolted vertically to the building that read "Baltimore Hotel."

It took me only thirty minutes to get home, where I tossed all my clothes in the washer and had a long hot shower.

I awoke the next morning hoping that it had all been a bad dream, but my clothes were still damp and there was a small amount of dried blood on the shower drain cover. The last clear memory I had of the evening before was heading to the staff Christmas party around seven. How or when I got to the Baltimore remained unclear. All I knew for certain was that my involvement had gone unnoticed to this point. It was then I remembered the Jag. The car was the only evidence that could link me to the scene, and despite the risk, it needed to be returned.

I headed back into the city without incident and found a nice parking spot a couple of blocks from the hotel. Making sure to wipe down all the surfaces, I tossed the keys on the front seat and manually locked the door with my knuckle. I took the bus home.

Later that same day, I began to ponder my next move. As curious as I was about the events of last night, it made no sense to go to the police. I had nothing to offer by way of explanation and would only be putting myself in harm's way. It was possible my presence there was a simple matter of wrong place, wrong time, but unless those memories surfaced, I doubted I'd ever know for sure. After much debate I decided to let sleeping dogs lie.

In the following days, there was barely even a mention of the incident in which multiple bodies had been found. No further details were ever released. No one ever came knocking at my door, so life carried on.

It was about a year later and just three shopping days before Christmas when I woke up to a news broadcast about some bodies being found in a motel in Pittsburgh. They said it could be the work of a serial killer. On the surface, I was sure it was just a coincidence that I had recently moved to Pittsburgh, but I thought I had better check my washer.

A damp pair of jeans, a shirt, a jacket, and a pair of gloves lay plastered to the inside of my Maytag. I examined the clothing with care and found a diffuse bloodstain in the interior right front pocket of the jeans. I guessed last night must have been particularly bloody. Turning them inside out, I added some more detergent and ran the entire load through another cycle.

I thought to myself that if this was going to keep happening, I should probably invest in a heavy-duty machine. The Boxing Day sales were on right now, so it would be a perfect time to upgrade. I added it to my shopping list on the fridge, then headed back to bed and slept soundly.

James A. Duncan
Crossing
AN EXCERPT

My eyes half open; it's hard enough to blink. Blank. Bright lights hurting, confusing my balance, I'm unsteady in everything I think and do. The excruciating light blinds me as a migraine forms. Everything takes twice as much effort as it would usually. They call it a blackout, but it isn't. You can recall some memories. The problem is that you have no idea if the morsels you do remember are factual or not.

What did I do? Where did I go? Did I go out? Embarrassment, shame, and dread usually follow, for me anyway.

They asked me if I was ready to go, but how can you ever be, really? The one thing that makes you available, capable of moving on, is the thing that you're trying to get rid of in your system. They told me that my time was up and that there was no way I could stay longer. What the hell am I still doing here, then? This is a recovery house, but am I recovered? No.

A knock on the door: is it doubt or fear this time? Fear. Fuck fear. The doubt is stronger—what if? There is a choice. I've made it. There's a sign. That's it. It's over. But not fucking here. Where? Where do I go? *Knock, knock*. It's time to go. *Knock, knock*, again. The knocks grow louder. Now it's over. I gotta go. I grab my backpack and force myself out of the room.

I'm at the terminal, waiting, looking at my watch. Five more minutes for the ferry to dock. I don't know how I made it, but I made it to the ferry. I stare at the tourist sign: the Bowen Island ferry, connecting Bowen Island and Vancouver. Bowen Island—a good escape and a great release from the monotony of the real world. The release from, but I now must go into reality.

My eyes scan around. I don't even know if I'm seeing straight. I see a face, someone I think I know. I don't know if I should say something. Even if I want to say something, I'm in no shape to speak. Mustering up something, I approach. "Sandy? Sandy from VHS?" I ask, waiting for Sandy's reaction.

Sandy looks up. "Shit, yeah. That's right. Alex? Right, been a long time."

"After high school graduation, I believe," I remind us both, wondering if I heard my name sideways, but my composure stops me from showing a reaction.

Sandy moves the bag next to me and sits close. "So, what were you doing on the Island?"

"I don't know right now. I don't know where home is." I pause. "What were you doing on Bowen?"

"I got a friend who has a cabin there. What about you?" Sandy asks.

"Working. You know, life is so strange. I haven't been here since a long time ago, with a different group of friends."

The ship's whistle sounds and we're off.

Sandy's face is perspiring. Turning to me, Sandy asks, "Hey, aren't you hot?"

"Seriously?" I ask, pulling up my sleeve, revealing track marks. "Okay?"

"I didn't know," Sandy says.

"You musta been the only one."

"When did it start?"

"It's a bit of a blur," I say. "Maybe high school. It's never really over. Even now, it's still rough. The Island was the only place I didn't want to use."

"I thought my high school years were rough." Sandy sighs, taking a deep breath. "You were a bully, you know that, right?"

"Oh come on, who wouldn't tease that strange kid?"

"You harassed me." Sandy's back straightens. "You know, it wasn't fun. You know it's a crime now?"

"Yeah, I did. You were so strange, though." I realize that maybe it wasn't such a good thing. "People, kids, complain about everything. Sometimes they just got to shut up."

"Anyway, I was just shy. Things change. People change," Sandy says reflectively. A seagull flies past us. Crying, it swoops down and picks up a fish in its sharp talons. "Our lives turned out differently. Differently than what we thought they would be. It's not bad, but it ain't great either. You know what I mean?"

My head still aching, I'm not really listening, but I need Sandy to keep talking so I don't have to.

"I think I do, anyway," Sandy continues. "It's been so long. Life happens, and I'm stuck going back and forth. Middle of a forest, stuck between a rock and a hard place, and I can't see the trees. Nothing changes. Sometimes I can't even get to the parking lot. You can't get stuck in the past, though." Sandy stops.

I grab on to this point. "Stuck in the past? Aren't you the one talking about high school?"

"I don't. I mean, I'm not stuck in the past," Sandy retorts. "So, all your mistakes are just from high school?"

"No. I'm just tired. Tired of battling. Battles in general," I lament. "With drugs. With everything."

"That's life. You gotta suck it up," Sandy cracks.

"Really? Suck it up?"

Sandy nods. "Yup."

"Sometimes I don't even leave my place, just drink."

"Everybody can have bad days."

"It's called the weekend," I say.

"Pretty funny." Sandy stops. "Uh, what was I...?" Sandy's got stuck on some thought. "We all worry about things that are unknown to us." Sandy pauses. "We've done this before."

"What do you mean?" I ask.

"I've been here before." Sandy takes a breath. "But I don't know how it ends. You know, like déjà vu."

"Well, think about it. Why am I obstinate? Sandy, think about it all. You know what's really going on. You need to try and accept it more. There's something about telling a stranger who knows nothing about you. Easier than telling a friend, somehow." I search for the right word. "There's no apprehension."

I carry on. "My mom lost someone. I did too. You know I had a brother? I killed him. I got him killed. I got him killed. It was my drugs … I tried. I was clean for so long. Nobody knows about this. My parents don't know that I was in contact with him."

I place my hand in my pocket, feeling a small instrument. I move closer to the boat's railing.

Sandy sees me and knows, for the first time, or so I think. I pull out a silver-edged exacto knife.

"This isn't the way out. Alex, come on. Don't do that!"

"I gotta do it now. No one will be able to stop me here. My life is over. I thought I knew who I was. I thought I understood what was going to happen. I realize—" I stop myself. "That's the worst part. My brother was killed for nothing. Think about it, just think about it. What's my name?"

Sandy looks lost, unsure of what I'm talking about, believing Alex is me, seeing so much pain. Still, Sandy is helpless to do anything about it. Sandy rises, hesitating. Hesitation fills the air between us. Both wanting to say something or touch me but neither of us able to get close enough.

Moving closer and closer to the edge.

"I know who you are, Alex!" Sandy protests.

"Do you? How do you know?" I call out. "That's not even my name! I don't know you. It's not about you, it's about me. It's about what I must do."

By this point, I've pulled myself onto the railing, pulling out the exacto knife. I unsheath the silver-edged instrument, slicing my neck as I fall backwards into the body of water.

☙

Falling from the top of the peak, the view, the clear picture, engages division. The abyss captures us, pondering the deepest, darkest chasms that we dare not think about. Proceeding not backward but forward. Releasing our thoughts, a vision of what could be. What if the concept is not something that you thought? What if the light ain't there? The pain starts and cries out to you. It needs you. The enticement of the bright light clouded. Enjoy the moment of not knowing. The process is too complicated for many to query. The final step, that's the crux. One final step to one last thought. Entertaining the idea of being idle, subterfuge, procrastination. Vacillate no longer. The choice. A choice made.

Faster, further. Louder echoes of cavernous black thoughts overpowering the balance of dark and light. Then it stops. After, it's all slow. The journey is completed; the decision is made, or so they say. You are at your destination.

Lost, not knowing where the destination is, the journey over. What's done has finished. Blame, forgiveness is all moot at this point. Let it be. What's done is done.

Sam Milbrath

The Tail of the Lake Monster

The bells on the door jingled when I walked into the diner. I nodded at Sheriff Louis in his dark brown park-ranger-like uniform, as he tacked a flyer on the community corkboard at the far end of the joint.

"Afternoon, Gail," I said to the waitress behind the long bar of banana yellow and stainless steel. She was an older woman but looked fit in her short white-and-yellow gingham dress and cream apron.

I pulled out a stool at her bar and sat a few seats down from a couple of out-of-towners consulting a map. Their little boy played with a stuffed toy snake with a head like a dragon.

"Hey, Al, been a while!" Gail said as she grabbed a heavy white mug, rubbed the lipstick stain off with the corner of her apron, and poured me a coffee.

I gestured toward Sheriff Louis. "What's that all about?"

Gail jerked her head back, incredulous. "You didn't hear about Bob?" She frowned and pulled her frizzy ponytail tight.

"No," I said. "What about him?"

She whistled. "Have I got a story for you!" She clapped her hands. "Here I thought I was the last in town to hear! What are you having?"

"The usual."

"One piece fish 'n' chips for our friend here," she called through the service window. Then, leaning in close, she lowered her voice and began.

☞

The lake was dead calm that day. Bob and Harry were the earliest birds out there on the glassy surface. The sun was low and pink on the horizon. Harry cut the outboard of his boat, a vintage 1998 red, white, and gold special-edition Lund, once they'd located their spot just south of Rattlesnake Island.

Bob was excited to try out his new spinnerbait lure, hopeful that its flashy colours might attract rainbow trout. The two of them sat there with their sock-tanned white feet up, leisurely holding their prize fishing rods and drinking the strong coffee Harry's wife Martha had made them, when all of a sudden Bob got a bite.

What started as a quick series of sharp jabs at the tip of his rod ended up bending the entire pole, nearly ripping it from Bob's sleepy hand. Jumping up from his morning stupor, he knocked his coffee on the red-carpeted floor and clutched the handle with both hands.

Bob braced himself, his old, bare knees jammed into the port side of the boat, his fat toes clenching the rough carpet. He let the line fly.

Harry watched as Bob's reel spun out of control, whizzing and zipping faster than he'd ever seen it go. Bob held tight. His eyes followed the light blue line before it disappeared from his sight—more than a hundred metres out past the boat. The fish began to slow, then it charged sideways, nearly tearing the rod out of Bob's now-sweaty palms.

The boat started to spin bow-first toward the fish's growing wake. They were being dragged across the lake. "Must be a giant sturgeon!" boomed Harry, clapping Bob on the back. "Heard they get up to three metres long. Say they're related to dinosaurs!"

Suddenly, the lake's surface flattened. The line, sixty feet off the boat, began moving closer and closer to them. The giant fish must have dove into the abyss of the bottomless lake. He'd lost it. Bob kept reeling, but the line went slack. Limp. He slowed his circling hand.

A minute ripple on the glassy surface began to rumble—like an earthquake jiggling a massive bowl of water. Out of the depths of the lake emerged a huge slimy, scaly, swamp-green snake-like torso, greater than the width of a car. Its volume and power parted the lake, creating two sideways walls of water, as what looked like a lake monster charged toward the boat.

Bob's jaw dropped. His knees threatened to do the same. Harry scrambled to turn the boat key, but his hands shook so violently that he ripped the keys from the ignition altogether.

He turned in horror as the lake monster undulated in massive rolling, slithering waves toward them. It was at least forty feet long, but before he could tell for sure, it disappeared, diving in front of the bow of the boat.

Bob squealed like a pig in panic. Terror reverberated through Harry's entire being as he looked up in the sky at a giant dragon-like tail whipping high above the boat. Water cascaded down the thick green tail, which came crashing down on the lake with a deafening smack, sending a tsunami wave under and over them.

The boat pitched sideways and sent both men flying. Split seconds before Harry cracked his forehead on the sharp corner of the open dashboard window and landed unconscious on the floor, he spotted a shiny yellow eye the size of a human head staring back at him in a wall of water. That was the last thing he saw before he passed out.

Another swift flick of the monstrous tail caught Bob's beer belly as he and his rod flew mid-air, sending him off course to land not in the boat like his dear friend, but into the depths of the monster's watery lair.

⌒

When Harry came to, the sun was high in the bright blue sky. In the distance, dozens of powerboats buzzed around the lake in circles, towing inflatable doughnuts with bouncing, laughing children in bright orange lifejackets.

Harry was parched. His head pounded. The light was blinding. He lifted his arm slowly and touched his aching head, wincing at the pain. His hand came back covered in blood. He looked down. His crotch was wet. There was a coffee stain on the carpet, two empty cups, and Bob's blue tackle box, but no sign of Bob. What had happened?

He got up slowly, grunting with effort, and looked around the boat. There was no sign of impact. He peered over the side of the boat into the cool, dark lake. All he saw was his own bloody reflection, warping in the ripples.

He found the keys on the ground and started the engine, motoring toward Lakeside Marina. Minutes later, he pulled into his slot, tied up the boat, and began the long walk to the marina office. What would he tell the sheriff? What would he tell his wife? Or Bob's wife? The lake monster was a local legend, but no one believed the folklore or sightings.

☞

Gail continued in a whisper, "Betty, the marina manager, told my neighbour that she just shrieked when she saw Harry walk into her office. Freaked her right out. She hardly recognized the man. I tell ya, she hasn't been the same since."

"How come?" I asked, dunking a piece of battered fish in ketchup.

"He was white as a ghost, shaking like a scared animal. Covered in blood," Gail said. "Confused and dreamy. Guilty for sure. Looked like a cold-blooded murderer. She let him use her phone, but locked him in there, just in case he tried anything, you know? Sheriff Louis came down, handcuffed him, and took him to the station, where he's been ever since. You wouldn't believe the stories."

She leaned in closer. "Martha, Harry's wife, was serving Bob more than just happy hour, if you know what I mean." She raised her eyebrows and pursed her lips.

To the boy down the bar, she said, "You done with that, sugar?" and took his empty plate. I watched the kid roar and pretend that his stuffed animal was riding invisible waves.

"Bob's body still hasn't turned up," she whispered. "Heard they found his fishing rod, though. It washed up on the lake's southern shores, near Cherryville. It's a tangle of blue line and rod. Tackles all gone. Jury's out on what will happen with Harry, but there's no doubt he's in a bad state of mind." She tapped a pink fingernail on her temple twice.

I thanked Gail for filling me in and paid my bill.

"Still can't believe you didn't hear," she called after me as I opened the door to the café. "You been living in a cave or what?"

Months later, on a dead-calm early morning when the sun was low and pink on the horizon, a patch of the lake began to ripple. In the blink of an eye, the elusive monster came up from the depths of the dark water to break the surface between two standing waves, before it dove down again. In the corner of its slimy, swamp-green cheek glittered a nickel spinnerbait lure, its silver and rainbow tassels spinning wild.

Emma Murphy

Rat

The city was cold. Each breath escaped from dark and waxy lips, the white wisps dissipating into the sky like sugar into water. Droplets of rain hung suspended from strips of black fur. Eventually they amassed on the congealing tips and sank through the strands to the tiny muscles underneath; the frigid beads hurt like rusted nails. His whiskers quivered. His small body followed. Another day like this and surely he would freeze. Numb to the roughness of the tar underfoot, he found it a conscious effort to put one after the other. How long had he been walking now?

How much further could he walk still?

Grey upon grey upon grey, as far as the eye could see. Concrete skyscrapers loomed over the streets; they could bend over like fingers forming a fist and it wouldn't seem any more suffocating. Waves of people seemed to roll in and collide from every direction. Ripples in the water distorted the reversed images of smooth dark feet pounding the pavement of the city's limits.

There was no escape from the dreary environment. Even if it was safe to close his eyes, the sounds of the city felt like a hurricane swirling around him as he teetered on the line between sidewalk and street. All of his weight went to his hind legs as he pushed himself upright, grasping at the top of the curb. With a short kick, he scaled the sheer vertical face. He waited for the people to pass. He must be patient. Though the margin was too small to do so comfortably, he took a seat on his haunches. Beside him, the mechanical beasts lumbered to a halt, obeying the red light in the sky that was so glaringly out of place. Perhaps it was their god, holding out its hand as if to say, "No more." Why else would such powerful creatures freeze in a jungle that never does? Blackened air seeped from their metal, hollowed tails and was subsequently dragged to the asphalt through the weight of the rain.

The stream of humans slowed. The gaps between grew larger. When he was brave enough to dare, he scampered across the sidewalk. It was long, maybe too long, and littered with spiderweb-like cracks that marred the surface. Each step was unsteady, and his heart raced faster than his feet.

What met him on the other side were long, verdant blades, but this wasn't grass. As it brushed against his whiskers, the surface was harder, smoother; each strand was designed to mirror the others and placed with precision. They towered over him, forcing him to meander blindly through the mockery of nature. Softer ground made his feet slide and sink. He felt a heaviness unlike any other.

Food. He needed food—if not for himself, some small morsel for the colony. The babes were growing, and help was scarce. The green pillars beat at his sides, until something else did in its stead. Grey and tall and coarse: the foundation for a human nest. He kept as close to it as he could. It provided some reprieve from the frost-laden gale, and the coat more water than fur. A few steps, then rest, the building bearing his weight for a moment, before moving again. Resting again. Moving again. Where there would have been passageways before was now covered by a thick white material that jutted out from the otherwise straight barricade. Five, maybe six times he saw it, but it was no less despairing with each repetition. He held out his hand overtop the material, as if to say, "No more."

Silently begging, "No more."

Finally, an opening. No larger than an inch across, a dark crevice in the stone slab. He wasted no time in crawling inside. Light did not exist in this place, but noise did; a faint hum, though he could not place its origin. No matter which way he turned, it never left his ear. The urban restraints were nothing compared to the shallow gap that circled tighter and tighter around his thin frame. He was out of sight; he thanked the red light in the sky for that much.

A brassy sheen appeared before him. The waves of heat emanating from it were palpable. Too hot to touch. Regretfully, he turned away, but he could not run.

Lost in the dark, wrapped with warmth and the faint mirage of light—was this death? He had only heard rumours about the experience in passing, though he had no shortage of memories. The crisp snap of bones under a metal rod. The acrid stench of burning fur as electricity coursed through a body. The sight of internal organs spread down the road from the paw of the mechanical beast. The taut grip of talons that separated you from another.

Truly, the colony had seen better days.

As he was standing there, he felt the heat seep into his skin. It was a pleasant distinction from the outside world, and it yearned for him to come closer. Glancing over his shoulder, he caught the metallic glow once more through the shallow slits where his eyelids struggled not to meet.

Air in this place was limited, and grew denser with every passing second. Tiredly he pulled himself through, his elongated nose sniffing at the rounded tube before him. Tiny beads of condensation cloaked much of the musty brass, and where they could not, there were traces of grime. Water. There was water inside; hot, gaseous water that made him anxious to be near.

For the colony, he must not be afraid. If he was dead, there was no reason for fear.

One hand met the surface of the pipe. The pain screamed up his arm, but he could not run. Quickly, he shoved the rest of his body over the cylinder, being careful that his naked tail did not skim the smoldering metal. His eyes darted across the darkness, meticulously scanning for another golden shine or an old wooden strut. Anything. All that faced him was the shallow chasm of darkness. He felt fire underneath his feet.

He took a leap of faith.

He landed.

Loose fluff barely cushioned the force as he collided head-first with a thin wall of plywood that bent under his impact. Once again, he found himself in the rain; however, in lieu of water there was a soft substance that easily stuck between the strands of his fur. So much of it was floating around him that he found it hard to breathe. Whiskers twitched, his snout wriggled, and he felt the sensation of some unknown force clawing in his throat, scratching and shoving, unable to rest. Coughing did not tame the beast; each attempt grew more violent than the last. He stumbled forward. It was hard to pick his legs up through the mountains of fibre swallowing them. Rapidly, he beat against the fluff with his hands and feet, trying to swim through it, but he did not feel as though he were moving anywhere. Only floating in space.

The itchiness of his insides caused his eyes—however useless they were at the moment—to tear up. He kept struggling, kept pounding against the down, for the colony he could not fail, for the hungry-mouthed children he must not fail.

A ledge appeared. It wasn't very strong, and the edges were chipped and warped. He reached out, and his whole body trembled. The rough wood dug into his hand as he wrapped his fingers over the corner. With great effort, he heaved himself up. Fluff tumbled down into the abyss as he sat precariously on the ledge. Dimly illuminated in front of him, there was a tilted beam with wires just grazing its worn face. There was a light.

Cautiously he approached the incline. He jumped and ducked through the gauntlet of vines, he supposed, in the jungle that never froze. The crack was small—they always were—and was stationed beside smooth plastic. That was the first thing he felt as he entered the portal to the other world. Off-white flooring was fractured in many places. Golden sparkles within reflected the light from the fluorescent bulbs sitting without a cover inside the ceiling. It too was fractured, and patched up with plywood in many places. Nevertheless, he still felt a draft. It must always be cold here.

Swiftly, he scampered across the floor, the stuffing from the walls trailing his every movement. An ominous presence hung over him; a massive wooden structure. Unlike the interior of the wall, which was worn down with age, this piece had ornately decorated doors where no dust called this home; it was purposely maintained in good condition.

A silver gleam caught his eye from the other side of the floor. Sitting inside this shallow bowl was a mountain of brown cross-shaped pellets, coated in a sticky powder and a chemical stink. Soft purrs rumbled through the human nest, and he knew his time was short.

He turned his head back to the rows upon rows of wooden doors. There were deep, entrenched triangles surrounding ovals sunk into the centre, circling a golden handle; a simple rod underneath flat metal flowers. Different kinds that tried to pull your eyes toward them with their screams for attention. Another disgrace to nature. It took up enough of the door's surface that if he could only reach out....

With a click, the metal holding the door in place was torn apart as the board swung open. His snout was assaulted by the warm, spicy scent of older wood. What he faced were shelves of unused dinnerware: fuzzy porcelain plates and teapots lurking in the shadows.

He clambered inside and rustled against the ceramics, which sang a melody of soft clicks as he turned around and closed the door behind him.

Kim June Johnson

How to Get From Here to There

An excerpt from a young adult novel

PROLOGUE

Do you ever wish you could turn the clocks back and back and back and fix one thing?

If I could, I would stay home the day Dane died. Mom and I had gone grocery shopping, and Dane was at home with Dad. It was April. In April, the rivers—the Red and the Assiniboine, which meet in the centre of Winnipeg—swell with melting snow. One year, before I was born, the rivers rose and flooded the streets for miles. Flooded farmlands and highways and seeped into backyards and basements. I've seen pictures. That was the worst year, but this year was getting bad, Mom said. People in the neighbourhood had started to put sandbags around the edges of their yards.

The banks were steep any time of year, and Mom and Dad were always trying to keep Dane away from the water. Dirty and brown from the farmland pollution to the west, it's not the kind of river you swim in in the summertime, although in winter people skate the length of it if it freezes smooth enough before the snow comes.

Dad had been up late the night before, and he fell asleep on the couch while Dane watched a cartoon on TV. Dad didn't hear Dane slip out the back door. I wonder sometimes if anyone saw it happen, Dane slipping into the churning brown water. I often wondered, in the days that followed his death, if someone was going to knock on the door and tell us they saw it from their house across the river. A few of the neighbours' yards had a view of our backyard. Had one of them been looking out their kitchen window and seen Dane reaching in to poke his small finger through the water's cold skin? Or throwing in a stone, before his feet slipped out from under him?

I used to feel a strong need to complete the story: if I knew exactly how Dane had fallen, I could understand why it had happened. The absence of knowing sat there inside me like an empty, aching space.

When Mom and I got home, Dad had just woken up and was calling for Dane. He was frantic. And then Mom got frantic and yelled at Dad. Did you not lock the doors? Yes, of course he's old enough to open it himself! And I stood out in the yard, not wanting to know what came next. And then Mom came out to the riverbank and started hollering for him. And she hollered and hollered until her voice grew hoarse. And the rest I don't want to remember.

CHAPTER I
"It looked better in the pictures."

Mom and I stand in the driveway looking up at the new house. It's evening, and even though it's late August and the light still lingers into the evening, there's not much of it coming through the dense trees.

But lack of light can't be blamed here: the house definitely looked better in the photos Mom showed me back in the spring when she learned that her Aunt Nan had left her this house in her will. "See, Scotia?" she said. "And just a short walk up from the beach."

The photos were old, mind you. Taken long before I was born, when Mom lived here with friends in the summers. When she talked about those days—everyone crammed into one house, making art and music and having beach fires—her face lit up.

We make our way up the crooked stairs to the front porch. One of the window screens is torn and a piece of mesh lifts slightly in the breeze. Mom pushes open the screen door and we step inside the porch, then she finds the key and lets us in through the front door, feeling around on the wall to find the light switch. The room lights up only slightly; there seem to be more than a few burned-out bulbs. To the right, there's a small kitchen with a wooden table. A living room area with an old plaid couch and a dusty wood stove. Walking through, I find another little room off the back, with a desk and a lamp. A small bathroom.

"Smells pretty musty," Mom says, pushing open a small window.

I climb the stairs to find two small bedrooms and another bathroom with just a toilet and a sink.

"It'll look better in the morning with a little natural light," Mom calls up from down below. I flick a dead fly off the windowsill.

Because it's late, we haul only the most important things in from the moving trailer: the bedding, the mattresses, the box with the tea and apples and cereal. We set the mattresses up in the middle of the living room because we're too tired to haul them upstairs.

"This will be a good place to read," Mom says, running her hand over the corduroy fabric of a cushioned window seat.

"Yeah," I say. But nothing feels even close to good. I push back tears.

I find my pillow and my duvet and lie down. Mom finds the kettle and puts some water on to boil. She rummages around in a closet for a broom and starts sweeping cobwebs out of the corners in the kitchen. The kettle whistles and she gets out the tea.

"Well, here we are, Scotia," my mother says, pouring water into two mugs. But I don't get up. I'm suddenly too tired for tea.

"Yup," I answer, the words catching in my throat. "Here we are."

Outside, the wind picks up and a branch scrapes against the side of the house. I shut my eyes and try not to think about the long, dreary three-day drive from Winnipeg to here, or this new place we're going to live—this small island, this strange house surrounded by dense trees. I try not to think about the things we left behind—my bed, the old brown couch. Mostly, I try not to think about my dad and how he didn't come with us.

Pruned

After the gardener came
to trim away the grapevines

which had grown too heavy
around the front windows,

the house was full of light again.
You couldn't stop admiring

the way it swept along the floorboards
in the hall, long stripes of it slicing

across the kitchen counters. How had you lived
in the shadows all this time without noticing?

It was like coming out of a depression,
or gulping air after a long, held breath.

Jessica Lemes da Silva
Books and Bocaditos

An excerpt from a young adult novel

An evening breeze greets the four of us as we pass through the arch of the wrought-iron gate and into the square courtyard. The sounds of a jazz quartet lure us further in. At each corner of the brick-laid courtyard are short palms and bougainvillea shrubs full of ruby-coloured flowers and hidden thorns. The bookstore itself surrounds the courtyard, entrances on the left and right. Mel goes right, to the art books, Teri goes left, toward the magazines, and I give Ricky a quick tour, ending at the café on the far side.

We grab two hibiscus iced teas and ham *croquetas* and find a table, centre courtyard. We have to raise our voices slightly to be heard over the tenor sax solo.

"Your friends are sweet," Ricky says as he settles into his seat, "but they seem like they're avoiding me."

"Avoiding you? How?"

"Like how my lactose-intolerant mother avoids *tres leches*. She admires from a distance but doesn't engage, you know what I mean?"

"Well, I'll make sure not to get a *tres leches* cake for your mom, then," I reply in between laughs. "But I'm not sure how you can assess that after a dinner that was mostly my father interrogating you and a fifteen-minute car ride."

I take a bite of the deliciously seasoned minced ham formed into the shape of a short cigar and lightly fried in breadcrumbs. God, I love *croquetas*. Just the right size, not too big—a perfect snack, or *bocadito*. "Unless you're channelling your sixth sense or something," I continue.

"I don't need my intuition to tell me your friends were pretty quiet in the car and now are … missing. They don't think this is a date, right?" He points his index finger back and forth between us.

I spit out some iced tea and slap the back of my hand to my lips to stop small chunks of food from flying out of my mouth and onto the table. "You're joking, right? I mean, do *you* think we're on a date?" I ask, wiping my hand and chin with a napkin.

He laughs, doubling over his crossed legs, and I begin to snicker, as this is … awkward. I mean, I came out to him at Janelle's party a few weeks ago, he has a boyfriend, and now he's laughing at the thought of dating me. Pretty clear.

"Look," he says, "I'm sorry. I just—I don't know what you've told Mel and Teri, because I totally got an *Is this Marcy's boyfriend?* vibe from your parents at dinner, and we're still getting to know each other." His eyebrows are arched so high as he says this that worry wrinkles have formed on his forehead.

The *shhh-sh, sh-shhh, sh* of the brushes on the snare drum fill my ears, making it hard to focus. Ricky takes a bite of ham *croqueta*, his hairy pinky finger sticking out, revealing a very thin gold ring. Even his pinky exudes elegance. "I just want to know we're all on the same page, that's all," he continues, his cheek full of mushed ham and breadcrumbs.

I mean, it wouldn't be completely silly to date Ricky. He's good-looking, easy to talk to, and a fun dresser. He's already met Papi, which is pre-approved in many books. I imagine holding his hand down the street and maybe borrowing some of his clothes now and again. But I wouldn't ever want to *kiss* him, and he wouldn't ever want to kiss *me*.

"I told them we're meeting up with your boyfriend Jojo later," I say. "There shouldn't be any confusion."

"Plus, we're going to a gay dance thing tonight," he adds.

"Well, I didn't quite get that far."

Ricky stops chewing and gives me a hard stare, eyes peering like a laser, analyzing my mind. Again, awkward. "Wait a minute," he says.

"They don't know about you, do they?" His eyes widen and he brings his hand to his mouth in surprise.

"I already told you at the party—nobody knows about me. I mean, *I* barely know about me."

"So what do they think we're going to?"

"They think we're going dancing at Bongos. Which is the truth, so don't worry. They won't be weird about it. And for the record, they aren't avoiding you. We do this thing when we come here, where we each pick something we think the other should read or look at. It sometimes takes a little while. So just *relájate*, okay?"

Ricky sips his iced tea, sits back, and raises an impeccably threaded eyebrow. His doubt pokes at me. Thank goodness there's music to fill our first moment of friend awkwardness. He's right, though. I should've told the girls about tonight's event. All of it, that is.

Both Mel and Teri come back with a couple of items each. Teri brings a *Bust* magazine for herself and an *Elle* magazine for me. She instructs me to read my horoscope in both. Mel hands me a children's My First Bible series and says to check out the Book of Revelation. "Girl, it reads like Harry Potter meets some Stephen King meets some true anger. The illustrations of the seven-headed dragon and the lake of fire are pretty dope."

This is a joke, of course. I glance at some of the graphics, then shift in my seat to take a closer look. "First of all, you can't ruin Harry like that. And secondly, how is this a kid's Bible? It's so graphic, complete with blood and guts!" I shake my head and take a sip of iced tea.

"Looking at all these stimulating finds, I should go find something myself," Ricky pipes up, making a slightly disgusted face at the picture-book Bible.

"There are some great photography books in the art section," Mel suggests, pointing to the right of the store.

"There's Cuban poetry just next to the café," Teri adds.

We all give her a look, as that seems like a very specific suggestion.

"Maybe he likes Reinaldo Arenas or something?" she says, looking away.

Ricky sits up and grabs Teri's wrist. "I love Reinaldo Arenas. *Before Night Falls* is one of my favourite books! How did you know?"

Teri gives Mel and me a side-eyed glance. This is the kind of glance that's fully loaded with some opinions. Slow to answer, she looks at us and then at Ricky. "Besides the fact that you have painted nails, metallic flamingos on your shoes, and a boyfriend—just a guess?" She gives a gentle shrug.

Ricky playfully pushes Teri on the shoulder, smiles, and says, "Not that anyone's stereotyping, right?" He gets up from the table with one bold movement.

Shit, this isn't going well.

"If you're into picture books, the kids' section is at the front," I say.

He takes one last sip of iced tea, winks, and says, "Got it."

Now who's avoiding who?

"Is it just me or was that super sarcastic?" Teri snaps.

"Dripping in it."

"Oh my God, Mel, that's not helping," I say.

"Kinda deserved," she replies, without even looking up from her book.

"Okay, okay, *jaa!* Let's all just chill," I plead.

Man, this is not how I wanted the night to start out, with my new friend calling out my old friend's bad habit of speaking in generalizations. Maybe Mel and I need to do more of that with Teri, call her out on her shit. *True friends call each other out, right?*

I get a whiff of something floral, jasmine or *algo de naranja*, and it pulls me out of the tension for a moment. I think it's coming from one of the servers. The smell relaxes me, and I feel my muscles loosen. I imagine the server leaving her number with a smiley face on our bill. *Do people actually do that?* The music stops and the musicians take a break.

Teri's knee is bouncing furiously, and I can feel the tremors by my foot. I place my hand on her thigh and squeeze. "Forget about it. It's all good. Okay?" I say, pushing my last *croqueta* to her.

Teri breathes out a big sigh and stuffs the whole thing in her mouth. Her cheeks puff out like a chipmunk preparing for winter. I see she's starting to blink quickly, tears beginning to swell. I look at Mel: *Mayday, mayday.*

"Gurrl, don't worry about it. I bet he's already forgotten," Mel says, taking Teri's hand and petting it gently, something my *abuela* would do.

"Tell me right now, how important is it that I like this Ricky?" Teri asks. "Because right now your new friend is *muy pesado.* He doesn't even realize how rude he was, Marcy."

Our server asks if she can clear our plates. As she collects the items on the table, her hand brushes up against mine. We exchange smiles, and my heart skips a beat. Teri and Mel fade and I'm lost to the speck of a moment: the smell of citrus, trumpet riffs, iced tea, seven-headed dragons, and misunderstood cues. *Ay Dios,* how am I going to tell my best friends I'm gay?

Non-fiction

Alaa Al-Musalli
Ghost in the Sky

The power blackout was longer than usual. I waited it out by staring at my coursebook by candlelight. I read the same lines over and over again, hoping that something would stick. I watched the black smoke of the cheap candle slowly twist up toward me, wrapping itself around my neck like a venomous snake. There was not much that I could do to resist its choking dance; it slithered into my mouth, seeping its poison deep into my lungs, filling my senses with shadows. The walls stared down at me as I fused with my sofa. I listened to the room, hoping it would cough me out into the front yard. I urged my adolescent brain to escape through the crack in the ceiling plaster. It floated toward the crack, lingered, then rushed back to me; there was nowhere to run to, nowhere to hide from it all but inwards. I closed my eyes, killed all thought, all desires and hopes, until I, too, blacked out.

The air strikes had robbed us of all comforts. I was numb to everything: the heat, the dark, the uncertainty, the losses. All I could do was focus on the little things, the simple pleasures. I came to at the image of my thirsty roses, which bloomed despite the turmoil. I mustered the energy to break free into the garden, leaving the dungeon to close in on itself.

I aimed the garden hose on my feet and let the cool water run wild on my thirsty toes. I stopped to wonder at how bizarre it was to find so much joy in such simple things. I looked up and took in the clear night sky, feeling resurrected by its might and serenity. I felt free. Alive. Nothing else on this planet was happening. It was just me, water running on my feet, and the Big Dipper right above my head. Grandma's story of this asterism made it my favourite night sky attraction, and if there was anything good about blackouts, it was the chance to see it without the polluting city lights.

"Once upon a time, there were seven daughters who lived with their widowed father, Na-ash; the girls were all very bright and beautiful, but one of them limped. The father suddenly died, and the girls, who couldn't find a single soul to help them, had to carry his coffin to the burial ground. Four of them carried the coffin at the four corners, while the remaining three trailed behind, following one of the corners. The one who limped was the last one on the trail. Look there! Follow my finger. Those are the daughters of Na-ash, Banat Na-ash, carrying their dear father to his resting place. One day, you'll tell this story to your children and grandchildren."

I squeezed the tip of the water hose to sprinkle the garden wall. Getting my feet wet was soothing enough, but the high point of the watering ceremony was letting the water coat that old brick wall. Its ridges and uneven surface were perfect resting grounds for dust that was unlike any other. The golden powder was, in essence, the exfoliating skin of Baghdad, a mixture of pollen from the green fields of Mesopotamia, sand from the desert dunes, war soot from the burning oil fields, ashes from the ruined homes, and the remains of the brilliant minds that built the crumbling city. The earth which birthed that dust was on fire, and when water from the River Tigris caressed that dust, magic happened. When the holy matrimony between dust and water is consummated, a warm, deep clay aroma is born, casting a smell no other two lovers could conceive. I transmuted into a palm tree. I stood tall, unyielding, and sent my roots deep into the earth, claiming land and water. My metamorphosis left me feeling invincible.

I moved on to the roses. I sprayed them with a gentle mist, only to tickle the leaves. The lime tree that Mom bought by mistake, thinking it was an orange tree, stood tall, demanding attention. It produced a hybrid fruit that was neither lemon, nor orange, not really lime nor narinja. Royal status was bestowed on it after its first yield, and its fruit crowned all our meals. It was the garden's queen. I sprayed the grass and all the other little bushes. Feeling thirsty, I drank straight from the hose. I was ready to go inside. I put the water hose back just the way Dad liked it—a snake coiled on itself in the corner of the garden.

I stopped to take one last look at the sky and forced a yawn out. I stared into the heavens, through the Na-ash daughters and beyond, trying to capture the farthest star I could find. I decided that this sky was mental-shot-worthy, as Dad called it. I loved watching him take these shots on and off set. He would use his pointers and thumbs to make a rectangular window in the air and zoom in and out before deciding on an angle.

"A good cinematographer always takes mental shots before wasting film. Besides, mental shots last forever," he would explain.

I took out my imaginary camera and zoomed in on collections of stars to find my perfect shot. As I was experimenting with the angles, I saw something strange through my frame. Some of the stars were vanishing. I zoomed out to cover more sky, but the stars were still not there. I put my hands down, thinking that looking through my fake camera was distorting my vision.

For the first few seconds, I didn't know how to react; I watched the heavenly blackout with amazement, without trying to make sense of it. I could make a triangular silhouette, swallowing the stars one by one, like a black eraser rubbing out the stars off the night sky, only when it moved forward, the stars were chalked right back on. It was moving from left to right in a straight line over our one-story house. It was slow and quiet— too slow and quiet to be real. I began to think I was hallucinating, after all it was a long hot day, and it was way past my bedtime. When I realized the stars were reappearing, I put my hand on my mouth to muffle a laugh, but by the time it came out of my nose, I didn't think it was funny.

The object was hovering only 500 feet above my head. Black upon black. One black I knew and grew up watching, the other a triangular alien mothership of some sort. I froze. I realized that if I moved, whatever was operating it might see me. I stayed calm and waited for it to float away, but it wasn't going fast enough. I didn't feel threatened. I stood there in complete silence, unexpectedly in awe of its beauty.

As the majestic silhouette cleared off the top of the house, a big ball of fire, as quiet as the sun, came out of its end. I watched it for a few seconds before I heard a low noise. It was like the hissing sound of a blow torch. I couldn't figure out how I was able to see the ball of fire first and then hear it. That sound suddenly made the object real. I wasn't dreaming. I was now ready to run, but I had to keep watching it—not only was I too terrified to move, but I couldn't seem to take my eyes off it.

"Sssshhhhhh; don't tell anyone you saw me!" it whispered.

I watched it disappear and tiptoed inside. I told Mom, who brushed it off as she did with most unscientific things. A figment of my irrepressible imagination, she called it.

Dad, the dreamer, was already fast asleep, which was good because he would have freaked out. I went into my room and drew the object, mainly to release it from my head. It became clearer after putting it on paper. The three-sided flying object invaded the page. I drew myself standing underneath it and filled the sky with dots for stars all around its sharp ends. I then erased some of the stars from above the thing, which animated it. I filled the page with descriptors.

"Big triangle! Flying low! No noise? Fireball? Sssshhhhhhh!"

I went to bed with so many questions. I could see the object in the ceiling even with my eyes closed. I buried my head under my pillow and forced myself to sleep. No more than a couple of hours later, I woke up to a nightmare.

Heart-stopping booms shook the ground beneath me. The sound of thunder, a hundred times amplified, a million times angrier, roared like lashes, slashing at my soul with every whip strike. The heavens were crumbling down, and the earth was opening up to swallow everything. I ran to my parent's room and jumped on their bed. They made room for me in the middle. I was shuddering with horror. Mom put her legs over mine to stop them from shaking. Dad held my hand.

We said good night; it always sounded like a goodbye. We never knew if we would make it through most nights. I fell asleep to the sounds of Baghdad being raped, wondering if what I had seen earlier had anything to do with it. I listened to the city cries until I numbed out.

I don't recall how long it took me to learn about what I had witnessed that night. The first mention of it was when someone described the ghost American aircrafts that were monitoring the movements of Iraqi troops in pitch black. The F-117 Nighthawk Stealth Bomber flew low over Baghdad for months, watching, planning, and making 'unintelligent' strikes without being detected by radar. It went down in history as the most successful aircraft bomber in the Gulf War. It scored direct hits on 1,600 high-value targets in Iraq, killing, and not counting, civilians.

In my history, the F-117, that mesmerizing, elegant aircraft that stole my stars 26 years ago, the machine that defies sense and gravity—my beautiful enemy—haunts my night sky till this day.

Tene Barber

Two Tall Pikes

AN EXCERPT

If anyone would have told me that I'd be taking my old man out for coffee three times a week, I would have laughed in their face. We've not
shared any remote form of the traditional father-daughter relationship
throughout the years. We have this last opportunity to get it right because there is no time left to waste.

"Ah, it's good to be off Derby turf," Dad says.

"It's a perfect day, Pops."

I start the car and roll down the front windows. Dad puts on his avia-
tors, a gift from his youngest granddaughter. We pull out of the driveway
with a bump and head down Cumberland Drive with the wind blowing
in our hair. Dad is smiling big as I turn on his favourite Johnny Cash CD.
"A Boy Named Sue" plays while Dad sings along and taps his feet, no
doubt remembering his glory days. We weave through the neighbourhood streets of Burnaby and New West. The rhodos and azaleas are in
bloom and no coats are required. In seven minutes, we arrive at our favourite Starbucks. On a weekday, I have no trouble securing a parking
space that allows me to easily manage him and the chair. With skilled
proficiency, I wheel Dad up to the green metal table complete with ashtray and umbrella.

I lock the wheels so he doesn't roll away on me, while I pick up our
coffees. I don't have to ask him what he wants because this is our thing.
Two tall Pikes in grande cups, leaving room for loads of cream and two
packets of honey. I ask for two cinnamon straws.

"Blonde and sweet, just like you like 'em." I pass him his coffee.

"Thanks T, gleep, gleep!"

This always makes me laugh, as he shrugs his shoulders in two quick successions to emphasize each gleep and his eyebrows follow along. It's the same every time; we each pull off our plastic lids and raise our paper cups.

"To the Queen," Dad says.

"To her corgis," I respond

We toast and take our first tasty mouthful, letting the golden nectar wash away any and all worries.

I watch him unwrap his cinnamon straw. He is now the epitome of domestication: Gap cargos, a T-shirt his granddaughter gave him bearing the words Old School, and an old-as-dirt ball cap I brought home for him from Maui. He looks like the dad I always wanted, mainly because I am his personal style consultant and purchase his wardrobe. He looks good.

"You look dapper today, Pops."

"I had my bath this morning. A new young one, scrubbed me just right, I pulled a bit of a stiffy."

He is so proud of himself.

"Jesus, Pops, that is way too much info for me."

He looks at me with an innocent face but with a crooked smirk that lets me know he is having a bit of twisted fun. Classic Pops.

"You're impossible."

"Always."

He fishes his pack of smokes out of his front pants pocket and sparks up his first gasper. Dad has been diagnosed with emphysema, but I don't say a word because he has sobered up to a great degree and the smokes are his last true vice. The administrators at the Derby Care Centre for Veterans are smart and have no interest in forcing lifetime alcoholics into withdrawal, so all residents are allowed two shots per day. This keeps the old rabble-rousers glowing instead of blazing.

"So, Pops, I hear there is a special ceremony for the 60th anniversary of the Korean War in a couple of months. You have to register if you want to participate."

"Hmmmm," he shakes his head in a "no" motion and looks down at his shoe, turning it from side to side, as if seeing it for the first time.

"Apparently there is an entire delegation from Korea visiting the Derby. It's going to be a big deal for all of the Korean Vets in the centre."

My father rarely speaks about his time at war. It is a mystery to me and leaves me with the impression that he is not proud of his time spent as a soldier. I know of his active service experience through an old cigar box containing his war mementos. Mom bequeathed this to me after their divorce and his subsequent disappearance. I love the images of him shipping out, a young eighteen years of age and handsome in his uniform and beret. Photos of his life at war reveal big artillery secured behind stacks of sandbags, muddy foxholes, camp tents, burnt-out buildings and his infamous imitation of Winston Churchill. His discharge photo, taken at the end of three years in this theatre of service, shows a man ten years older. He returned with malaria and a buggered disposition.

He looks up at me with alarm, his eyes as large as loonies.

"I gotta piss."

"Oh, come on, I just…."

"Now."

"Now?" I realize that he is not kidding or attempting to change the subject.

"Now, *now*." He is panicking.

He refuses to wear the pull-ups that Derby supplies. I do not press him because I know it hurts his dignity. Today in this moment I want to say, *fuck your dignity, wear the goddamned pull-ups.*

I rush to unlock his wheels and push him to the entrance. I've learned to wheel him backwards through doorways, so I spin around, pull the door open, wedge my right foot against the door frame and back him in. I spin him forward again and we are at top speed heading to the bathroom. Thankfully one is unoccupied, and Dad leans forward, turns the handle and opens the door. God bless Starbucks for equipping all of these bathrooms for wheelchairs.

"Oh shit." I speak out loud as I realize that I have to help him.

"Never mind, just stand me up." I help him to his feet from behind the chair.

"I'll hold you up, but I'm not holding your schlong, that's up to you."

He is frantically working his fly and whatever else is in the way and I finally hear his stream hit the bowl. I relax a little too much and he begins to fall to the right.

"Jesus Christ, hold me up goddammit or I'll paint the place."

"I'm trying." I struggle to get him completely vertical, as I'm bending forward over the chair at a 50-degree angle, a seat length away from him. He sways to the left. I can hear his urine hit the floor, the wall, and the sink before I can manage to get him up straight again.

"Fuck me, I hit my pant leg."

This is so ridiculous; I feel a deep laughter welling up from my belly and before I know it, I am laughing so hard that it is impossible to keep him straight. I try to say they'll wash but I can't get it out.

"Have a good fuckin' laugh, asshole."

He sounds angry but his shaking body lets me know that he is beginning to laugh with me. As I sway back and forth behind him struggling while weeping with laughter, he manages to tuck and zip. He sits down and we both laugh uncontrollably. I wrap my arms around his shoulders, tucking my chin into his neck and give him a kiss on the cheek.

"Well that's a first Pops."

"It better be a fuckin' last."

The bathroom was a disaster when I pulled the door open and backed the chair out. I spun him around and we rolled nonchalantly past the order-up counter. I looked at the poor kid behind the counter.

"That bathroom needs attention, it's pretty bad in there," I said like we found it that way.

We are not sticking around when we reach the table. I hand our half-empty paper cups to Dad. I wheel him to the car, place our coffees in the front cupholders and work through our routine with the chair. I sit in the driver's seat and expel all the air from my lungs through my lips.

Dad looks at me sheepishly and we break into a fresh round of hysterics. As I regain my composure, I start the car.

"Want to go for a drive?"

"Ya."

I'm staying local after the bathroom incident and we drive through Queens public garden. I park under a tree fully loaded with blossoms and we watch the petals drop like rain while sipping our lukewarm coffee.

Madeleine Lamphier
Vipassana
AN EXCERPT

In the last hours of a night shift, we're often too tired to talk. Maybe it's the collection of crew members, whether the calls were uneventful or overly so, or how much downtime we've had between them. No rest is often better than the promise of it being broken over and over again until dawn. We might come home from a call, clean up and put the truck back together, just to be tapped out the minute we're ready for service. That's one recipe for the giddy delirium that makes some mornings almost rowdy. Maybe perpetual motion is the secret to life. At least sometimes.

We got slammed last night and the crew sounds lively this morning. I hurry to change and join the fellas before they head off for home. I push my black socks, fire T-shirt and men's underwear shorts into my bag, then hang my uniform and kick my boots into the locker. I consider bringing my gear home since I won't necessarily be assigned to this hall when I return from holidays, but a roar of laughter comes from the kitchen. I grab my bag and walk out of the dorm.

Alex's massive frame leans against the counter as he tells Rohan the highlights of the night. I make an ineffective attempt to wedge him out of the way so I can grab a mug from the cupboard he's eclipsing. I turn my body sideways and lunge with my arm outstretched towards the handle.

"I thought the smell was coming from the laundry room when we got into the building, but we walked down the hall and it just kept getting stronger and stronger." Alex keeps talking to Rohan while he drops his shoulder, shifts to his right foot, and pins me to the wall. "We finally get down to the suite and the door's open. I look in and there's shit *everywhere.* I make Maddie go in first, and I'm holding the medical forms up like this," he says, releasing me to peek his eyes over an imaginary folder. "I'm like, 'I'll be in the truck if you need me!'"

He laughs and slaps his giant hand on my back.

"You were halfway down the hallway when you said that!" I say, as I get a mug from the cupboard and pour myself a utilitarian cup of coffee. I pull out a chair beside Mike, who is sitting kicked back from the table with his hands folded behind his head.

"So, me and Maddie go in with the Cap and this old lady is on the bed, and there's literally shit everywhere," Mike says, spreading his arms over the table. "There's shit all over the bathroom floors and the walls. There's a shit trail on the carpet leading from the bathroom to her bed, and she's got, like, this fuzzy, light green carpet. There's the main trail and then some puddles around," he says, slapping his hand down randomly.

The oncoming crew has arrived for their day shift and the eight seats around the table are now full. Alex still stands against the counter blocking the mugs. Like an enormous puppy, he places his already un-avoidable body in high traffic areas to force social, and usually physi-cal, interaction. I suspect it's a need ingrained from decades of playing rugby. Anyone who wants a cup of coffee now has to say good morning to him directly, if not actually touch him.

"Cap's in the bathroom looking for the lady's meds, and I'm filling out the FR form when the paramedics arrive," Mike says. "This lady's got some gauze, or toilet paper, or something stuck to her, and the one paramedic goes, 'Well, if she were my grandmother, I'd want her to be cleaned up,' and he goes to wipe it off, but it's attached. Turns out it's her prolapsed bowel."

He drops his forehead down hard on the laminate table. I bury my eyes with the heels of my palms to darken the fresh image.

"So, we get back to the truck and start driving, and it reeks like shit in there," Mike says. "Cap's like 'Jesus! I've got shit all over my boot!' so he takes it off and holds it out the window the whole way back to the hall. Alex is gagging and his eyes are watering, so he's driving all over the road. We were *dying* we were laughing so hard. We felt so sick."

"Yeah, that was awful," I say, my eyes still covered. "One of my worst shit calls for sure."

The conversation spurs on a stream of one-upmanship, each recount as awful as the next. Damon tells a story I'd heard before, about riding with the paramedics one hungover morning. Their patient had explosive diarrhea for the entire twenty-minute trip. There are no windows in an ambulance, he reminds us. We cringe and laugh; every story is so familiar and relatable. I love mornings like this, when fun and laughter trump our desperate need to get home to rest.

"Hey, Maddie," Rohan says smiling as he pulls up the seat beside me. It's always nice to see him when our shifts cross every fourth morning. We talk about kid stuff mostly, his three littles and my two preteens. He and my husband used to play soccer against one another as teenagers. His wife is a shift worker too, so we have lots to talk about and rarely resort to work gossip.

"I heard you're going on some crazy meditation thing in the middle of the desert," he says, obviously having gotten wind of my imminent holiday plans.

"Yep. Wanna come?" I smile back.

"There is no way I could not talk for ten days," He says, eyebrows raised high above his dark brown eyes.

"Well, that's exactly why you should come!" I laugh.

"You're seriously not going to talk for ten days? What are you going to do?"

"I mean, I think that's the point. To learn how to observe your thoughts without being a slave to their noise, and not having to distract away from them."

Ro's eyes have glazed over. "Can you call home sometimes?"

"Nope. No cell phones. You can't even bring any reading or writing stuff."

"That's fucked," he says, shaking his head. "You're totally going to go nuts."

"I totally might."

⌒

Almost three hours into the flight to Palm Springs, neon green de-icing fluid still sputters through the fins of the airplane wing. I look out the window, amazed by how different the shallow, brown mountains are from our imposing blue ones. The low, jagged peaks interrupt the monochromatic landscape; veiny roads are carved into the surface where they wind and intersect.

I press my forehead to the plexiglass, unsure if it's because we're still too high up, or that the area is too remote that I can't make out a vehicle. As we descend, patterns of neighbourhoods appear along with strip malls and wide streets, megamalls and their immaculate blacktop parking fields. America even looks like America from 10,000 feet in the air.

I pick up my rental car and drive east from Palm Springs for about an hour. Jubilant with freedom, I loudly mangle lyrics to Ariana Grande songs that crackle through poor radio reception. Towns become intermittent and grittier, sand covers the sidewalks and slopes up curbs like red snowdrifts. I pull over and throw my hazards on, jumping out to take a picture of where Jazzersize and Independence Guns & Ammo share a building.

It's just after three o'clock when I see the sign for the Southern California Vipassana Centre. I park and find my way to the registration area in the dining hall. After waiting my turn, I submit my form to a woman wearing a well-loved knit cap and similarly tangled eyebrows. She marks arrows on a map which direct me to my residence and explains that although I'm in the shared accommodations building, my roommate has withdrawn at the last minute and I'll have the room to myself. This feels auspicious.

She reviews the code of conduct with me, including the five precepts which I commit to observing during the course. I vow abstinence from killing any being (seems easy enough, even in its vicarious expressions, so vegetarian meals only), from stealing, from sexual misconduct (I'm married, will have no roommate, and the men are literally off-limits), from telling lies (not talking should do the trick), and abstinence from all intoxicants.

I hand over two books, my journal and cellphone, which she logs and labels, explaining the process for collecting them at the end of the sit on day eleven. Eyebrows smiles at me with unaffected warmth and wishes me well.

Jordan Smith

də'sent

AN EXCERPT

It is winter and the rain sweeps in out of the darkness from the long swells of the open ocean beyond. On the other side of the island the house I am building with my father sits half-finished in the rain. I am hunkered inside the "Hilton," near the wood stove, waiting for a break in the impenetrable cloud of my thought. Al is here too, outside on the porch smoking, waiting for the blue light of his cell phone to tell him that he exists.

Al leans inside the door.

"Have you ever considered that you're missing something?"

"What, like something tangible or just the point?"

"I don't know. Just something."

Al's head disappears back behind the door, but before it does a sly grin creeps onto his face. I wonder if Al is fucking with me again.

The sound of his footsteps recedes down the stairs, his shoes squeaking with each tread. *Fuck you* his shoes say. Couldn't care less how unpleasant I am. His shoes squeak along the side of the building, eventually fading beyond the limits of my hearing. About thirty seconds later the squeaking returns. The door opens and Al spills through with an armful of firewood, kicking off the offending shoes. He thumps in, his great pink calves pounding his feet into the oak floor, the joists sagging with each blow. He dumps the firewood into the box beside the stove and carries on into his bedroom. I can hear him fumbling around with a CD case and then the sound of the CD player tray sliding shut. He reappears as Miles Davis's horn echoes out of his room and he slumps down in the vinyl recliner across from me, brushing wood bits off his threadbare work shirt and tattered old gym shorts.

He sits smirking.

"What?"

"Nothing," he says.

"Well you're smiling about something."

He shifts his substantial girth around in the old recliner, the vinyl protesting. He reaches into the breast pocket of his shirt and pulls out his cigarette case. He removes a cigarette and taps it three times on the coffee table. A silver lighter emerges from another pocket and he flips the top back, sparks a flame, and lights the cigarette, exhaling a cloud of smoke with a great deal of satisfaction. The cigarette case goes back in a pocket, the lighter he leaves spinning on the table.

"Still stuck?"

"Yeah. What was your first clue?" I say.

Al looks above this response and carries on smoking his cigarette with dignity. "Well, what's the problem?"

"The problem is I hate everything I write," I say. "It always reads so poorly."

His smile returns. "You mean to say that you always write so poorly. Beer?"

"Yeah, please."

Al is a year younger than I am and he works at the Christian camp on the island. We are both stumbling headlong toward 30. They don't like him much around here, mostly because he smokes and carries himself with a certain je ne sais fuck you, but he survives because the head of camp operations is something of a father figure to him. His hair is a thick brush fire of copper burning skyward, mostly because he only washes it occasionally. His heavy side burns add to the already impressive width of his jowls and when he smiles it is often through his small teeth, because, well, because fuck you. He is built like a rhinoceros, and would be just as dangerous if he chose to be.

He has been the boat driver for the last few years, which consists of driving the boat back and forth from the mainland to the island and doing odd jobs around the camp when he is not in the boat. In the summer he tows screaming kids around the sound on a giant, inflatable banana. This year, they fired the caretakers before Christmas and Al will be here all winter long, filling in until they find someone new. He stays in this outbuilding, the "Hilton," which is just behind the farmhouse where the caretakers usually live.

☞

Al retrieves a beer and a can of Coke from the fridge. He pulls a bottle of Wiser's DeLuxe out of the freezer and mixes himself a rather liberal rye and coke. He pops the cap off the beer and hands it to me, and then falls carefully back into the recliner with his drink held aloft.

"Tell me again why I'm doing this?" I ask.

"Well, I was under the impression that you think God told you to," Al says wryly.

I can't help but laugh because it does sound totally ridiculous when spoken aloud. And I can't totally deny believing this.

"Perhaps you ought to quit wearing that foil helmet of yours," he adds, enjoying his wit.

☞

I do look the fool. I just dropped out of university for the second time in ten years, this time probably for good. People tell me I can do anything I want. And sometimes I believe them. But none of it matters now. I have thrown all of that away and now I am stranded on this dismal island with no one else but Al and his cigarettes, and perhaps a vague notion that God thinks it a fine idea for me to write an epic tragedy about a father and son and a house that never gets built.

"Well, it's all I've got left," I say. "It's like I can feel him up there fingering a thunderbolt, or the sword of Damocles. If I don't make good on this I might really be done for. Or worse yet he might give up on me ... and then I'd really be fucked. I'd probably wind up living on the street. I really feel like that. For the first time in my life I feel like total failure is within my grasp. Do you ever do that? I mean when you're driving around ... think of places where you could sleep if you were living on the street?"

Al, unmoving, looks at me. And then he chuckles.

"Do you even like this God of yours?"

"I'm not sure anymore. I thought when I signed up for the program there would be a few more perks involved."

"Like what?"

"I don't know. Just something more than this."

"It might be worth noting that not many who do sign up for the program find it all that rewarding. Consider, for instance, that God asks Abraham to kill his only son. It really doesn't get much better from there. Jacob, Joseph, Moses, Elijah, Hosea, Jeremiah, Jonah, and, of course, there's Job, the proverbial king of suffering. None of these guys had a lot of fun. And then we have the big show himself, Jesus. God doesn't even give his own son a break. It's not a lucrative relationship."

"I'm starting to pick up on that."

"Well, that's good," Al says, carefully putting out the remains of his cigarette in the ashtray on the coffee table.

"I fear God, I really do," I say staring at the floor.

"Isn't that supposed to be a good thing?"

"I suppose so, but it sure doesn't feel good."

"Well, perhaps you have finally reached the dead end of things. Perhaps now you are desperate enough to actually write something."

Kadee Wirick Smedley

Juliette

A MEDITATION

One day you are moving on, ready to close the door on childbearing and child-losing and open a new one that places fewer demands on your body and soul. You need to be done with fissures and blisters and the exhaustion of full-term pregnancy and childbirth. You especially need to avoid positive pregnancy tests and heartbeats and ultrasounds that end in bloody loss and death.

So you pack up your crib and your boxes of baby clothes. You clear out the plastic toys and baby bedding, the bibs and bouncy chair and teething rings. You go through these emblems made precious because your children wore or chewed on them, but in the end everything is boxed up and taken away. Your husband drives the whole load to a local thrift store where, hopefully, they make their way to families that want to enter the season you so badly need to leave.

Then you move to a new house, and you set up rooms for a family of five. You plan a trip abroad. You settle into the bodily independence you haven't been able to enjoy for a decade. You look forward to a less complicated future than the past you are leaving behind.

⌒

And then one night at your still-new home, you pick up the phone to order sushi and, because your period is a few days late, put the phone down and walk to the pharmacy for a pregnancy test. Just in case. And you come back and take the test out of the box and pee on the stick like you have ten or eleven times before. You hold the urine-coated stick with one hand and wipe with the other, pull your pants up and set the test on the counter.

When you return two minutes later, you pick up the test and find it positive. Unbelievably positive.

And you stand in the bathroom and cry because that part of your life you wanted to close has been reopened; the loss you so badly needed to avoid remains a possibility.

But then your husband—your good-natured, steady, immoveable husband—comes in. He sees the positive pregnancy test and gives you a hug and tells you everything will be okay. And you try to believe him. At the very least, you stop crying.

⌒

Thirty-five weeks later, you give birth to a perfectly perfect, light-haired, big-eyed baby girl. A girl you can't bear to put down. A girl who spends her first night and every night for 17 months cradled in your arms. A girl who loves her daddy and her big brothers but saves her biggest smiles for you. A girl without whom you can't imagine life. A girl who learns to dance almost as soon as she learns to stand. A girl who transmits sunshine and steadiness from the palms of her tiny hands.

⌒

And one day, your baby girl isn't a baby anymore. She is a golden-haired, delicate toddler whose courage and tenacity surprise those who judge by her fragile frame. A girl who misses nothing: not the subtle changes of your mood or the drama-ridden conflicts of her siblings. A girl who, by eighteen months old, can identify every article of clothing in the house and who they belong to. A girl who comforts herself by climbing into your lap and pinching the tiny folds of skin on your neck.

She bundles her sunshine and steadiness into words now—clearly communicated, easily understood. You know what frustrates her and what gives her joy, what she wants and why she wants it. You see how attentively she follows the conversations and quarrels of her brothers because she uses their vocabulary to press her own case against them (and you).

She still goes to sleep in your arms. She allowed her daddy to put her to bed for a few months, but when he went away on a trip she staked you out as her permanent night-time companion. And you mind … but you also don't mind, because you have medically closed the door on child-bearing and child-losing, and she is—and always will be—your baby.

And one day your toddler is a scrappy preschooler, and the strength with which she was born reveals itself in preferences on what to eat and read and wear. And you wonder at every new revelation: that actually she hates dresses and the colour pink and can you please buy her more clothes in black? And no, she won't play with so-and-so even though they want to play with her because they cry for their mom every day, and she doesn't play with kids who cry. And she prefers witches to princesses and scary stories over fairy tales, stories you could never have endured at her age because you were timid and easily terrified.

But she is not you and you are not her. So you tell her scary stories and let her be a green-faced witch for Halloween and you stop buying her dresses and add a few pieces of black to her wardrobe.

And then one day your preschooler is in elementary school where she triumphs on the monkey bars and joins a trinity of playground warriors. She makes you walk her to the door and sometimes past the door of her classroom every morning because even warriors need their mommies at the beginning of a long day. And she fights you on brushing her hair and, when you warn her about tangles that look like bird's nests, she tells you how happy she would be if a bird made a home in her hair.

And when school is over, she demands you be no more than ten feet from her at any time. She likes to stay and play at the playground and is one of the smallest kids there, fearless in climbing, jumping, swinging. But that fearlessness depends on you being close by, and if you aren't close enough she comes and takes your hand and pulls you to an accept-able distance from her chosen activity. When she falls–losing her grip on the bars or getting knocked down by a passing child–she stands up and locks eyes with you. And of course you ask, "Are you okay?" and her mouth tightens into a half smile. She doesn't cry, refuses to cry, instead she runs towards you, declaring "I'm FINE, Mommy," burying her dry eyes in your neck before going back out to play.

She still goes to sleep in your arms. But now she spends only an hour or two in your bed before her daddy moves her to finish the night alone in her own room. Her last waking request is to "please tell me a story I've never heard before and it can't be a Bible story and it has to be scary." So you lull her to sleep with tales of demogorgons and dragons and fight to stay awake yourself. Because you never feel so safe and relaxed as when you are next to this tiny, monster-loving little girl.

⌒

And people tell you that life with her will be difficult someday; that girls have more attitude and drama than boys and you will have to worry about her when she reaches adolescence. They reinforce what you already know: that the world is less hospitable for her than for your boys; that her body is more likely to be violated and her voice quieted or ignored than theirs. That in much of the world her thoughts, her perspective, her very life are measured of less worth than these three brothers who came before her. And this strikes you as the most foolish of all follies, because how could such a beautiful, remarkable person be less valued than any other?

So you determine, each and every day, to let her know how important she is. How loved she is. How carefully you pay attention to what she says and what she does. How seriously you mind what she wants and what she doesn't want. How much her voice, her thoughts, her feelings and her perspective matter to you and to the rest of her family, and how this will be true whether she is a toddler or a teenager, married or single, gay or straight.

And you think back to that moment in the bathroom, when you wept over what her impending life meant for yours. And you thank God that your fears weren't in any way realized, that rather than losing her, she lived. And that her life, far from impeding or disrupting your own, has made it utterly, gloriously complete.

Kathryn Robbins-Pierce

Dancing to My Own Drum

AN EXCERPT

My bedroom door is pounded. The morning ritual has begun. Opening it, Mom yells: "Get up! You're going to miss your classes. You'll never graduate at this rate."

The door slams. She stomps down the hall toward the living room on her way to the kitchen at the back of the small wartime house on Young Street. I resent her assault and pull the sheet over my head. I can outwait her. She must leave for work by 8:20 a.m. There will be one more series of yells and dire warnings before the slam of the front door brings peace and silence back to the house. I victoriously go back to sleep.

Awake at ten, I make my way to the University of Winnipeg for the last of my morning classes at eleven. I had mistakenly, in a fit of freshman eagerness, signed up in September for all morning classes in first-year arts. It's now April and my morning eagerness is being seriously challenged by the workload, with papers still to write and final exams pressing down, in addition to a part-time job as a waitress.

After class, I meet up with Brian for lunch in the cafeteria.

"Mom's still at it, every morning, the same old routine."

He rolls his eyes; he's heard it all before.

"Your mom always seems so polite when I've been at the house."

"What you see is her proper English façade that she presents to the world. I get the dark underbelly."

We have been dating for a few months. Early on in our relationship we spend a night in a room in the residence, but not in his room which he shares with a roommate. We stay in a vacant room. We are so new to each other; we are tentative in our touch. Lying in the single bed after some gentle necking and exploring, we fall asleep in each other's arms. We wake in the early morning to a knock on the door. Females are not allowed in the male residence.

Half clothed, we stumble out of bed in panicked confusion. Pulling on my shirt, I move toward the closet out of sight of the door as Brian searches under the bed for his shoe and a lost sock.

"Hello?" Brian responds, the rise in his voice implying the question, who's there?

"Housekeeping," comes the response.

"Shit," we whisper under our collective breath.

"It's my mother!" She works as a housekeeper in the men's residence.

"Just a minute." Brian pulls himself together and answers the door, partially blocking the view into the room, one shoe still in his hand.

"Oh! Brian?" says mom, confused at finding him there.

"Oh hi, um … I was locked out of my room last night. I'll be out of here in a minute."

A few minutes later, we check the hallway. The coast is clear. We tiptoe out, down the stairs and out of the building into the early morning.

"Oh my god, that would have been just too embarrassing," I say as we walk hand in hand down the street laughing at our close call.

Brian feels the same way. "No kidding. Shit! I just about died when I saw your mom standing there."

By summer he has moved into an apartment with his friend Jerry, a short distance from my mom's house. While I still live at home, I begin staying over at Brian's on weekends. I hear from my sister Janet: "Mom's really pissed at you."

"What's she pissed about now?"

"You and Brian, what do you think? She keeps bending my ear about you staying over there."

"Don't worry about it, but thanks for letting me know." Janet, at seventeen, is the only one still at home full-time now. My older brother Jeffrey, 21, moved out a few months ago.

One evening Jerry, Brian, and I are driving around in an old black hearse that Jerry uses as his personal vehicle. We are south of the city on the floodway, a large concrete culvert that the city has developed to divert the spring floodwaters that have been a problem for years. Around us is flat, open prairie. Parked on the grass beside the culvert to watch the sunset, we run out of gas. Jerry and Brian opt to leave me in the hearse while they hitch to the nearest garage to get some fuel. Sitting alone in the gathering dusk, I have visions of the ghosts of dead people who had been in the hearse, rising from the rear. I can't turn around. Just as my imagination is about to get the better of me, they return. We stop at the first service station as we get into Fort Garry, a suburb on the south side of Winnipeg. The place is crawling with cops. There had been a major jewelry robbery that evening, and they are out looking for the culprits. The black hearse draws attention. Stopping us, the cop flashes a light into my face as I sit between Jerry and Brian.

"How old are you?" he demands. My long blond hair, blue eyes and fair skin belies my age, casting me as younger than I am.

"Nineteen," I reply. The age of majority is 21, but he seems satisfied. He passes us on. Later, at home, I recount the adventures of the evening to Mom.

"Did you know there was a major jewelry robbery this evening? We were stopped by the cops; they were looking for the guys who did it."

The words had barely left my mouth when she responds, yelling, "I didn't know where you were. What if the police had called here and I didn't know where my daughter was? What would that look like? What would the neighbours think?"

Stunned by her response, I reply, "That's what you're concerned about? What the neighbours think? Who cares what the neighbours think."

A few weeks later, Brian and I attend a friend's wedding on a Saturday evening. Sunday morning finds me at Brian's with a party dress and dress shoes, but no real clothes to wear. A phone call to Janet to bring over a T-shirt, a pair of jeans, and some runners, solves the problem. That evening, as Brian and I are standing in the enclosed veranda of my mother's house kissing goodnight, the front door flies open and my mother screams, "If you can't obey the rules of this house, then you can get out!"

The door slams shut, rattling the window set into it. Brian and I stand holding each other as the shock waves of sound dissipate.

By September, I have a room rented on the third floor of a walk-up in a rooming house on Assiniboine Avenue, a nice tree-lined street behind the Manitoba Legislative Building. As I enter or exit, several of the doors open a crack and elderly eyes peer out, noting my comings and goings. I last about a month.

I have been spending most of my time with Brian, who has rented the top floor of a house near the trendy Osborne Village area of Winnipeg. He was to share the three-bedroom apartment with two roommates, but they bailed on him.

Having breakfast one morning, Brian asks: "Would you like to move in here? There's lots of space and no prying eyes."

Pausing for a moment, as if seeing him for the first time, I smile and nod my head.

"Yes, on one condition."

"What's that?"

"We don't tell our parents. Deal?"

"Deal."

J. G. Chayko
Finding Nellie

An excerpt from a work in progress

The bright lights over the dressing room mirror illuminate my reflection. I perch on the edge of a chair and apply my makeup, listening to the theatre come to life. The stage crew thumps on the ceiling above me, tromping over the stage floor. The other actors bounce into the dressing room, giggling and laughing over some recent flirtation, and the house music creeps in through the speakers, mingling with the rhythmic murmur of the audience. There is an odd nip in the air backstage, and I shiver in my crimson lace dress. The stage manager flips the pages of her script, and her voice rings out with the anxious tone of a woman keen to present a first-rate show. The whispers of technicians, and actors reciting their lines dissolve in the high ceiling like a fine mist. Just before the curtain lifts, I look across the stage into the wings and see a figure of a woman with dark hair wearing a high-collared dress, her hands clasped in front of her chest, eyes closed, chin slightly lifted, mouthing silent words.

⌒

My great-grandmother Nellie looks down from the white walls of our living room, a small but commanding image amid the many photos. The picture encased in a silver frame reveals a stylish lady with a pretty face and dark hair piled on her head in waves. Her fair skin is illuminated in the sepia film, her body deliberately turned towards the camera lens. She wears a high-collared dress that streams down her back and fans out behind her like the train of a wedding gown. A fur-trimmed shawl hangs over her shoulders. She was a vaudeville performer on the London stage.

I was fascinated by her. In my childhood, I climbed onto empty stages and twirled in front of imaginary audiences, piling my hair on my head and emulating her posture. She was the catalyst for my own journey to the stage.

In the early 1900s, after a scandalous separation from her husband, Nellie travelled to New York to start a new life. Family letters traced her journey as far as 1909. No one knew when she passed away. Ads placed in the paper a few years after her disappearance led to her final resting place in the Evergreen Cemetery in Brooklyn. When my partner and I had the opportunity to travel to New York, I set out to find Nellie, the mysterious relation who enchanted me from the first time she looked down from our living room wall.

⌒

The small plane bounced over the murky waters of the Hudson River, the wind currents tossing its small frame like a ping-pong ball in a lotto machine. The commanding silhouette of Lady Liberty stood in the haze, her torch raised in welcome. New York loomed before me, swallowing the sky with its soaring buildings. The flash from a visitor's camera blinded me when I exited the plane, and in the spark exploding behind my eyes, I thought I saw an image of a woman in a long dress disembarking from the ramp of a cargo ship. Yellow cabs swarmed through the streets and in the hum of their engines I heard the rumble of carriage wheels rolling over the muddy ground from a bygone era. The crowds on the street surged around me like the torrent of new immigrants pouring onto Ellis Island. I envisioned Nellie amidst the chaos and wondered if she felt as overwhelmed as I did.

I emerged from the darkness of the coiled subway tunnels into a barren section of Brooklyn. Scattered remains of broken houses and flat-roofed industrial buildings decorated the landscape. The only beauty was the lush green cemetery that sat on a hilly knoll overlooking the street. Great stone pillars hung over the entrance. The winding driveway led me past huge mausoleums and impressive stones, a grave reminder to be respectful of the sleeping souls beneath the ground. The administrative building emerged like a majestic stone castle from the Middle Ages. The reverent silence within its walls was occasionally disrupted by a loud woman with a Virginian accent barking at a timid man about a death certificate. The patter of soft-soled shoes and turning pages echoed in the high ceiling.

A woman with bleached hair and glasses stood behind a plastic window cracking her gum and writing in a ledger. I handed her a piece of paper with the name of my great-grandmother. She entered it into the computer, and then pulled a large blue binder from a metal cabinet and plunked it on the counter. She skimmed her long red fingernails over the pages, but she couldn't find Nellie. She said we should consult with someone who was more familiar with the historical graves. She turned to a doorway near the back wall and hollered for a man named Anthony.

Anthony was a short stout man wearing jeans and a green flannel shirt smattered with specks of blue. His enthusiasm was infectious and his knowledge on the inhabitants of the cemetery was limitless. He prattled on about the history of The Evergreen, spilling out stories of famous people buried on the grounds—he thought Nellie might be amongst them in the old actor's plot. He vanished into a back room and returned ten minutes later, staggering under a heap of binders, notebooks, ledgers, and poster cylinders. He spread out a selection of maps displaying the names and dates of all those who passed nearly a century ago. The paper smelled fresh, but the mottled stains and discoloured ink revealed its true age. The bumpy texture of the parchment grazed the tips of my fingers as I studied plot outlines for over an hour with no success. Anthony unfurled one last chart and spread it over the table. The ends curled in defiance, as if the phantoms of the past did not want the living to find one of their own. This was the last clue to her whereabouts. I was resigned to the possibility that she might be eternally lost, existing only in the mystifying letters left behind—and then my eyes swept over a rectangular box with her name, glowing like the Broadway lights.

◞

Nellie lay under a modest rectangular stone, her name hidden beneath a patch of wild grass. She was one of many forgotten souls beneath the giant obelisk looming over their final resting place. The dry leaves rolling over the ground were the only visitors to the forgotten artists of Vaudeville. I sat on my heels, closed my eyes and traced the rough etching of her name with my fingers. The breeze lifted my hair and crept beneath the layers of my coat. The bitter cold of a New York winter ached in my bones; I heard the clacking of horses' hooves on frozen ground, the chatter of the upper class out on the town for a night at the theatre; in the chill air I caught the faint scent of garbage mixed with the decay of an overpopulated city. I saw a woman with dark hair, a wool cloak, and tattered leather boots exit from the back door of the theatre. The fog rolled in and her shadow evaporated like the world of Vaudeville fading into oblivion.

Curtain down, lights out.

Emelia Symington Fedy
The Tracks
AN EXCERPT

We always met at the same place on the tracks. It was a spot hidden away from the road by a bend in the railway about the length of a city block. Our spot was a quiet place that got dappled sunlight through the cedar trees. We couldn't hear the cars on the road or the kids from the nearby playground; the forest dampened all sounds except for the honeybees and mosquitoes.

In the spring, Nootka roses and lupines and daisies grew along the tracks and when summer hit huge bushes of rosehips and wild blackberries took their place.

If I got to the tracks first, I'd sit down on the hot rails and wait for the girls. I might throw a few stones into the woods trying to hit a tree or maybe I'd collect a little pile of twigs and build a log house for the fairy people. The air was softer and sweeter and the light was dimmer, almost as if upon arrival a veil transported me into a kinder realm.

When everyone arrived, we'd get up en masse and start walking—always—out of town.

We walked double file along the tracks. Emmy and Cristal. Mounce and Aimes. Anne and Kay.

This pairing was one of many undiscussed rules we followed. We were a girl gang, but we also split into best-friend groups and this was not something to be jealous of or questioned.

Cristal was my best friend. She had short white-blonde hair and wore 501 blue button-fly Levi's jeans, and a cotton plaid short-sleeved shirt with white runners. This was her uniform and all that ever changed were the colours of plaid shirts and a new pair of the exact same sneaks on the first day of the school year.

Cristal was lithe with square-ish hips and no boobs. She played high school basketball but she didn't do soccer or softball because those sports cost money and would've meant her parents had to drive her places. If she wasn't home by four p.m. every day after school, she'd be grounded for a week so she was always checking her watch.

☙

Cristal's room was in the basement of her house and I'd only been invited down there once. It was a functional cement room. It had a single bed that was tightly made and a small dresser for her uniforms. There weren't any posters on the wall or anything that hinted at her personality. I remember the high small rectangular window the size of a box of chips that let some outside light in and if you stood on her bed on your tippy-toes and looked out of it you could see her parents' car tire. I don't think her parents abused her but the starkness of her life had an aggression to it. It was like she had to be a pencil at home: narrow, sharp, and fit into her little case.

Cristal was grounded once because we all prank-called a substitute teacher from my house. We looked up the teacher's name in the phone book and left a creepy message on her answering machine—deep whispers about how we were going to kill her dog and fuck her grandma— but before we hung up we started giggling uncontrollably and someone in the background yelled Cristal's name. She got caught and was suspended from school. After that, she was on lockdown and had to be in her bunker by three p.m. every day and she wasn't allowed to leave the room until school the next morning.

After a week two of her confinement I started to miss her so I went over around nine p.m. one night and slid a love letter down through the crack of her chip-box window. Standing on her tippy-toes on top of her bed, Cristal reached for the letter. The movement of me crouching outside made the motion sensor light come on and her mom opened the side door to check out who was messing around outside. She saw me and screamed. I scrambled up and booked it down the road, but she chased me for at least two blocks. What scared me the most was that she didn't give a shit who saw her trying to run down a thirteen-year-old girl.

Cristal spent all her free time at my house. Mom let her smoke in the breezeway and she'd help Mom pull weeds in the garden. I'd come home from speech and drama lessons to find them sitting in our screened-in porch eating cheddar cheese and Wheat Thins and drinking strong black tea. They'd be talking in hushed tones, knee-to-knee on the porch, closer to each other than to me, which made me want to smash their enjoyment.

I had to keep a wall up with my mom, to protect her as much as to protect me. Beside her single-parent chutzpah sat a fragile bird. I was a bulldozer and if I truly turned my engine on I'd flatten her. I wanted to love her but I also wanted to destroy her—for being sick, for not protecting me from my dad—but mainly for not being strong enough to let me be my big bulldozer self.

"I'm home. Let's go upstairs," I'd say, interrupting their close-knit whispers and turning to go. Cristal followed; if she didn't have me, she didn't have my mom either, so she acquiesced.

Cristal picked me up for school every morning and walked me home every afternoon. Like the love letters we passed in class, proclaiming our eternal devotion, this would have been a romantic gesture if she was a guy. When we had the occasional sleepover, we'd spoon and whisper the same phrase over and over again.

"Let's be gay together."

I thought it was hilarious. She'd say it and I'd laugh into my pillow and snuggle my back into her tummy. It was the sound of the words that made me laugh. I didn't really know what gay was but I knew it wasn't me or anyone I knew. It was the equivalent of saying, "Let's be purple together"—a nonsensical phrase that was ours alone.

I see now that she was gay. Super gay. The gayest gay in gay town. Population her. And no one else *could* know and if they did, she'd have had the shit beaten out of her. So for her, the phrase was a fervent prayer, repeated again and again into the safety of my ears only. I never heard her plea.

⌒

I see us all now from the view of a circling crow, walking and talking along the tracks, headed nowhere in particular but in the direction of away.

When I fly down and land on a branch to listen in, we talked about *everything* but shared *not much*. There was a deep pool from our necks down that was murky and motionless and held words like "gay" and "death" and "rage" and "terror."

We felt like we were best friends but we really only shared ourselves from the neck up. We knew—and I don't know how we knew—that we couldn't bear each other's pain. We didn't know what to do with those hot rocks we held in our bellies so we kept them submerged. The laughter kept them down. The slushies kept them cool. The walking kept them tired. We did everything we could to protect each other from the pressure that was building—until there was nothing left to do but explode.

Melanie L. Walker

On the Day She Chose to Go

AN EXCERPT

Ellen asked me to stand outside her bedroom door while she dies. I clench my dress and stare at the walls with scuff marks at wheelchair height. Memories of people who have died before are kicking up like dust in my mind. This is not their time. I shut them out. I want her plan to work.

Inside the bedroom, Ellen's three children, and four of her grand-children, are circled around the bed. Their voices lower and fade as the Rabbi speaks.

Outside the bedroom, I stand with a small group of family and friends. We are barely-moving shadows in the winter dusk. It was part of Ellen's plan to have some people in the bedroom and some waiting outside. After she has "gone upstairs" as she calls it, Ellen's son, my part-ner, will walk out of the bedroom and I will hold his grief with mine. I don't want to watch her die. This woman who loves me because I love her son. This woman who loves me even though I am not the mother of her grandchildren. I focus on the linoleum until I find a flaw in the pattern on the floor.

The Rabbi pauses, there is a small shuffle, then other voices speak. I strain to hear them but my heart is thumping steady in my ears. Again and again, over the past few months, I have been chanting the words: this is what she wants, this is how she'll go.

I remember the day she told me about her choice to die. Her text message said, "Come over when you can. We have to talk about unspeakables." Unspeakables was our word for the dark stuff no one else wanted to talk about. By then, because of the downward trajectory of primary progressive multiple sclerosis, her fine motor functioning was more limited and her messages often had typos to decipher. But this message came in clear.

Later that week, after a long day at work, I arrived at Ellen's apartment. Even before Ellen had announced her plans to die, I had been in my own depression for months. On the day she called me over, my muscles ached as though I had a piano tied to my waist and my skin felt like it had been flipped inside out so that everything felt like too much. The last thing I wanted to do was cross town on the bus on a grey November day but I was not going to complain about long days, public transit, and depression to a woman who had slowly lost the use of her legs.

Over the years, I had watched my partner Jesse transfer his mother from wheelchair to bed many times. Whenever he lifted her and she surrendered, it softened me. It hurt to see a strong woman being put to bed by her grown son but it helped me get outside of my own pain.

When I arrived, Ellen's bedroom was filled with the last rays of the sun. Ellen was propped up in bed against the orange sheets, looking out the window at the perennials in the garden. She turned and gave me her cheeky but genuine smile. Her grayish short hair was swept off her tilted face. As she lifted her arms for a hug, it caused a sway in the soft folds of skin that once held her muscles. While I leaned on the bed rail, she held me long enough for me to try to pull away a few times, only to be squeezed harder. Her hugs were getting longer and longer.

After she had me straighten out her legs, rearrange the blankets, and spill two tic tacs into her mouth, she got right to it.

"When your dad—" She stopped and fumbled with her cell phone. "What time is it? Oh good. Not bedtime yet. We have enough time to talk. So when your dad.…"

"Killed himself," I finished. She knew I didn't like the term "committed suicide." My dad had not been convicted of a crime.

"Did you blame him?"

"No." I crossed my legs. "Why?"

"You know how I've been talking to the people at that clinic?" She pushed her chin toward me, deep valleys of questions in her eyes.

I nodded, staring at the painting of the little bird above her bed.

"I'm past what I can cope with. I don't want to break my neck and end up in the hospital where I can't make the choice."

As I tried to focus on her face, I thought about the many times my dad had been in the hospital for attempted suicide. Eventually, he succeeded at dying.

"I'm losing myself inch by inch and I'm kinda up to about here," she gestured to her abdomen, referring to the effects of MS. "The further up it goes, the more we're talking about organs that are pretty necessary. I want to be present when I go upstairs."

"I understand," I lied. I wondered what she looked like walking around. As long as I'd known her, she had used a wheelchair.

"And I'm okay to go," she continued. "But I think about my grandchildren. My kids, they understand. They're sad but they're grown-ups. They'll be okay."

"Yes." I agreed, even though at home, I saw her son in a fog.

"But I'm worried about the grandchildren," she said. "That they won't understand. I'm worried they'll think...."

"You're worried they'll think you didn't try?" When she gave a small nod, I said, "It's not the same. My dad was depressed for a long time. But he didn't choose to die to hurt me. Even if it hurt me."

"You don't blame him?"

"No. It's different. You try at your relationships. He didn't. Or couldn't." The back of my head felt heavy. I rested my elbows on what would become her deathbed, smelling her lavender soap.

Just months before this conversation, the Canadian government had passed legislation that allowed medical assistance in dying. In her irreversible state of decline, Ellen knew she was eligible for the procedure. In her bedroom that day, the tree outside her window was waving its branches in the last bit of sun. I looked back at Ellen and wanted to run. Maybe she did, too. Instead, I rested my palm in hers and hoped my face was saying what my voice could not.

"I wanna have the choice." She squeezed my hand and said, "Can you get me two more Tic Tacs?"

I stood at the low dresser beside her bed. As per Ellen's system, the prescription bottles marched a straight line past the two water glasses toward the ointments and creams. With one hand I picked up the square plastic case of candies, with the other I caught a tear rolling off my cheek.

When I turned to her, she tipped her head back and opened her mouth. A woman shaped like a baby bird. I dropped the vanilla-mint candies in her mouth and the tiny ovals clicked against her teeth. Two at a time was the rule. I wondered how many pairs of Tics Tacs would melt on her tongue before she died. She closed her mouth and sighed with pleasure.

Looking down on Ellen as she smiled with her eyes closed, I imagined her younger face. There were stories of her marching in the streets for things like free daycare, her legs propelled by a fierce belief in equality. Now this feminist, humanist Jewish writer, activist, and grandmother was choosing death. Euthanasia. This word echoing inside my head made fear crackle across my chest. Although I wanted to tell her that she shouldn't have to demonstrate her feminism with this kind of choice, I saw her lying there, and I knew what was equally true: she shouldn't have to feel guilty for wanting to choose.

So I smiled, picked up her hand again, and said, "When?" I wanted to know how long I had to prepare her son for his mother's death.

"I think January. February will not work, two grandchildren's birthdays that month. March is too close to Passover. April is Passover. And I don't know if I can make it until May."

"Okay then. January it is."

⁓

Two months later, death day is here and, as planned, I am standing outside Ellen's bedroom door. The Rabbi sings the final song. Ellen is singing too. She was looking forward to this part.

Outside, the rooftops are crisp, dark edges against layers of silver and blue sky. Here in the next room, the living have their heads bowed. Only five feet away from me, the doctor is staging her part of the plan by lining up the medical supplies on a makeshift table. As the Rabbi sings Ellen away, I make up my own words for the Hebrew song I do not know: this is how she wanted it, this is how she'll go.

Once the ritual is over, the doctor will conduct a different sacred act. She will inject Ellen three times. The first injection will put her to sleep. The second one will put her in a coma. The third one will kill her.

We are all prepared for this. We are all, not at all, prepared for this.

Terri Taylor
Dreaming Myself Awake

AN EXCERPT

My ex-husband was in all my dreams last night, like the guest star in a sketch comedy. Without the jokes.

I haven't been sleeping well. I spend the night dozing and dreaming and when I walk downstairs in the morning, it's as if I never left the day. Or the day never left me, it just turned dark and took me with it. There's no disappearing into sleep, no falling into sleep. No waking up rested and refreshed.

In the first dream, he and I are in the kitchen of my stepfather's diner, standing in front of the one-way mirror where we used to spy on the people eating. "Not spying!" my mother would say, "We're checking up on who needs coffee refills." Right. We're surreptitiously watching.

In real life my used-to-be husband isn't tall, but here, in my dream, he's looming over me. Actually, it's less that he's looming, and more that he's disregarding. Me, I mean. In a way that feels physically big.

Implacable, I realize now. I love that word. Implacable. Like nothing sticks to it. Everything just slides right off. That's what my words always did in real life. Came out of my mouth and slid right off him into a pool at his feet. There must be an ocean of my unheard words somewhere.

In my dream he's both looming and implacable. It's more like he's a living, breathing wall, a solid apparition in the shape of a human. I'm talking. Or trying to talk, but gobs of gum keep getting in the way. And each time I reach in to take it out of my mouth, there's more and more of it, like a big wad of taffy gum. I keep pulling it out of my mouth but the gum just keeps growing. It's sticking everywhere–my teeth, my hands–

there's no end to it. I can't understand where this gum is coming from and I'm so embarrassed.

But he doesn't even notice. He's just staring at me like the implacable, disregarding wall that he is. Waitresses brush past us bringing dirty dishes with soggy leftover bits of burgers and coleslaw. I can smell the coffee cutting through the thick layer of short-order grease and deep fryer oil. I used to come home from work smelling like that and no amount of showering could wash it out of my pores. Sometimes I can still smell it.

Then the dream shifts and we're in our bedroom. The real-life bedroom where I night nap now. And again, I'm trying to tell him something important, but this time he's not even looking at me. This time he brushes his hand in front of himself like he's waving away a small swarm of gnats. He doesn't even see me standing in front of him. Maybe that's what my words were to him in real life. Gnats.

In the last dream we're driving along a winding canyon road. Like Fraser Canyon Highway or the old Sea to Sky highway to Squamish before the Olympics, except with more trees on the drop-off, cliff side and no river or ocean below. Just a yawning chasm of thick spruce and needle-point fir trees. Suddenly we're careening off the edge, suspended, micro-moving toward those trees and the Grand-Canyon abyss below. "This is it," I think. "I'm really dying this time. This isn't a dream, this is really happening." And then I wake up.

I had many variations of this dream throughout my marriage, where I'm voiceless, unseen and unheard. Like I'm a ghost haunting my own dreams.

I married a slight man, 5'7" and maybe 160 pounds soaking wet. If I wore two-inch heels we could balance a ruler across our heads, but in my dreams he towers above me. After he leaves me, after the detonation of his affair, he grows even bigger in my dreams. I beat my hands on his dream chest and it's like I'm not even there. I yell and yell and nothing comes out.

Carl Jung says in the *Red Book* that dreams are the "speech of my soul.

I must carry them in my heart, and go back and forth over them in my mind, like the words of the person dearest to me."

After my ex left, I began to study the teachings of Carl Jung and Joseph Campbell, delving into the world of symbols, myths, and archetypes. I felt a deep need to withdraw from the world and go within. Joseph Campbell is often credited with saying, "the cave you fear to enter holds the treasure you seek." My ex's betrayal was my call to awaken to my own hero's journey. I needed to understand how I got to where I was, to this painful, broken-open place of shattered illusions. Discovering the language of my soul was one avenue of exploration, and analyzing my dreams became an important spiritual practice.

The power of dreams crashed into my life more than a decade before my ex's deception and the end of my 24-year marriage, when the deep impact of one dream catapulted me overnight into a long period of depression and anxiety. My twin boys were just six years old, and the girls were nine and eleven. We'd just finished renovating the first house we'd ever owned and I thought I was happy and content with my life. I didn't feel heard or appreciated in my marriage, but I thought that was just a normal phase in all marriages, when our lives were overflowing with the responsibilities and obligations that came with four children.

I remember a snippet of the dream: I am sitting on the toilet and great gushes of blood come streaming out. I am a never-ending waterfall of blood, overflowing the toilet and running rivers across the floor.

I woke up suddenly terrified, the sound of my heart beating inside my head, detonating bombs of desperation and panic. I was instantly convinced that I was dying. I was sure that the dream was prophetic in the worst possible way. I went to bed happy the night before and woke up the next morning filled with terror, as if the blood-draining dream was a doorway to another dimension, another realm of existence.

On the outside looking in, nothing had changed, but inside me was an apocalyptic wasteland. I went through the motions of my day, taking my kids to school, making dinner, even volunteering in their classrooms.

I was a zombie, going through the motions with my body while my mind fixated on Armageddon, and only one person even noticed that my world had changed—my dear friend Mary, who has spent too many days, weeks, and years walking through the darkness of depression herself. She recognized herself in my eyes.

I knew the dream was trying to tell me something, but this was years before the instant power of the internet and before I started studying Jung. I didn't think to look for books on dream analysis, and I didn't have the tools and spiritual community around me that I have now.

I learned that you can go to sleep an optimist and wake up a pessimist. Depression and anxiety don't always sneak in sideways, or tiptoe silently into life. Oftentimes the pendulum smashes in with all of the eloquence of a hurricane, obliterating all evidence of common sense and logic. It sweeps in and takes hold like a wind witch of horny burrs, latching onto any small place within me that harbours the slightest doubt or fear. It rips and shreds as it sticks tight, burrowing deep within my psyche.

That dream haunted me for over a year as I slowly eased out of the dark bowels of anxiety and depression. It changed how I moved in the world. It taught me compassion and empathy, and it also left me with a desire to understand my dreams.

Now, when I revisit this blood-flowing dream, it's clear to me it's about the loss of power I was feeling in my marriage. My soul was trying to wake me up, telling me that I was losing energy in my root chakra, the foundation of safety and security. She was screaming at me through my dream. Eleven years later, I finally learned how to listen.

Kelly-Anne Maddox
Saving Avi
AN EXCERPT

Avi stopped nursing when he was five days old. Every hour, I undressed
him, tickled his back, and laid his soft warm skin on the cold leather ot-
toman to wake him. Every hour, his mouth and eyes half open, I put him
to my breast and he mustered a little suckle, closed his eyes and drifted
off to sleep. Every hour, I begged him to thrive.

I paged my midwife, Celine, early that morning after a night of lack-
luster feedings. When she arrived at the end of the day, I was pacing the
floor waiting for her. My mother had just died of metastatic breast cancer, her illness and my pregnancy overlapping almost exactly. I couldn't
help but fear that Avi was slipping away too.

Celine laid Avi on her lap, cooing at him, tracing her finger along his
windpipe, examining his lips, his skin tone. I sat across from her, studying her with equal intent, the changes in her mouth, her eyebrows, trying
to decipher what she was thinking.

"Look at this," she said, pointing to a chapped spot on his lip. "He's
starting to get dehydrated." Her finger moved to his collarbone to show
me a slight indentation when he inhaled, a sign of possible respiratory
distress.

"I think you should take him to emergency," she said. My husband
David and I looked at each other in shock. I could feel the blood draining
to my feet as I relived the past year of my mother's illness in those few
seconds—the call to tell me her cancer had come back, the sickness after
each chemo treatment, the last month of her dying.

"Is he going to die?" I asked Celine in a voice so small I could barely hear myself. I needed her reassurance, needed to hear this woman (whose title in French is *sage-femme*—literally, wise woman) tell me that everything would be okay. I was sure that if my mother, the one person who always told me that things would work out for the best, the one person who I believed was eternal, could die, then that meant anything bad could happen from now on. Celine took both my hands in hers. Looked me in the eye.

"Oh sweetie, no. We'll go to the hospital, they'll find out what's wrong and treat him. He's going to get better."

⌒

After my mother died, grief enveloped me like a second skin. In the six weeks after her death and before Avi's birth, fear often overcame me. Fear that he had known nothing but sadness even before he entered the world, that I wouldn't be able to take care of him, that I would sink under my sea of tears. I would caress my bulging tummy, try to transmit thoughts of love, "It's okay, baby. Please don't be sad."

During my weekly visits with Celine, she urged me to prepare for the baby, to make room for him in my life. Physically, he took up all the space inside of me. He would poke his feet into my right side, stick his bum out on my left, dig his hands into my hips. Emotionally, though, I was empty.

When the time came, Avi's birth was fast. Pain crashed over me like an ocean storm, keeping my grief at bay. But in the early morning hours of postpartum exhaustion, as I rubbed my cheek against Avi's downy head and filled my lungs with his scent, I thought of how my mother would never get to hold him. I remembered when my daughter Zoe was born in 2010, when we lived in Kamloops and Mom worked in the oil patch, how she hopped on an overnight bus to come meet her first grandchild and take care of us. Knowing that she would have immediately flown to Ottawa from her home in Newfoundland to help with Avi, especially since his birth ended in an unplanned c-section, made what should have been a joyful occasion all the more bittersweet.

From his first moments, Avi was a sleepy baby. Accustomed to Zoe who, as a newborn, would wake every two hours and demand to be fed, I expected the same. But Avi would doze for four or five hours at a time and I naively congratulated myself on having one child who slept well. As a devotee of attachment parenting, I believed in following the baby's cues. When his eyes peeped open he would nurse, suckling for a couple minutes and then falling back to sleep. I believed he didn't need more than that.

There were no signs of problems in the days following his birth. The routine hospital baby tests were stellar. During the midwife's home visit on day three, she weighed him, looked him over, said he was fine. She recommended I visit a lactation clinic for a refresher. My daughter was three when I weaned her, and by that age we were both breastfeeding experts. Learning to nurse a newborn was a steep curve, even the second time around.

At the clinic the next day, a wave of grief crashed over me when I went to the bathroom and saw my reflection in the mirror. I burst into tears, bending over the sink to brace myself. I took a few deep breaths, splashed cold water on my face. "Okay, hold it together," I told myself. I walked back into the crowded waiting room, hoping I looked composed, but convinced I was fooling no one.

When it was our turn, the lactation specialist watched me feed Avi. She checked the latch and my posture. She noted that I was doing breast compressions, a massaging technique used to express milk into a baby's mouth. She told me that at four days old he would be able to draw the milk out himself and that I should stop compressing.

When I got home, I followed her advice. I tried encouraging Avi to suckle on his own but he could barely manage a few swallows before his eyes would shut and his mouth fall open. Looking back now, four years later, it was almost as if he didn't want to impose on my grieving.

The next day, the day I thought I might lose Avi, we headed to the hospital. During the ten minute drive I kept turning around, asking Zoe periodically to hold her hand under Avi's nose to make sure he was still breathing. I cursed under my breath at the red lights.

Celine met me in triage as David left to drop Zoe at a friend's house for the night. My midwife's presence served as reassurance that Avi would be okay and I convinced myself that if she left then that guarantee might leave with her.

David returned and joined us in the examination room. When the pediatrician came in, she listened to Avi's heart and lungs. Both were normal. She pondered the possibilities: an infection perhaps, or a reaction to the antidepressants I was on. She ordered blood work and a urine sample, then told us to come back to see her the next day to check him again and review the test results.

While we waited for the nurses to come back and shove a catheter in my baby son's penis, Celine made me lie down on the bed and relax. She had me try nursing Avi and he sipped for a couple minutes on both sides. The three of us agreed that this was an improvement.

She then set out a plan to get as much milk into Avi as possible: rent an industrial pump; use it after every feeding, then give the milk to him by bottle; keep a detailed log of each feeding; meet with a private lactation consultant. But her most important piece of wisdom was for me to start sleeping, to start eating more, to nurture myself so that I could nurture Avi.

By the time we got home I was starving. Instead of nibbling on carrots or almonds like I had been doing, I heated up some leftover lasagna and ate two helpings at midnight.

Avi seemed more alert the next day, perhaps in response to my reinvigorated sense of purpose. When we returned to the hospital that afternoon, I could feel the knots in my shoulders relaxing as the doctor said the test results were negative. Those 36 hours which I lived in slow motion shocked me out of my haze of grief. I realized that the last thing my mother would have wanted was for me to wallow and give up. Instead, I channeled my sorrow for her and my love for Avi into a fierce determination that he flourish.

Saving Avi became an operation of precision. David and I followed Celine's instructions to the letter. After every feeding I hooked myself up to the massive double pump like a dairy cow. Then David fed Avi while I went back to sleep. I nursed him every three hours, setting an alarm at night to keep us on schedule. I meticulously recorded the time, how long each session lasted, whether he was awake at the end, the amount of milk he drank from the bottle. I hired a lactation consultant who showed me how to increase Avi's milk intake by threading a slender tube, one end in a bottle, into his mouth while he was nursing.

I looked for any sign that he was gaining strength over the following weeks. I watched every day as the shrivel on his lip receded and disappeared, as colour returned to his cheeks. I reviewed my notes daily, checking that each feeding was longer, that he was falling asleep in the middle of nursing less often, that it was he who was waking me at night, not the other way around.

Nearly two months later, it was my mother's birthday. A day I was anticipating with dread, certain it would swallow me whole. Mom would have turned 64 the same day Avi turned eight weeks old. As I changed his diaper that morning, kissing his little toes, he looked up and smiled at me for the first time. I noticed that his eyes were the same blue as hers, the colour of the sea glistening in the sunshine. I smiled back.

Karen McCall

A Night in Lower Labovia

AN EXCERPT

I pull my eyelid tight and apply the black Maybelline liner with heavy-handed care. I like it nice and dark around my eyes. It's so hard to get the top just right. The thick lines smudge and go crooked so easily. Sucking in my lips and cheeks, I smear pink rouge into my cheekbones. A little bright maybe, but it lasts longer that way. Peach Delight gloss on my lips and I'm ready.

I look at myself in the mirror, and feel pleased to be fifteen. It took a lot of work, but tall and plain is now sleek and pretty. My long brown hair, ironed straight, is covered with a bowler hat, straight stovepipe pants hang right over my new lace-up Ingeborg shoes, and my mom's black umbrella twirls coolly in my hand. I've got the look I want, thanks to having my own money working part-time at the movie theatre. Now all I have to do is sneak out of the house without being seen.

I grab my Export A's and bus tickets, then take each stair down from the bedroom slowly, careful to miss the creaks. My parents are talking and watching TV in the den one floor down. I stop at the front hallway to check my father's jacket pocket for spare change, before opening the front door, and booting it up the street. I count one thousand and one, one thousand and two, and know if I get to one thousand and fifteen, I'm far enough away from the house that I can't hear my name being shouted. Nobody calls. I'm free.

I've never gone out in the middle of being grounded before but, hey, you gotta go, where you gotta go. I take the 49 Islington north and transfer to the Westway bus that will take me to my destination: Martin

Grove Plaza, the best place to hang out in the world. School is so boring, and I've been waiting all week to get there for a sweet Saturday night.

This is the first time I've made this trip without my best friend, Brenda. Without an ally, I'm a little nervous. My heart is beating and my stomach is sore. I can't wait to get off this bus. I'm dying to see Dave. Just to stand next to him, and hope he talks to me. I met him at the community swimming pool last year, and he kissed me later at his friend's house. Once he actually called me to go listen to music in his car. Rain was streaming down the windows in the dark, and we necked as "Light My Fire" by the Doors boomed out of his car speakers. I was too overwhelmed and awkward, and hardly spoke. He never called back. I peer through the bus window, scanning the parking lot for his marina-blue Corvair. It's there.

The little alleyway in the middle of the strip mall is full of kids wearing lumber jackets, leather jackets, bowler hats and stove pipe pants under trench coats. I move towards them.

"Hi guys," I say. A few heads turn in my direction; some nod, but nobody answers, so I just blend my way in, and stand there trying hard not to do anything stupid or uncool.

I'm too nervous to pull out my cigarettes yet, just in case I don't light up right, so I listen to the conversation, and move my head like I know what's going on. It doesn't matter here that I don't have much to say. They accept me. Somebody asks me for a cigarette, and I light up too, then the group moves by osmosis across the street to the benches and picnic tables in Westgrove Park.

Everybody is talking about the bonfire and the beer last night. I wish I'd been there. I'm just getting used to drinking, but I can do it. A few months ago, I stole my parent's Scotch whisky. Siphoned it off bit by bit into an empty peanut butter jar, and brought it here to this park. My friend Brenda and I plugged our noses and took turns chugalugging. I was drunk in about one minute. It was like magic. We laughed in the darkness, and fell down because we both had the spins. I spewed on

Brenda's sweater but she didn't get in trouble. Her mom hasn't talked to her dad in nine years because he had an affair with the neighbour. She's lucky. It's easier to get away with stuff when no one is paying attention.

After a while I hear whistling and clapping, and see Dave coming up from 'Lower Labovia.' It's what they call the little ravine just down the hill from this picnic table. I've never been there. Nobody's asked me. Sometimes when they drink beer, I can hear the guys clink their bottles and toast one another, shouting nostrovia.

Dave is running toward us. I like that he's tall and love his crystal-blue eyes, and the sharp angles of his face, even with a bit of acne. He lifts up his arms, forms two fists then does a little victory dance in a circle. The guys slap his back, and give him power handshakes and high-fives. I wonder what's going on.

Everybody starts yelling, "Sooey, Sooey, Sooey, Saunbie Zombie," in high pitched voices like they are calling a pig. I don't join in. Then I see her coming up from the ravine alone. It's Suzanne Saunbie. I know she hangs around here too, and lives in the apartments across the street, but she never talks to me. Her matted curly brown hair, sticking up on all sides, is full of twigs. She moves closer to us in the dark. Her white blouse is ripped a bit, and there is dirt on her hands and along her legs under the black-and-white checkered skirt. I sit there frozen, then realize I'm the only other girl. I feel afraid for her, and mad at all these people. She is smiling.

"Hey Saunbie, wasn't getting it last night good enough for you?" laughs Mike. He turns to us, "I pissed on her last week and she liked it."

His blond hair is slicked back. I used to think he was cute and nice. But, now my stomach is churning, and something catches in my throat. I can't talk and I'm afraid to look at Mike or Dave or the others. I glance at Sue. She gives me the 'what the fuck are you looking at' stare and says, "Does anyone have a cigarette?"

"You were smoking pretty good last night, Zombie, but after to-night, looks like you're a chain-smoker," somebody says, smirking from the other side of the picnic table. Stit, the youngest of the group, with his slow moving green eyes, and oversized red and black lumber jacket, leans in and hands her a cigarette. She lights up, sits on the bench and blends back into the group.

I don't know what to do. I want to get up and leave. I'm afraid they'll find out I'm still a virgin. I'm afraid they'll think I'm not. They talk big, but I didn't know anybody here was actually having real sex. I'm busy twisting a Kleenex into a long damp string in my hands, and wish I could find my way home without anyone noticing.

Jane Shi

How to Make
Strawberry Dumplings

I like strawberries. Don't make me eat anything that's strawberry-flavoured, though. It smells wrong, shimmies too closely to the territory of cough syrups and other sickly sweet medicine genres of flavour. On this glaring hot day in June I'm watching a friend's cat and watering their garden where strawberries grow and glisten in the sun. It's hotter than it was a few years ago here in Vancouver, where large rays angrily tattoo my skin with shadows of melanoma. Even so, the heat adds a pep to my step. I've even invented a new recipe that's gone quite well with friends: strawberry dumplings.

What you do is chop up a bunch of strawberries and mix them with honey. You fold them up with round wrappers and pan fry them. So simple, as easy as apple pie in a Midwestern movie. You can figure out the rest. Hint: NOM.

You know what *is* puzzling? I've never understood what people meant when they said "lover." There's a passionate strawberry surprise in the word that exceeds the private, gender-neutral term "partner." *A sexual or romantic relationship, but not married.* These days, few decorate the ambiguous sexts, many-months stands, and intense bouts of affection squeezed onto the warm sheets of a dorm room twin bed with such a tender fruit.

Save for a few people who are presumably incapable of loving (a cruel kind of othering that lumps asexual and aromantic folks with ruthless psychopaths), "lover" sounds like something that could be anyone at any point in time. Yet in common parlance, it nonetheless has an elevated, special meaning that differentiates it from other forms of coupledom and friendship.

Strawberry dumplings are special treats not served in traditional Chinese or Chinese diaspora family settings. I mean, they could be, it's just that I invented them, and I haven't yet seen it done. If you take this recipe home to your family, do foodstagram it and tag me, won't you? If you're allergic to strawberries, you could still try mangoes or peaches or even durians—what's most important is that you post it on Instagram!

I'm allergic to mangoes. Nothing bad would happen if I made mango dumplings and ate them, though my skin would get hot and strawberry red if I mushed peeled, ripe mango flesh against my face. Nothing bad would happen either if I boarded a plane to Toronto and met up with [redacted], where we would roam the queer corners of the city together, shuffle into the gladly open arms of a giant bookstore, and look awkwardly at nudes of men with skin as delicate as ours.

How do you know that somebody is doing a thing, and not just doing a thing, but doing it for *you*? How do you know a thing that takes a whole life to understand is real, and could be described with language?

Some would say love is not meant to be understood, only felt. I guess the thing about feeling things is that everyone feels a different thing, like blind men feeling different parts of an elephant and determining its ontological limits based on what their hands know. For some, love is sturdy like a tree trunk. For others, it's so sharp it could pierce right through you and be utterly gruesome. Then there are those who feel they could use it like a cat-o'-nine-tails, or a big flat leaf on which to put dinner, or a cool marble wall to rest your back against on a roaring hot summer day. And let's not forget about those for whom love is a hose you use to water a suburban garden. Where strawberries green, and ripen, and become early June Christmas decorations for a family that doesn't believe in Christmas.

I've always wondered about this elephant story. A parable possibly older than the Buddhist, Hindu, and Jain texts in which it first appeared, its various visual depictions paint remarkable tableaus of a group of people coming together to understand a thing, the unexplained intimacy between a group of men and a giant, almost fantastical creature. In some paintings, the elephant's back is as large as a boulder and several men have climbed on top of it to get to some faraway, coveted destination. Growing up, I always thought that the story was Chinese in origin, but now that I'm older, I am learning that a lot of things aren't Chinese, and are just taken from elsewhere and called that.

I don't like that in some versions of this story the men start to erupt into physical fights over what they believe an elephant *really* looks like. Maybe it's improper of me to want to rewrite an old story, to want these men to resolve conflict and collaborate to understand the larger problem before them. Or maybe it's just foolish. After all, they're *men*. Count on toxic masculinity to ruin what could be effective disability justice organizing, any day. Which brings me to what nobody seems to be asking: What is the elephant feeling? Does it care what it looks like? Is it tired of being touched by strangers? Does it want to go home?

Eventually, I'd go home after hanging out for a few hours with [redacted]. I'd stare at the ceiling and stare at the wall and because I wouldn't have eyes looking inside myself, I'd pretend-stare at my soft, cool elephant walls. I'd stare and stare until I'd get bug-eyed and watery. How annoying would it be if a moth were to fly inside my mouth right then and just tickle me silly?

You see, a lot of philosophical thought experiments don't bear the scrutiny of the ripple and fall of waking. The kind of waking that tumbles out of your mouth like piping hot fruit or a chorus of moths bursting from a broken nest. I swear for any philosopher to understand what's going on in their thought experiments, they'd have to take first-year biology at the very least, but then I'm sure university wasn't even invented yet when philosophy lumbered along. I suppose you don't need a PhD in lepidopterology to be equally fascinated and horrified by the nearly strawberry-red wings of an elephant hawk moth.

I've decided I've never had a lover in my life, unless the lover were a cup of warm coffee or a round dumpling skin or a poem that spoke to every part of me and held me in its inky arms. Right now, I'm thinking about that line in Dina Del Bucchia's "Remember When": "You held my hair and another time me when I couldn't stop crying / about that boy I barely loved." Are poets just body-pillow manufacturers? Artisanal boutique craftspeople of language furniture? Designers of feeling? Cats on a page? Mass producers of word-dildos? I know a lot of people would object to the idea that love has anything inherently to do with sex. I certainly do. Nonetheless, that word "lover" sticks stubbornly to sex, which sticks hard, too, to romance. Language can be an utter culinary disaster.

The truth is, even though I've made peace with moths (and can accept that the elephant hawk moth is a different species than a *small* elephant hawk moth), I never want to be anybody's lover. The R is too much like a rickety armrest attached with super glue that's not super at all because it could melt at any moment in the climate crisis. But it's also because I don't need or want love like a lot of people need or want it. I'm like singer Moses Sumney, whose album *Aromanticism,* and his own coming out, puts my orientation in the headlines. In his album, moths have plastic wings.

My own album is demiromantic. It's like how I absolutely will not eat dumplings with green onions in them—not even with bribes—but on the odd occasion will make an exception for a friend who's chopped them up real thinly for me, handing them over with a knowing smile in a still-steaming Tupperware container.

The elephant in the room is a banal question. What is the difference between being someone's lover and being their truest friend? In Dina's poem, the "you" and "me" aren't lovers. If you read the whole poem in *It's a Big Deal!* you'll know there's no need for any gay innuendo for the hair-holding and me-holding to mean absolutely everything to the speaker.

This business of being aromantic feels fraught in our romance-obsessed world. It doesn't seem fair that eventually, even your closest friends will drift apart and live routine lives with a partner, married or not, whom they don't ever call "lover" either. It doesn't seem fair you can't call all your closest friends lovers—an elephantine word perfectly suited for the ooey-gooey surprise of trust that goes on between you. Maybe it's not love that we need to understand better, but friendship. What if we tried to get rid of the nauseating connotations "lover" has, reclaim it from those who take it for granted, or stop using the word altogether? Maybe then I can believe that I'm enough as I am. Either no one is a lover or everyone is. But then I wonder if I am asking too much of language, too desperate to belong in words that don't belong to me. I wonder if moths insist on flying in because they smell the sweetness of honeyed strawberries, or if they mistake the scent of melting ice cream on the counter for the real thing. I wonder if they are waiting to sleep on the back of an unsuspecting elephant, ready to fall in love with the language of their wings.

I always fry my dumplings on non-stick pans. After lining the pan with them on high heat, I pour in half a cup of water before reducing to medium for about fifteen minutes, until the bottom turns golden brown. Putting oil on the bottom is very important. It's just as important as the water.

Don't forget, okay?

Hailey Rollheiser

Omelette

We woke to a rainy, dark morning, the sweet scent of sweat hanging in the air. I opened my eyes with a feeling of dread. I was awake, again. A weight had settled on top of my chest, and there was a heaviness in my bones. I lay for a few moments without moving or speaking. I wanted to savour the time before I had to face him, and think about what he had done.

But it was too late. The thoughts rushed into my head with the opening of my eyes. They would stay with me until the moment I closed them again, only to have a restless night full of vivid dreams. I was starting to lose sleep. Reality had begun to feel unreal; I was detached from my body, a mere wisp of myself, floating through space. I stretched my fingers in an attempt to feel present.

My fingers cracked and then I felt his weight shift on the bed as he moved, pulling me closer to him. We were both awake, but we did not speak. The rain sneaking in through the slight crack in the window made his room feel damp—the room, the bed, us, permeated with a gloom. I pulled the comforter tighter but it couldn't ease the shivery dampness in my chest. His arms were around me, but I didn't feel the warmth of affection. I felt hollow.

I looked around his bedroom, covered in lasting relics of his childhood—the narrow single bed in which we lay, a lampshade printed with soccer balls beside us, the dinosaur stickers on his bed frame. We were both seventeen, yet he had not redecorated since he was a child.

We had spent so many sleepy summer days here in his room, having sex in his single bed, licking the sweat off each other's shoulders. It had been stifling, but we were comfortable stuck to each other's skin—

thinking there was no one else we'd ever spend our days with, desperately clinging to the idea of forever, wanting it to be true.

Sprinkled in between our slow, sex-filled afternoons were boozy, jealousy-fuelled nights: slurred words, shouted names, slammed doors. Looking into each other's eyes with a crazed energy we mistook for passion. Crying together and hating each other, while slipping a hand inside the other's pants. Making each other cry and then moan, pushing him away then pulling him deeper. We'd fight then we'd fuck, and it all felt so urgent, and passionate, crazy and feral. We mistook it for love. Now, summer was over.

"Are you awake?" he asked.

"Yes," I said.

"Are you hungry?"

He wanted to do something nice for me that morning, so we went downstairs and he started to make breakfast. I helped grate cheese, as he chopped vegetables and cracked brown eggs into a frying pan. An air of fragility hung over us, like this moment was a bubble that could pop in a moment. He was trying so hard to make things right, but there was nothing he could do that would fix what he had done. We shouldered the weight of this feeling together, but it didn't make it any easier to bear. We both pretended that cooking an omelette might make things a little bit better. We pretended not to know we were pretending.

But the thing he was trying to do right went wrong. The pan was too hot, and when he flipped the omelette, it was burnt. All of the ingredients that we had carefully prepared went to waste. He scraped the singed omelette out of the pan and into the garbage. The smell of burnt eggs filled the dimly-lit room and made me feel sick to my stomach. Now more than ever I wanted to escape this room, this relationship, this situation. Fucking fly out of the house, floating away, anywhere else.

"Fuck," he said. "I can't do anything right." Tears filled his eyes and his expression became strained. He dropped the pan into the sink and I flinched when I heard it clatter. I went to him, and put my arms around him, and held him without saying anything. I was the one comforting him after all he had done. This was how it always worked; I somehow found myself in the role of picking up the pieces that he so carelessly shattered.

So I took his hand and led him upstairs, and we crawled back between the sheets of his narrow bed. The first time we had ever had sex—drunk, in this same bed—I had hurriedly yanked up my dress and as he entered me, his face close to mine; he looked at me and brushed my hair out of my face. In this moment of tenderness I knew something had shifted. I was used to rough sex with older guys, but here was something different.

I didn't know how to relieve the anguish of the situation I so badly wanted to escape, so I tried the only way I knew how. I started touching him, and he started touching me, and we kissed. We wordlessly undressed, kissing and caressing each other with increased intensity. Then he reached over to the drawer in his desk and I waited as he rolled a condom on, and it felt altogether tragic as I thought about the reason why I wanted him to wear one in the first place. He had fucked another girl without one, and the results of his STI test hadn't come back yet. I watched him roll the condom on and was both present and in my head, imagining what he had done with her as he did it with me.

He was inside of me, but he was inside of her. We were both quiet and neglected to look at each other. He laid his face on my shoulder, and I stared at the picture of us hanging on the wall behind him, smiling at me, as I ran my hand limply up and down his back. I kept thinking about her, and how she felt when he was inside of her, and if he looked at her, or brushed her hair out of her face, then kissed her, and where he put his hands on her, and where she touched him. I felt the stain of her body, and the mark her fingerprints had left there. And then I thought about the omelette, how all he had been trying to do was make it right.

I started to cry, silently at first, so he couldn't hear me. There was a sick desire in me to keep it hidden, so maybe he could enjoy himself. But a gasp escaped from between my lips, and he moved to look at me, and saw the tears running down my face. He stopped, laying his face beside mine, and held me as he began to cry too. We both cried silently, holding each other and the burden of what he had done, the weight shared between us. I knew then that there was nothing he could do to make anything better.

I wanted to go back to the way we were, so jubilant in first love. I wanted to go back to the version of myself I had been before I'd experienced heartbreak. I had been so confident in my belief of true love, in the decision to put that love, and all of myself, into another person. I didn't know anything about love except for the way it felt when he held me, and how happy I was when I opened the front door to find him there.

But I could not return to the past, to a place unmarked by pain, no matter how hard I longed for it. The scar on our relationship would never go away. The hurt was always there, lurking shallow beneath the surface, ready to re-emerge at any moment. The pain felt permanent and it changed me. The illusion of love had been lost.

And I still don't like the smell of burnt eggs—they make me sick to my stomach.

Adriana Añon
A Tray of Sweets

The tray carried a small plate loaded with a silver-plated fork beside two varieties of sweet Arabic treats. There was orange juice too, served in a basic wine glass. Even in its simplicity, there was something lavish about such an offering—in this unadorned home, the bright-coloured juice and the glossy coating on the pistachios stood out like a brooch on an apron.

Excusing herself for a moment and going into the kitchen, Rima had emerged bearing the tray of sweets, which she placed in front of me, on the table where we usually put our books and pencils. Not fully knowing if the tray was for me, it lay there untouched for a while, as we continued with her English lesson. I'd been coming here twice a week for a couple of months, and this was the first time a tray had been brought out.

Rima's eldest daughter, Salma, had the day off from school and had just joined us on the sofa, where her sister, Tala, a vivacious toddler, had already been running circles around us for the first part of the lesson. It's this happy toddler who keeps Rima home, unable to attend the daily English classes offered to all refugees. For the program in which I volunteer, I drive to Rima's twice a week and teach her English, so she can continue to improve her language skills and one day hopefully pass the Canadian Citizenship Test.

On days like today, with her two daughters home and the English lesson that must go on, I worry about my student. She is a driven young woman. Her interest in learning is most evident when her toddler climbs on her lap demanding attention, and she settles her on her right knee, holding her tightly with one arm, while with her other hand she grips her pencil with resolve, and finishes writing the sentence we are working on.

Although flustered at times, Rima doesn't lose her patience. When Salma is also home, her attention is doubly requested, her hands both full.

I think about my own life—how easy in comparison, how free. I learned languages because I was interested, because I loved them, and my parents could pay for lessons. But this is a matter of survival. Rima has a family to raise. At 24, a daughter on either side and a third child in her belly, she is trying to make herself understood in a language that doesn't come easily. I struggle to remember that she is among the chosen, the "lucky ones." She lives in a safe Canadian city, she has a heated home for her family, more than her basic needs met. I know her children will have a future in this country, and yet, "lucky" is not the first word that comes to mind.

Since October, her first comment has always been "It's cold today," and I worry that in her third winter in Ottawa, October still feels cold to her. I worry, but I understand.

"This for you," she finally says, pointing with her hand at the tray. "Please try."

"Oh really?" I say and emphasize the surprise in my voice. "It's beautiful. You shouldn't have. Thank you."

"They Arabic sweets. You like?"

"I think I will."

"This favourite mine," she says, pointing to the one that looks like a pale pancake. "And this favourite my husband." The husband's favourite looks like a miniature nest holding glossy pistachios.

I realize even the little girls have paused and now focus on me, expectant. I take the first bite of Rima's favourite velvety cream-coloured sweet, and smile as I chew it. The relief at my approval is palpable. The little girls smile with excitement as they watch me. Rima giggles nervously.

"Yes, you like?" she asks.

"It's delicious, Rima. Really good," I say, exaggerating the body language with thumbs up and smiles. "I love it."

"This we eat," she says, "we eat in our home."

I'm not supposed to ask Rima too much about her home. She has left war-torn Syria, she has been a refugee in Jordan, she has been away from the rest of her family for three years. But I know this only because, slowly, she has shared it with me. I'm curious, of course, but my job is to teach her English. Still, in the process of learning we share so much more.

"Here is Uruguay," I tell Rima, pointing at my country on the world map. "That's where I'm from. And here is Syria, where you're from." And then moving both my index fingers simultaneously across the world map I make them meet in Ottawa, where we both live today. "Look at all the distance we had to travel so that we could meet each other."

"So far away," she says in astonishment. When I look at the map, I'm reminded of an essay by the poet Al Purdy I'd once read, about all the movements of people from one side of the world to the other: "I have an inexplicable feeling ... because of all these eastward and westward movements that everyone may have been looking for everyone else on the face of the Earth ... because humanity has always been searching for itself."

In the process of learning the Canadian provinces and their capitals, learning verb tenses, and learning new words, Rima and I share stories of what we did at the weekend, we share laughs, we share worries.

Today, Rima has shared a piece of her home, her identity, all in a simple tray of sweets. I teach her meanings and she, without knowing, gives my life more meaning.

The names in this story have been changed to protect the identity of these real-life characters.

Isabella Mori

Believe Me

This is an excerpt from a book project,
"Believe Me—A Mental Health Trifecta: Poems, Short Stories,
Interviews and Research on the Topic of Mental Health"

A quick introduction: Humans are not one-dimensional. Neither are those who have encountered difficulties with their mental health. With a background of over 25 years of working in the field, and taking a Narrative Medicine approach, I look at individuals' experience through three different lenses. Each chapter contains one of my poems or short stories about a topic that touches on mental health or addiction; an interview with someone who resonates with the topic; and a taste of the research on that topic.

People with lived experience of mental health or addiction challenges will see themselves and their peers reflected in this book and can see how research connects with some of their lives. Those without personal experience as well as health professionals can get a more rounded view of mental health, mental illness, and addiction.

What follows is a text in the form of haibun, a Japanese form of lyrical prose combined with haiku. After that, you will find an excerpt from the interview that was prompted by the text.

"DEPRESSED"—A HAIBUN
It cannot be done. The blanket is too heavy, the legs too tired. "The fog—" you want to add ... but you need to rest. You close your eyes. You cannot think long sentences.

The fog too thick.

Like cotton. Not fluffy-cloud cotton; dusty cotton stuffed in your mouth. You can hardly breathe. How can you lift a blanket?

The alarm goes again. You are, indeed, alarmed. Alarmed at the cotton. Alarmed that you can feel nothing yet sense your heartbeat with dread at the same time, and that all-consuming tiredness. This is when you can think long sentences: when they are about a never-ending, boring ugliness.

You hear yourself, though distantly, explain to yourself and a world that does not care, how your limp hair will repel anyone mistaken enough to feel attracted to you; how you know that the letters on your laptop will dance in front of your eyes again, utterly unwilling to reveal any meaning; how you will buy a cinnamon bun and it will just taste bland, and your response will be to buy more with money you don't have and stuff your pimply face until you burst.

But you will not burst. Even that cannot be done.

> endless landscape
> icy wind blows dust
> across the tundra

Thirty minutes later you find yourself out the door. Somehow you ended up in clothes; you even thought to put on rubber boots and bring an umbrella. You look up. The rain has stopped. For now.

> beetle crawls
> over the dung heap
> a rainbow brightens its carapace

THE INTERVIEW—AN EXCERPT

Lucinda is a university student in her early twenties. She has battled anxiety and depression since she was a child. In the last few years, she has had moments of thinking about ending her life. She has found a combination of medication and Dialectic Behaviour Therapy helpful in dealing with her challenges.

What were your reactions to reading this story?

It's about a person struggling to get up in the morning because what's the point, you'd rather be hiding under the blanket or somewhere safe.

"You hear yourself, though distantly, explain to yourself and a world that does not care, how your limp hair will repel anyone mistaken enough to feel attracted to you" ... there's no way I can be attractive enough, I won't be able to focus.

There's stress eating—at some point eating was enjoyable but not anymore. Enjoying is a difficult concept for this person. That's relatable.

"Even that cannot be done"—as much as you want to kill yourself, it's not possible, as much as that seems nice or stress relieving.

Then the part about somehow managing to get up, to be prepared ... the intensity is over but not totally gone, the wanting to escape is not totally gone.

The last poem—there's some semblance of possibility with the rainbow. The person feels insignificant, disgusting, trying to get through life but it's hard to feel. The person is still focused on the dung heap.

What would you say is the main theme?

Being stuck between the part of you that wants to do something, to be happy, be productive and the "I don't want to be here, don't want to deal with anything"—but you don't burst. The inner struggle between wanting something positive and just to live ... the teetering line between I don't want to live and the part that wants to live, feel joy.

What's a positive message?

"But you will not burst"—there is a glimmer of hope. It has promise.

The amount of times I've thought about totally ending it, there is a part that stops me. Or when I tell someone: can you please take this knife away from me. There is some sort of internal break or barrier. I always find ways to tell myself, no, you don't want to jump into traffic, no, you don't want to hurt someone else by killing yourself. As much as it sounds so much easier and pleasant, there is this obstacle, there is possibility for happiness or less stress.

Lindsay Borrows and John Borrows
Border Crossings

An excerpt from a father/daughter collaboration

I never expected to end up here in Mexico, visiting for the weekend from Phoenix—yet another place I am just visiting. But isn't that how it goes? We dream, plan, and work until we find ourselves in a place that we never knew existed. And how could we ever know what lies beyond the borders of our imagination? Borders. Or as they say in Spanish, la frontera. It is a line that can separate worlds.

One night, I biked a few miles down the road from the casita I was staying in, to the wall that separates Nogales, Sonora from Nogales, Arizona. I laid my bike on the ground, climbed a pile of rocks, and looked over the fence. Behind me to the south, was a maze of run-down houses, their bright colours paled in the soft moonlight, dogs barking, car horns and banda blaring. To the north of the fence there were fewer houses, less noise. I took a handful of sand that had gathered in the crevices of the rocks from various windstorms and tossed it gently into the air. The granules scattered and disappeared.

Every day, people from all across Central and South America make the journey to this border. Many spend years dreaming of a better life in a land without drug wars, rampant homicides, and less worry of where the next meal will come from. A land of promise and hope. I breathe deeply, like the breath that the 25-year-old schoolteacher from Jalisco took as she arrived here after days of walking and taking various buses. She had a black backpack with lip gloss, a photo of her family, a small water bottle, a plastic garbage bag, and garlic. She only took the photo out of her bag in the early morning as she started walking for the day.

The image of her family kept her spirit alive while the water did the same for her body. The garbage bag was to prevent anything from biting her as she slept on the ground at night, and the garlic smell helped ward off snakes and critters. The lip gloss was a luxury, and everyone needs a little of it.

People die crossing la frontera every day, shrivelled in the heat and unrecognizable to the few passersby that may venture into the Sonoran Desert. The voice of an elderly woman who has nurtured me comes to mind. Acuérdate mi hija, una historia buena es más poderosa que la muerte. Remember my daughter, a good story can be more powerful than death. I felt that to be true, and was filled with some peace as I looked out across this land that has both taken and given life to thousands. My parents have learned to let me cross borders to walk across deserts since I was a little girl. Every year they not only allow me to wander a little further into the unknown, but sometimes they even encourage it.

I pulled out the note he mailed me shortly after I moved to Phoenix, and shone my headlamp on it.

⌒

My Child. I remember the day you came into this world. You were all points and angles. You seemed to unfold from your mother's body. You expanded, preassembled, as you were drawn from her womb. Have you ever seen a featherless newborn bird, eyes closed, straining upward, reaching for the light? That was you. Your chin, beak-like in birth, was somewhat sharp and pointed. Your shoulders were very wide; their future power prominent, even through those first few moments of life. Your skeleton sprang on its hinges, ready to take flight.

But you were silent. Not a peep. You didn't cry, or take a breath, or move. I think my heart stopped. They rushed you to a small table at the edge of the room. They rolled you over and nudged your chest. They pushed their fingers inside your mouth to clear your throat. Eternity passed in those few seconds. My happiness crashed to the ground. It soon gave way to fear. And when you didn't immediately respond I found myself in the deepest sadness I have ever experienced. We already loved you and I thought you were gone. Your mom was still, anesthetized on the table. What would I tell her when she woke? She would be heartbroken too.

And then you cried—the sound of life. It was the sweetest song I ever heard.

They bundled you in a soft, downy blanket and delivered you to me. You soon stopped fussing and nuzzled against me. You were solid, physical, and aware. I studied your every feature. I felt the strength of your body and spirit. I knew you would soar. It was one of the greatest days of my life.

With your head in my palm, and my arm at a right angle, your feet barely reached my bicep. I loved to carry you like this and then fold you into my body. I thought of a scripture, "How oft ... I have gathered you." As you grew from a baby into a child, I would prop you over my shoulder and hug you with my hand on your back. Sometimes you liked to be cuddled in this way, but at other times you would rear back. You wanted your space. We called that your "catamaran," as if you were straining against our bodies, using them as an outrigger, learning how to steady yourself for the journey ahead. But other times you would quietly settle against me and I would rock you to sleep.

And as you slept you would grow. I can't tell you how fun you were as a three-year-old. I loved when you sat on my knee. I would bounce you around. You were so bright: all those questions, and a million smiles. Easy to laugh, always a song, your eyes shining brightly, your joy was full, and so was mine.

Heaven was to watch you read, colour, do crafts, and play house. Your mom would tell me about your every success when I wasn't there. You were enthralled with nature when we went to the farm. You lived scripture; you would "Consider the lilies of the field, how they toil not, neither

229

do they spin." You watched the swallows swirl around you, on the lawns around the barn. I'm sure, God-like, you would know if even the smallest sparrow fell to the ground. Do you remember the time we buried one with iridescent yellow wings? You were enthralled. Back in Toronto, you followed your sister around the Charles Street Daycare, catching up to her in those first two-and-a-half years of your life. I watched you ride up and down student housing halls, fearless, on your plastic pink-and-purple Fisher-Price bike. I will never forget your yellow, one-piece pajama suit, when we dressed you for Halloween. We painted a few whiskers on your cheeks and coloured your nose black and put mouse ears atop your head. I carried you home when you got tired of knocking on doors asking for candy. I hope you feel your Heavenly Father's arms around you when you get tired of knocking all those doors throughout life. He will embrace you and carry you home.

And then we moved home to Barrie. To ensure you were safe, I fenced the yard. You never liked fences, and I've since seen you twist your body and soul so you could be on both sides at once.

And now, only a few months ago, you walked through airport security to fly away once again. We had the same feelings deep in our hearts. You went to Phoenix. What a great name for a city: named after a mythical bird, rising from the ashes. You have soared. And, like an ancient phoenix, you are continually reborn wherever you serve. Life does not end, and we are for eternity.

Tears filled my eyes as I folded the letter back up. The wind picked up more dust, which swirled around me before settling again. I took one last glance across the desert to the north, climbed down from the rocks, and biked back to the casita. It was time to sleep, and dream some more.

Fiction

Jacqueline Mastin
Bone & Earth

AN EXCERPT

A mouse got inside once. It took us six months to catch it. It was 1996. I remember because that was the same year I found the teeth in the wall.

At the time, my husband, Sam, and I were living just off Westcove Drive, south of downtown Fredericton. The house was old, a 1950s bungalow, which is probably how the mouse got in—all the holes. It was a small house, and it didn't look like much from the street, its greying stucco and concrete front steps not unlike the rest of the houses that lined Creekside Road. But if you'd ever stepped inside, you would've known it was perfect—one of those houses that made you feel like you lived there, even when you didn't. The polished fir floors drew you in toward the living room, where the walls rose to meet the ceiling in smooth curves. A single glass-panelled door led to the kitchen, and another to the dining room, where there was a tall, narrow window with a deep sill. The thick cedar hedge that lined the side of the house blotted out the light from the streetlamps and somehow from the moon too. At nighttime you could climb right up and sit inside that window sill, cross-legged with one knee almost touching each side and your back to the dark.

❧

"You're better off now that the museum's fired you, you know," he says. "That job was wearing you down for years, Joanna." Sam is leaning on our aquamarine-blue kitchen countertop, its chrome edges leaving impressions in his thick, tanned forearms. He turns his head to look at me in the dining room.

"Yeah," I say. But I can barely hear him over the ringing in my ears. It started when they told me that morning, my termination papers lined up in a perfect row at the edge of the oval conference room table. The words, spoken without emotion, were like a strong blow to the side of my head. For a moment I couldn't hear anything, and I wondered if I might die right there in that oversized chair in the basement of the Museum of Natural History. I imagined the coroner filling out my death certificate. Cause of death: blunt force trauma. And then maybe they'd drain my bodily fluids and pluck out my eyeballs before peeling off my skin and mounting it on a mannequin made of polyurethane. I'd be just like the birds in the exhibit upstairs: suspended from the ceiling where I could watch each of the museum visitors pass by below, my glass eyes fixed and staring.

None of that happened though, because I didn't die. My hearing came back and that's when the ringing started, probably because I couldn't cope with the sound of my own heartbeat rising up from my chest and into my head. I'd once heard in one of those nature documentaries on the Discovery Channel that sharks can sense the heartbeats of their prey, and I wondered then if that was true for any other species.

"Well, this calls for champagne," Sam says, "because some losses should be celebrated, not grieved." The pop of the cork sends a jolt from my ears down into my feet, and I'm suddenly aware that the ringing is gone. He pours me a glass without saying anything, and it occurs to me that I'm not sure when he'd bought it. After all, champagne's not really something you keep around. I wonder then if Sam saw this coming, and I think about who else might've expected it, who else knew how it would all end before I did.

It's still dark when I wake, cold and breathless on the living room couch. I can smell the stale champagne in my glass on the coffee table behind me. I roll over, and that's when I see it: a small, grey mouse in the middle of the living room. It's not scurrying, as mice do, not erratically sniffing out food. It's just staring at me, casually, as if to say, *You're too drunk to catch me.*

"I probably am," I say out loud, before falling back into a silent, dreamless sleep.

⁓

"I bet it got in last week when I was replacing that weatherstripping on the backdoor," Sam says. It's the next morning and we're sitting at the kitchen table. I'm clutching a coffee cup between both hands, its aubergine rim paused on my lower lip.

"Yeah, probably," I say.

"He needs a name, you know."

"What?" I say.

"A name. If he's going to be living here for a while." Sam sounds defeated, like he's already accepted we'll probably never be able to catch the mouse.

"Grey," I say, without smiling.

"Very creative."

"Silver, then."

"No," Sam says firmly. "We're not calling him Silver."

"Why not?"

"You know I had a guinea pig named Silver when I was growing up, Joanna. We're not calling him that."

"Okay, fine," I say flatly. "Henry." Henry was the name of my golden retriever who'd been hit by a car when I was eight years old.

"Really, Jo? Henry?" Sam says. A few seconds pass before I realize he's speaking to me, and when I do I give him a blank stare and a small, unapologetic shrug.

⁓

One morning late in the summer I'm doing laundry in the basement—the second or third load—when I hear it: a quiet sound, a faint scratching coming from inside the laundry room wall. I move silently from where I stand in front of the washing machine, crossing the room to lean into the now-soundless wall, eggshell white and cool against my ear. I slide slowly down the wall, my left eardrum leading the way, until I'm crouching on the laundry room floor. There it is again. Here the wall looks soft and damp and smells faintly of dirt. I press into it, first with my nail and then with the tip of my finger, which sinks into the wall violently, as though it's made of loosely draped, decaying skin. I press my body flat against the floor until I feel it push back against my hip bones, tilting my head until my right iris turns the hole fern-green. I see only darkness, and I think about what it might look like to Henry if he's behind there now, a single giant eye appearing in his world.

I brace my thumb against the wall and begin to break off pieces of the moist drywall, one palmful after another, until I can fit my entire head, my shoulders, my chest, inside. I move my hands around in this dark space inside the wall, feeling the coolness of the concrete that separates me from the outside. My fingers snag on a crack, an opening—part of the foundation had crumbled where it should have been solid, continuous. Sliding one palm toward the other, I touch it with both hands at the same time: the Earth.

My fingers sink into the soft dirt and touch something jutting out into the empty space that surrounds me. It's sharp and smooth, and even in the dark I can tell it's brilliantly white. Like an artist painting with my bare hands on a canvas, I trace a nearly perfect rectangle around it, my fingernails outlined in dark crescent moons as I extract the beautiful shape from the Earth's raw grip. I climb out from the wall and the bright laundry-room lights illuminate the palms of my hands and in them—a complete human jaw. I hold it up in front of me and think about how it might look in an exhibit at the art gallery, framed by a beautiful rectangle of crumbling dirt.

"Have you called the police?" Sam asks when he gets home from work. His face has a slightly grey hue to it, and his eyes have that faraway look they get when he's distracted.

"Not yet," I say. I'm leaning back on the couch with my feet up, crossed at the ankles. My sketch pad is on my lap and I'm staring intently at the jaw where it sits now—in the middle of the coffee table in our living room, the earth peeled back from its edges.

"Well ... when did you find it?"

"Just a little while ago." It's six thirty in the evening and I don't tell him that I'd found it just after he'd left for work that morning.

"Jesus, Joanna. We need to call the cops about this." Sam's normally even voice wavers with concern.

"Mmhmm," I reply, without looking up. I can feel Sam's eyes searching my face for a sign that I agree with him, but say nothing.

"I mean, you find a human skull and you're using it as a goddamn paperweight," Sam continues.

"Jaw."

"What?"

"You said it was a skull, but it's a jaw." Sam winces at the chattering sound the teeth make as I lean forward to brush the dirt that has spilled onto the stack of sheets beneath the jaw. "What I'm drawing is a skull," I add.

"Come on, Jo, I—"

"Okay, tomorrow," I say, relenting. "First thing."

Ingrid Olauson
With the Horses, Blondie

"What did your beloved say this time?" Louise sometimes referred to Sheila's client as "beloved" because Sheila would so often, these days, sneak away from their bed, late at night, to call the office in Manama. Because their business spanned several time zones, there was a sordidness to the phone calls that Louise liked to make Sheila aware of.

"I think we've found a new investor, which is exciting. Moe says we'll meet him tomorrow." Sheila's face disappears momentarily on FaceTime and is replaced by the words "Low connection."

"Sorry, honey, I didn't catch that last bit. How much longer are you staying?"

"I wish you were here. Moe's hooked me up with a really nice apartment. There's a pool and—" Sheila tilted the camera so Louise could see the expanse of palm trees and desert sand. The sun was setting over a crystalline blue sea—"look at my view."

"It's beautiful," Louise exclaimed. Maybe she should have gone to Bahrain with her. Louise knew how much it meant to Sheila to have her by her side on these trips, but it was a long flight and the dinners and meetings with clients were not Louise's particular strength. And she had the illustrations to finish. Though, she supposed she could have done that on the plane and in the apartment while Sheila was working. Still, it wasn't worth it to go now, get over the jetlag, and only be there for a couple weeks.

"Moe really wants to meet you. You're practically all I talk about." Sheila's beautiful, full lips protruded into a pout as she said this, causing Louise to ache for her like she did when they first met. Sheila was a beautiful, radiant force. On the third day of seeing Louise, she rested her ear on Louise's chest, to her heartbeat, after they had made love and told her she loved her. Louise moved in a week later.

"Really? Good things, I hope," said Louise. She never liked the idea of Moe. She didn't trust him.

Almost as long as they'd been together, there was Moe. Mohammed came from a wealthy family who, after suffering a near fatal skiing accident in Switzerland, abandoned his Olympic dreams and turned his interest to business, partnering with a U.S.-based sustainable technology start-up. That's when he had called his cousin's husband in Vancouver. Sheila had received the call at Louise's parents' house as they were drinking eggnog and brandy in front of a slow-burning fire. The Muslim called the only Jewish lawyer he knew, who would be working on Christmas Eve, the husband had allegedly said. He didn't practice that kind of law, but boy did he know the right lawyer who did. She had worked all Christmas while her office scrambled to get the contracts in order.

It was usually like this; Sheila worked around the clock. She had lawyer's brunches on weekends and teaching engagements out of town. Louise worked from home or at a nearby coffee shop. She'd usually be finished for the day and itching to go out when an exhausted Sheila got home. Usually, Sheila would get a second wind to go out for dinner or drinks or meet up at a friend's house. They took trips when they could. Louise introduced Sheila to camping and they both discovered a love for fishing, even though they rarely caught anything. They would sit in their campsite after the day's excursion, Louise reading one of the books she brought along, Sheila absorbed in her tackle box. They enjoyed each other's company so much that when one of them had to leave for more than a few days, it was almost unbearable.

"I think I'm going to go to bed early," Sheila said, yawning. "It was a long day of talking. People here take their time. There's usually at least an hour of talking and drinking tea or coffee before anything is discussed. Will you stay with me until I fall asleep?"

Louise stayed on while Sheila prepared herself for bed, washing her face and brushing her teeth. Louise made a second cup of coffee and sat at the kitchen table in front of her sketchpad. The pages for the children's book were spread out in front of her. "Is it okay if I work while we talk?"

"What's it about? I still can't believe that you—an artist who paints women in ecstacy, going down on each other—you, of all people, were commissioned for a children's book. "

"Oh and you're so decent. My correspondent in the Middle East."

Sheila laughed. "What we do is technically legal here."

"Phew! Well, if you must know, the book is about a farmer who has a special cow who thinks she's one of the horses. Here, it'll just be easier if I show you." Louise held up a drawing of horses running through a prairie landscape.

"Once upon a time, a long time ago, there was a farmer with three beautiful horses. Every morning, he would open the pasture gate so they could run free until they tired. He also had a blonde cow that grazed in the pasture." Louise held up a drawing of a golden-coloured cow with long eyelashes. "She was very dear to his heart and every time he let the horses out, she saw them running. Whenever she saw their joyful galloping, she would lift up her tail just like the horses did and run. The farmer would laugh and say, 'With the horses, Blondie!'" She showed a drawing of the cow running with the horses, her tail triumphant with the flourish of Louise's pencil.

Sheila beamed. "That's one to read to our kids!" They'd talked about what kind of mothers they would be. Whether they would enforce the playing of instruments, athletics, or encourage a more wholesome play that would involve climbing trees and digging in the dirt. Every time Shelia held a baby, she was at one with herself. Louise, unlike Sheila, was challenged to find the desire to be maternal. Wasn't it enough to be that way with Sheila? Louise felt good when Sheila asked her for little favours. The sweetness of opening a package or a jar for Sheila—though Louise knew she was capable of opening it herself—was a kind of salvation.

"I went to a mosque today." Louise could tell by Sheila's slurring speech that she would soon be drifting off. "It was stunning. At first, I went to the wrong section."

"What's the wrong section?" asked Louise, who didn't know much about mosques either.

"I went to the men's section." Sheila laughed. "It was pretty embarrassing. But a nice man who worked there showed me to the women's side, where there was this stone barrier you could see through in this Andalusian design."

"Sounds lovely." Louise attempted to imagine Sheila in an abaya. "At least they make it look nice when they separate us from the men."

"Mhmm …" Before long, Sheila's eyes started rolling back into her head and her lips parted into peaceful snoring. Louise let the call go on for some time, daydreaming about mosques, the desert, and the sea while she sketched galloping horses. Just then, Moe's face ventured into her head. Why on earth was Sheila following this man to the Middle East? Surely, a failed athlete with his parents' money wasn't the basket Sheila should put all her eggs into. She failed to understand Sheila's devotion to her business partner—what else could she call it but devotion?

"Shit!" Her pencil broke over the page. She had been pressing too hard. "Sheila, wake up!"

Sheila stirred, but didn't wake.

"Sheila!" hissed Louise, louder this time.

"I'm not a follower," murmured Sheila.

She must be dreaming, Louise thought. No—it was less work and less energy to convince herself Sheila was being influenced by his congeniality, his cult image. Your beloved prince, thought Louise. That's what he was in her mind. A prince who swept her Sheila off to a faraway land. Louise could only think of the sweet somethings Moe would be saying to his future lover, the kind of things a lover says before departing one bed for another. Oh God, was she being Islamaphobic?

Sometimes Louise pretended to call upon a glorified, Marxist past, being constantly critical of what her life was producing and how she was producing it. Now, that same overbearing eye was watching Sheila as she slept. "I look at you, and so does he," she said to the screen in anger. Moe's sustainable energy start-up had to be a scam. He was probably ripping off the factory workers in China who were building his machines to pay Sheila's paycheque. But then again, Sheila's paycheques were paying for their lifestyle. Was that what she was really angry about?

Louise was living her dream. She was an artist and she was with the woman she loved.

She examined the drawing on the table in front of her and debated if it was worth salvaging or if she should start again. I wish I could run away with you, mused Louise, afraid she was somehow being left behind.

"Sheila?" Louise said to dead air. "I'm coming to Manama."

Rowan McCandless

TEOTWAWKI

An excerpt from a collection of 12 short stories exploring the lives of the obsessed and the dispossessed. Humourous and heart-breaking, weaving literary fiction with speculative elements, readers can expect the unexpected in "The Mausoleum of Lost Souls"

I hate to break it to you, but it's a fact, plain and simple: in this world, it's survival of the fittest. Another simple fact? Jamie Barnes can't climb a rope worth shit, and our jag-off of a gym teacher knows it.

"Come on, Barnes," Mr. C. says, glancing at his Timex wristwatch. "Time's a-wasting and I'm not getting any younger."

Jamie's face turns beet red as he white-knuckles the rope suspended from the ceiling. His arms shake like Mom's Jell-O ribbon salad. He's giving it all he's got—not that it matters, cuz I'm pretty sure if he straightened his legs his feet would still brush the floor.

"I can't," Jamie says, twirling in circles like one of Dad's Old Spice soap-on-a-ropes.

Mr. C. removes the Bic pen attached to his clipboard, starts poking poor Jamie with the capped end like he's the Pillsbury Doughboy.

"Don't"—*poke*—"you dare"—*poke*—"let go of that"—*poke, jab*—"rope," Mr. C. says.

Things go from bad to worse, cuz the higher Jamie reaches on the rope, the lower his gym shorts slide down.

My best friend, Charlie, elbows me in the side. "His ass crack's showing, for chrissakes."

Some of the boys in our Grade 8 gym class grunt like little piggies. The Ashleys start giggling. Ashley H. laughs the loudest.

Geez Louise, now Jamie's crying. He's got snot dangling from his nostrils like bungee cords.

"You know," Mr. C. says, "my 86-year-old grandmother could shimmy up and down that rope faster than you. Pathetic, Barnes. Absolutely pathetic."

Dad says some people are like that—you know, pathetic. They're weak-willed and soft, and that makes them a target. Still, it doesn't seem fair that Jamie's gotta suffer just cuz he's cursed with the same sorry physical constitution as the rest of his family.

"This is bullshit," I whisper to Charlie.

"Something you'd like to share, Westerberg?" Mr. C. says.

I shake my head. No.

"Didn't think so."

I stare at the criss-cross of lines on the hardwood floor and can't help wondering: Would Mr. C. and the rest of the class be a whole lot nicer to Jamie if they knew what I know? That TEOTWAWKI's coming. Dad says it could be any day now.

The
End
Of
The
World
As
We
Know
It

"Come on, Barnes. Before it's Christmas."

But Mr. C. doesn't know TEOTWAWKI's coming, any more than he knows last Christmas could very well have been exactly that—the honest-to-goodness last one celebrated on the planet. So I guess Jamie's just SOL in more ways than one.

Except for Charlie, who's been my best friend since kindergarten, they're all SOL. They just don't know it yet.

There's this thud as Jamie lands butt-first on the mat. "May I be excused so I can go see the school nurse?" he says, cupping and cradling his hands cuz of some nasty rope burns.

"What are you? Some kind of baby? Suck it up, Buttercup." Mr. C. looks my way. "Westerberg! Show Barnes how it's done."

I take a step forward.

Jamie takes two steps back, blowing onto his palms like he's trying to snuff out lit candles on a birthday cake. He's got this pleading look on his face, like I'm the only one who can save him and his reputation from total annihilation. But what can I do? I'm not about to be anyone's target, cuz I'm not weak—or soft.

I grab the rope. It's thick and coarse in my hands. I loop it under my knee, over my foot.

"Go, go, Westerberger," Charlie cheers from the sidelines.

Dad would have a major conniption if he knew I told Charlie about TEOTWAWKI, but I know Charlie'd never betray us and I can't imagine surviving the end of the world without him. I'd warn everyone like I did Charlie (well, maybe not Mr. C., and if I'm honest, I'm kinda on the fence when it comes to saving the Ashleys, especially Ashley H.), but I can't. Dad says we gotta keep it on the q.t. Says, "The last thing we need, when the GD shit hits the GD fan, is a bunch of pie-eyed, shit-scared townies after our supplies."

Mr. C. blows the whistle around his neck.

I pinch the rope between my feet and look up at the rafters, testing my weight and my hold on the line.

I start my climb. Find my rhythm. Super star.

Dad says, when the time comes we gotta be ready. Only the strong will survive. So I've been working out, big time. I can do 98 push-ups, 117 sit-ups, and 143 star jumps. No joke. I'm serious. I'm not lying. And I'm sure as hell not some pathetic cry-baby like you-know-who.

From the top of the rope, I look down at the Grade 1-ers tossing bean bags at one another in barefoot gym, at Mrs. Rempel's Grade 4 class playing murderball.

Mr. C. gathers everyone's attention like a barker at a carnival. He says, "Ladies and gentlemen, our Mr. Barnes has just been shown up by a girl. Do me a favour, Barnes, and get out of my sight."

Jamie starts his walk of shame toward the exit.

I wave at Charlie but get no response, cuz he's too busy making googly eyes at Ashley H., who's the first girl in our class to smoke cigarettes, and sneak booze out a parents' liquor cabinet, and five finger discount Bonne Belle makeup from Selkirk's five and dime store. She also looks a whole lot different wearing our school gym uniform than the rest of the girls in our class; the infamous greenie, the bloomer-bottomed bane of my very existence. I'm still flat as a board and skinny as a rail. My hair is super curly and my nose is too big. Ma says, good things come to those who wait and I'll grow into my beauty. That I'm just a late bloomer like she was. But what's the point of being a late bloomer if the world is coming to an end?

Ashley H. touches Charlie on the arm, and my temples start throbbing, my ears start ringing, and pinpoints of light cascade from the rafters like shooting stars.

Jamie's almost at the exit when this blast shakes the gymnasium. Before I can warn him, he opens the door. A tidal wave of heat roars into the gym, followed by a river of hellfire engulfing everything and everyone in its path. The smell of sulfur, of smoke, of burning flesh makes me want to puke. Jamie looks like the Human Torch. *Snap. Crackle. Pop.* He's toast.

Flames spread across the hardwood floor, lick the gym bleachers.

"Run!" I tell them. "Run!"

Mr. C. melts like a wax mannequin. So do all the Ashleys. Especially Ashley H.

I close my eyes, trying to shut out the carnage, but there's no way to rid my nose of the smell, the images seared into my brain. I feel like bawling, but I can't. Cuz bawling's for wusses—and Dad says there's no room for wusses, before, during, or after the apocalypse.

"Way to go, Westerburger!" Charlie says.

I squeeze my lids as tight as I can. *I'm sorry, Charlie. I'm sorry.* I hear screams of torment. Howling. The sound in my ears blares like sirens, like ringing bells, the recess bell, like static, like the high-pitched nasal whine of the secretary's voice coming over the PA system. "Will Cassie Westerberg please come down to the principal's office?"

"Zip it!" Mr. C. says. "Westerberg, get down here!"

I open my eyes. Everyone's staring at me.

"Today, Westerberg!"

I climb down and land feet-first on the mat. Mr. C.'s looking at me like I'm some kind of nut job. So are the Ashleys. Especially Ashley H., with her nose in the air like I smell bad or something. Like I said, it's survival of the fittest.

K Ho

Lunch with Hot Girls

*Author's note: This excerpt contains the opening pages of my current
book project, a novel that explores the impact of a homophobic incident
on four Chinese Canadian protagonists. Contrary to the working title,
lunch will not be served in this excerpt—unfortunately*

When Lindsay Campbell elbowed me aside in the phys. ed. hallway and
saw her name absent from the junior volleyball roster, she ran into the
locker room, screamed at everyone to get out, and sobbed herself hoarse
for the rest of lunch. No one could get in, not even the school janitor, for
it was soon discovered that Lindsay, by some remarkable feat of strength,
had uprooted three wooden benches from their resting places, dragged
them across the locker room, and jammed them against the door. News
travelled fast. By next period, every student in Mr. Matthews's gym class
had heard about Lindsay Campbell's astonishing strength and more formidable disappointment, and knew better than to knock on the door to
ask if they could change into their gym strip or pee in the toilet or so
much as breathe the same air as her. For the rest of class, the girls stood
around the perimeter of the gymnasium smoothing their pleated skirts
while the boys, remaining in their uniforms more out of laziness than
solidarity, unknotted their ties like bachelors at a wedding reception and
hurled styrofoam balls at one another until their armpits soaked through
their starched shirts and the ripe smell of overheating teenagers curled
out the hallways and floated through the early autumn air.

The date was September 2006, some twelve years ago, and I was
starting tenth grade at Milton Academy, a private school nestled in
Vancouver's gleaming West Side. It turned out Lindsay Campbell was

248

devastated not only because all the hot girls in our grade had made the volleyball team except her, but also because it was her birthday. Her lunchtime spectacle had been so head-turning that no one had seen the team list, but the news came to me the next day in the form of Lindsay Campbell herself.

It was morning break. Striding to my locker as a newly minted fifteen-year-old, Lindsay took a deep, impressive breath and declared, "Well. I'm not mad you got on the team." Before I could respond—not that I knew what to say—she spun on her heel and stalked off. Everyone resumed their hallway activities. I leaned my forehead against the cool metal grate and exhaled in relief because fourteen-year-old Lindsay Campbell was known to have a keen eye for detail and revenge.

After classes that day, I went to see the team list, feeling a seed of excitement burrow inside me. My friends—Adeline, Mia, and Vivi—had all been out of town that summer, and I had spent the long hot months drilling a volleyball against the back of the house while my parents worked at the restaurant and my thirteen-year-old twin brothers played video games and fought upstairs. Once, my brothers had become especially combative and I overheard them wrestling and banging about in their bedroom above my practice wall, until at last, one of them came away clutching a fistful of ripped hair and flung it out the window to the ground below, where I stood on the hot pavement holding my volleyball, the thin black hairs falling around me in soft needles of rain.

It had been my goal to make the junior volleyball team since tryouts last September. I didn't have a sliver of chance then; the two girls who played my position had been starters the year before, and could kill a ball down the line with lightning-quick accuracy. My line shot, on the other hand, was like a luggage cart with a loose wheel: it could reach its destination eventually, but never on the first try. The older girls had moved on to the senior team, and now, as I stood under the bulletin board and scanned the list, anticipation sprouted in my chest. Squeezed between Rebecca Sullivan and Yvonne Watkins-Yonge, was my name, xxxx Sun.

I had made the team. Our first practice was tomorrow. The lonely summer had paid off.

⌒

Despite Asian students comprising over 60 percent of the school's student body—a statistic that was either debated or reviled, depending on which Vancouver newspaper one sought out—we were considerably underrepresented in Milton's athletics program. As such, I was one of three Asians selected for the team. It was surprising (or maybe not so surprising) that immediately the three of us discovered we didn't quite fit in, for the moment the hot girls entered the gym they flocked to each other like beautiful birds and partnered for warm up so efficiently that I thought their pairings must have been preordained. The cues were clear. My Asian teammates and I were to stick to ourselves (while the hot girls stuck to themselves), and we would fumble through the two-person warm-up as a clunky group of three. It wasn't that the hot girls were unkind or scathing in any particular way. It was just the natural order of things: that old high school machine revealing all its coded and well-oiled parts.

We were soon relieved of our triangulated misery by a recently excommunicated hot girl. On the third practice she barged into the middle of our trio, snatched the ball from the air, then pointed at me and said: "Dibs. For warm up."

"No problem," my Asian teammates squeaked, backing away.

The girl was white. She was a controversial figure. She had a big butt and big boobs and had slept with numerous boys over the summer (as well as after classes now, allegedly), and she liked to arrange her ponytail at the very top of her head so her hair cascaded in all directions like a fountain at a casino. The hot girls held a meeting. The hairstyle, they determined, was so eighties, and not in the cool, strategic way, and the cleavage and after school activities simply too flagrant. And so, because my new warm-up partner had gotten her decades all wrong, and hummed too loudly when she applied lip gloss before practice (as well as the other things), the hot girls proclaimed their evaluation. A slut. Ejected.

By the next week, the ex-hot girl was sitting with me and my Asian teammates at the front of the bus while the ongoing hot girls screamed to country pop in the back. I didn't mind the ex-hot girl's company; it was nice actually, having another person around, as if her reputation could shield me from being scrutinized and gossiped about. Back then—and still now—I believed being invisible was not only easier, but smarter. I couldn't understand how the ex-hot girl navigated her infamy, or why she didn't care she was hanging out with Asians, but it seemed she had grown up that summer, had jumped a fence and rooted herself in a wilder, more unruly field of maturity—cars with older boys, innuendos I didn't yet understand—and had attained the self-possession of someone who no longer bothered to cultivate her high school cred, never mind what the junior volleyball team thought of her.

I wish now that I had been more aware of everything that was roiling under the surface, all those little cuts and invisible alliances weaving around me. I didn't know I would not last a half-year at Milton.

But I was fifteen then, and enamoured with a sport and the sense of belonging it gave me. I loved the feeling of the ball, that split-second sensation of my hand connecting to leather, the way the clear snap of a spike rang through the gym, how it differed from the muted thump of a float serve. I loved the skid of skin against floor when I dove, how the ball sprung from my hands when I set, and the way, once airborne, it glittered against the gym's fluorescent lights and hung at its peak like a chandelier. I also loved how, unlike other Milton sports teams, we didn't run into the change room before a match but undressed out in the open, on the sideline of the court, bra straps sliding, hair elastics loosening, pulling off our warm-up shirts and slipping into our maroon jerseys before the huddle. Most of all, I loved that once we walked onto the court, everything would drop away, all those pointed comments and hushed conversations and stink-eyes aimed specifically at the ex-hot girl, and we would become exactly what we were chosen to become: a team. Cohesive. Undivided. As my teammates leapt and tumbled and panted around me, I would think to myself, how lucky I was, how lucky to be part of this smooth, thrumming unit.

Looking back, I see how that year at Milton Academy was a little like a mountain materializing through fog: vivid in the patches I could see, looming and treacherous where I could not. I wonder if everything might have remained like that, dormant and woolly, had Jessica Copeland not come along.

Tamara Lee

This Close

Her mom liked to say you couldn't really see the mountains unless you stood farther away from them. At age ten-going-on-eleven, Becks was eager to test that theory. It wouldn't be more than a couple of years before she'd be sitting on the Granville Street sidewalk outside McDonald's, with people she'd call friends, looking over to the snow-capped mountains, trying not to think about what her family was doing.

Becks started going downtown more regularly when the SeaBus started shuttling North Vancouverites from the sleepy suburbs to the real city. Her mother took her on the inaugural trip because her father had gotten a special invitation from Transport Canada and would be on the crew. Her brother, Paul, was sixteen and too cool for that sort of thing. But Becks, still not the thirteen she pretended to be, hadn't yet reached the age of full resistance.

"We'll make a day of it," her mom said, pulling out a package of Big Red gum from her white summer handbag. "It's $1.49 Day at Woodward's. We can get a hotdog." She stuffed a stick of gum into her mouth then offered Becks some.

It had that sharp cinnamony flavour that burned her tongue so she couldn't properly taste anything for hours after. Becks took two pieces and corralled them into her mouth.

By way of disapproval her mother said dryly, "I hope you don't choke."

Her mom dressed up for the occasion and asked Becks to change her shirt, at least. The jeans would do but the ratty T-shirt would not.

They made their way slowly toward the gangway amidst the throngs of other dressed-up adults and squirmy kids. Becks had on the most casual outfit, and she took pride in her achievement.

"Hold my hand," her mom said with authority.

"No. I'm not a baby."

"I don't want to lose you."

"We're going to be on the same boat. I can't get that lost."

Her mother couldn't argue with the logic but refused to give in. "Stay close then. I don't want you to get swept away."

Everyone else was vying for what they thought would be the best seats, but Becks and her mom had been given reserved ones in the middle of the first row, facing the downtown harbour.

Near the bow of the vessel, Becks thought as they settled into their seats. Her father had taught her the language to use. Berth, bow, stern. *Know where you are at all times, Rebecca. If a ship goes down, you need to know where you are so they can find you.* It seemed to her if they had found her to ask her where she was, they already knew. But she didn't argue. Her dad wasn't someone anyone enjoyed arguing with.

"There's Daddy." Becks pointed toward the stairs leading to the wheelhouse. "Dad!"

"Becks, don't holler."

"But I want him to see us."

"Leave him be. Now turn around and sit properly."

Becks straightened up as much as she could, but her feet dangled so it was harder to pretend she was a teenager. She watched younger kids turning around on the long front row of bench seating to look out the window, their knees tucked into the backs of the seats. Mixed in with the crackly voice on the intercom calling for the captain and deckhand to prepare for sailing, Becks heard children's laughter, a baby crying, and women speaking excitedly.

Her mom had taken up a conversation with the matronly woman beside her, bragging that her husband was one of the captains of the vessel and, "Isn't it about time this happened? It's so nice not to have to drive over the Second Narrows Bridge."

The ship's horn blew and the SeaBus lurched forward. The crowd hushed as the vessel pulled out of the berth into the brightness of the afternoon. The water gleamed, and a halo of light diffused behind the downtown buildings.

"Psst." Becks heard something above the engine hum. She looked to her right past her mom. "Becks. Hey, Becks."

She looked to her left and saw her father standing near the bridge stairs, signalling her to join him. She smiled and tugged at her mom's jacket, but her mom was still talking with the stranger about progress and didn't notice her daughter's attempt at attention. Becks walked quickly over to her father, who lifted her up to the third rung of the ladder to the bridge.

"Hold on tight. Jimmy's up there. He'll get you."

Jimmy, her father's friend and long-time deckhand, had convinced Becks's dad to leave his job on the tugs for a job with the SeaBus. Jimmy had been made a captain, so it was an easy choice for him. Becks's father, though, wasn't sure if he'd get bored just driving back and forth all day long. Becks's mom had to convince him it would be the best thing for the family. No more weeks of on-calls; no more eighteen-hour days. A nice uniform that looks like a pilot's. It took several goes, but her mom won out. Becks wasn't convinced it would be the best thing for the family. Paul said Dad would get bored within the year and regret leaving the tugs. And eventually, Paul would be right.

"Give me your hand, Becks." She didn't mind Jimmy taking her hand. He was a big bear of a man with a deep jovial voice and a dimple in his right cheek. It seemed strange that a grown man could have a dimple, but it made her love him even more. He hauled her up like she was a round of tugboat line and it made her laugh. "Bud's acting third mate on this trip. You remember Buddy from the tugs, don't you?"

Becks felt her stomach knot at the sight of him and nodded an obedient yes. She immediately felt relieved Jimmy was there.

"Best view in the house, sweetie. Bird's-eye," Bud said, his stale smoke-and-beer breath filling the air. He gave up the helm for Jimmy to take over and Becks squished up on the other side.

Her father had joined them looking like he did whenever he finished having an argument with her mom. He instructed Becks to stand over on the left of the helm.

"Tight fit. Don't mind Bud." Bud stood back a little to give her some room.

She dutifully moved over, and decided to study Jimmy's captain's hat. It did look like he could be a pilot.

"What direction are we facing, Becks?" Her father was going to turn this into yet another lesson.

"South. Mountains are always north." She turned around in a full circle noticing that the wheelhouse had windows on all sides.

To the east, she could see the Second Narrows Bridge and two tugs guiding a ship out of the inlet. She knew the need for rapport between tug captains, the expectation of trust just to navigate the waters. The few times Becks's dad had taken her out, through the tight squeeze below the bridges, he'd hollered at her to keep quiet.

To the west, she could see the huge yellow sulphur pile and, beyond that, the Lions Gate Bridge. Depending on if you were coming or going, the Lions Gate was the first or last obstacle in the navigational dance. Beyond the Lions Gate was the Strait of Georgia and, beyond that, the Pacific Ocean. There was a lot to get through before finding open seas.

Looking to the north, she could see the wide expanse of the coastal mountain range, formed in a semi-circle, like arms reaching for a child. She could really see them then, like her mother said, but all she wanted was to push them away.

Sometimes Becks looked back at those mountainous arms, remembering how it felt like they'd crumbled all around her, carrying her atop their rubble, all the way down and over the Burrard Inlet.

She looked up at the buildings surrounding her—downtown Vancouver, with its noise and hippies and protests and punks and every kind of curiosity Becks couldn't yet conceive of, on that first trip across the water. All she knew then, was that she was driving toward it. And all she knew now, was that she was unsure if she was being pulled back, or if the arms of the mountains were pushing her forward.

Kerry Furukawa

What Else to Do?

*An excerpt from a short story about a bank teller who
must deny her mother's request for a loan*

It's my mother calling. She wants me to take another loan for her at the
bank where I work. She doesn't know that I know this. But my big sister
pinch me and tell me that Mummy's been bemoaning the shameful condition of the house lately. The inside bathroom needs tiling, the walls in
the rooms need painting, the roof in the kitchen is leaking. All true. But
I don't get the shame part.

They brought that house from one room with a kitchen and bathroom outside, to four bedrooms with everything inside, while raising
the three of us.

My mother started out wiping floors at the branch library in our
community. As for my father, he was always a cow man. Raise, sell, buy.
Every time he sold a cow, he would go straight to the hardware store or
to the carpenter's house, or to the woodwork shop. My mother would
go straight to the wholesale and market after she got her two weeks' pay.
That's how they built the house and raised us. They told us these stories
over and over.

My father would sit on the verandah after coming home in the evening, take off his boots, roll up his pant legs, lean back and just look out
onto the street. One of us would bring him some water—he would drink
a bit, hold the glass in one hand, and pass the other back and forth over
the arm of the rocking chair.

"What a thing, eh? Verandah. I remember when we only had one
dege dege room. All a we inna one room. Now we have room for all you

children plus verandah." You couldn't mistake the look in his eyes for anything but pride. And we all felt proud of all of us when he spoke that way.

But, according to my sister, my mother has been saying all her children are big now and working, and people must be saying they can't even fix up the house. But she's not asking us to, she is just saying people must be saying that. No, what she is going to do is get a loan. The same way she got a loan to raise the pigs, a loan to buy a little car so she could drive to the market and doctor, she is finally going to get a loan to fix up the house. But my mother's salary can't really support a loan. Gout ended my father's cow days. My sister is struggling with her family and my brother is not approachable. So I've been waiting for the call.

"Mummy, morning."

"Sleep, you sleeping?" She won't get straight to the point.

"Mummy, it's 6:30 a.m. on a Saturday, of course I'm still sleeping. Like I was when you called twenty minutes ago."

"Oh, so you saw the call and didn't answer. Suppose I was down here dying? Anyway, is a little business I want to talk to you about."

"Yeah? What's that?"

"The house, man. Time to just band my belly and fix it up."

"Oh. That don't sound bad." I don't have to ask how the "business" fits in.

"If we use the house as security, how much you think we can get from the bank?"

"Not sure, you know. Would have to ask."

"Okay, find out and let me know, you hear? And I know you tired, but remember it not so good to sleep too late."

I can't say no from the get-go. I'll feel bad about it. Even the eventual "No" is going to have to be real soft. The time with the pigs was different and, in all honesty, she helped me to pay it back with some money from her sister in England. With the car, it was the least I could do for my mother. She paid the down payment, which was only five percent of the cost, and I handled the rest. But now, I'm thinking about getting an apartment. I don't expect her to like the sound of that, by the way.

Apartment? You alone going to buy apartment? Those little boxes with no back door, where everybody can see your business? It's just like living in a big yard. How can you buy apartment when your parents living in these conditions? Fix this up first. When we dead and gone, you can have something nice to live in. In fact, you don't even have to wait for that. With the new highway, you reach Town quick quick.

I have never expressed any interest in going back to Jackson Town to live. And the house really is not that bad. It has seen better days for sure, but it also survived Hurricane Gilbert. Anyway, since I haven't said no at the beginning, I have to save it for the end. My friend Taneisha, over in Loans, once found a technicality to get out of borrowing some money for her brother.

Of all the working people whose families see them as a door to all kinds of opportunities, those of us who work in banks have it the hardest. Never mind that it isn't our money we are counting or lending all day long, as far as they are concerned, they have a link on the inside. All that is fine, but I want something for myself now. I don't have a family, but I can get property. In the evenings I can change into a loose dress, go out onto the balcony, sit in my wicker chair, drink some wine, and feel the day ending. I can invite friends over, we can play games in my smartly furnished living room, eat food prepared in my modern kitchen with my stainless steel appliances. And me and my friends can feel proud of me together.

In my nine years at the bank, I have taken the two loans for my mother and more recently one for my big sister. My sister was unlucky enough to have a child with special needs in a country that doesn't really know what that is. She had to stop working for a while. True, she had barely helped with the repayment, while my mother had. But you know when somebody does something for you and "Thanks" just isn't enough? My sister heard the man's wife call me all kinds of names right there in the nightclub parking lot. She saw the man stand there until his wife was finished, and then drive her home. Nobody in the family heard a word about it, even though my sister's mouth was made for talking. In a sense, I wanted to buy out her memory. The loan meant I didn't owe her anymore.

My mother has her ways, but she hardly makes us feel like we owe her anything. I'd say she's really interested in us. Even my brother, who makes fun of her plastic flowers and figurines on doilies everywhere in the house, gets the question when he visits: "So tell me, what's going on with you?"

"Well, just like you said she would, Mummy called. Long and short is she wants to know how much we can get."

"What you tell her?"

"That I will find out."

"Listen girl child, Mummy and Daddy done built their lives, time for yours. Simple."

"I know, and with this special employee interest rate, and 35 just sneaking up on me, now is the time to get serious."

"A bit dramatic there, but I get you. Looking at any apartments this weekend?"

"Just the one in Barbican. Gated, of course, and it even have a pool."

"Like you can swim."

"Anyway, I'll let you know how it goes."

Mummy knows I can have an answer soon, and I can imagine her humming and turning the roast breadfruit on the stove, humming and picking the ackee, humming and putting the saltfish to soak, calling, "Morning," to Sister P. All the while waiting.

My friend Taneisha who works over in Loans says we can get eight million easily, ten if we try. As for a way to get out of borrowing any money at all, she sends me a snap from a customer brochure that lists quite a few methods. And there's one I'm sure I can use. An application for a home improvement loan may be denied if the building doesn't comply with the restrictive covenants on the title; i.e., prescribed building specifications were not adhered to. Our house was not only built haphazardly, but also according to how much rum Gideon had had. He was who everyone called upon to add on to their house. And he was generally good at it. But my father always said, especially with the last room, Gideon let the waters get the better of him. The only problem in that technicality are the words "may be denied." It's not categorical.

The house sits on a nice piece of land in a community where everybody knows everybody. A new face is always identified by who they are related to. That's so-and-so's granddaughter, and so on. There's a primary school and several churches. There are no supermarkets or pharmacies or gas stations. Just little shops where you are served over a counter and instead of your choice of cooking oil brand, you get an unmarked plastic bottle or a little plastic bag, depending on how much you buy.

Everything else—high schools, hospitals, market, banks—is a thirty-minute drive away. My mother has one of the few cars in the community. Others take taxis that squeeze in as many people as are willing to be squeezed in, and drive too fast.

Montana Rogers
Forever No More

AN EXCERPT

The water rolled across the sand, scattering the scavenging seagulls
and erasing their tiny footprints. Families lounged all down the beach
in bright swimsuits, talking and laughing around coolers and the occasional portable radio. Boys played catch or tag in the shallows of the
water, while girls swam about pretending to be mermaids and dolphins.
The groups of families grew further apart as Mayflower Cove Beach
stretched into the private sector along the wooded point. Halfway between the dunes and the water, Alice sat with her mother and her younger
brother and sister, soaking in the sun, enjoying the soft, salty breeze.

At fourteen, Alice was the eldest child of the McDowell family. She
squinted at the water, which glinted in the early afternoon sun. Her eyes
began to hurt and she looked away toward the end of the beach. It was
low tide and she could see the trail of large rocks, pier-like, an extension
of the beach, weaving into the water. The waves lapped at them and a
seagull dove down to a pitted mound of coral, swooping in on some unsuspecting fish or small sea creature that had been trapped in one of the
tiny pools left behind as the water was pulled out to sea. Alice and her
brother, Danny, who was only a few years younger, used to climb on the
rocks searching for lost treasure and, on the weekends, their father had
occasionally taken them out there to fish, but Alice was too old for that
now.

Alice sat in a contented silence next to her mother, listening to
Danny and their six-year-old sister, Sarah, squabble over whose turn it
was to use the bucket and shovel. Alice squished her toes in the sand,

dragging her finger in twisting patterns through the damp grains, wishing the day—the summer—would last forever. She was not eager for the start of school, schedules, homework, bedtimes. She wondered what time her father would arrive home from work and if he would take them stargazing or if they could have a bonfire tonight, preferably with a bag of marshmallows. Her stomach began to grumble.

"Lunch time," Alice's mother said, sliding a bookmark into the novel that Mrs. Williams from next door had lent to her last week. It was *that* book, *Peyton Place*, by Grace Metalious. She had heard Mrs. Williams describe it as "quite shocking," and Alice couldn't wait to read it. Everyone was talking about it and, at Alice's nagging, her mother had promised to let her read it next summer *maybe*, when she was a little older. Her mother stood and began to shake out her towel. "Danny? Sarah? Time to go inside."

Alice watched as her brother and sister raced across the sand. "Mom, can I stay out for a little longer?" she asked, as Danny came panting into the shade under the umbrella, Sarah trailing a little ways behind.

"Me too?" Danny pushed up his glasses. "The tide is low enough for me to go to the rocks now."

"I suppose we could bring lunch out here, have a picnic." Alice's mother stepped into her sandals. "Just stay out of the water until I get back."

Danny and Alice both nodded. Though Alice wondered why she couldn't go swimming. She was a strong swimmer. She had swum on her school's team for the past two years; she didn't need her mother to babysit her.

"Me too, Mommy?" Sarah pulled at her mother's manicured hand.

Her mother pursed her lips, thinking. She hesitated before saying, "As long as you keep out of the water. I'll only be twenty minutes. Alice, Danny, keep an eye on your sister."

"But Mom," Alice and Danny said in unison.

"Or, you all come inside right now and help me make lunch." She arched a thinly shaped eyebrow before sliding her black cat-eye sunglasses on to her nose.

"Fine. Danny can watch her first." Alice stood. "I'm going to sunbathe."

"Come on," cried Danny.

"I'll help you with your castle." Sarah planted her small hands on her hips, ready to work. "Mine is done." She pointed to a circle of variously sized heaps of sand a few yards outside of the shady circle that the beach umbrella provided.

"No!" Danny's eyes grew wide as he surveyed Sarah's castles.

"Or ..." their mother said as she started walking toward the little path that led between the sand dunes and up to the street where they lived.

Alice gave Danny a pointed glare.

"Fine," Danny clenched his fists. Sarah bounded over to where Danny had been building his castle and Danny followed. "No, don't touch that!" Danny held out a hand to stop Sarah, but it was too late.

Alice shook her head as the tallest spire of Danny's nine-towered masterpiece disintegrated under Sarah's touch.

"Sorry." Sarah's eyes began to water.

"Don't cry, Sarah. Just go over there and play." Danny looked down at his castle, waving Sarah over to the dunes.

Alice snatched up her towel and jogged in the opposite direction of the sandcastle construction site. She spread her towel on the ground and lay on her stomach, resting her chin on her elbow. She wiggled around molding the sand under her towel to fit the contours of her angular body and snuck a quick peek down to the public end of the beach where a throng of sunbathers sprawled. The older girls had sunglasses, which Alice's mother had refused to buy her, and some had hats. Others flipped through magazines, probably *Seventeen*, she thought, but she could not make out the titles from this far away. She felt like she was mirroring the sunbathers' general positions well; however, and assuming she was doing this correctly, it was quite uncomfortable and she was not sure why anyone would voluntarily lay out in the sun for hours and hours. It felt like what she imagined torture must feel like. Her back burned and grits of sand kept getting in her mouth. Her long, blond hair, though it had dried quickly in the sun, felt sticky like it always did when ocean water dried in it, and every time she fidgeted or shifted her body to get comfortable, it caught in her armpit or at the nape of her neck and pulled at her scalp. It was frustrating.

She was about to sit up, go to the house, see if her mother would let her make lemonade to go with lunch, when a shadow fell across her. She turned her head and looked up. It was Danny. He held up his suit, which threatened to slip off his scrawny hips at any moment, with one hand and in the other hand he held his magnifying glass. "You're in my sun." She flicked his big toe.

"It's your turn to watch Sarah." He ignored her, jerking his magnifying glass over his shoulder.

Alice peered around his ankles. In the soft sand by the foot of the grassy dunes Sarah stood on her tiptoes, hands held above her head for balance, pirouetting and curtseying in her polka-dot swimsuit. Her brown curls bounced as she spun and her round cheeks were pink with exertion. She twirled faster, the blades of grass beside her swaying in her wake. Alice frowned. Being a ballerina was such a childish dream.

"I'm busy." Alice flipped onto her back.

"It's your turn," Danny repeated and walked away, brushing stray sand out of his hair.

"Danny!" Alice shouted after him. He started running toward the rocks. *Great.* Alice sat up on her elbows and glanced back at Sarah. She had her doll now and was doing something that looked like a waltz. She was fine, not even near the water. Alice lay back down and turned her face toward the sunbathers again. From this angle she could see all their colourful beach umbrellas, silhouetted against the sky, like strange caricatures trying to mimic the stars.

A seagull jumped into the air, floating over the umbrellas and she followed it as it drifted above her head. She tilted her head back to watch as it soared over the dunes toward the houses and disappeared. As she shifted her gaze back she noticed that Sarah was no longer playing by the dunes.

Alice sat up and looked around. There was her doll propped up against the umbrella, but she didn't see Sarah anywhere.

Alice stood. *Maybe she went back to the house?* She reasoned and walked to the foot of the path; it was empty.

Where did she go?

Alice turned toward the water.

Lindsay Foran

Heather Ryan is Reborn

An excerpt from a humorous literary novel

According to the Rebirth Nation website, we all need to consciously experience "the constriction of birth and the euphoric release of pushing your head into the world."

Have I been in a bit of a rut? If a rut means "nothing is going right, and some days I just want to scream for help from the window of my basement bachelor-size apartment," then yes—I guess you'd say I'm in a rut. But Trinity's probably right; the state of my underwear reflects the state of my inner being. Maybe the rebirth will give me a renewed sense of energy and purpose—maybe I'll have flowing hair like Trinity? I mean, obviously I don't expect my hair to change, but that would be pretty awesome. My hair has always been short, just a few inches long, and I just let it air-dry into a frizzie puff ball, as Mother called it. If I had golden, pony-like hair like Trinity, then I'd let it grow so long that I could lie on the grass and use my hair as a blanket. Like some sort of Disney princess, animals burrowing inside my mane. I'd just be walking down the street and birds would fly out from under my waves. I'd definitely have a father (because only mothers die in fairy tales), and I'd find some strapping young prince to fall in love with me—have hot prince sex. I've said it once, and I'll say it again: life as a Disney Princess would be everything.

I pull off my torn purple Hanes Her Way underwear, and now Trinity stares at my unkempt pubic hair area, her brow scrunched and her lips curled. Maybe it's just that she's never seen another woman's vagina. I can appreciate that. Maybe I wasn't meant to take off my underwear?

She's still staring. My heart races. It's too late now to put them back on. They're already crumpled on the floor of the tent with my jeans.

"The next time you have a weekend off, Heather, it might be fun for you to treat yourself to the spa. A good wax goes a long way, you know."

I nod. A spa weekend! "Yes, we should!" I say. "We could make it a girls' weekend, right? Unless Jesse wants to come too. I'm totally cool with that." I knew this trip was a good idea. A way to make friends. Isn't that the point of life? Friends: putting the life in life-preserver. I have to remember to tell Jesse that—he seems like he'd appreciate little mantras. The tattoo on his forearm reads: "Take these broken wings and learn to fly." Maybe a tattoo would be a good idea. Although Mother hated tattoos—trash.

"I really wasn't expecting to get totally naked," I say, my clothes in a pile on the tent floor, my shoulders and neck awkwardly hunched over. There's a robe next to Trinity, but she doesn't pass it to me, and to get it would require me to bend over, and I know from past experiences that bending is my least flattering position.

"I was never supposed to be here," Trinity says, staring right at my tummy flab. Suck it in, Heather. I take a deep inhale, and look down. The flab is still there. From this angle, it looks bigger, with a trail of curly hairs trying to escape the deep cavern of my belly button.

"Hairs, right?" I laugh, but Trinity isn't looking at my belly button. She's looking right through me.

"I always thought I'd die at 27. You know—like Kurt Cobain," Trinity said.

"Is he that actor from Stand by Me? I love that movie."

"No. Nirvana."

"Oh, right. Like the Buddha."

"No, like the band. Do you know Amy Winehouse?"

"I'm not really into music."

"Janis Joplin? Jim Morrison? Jimmy Hendrix?"

"Sorry." Never apologize for being yourself, Mother would say. But

Trinity seems suddenly desperate, and these names sounded familiar, as though I'd bumped into them along the way. But I can't see their faces, or hear their songs.

"Anyways, all those singers died at 27. It's a thing. You should know that, Heather. My dad was a huge Nirvana fan. That's what I grew up listening to. It defined me."

"Oh, I hear ya. My mother always listened to Cher. We watched Mermaids so many times that I swear I could recite it for you right here and now."

Trinity shakes her head no, but doesn't speak for a few moments.

"Should I perform a scene?" Sometimes when people don't respond, it's because they're waiting for you to step up and wow them. This feels like one of those moments. I take a breath and belt out my dramatic monologue: "What the hell were you thinking about, huh? Your sister, who you were supposed to be watching, she could have died!" Nailed it! I'd even go so far as to say I outshone Cher. Mother was right; it's important to have a prepared parlour trick of some kind.

But Trinity isn't paying attention.

"And then I turned 27," she says. "I waited. Nothing. I'd step off a curb, convinced a bus would take me out." Trinity holds back tears as she speaks, her hands tucked under her bum, her knees pulled up to her chest. "I'd buy my stuff from the shadiest dealers, thinking, this time I won't wake up." The bright sunshine girl from three minutes ago is suddenly gone, and I'm left with this broken shell of a child. She probably needs a hug, but again, that would require some bending. "Then I turned 28, and I realized it was all a joke. I wasn't important enough to die with these legends. I was a nobody."

"I don't think that's true," I say quietly, very aware of my nakedness and forgetting the lines to the rest of my scene.

"And the worst part? How do you live your life when you never thought you'd have one? I spent most of my life thinking this was the end, and then nothing. I wake up the next day and there's life. More life.

Day after day. The only thing that made it better, that filled the void, was drugs. But god-dammit, drugs are expensive. In more ways than someone like you could ever know."

I watch Trinity speak, and I wonder for a moment why I was paying her to help me through the rebirth session. She sounded more lost than I was. But there had to be a reason. Something or someone led me to her. Maybe I was meant to save Trinity. Maybe this is the moment when my empath gift will finally work. The plan is bigger than me, so I can't question it—I just have to go with it.

"I think I'm here to save you," I say, suddenly sure of my path. "Jesse found me, showed me the light. You know? The rebirth, it's magical."

She lifts a small hand to her face and wipes away stray tears. "I'm so jealous of you, Heather."

"Jealous?" No one had ever said those words to me.

"Yes—you're in for a treat." Trinity stands, her legs shaking slightly. I reach out to touch her. If ever I'm going to feel my gift, this would be the time, but she steps aside, and folds into herself.

"Do you think the rebirth will help me find the answer to a very pressing question?" I ask. "About my father? Did I tell you he just died? But I didn't even know I—"

"You should put on this robe." She throws the white robe in my direction before quickly crawling out of the tent. The robe is matted and worn, not fuzzy and warm like the ones I imagine they give you at hotels.

The only time Mother and I ever stayed at a hotel was when our house was being fumigated. I was eight. Lice. An infestation, they'd said. The hotel we stayed in seemed like it would be more likely to have a bug infestation. "All we can afford at this point," Mother said to the teenage clerk, as though he really cared.

"Totally," he'd replied, his eyes slowly following the curve of Mother's neck down to her low-cut blouse, the top two buttons open, the tip of her lacy black bra brushing up against the silk of her blouse.

"Take a picture. It lasts longer," I'd said, laughing loudly until Mother jabbed me in the ribs with her elbow.

"Manners, Heather." She'd pulled me out of the motel office, down the parking lot to our room. "Everything I do—it's for you. And you can't even allow me the tiniest amount of fun."

My teacher had assured me that lice had nothing to do with uncleanliness, but Mother wasn't convinced. "Purely disgusting," she kept reiterating for weeks after the fumigation. Every day she would check my scalp, brushing until it bled, small scabs forming. At the time, I thought it was my penance. Like those monks who whip their own backs. So I never cried, never screamed, never said a word. I sat on the bathroom floor, my teeth clenched, digging my fingernails deeply into the palm of my hand, creating small half-moon slivers that, if I look closely, are still faintly outlined on my palms. The bronze comb sat enshrined on the bathroom countertop for years, a reminder of all the ways in which I'd failed her.

Alli Vail

Brooklyn Thomas Isn't Here

*An excerpt from a contemporary novel about a young woman whose
heartbeat has disappeared; things are getting weirder for Brooklyn*

I beat Kailey to yoga. I take up a spot in the back corner next to the white
wall, so I'll only have neighbours in front and to my left. The sign taped
on the mirror at the front of the room says: your mat must be twelve
inches or closer to your neighbour. The room already smells hot, wet,
and dirty—like reheated gym clothes. Hot yoga in July. Brilliant idea. So
far, the class is only partially full, and pretty much everyone is on the far
side. The area next to me is mercifully empty.

I watch the women come in while I pretend to stretch my quads.
They're vibrant in pink, blue, and orange Lycra. Excuse me—Luon. Lycra is so not a thing anymore. They pose seriously on their mats, staring
intently at themselves in the mirror while they tuck their feet into their
thighs, seated or standing. The few that come in chattering and giggling
are silenced with a sharp look from the regulars. Here is a place of sanc-
tity, like libraries used to be. Now, you can have a phone and snacks in
the library, but not in a yoga class. Talking is forbidden unless you are
the instructor speaking in careful, sing-song, non-offensive tones. At
least that's what the sign said on the door. No talking. I don't know how
Kailey manages.

The room is starting to fill, but there's still plenty of space near me and
I mentally chant, stay away, stay away. Just when I think I'm in the clear,
a short man walks into the room. He makes a beeline for my direction,

and flops his mat a scant ten inches away from mine. He doesn't look at me. He's businesslike, spreading his mat briskly. He's not wearing a shirt and I can see the hairy pad of black hair on his chest and his arms. Everyone can see everything else in the outline of his tight short-shorts. It's in the mirror, and in my peripheral vision.

"Of course," I mutter. He *would* stand right next to me.

The thick gold chain around his neck catches light from the ceiling lamps and bounces it into the mirror. The beam momentarily blinds me, but nothing will obliterate his image from my brain. It's too late to move now. The girl in front of me is so close I could reach out with a toe and push her over in the guise of preparing for half-moon pose. Kaylie swoops in just as the instructor closes the door. She mouths me an apology from the front of the room and whips her mat out of its curl; it hits the floor with a flat and heavy thud.

For the first fifteen minutes, we drip onto our mats and stand in our own sweat. My toes wrinkle in their puddles. Then the real horror begins. The man beside me flings his arms out to his sides, mimicking the instructor at the front of the room. His fingertips do as requested—they stretch over my mat, filled with fizzing energy. I watch in horror as the sweat rolls down his arms—undeterred by the thick sprouts of hair—crests over the edges of his bones, and lands on my mat right next to my feet. The girl in front of me, in deference to her neighbour, has kept her arms vertically pointed and inside the boundaries of her neon purple jute mat.

The instructor is oblivious to the drama this man has caused. Surely, I cannot be the only one disgusted about the *drip … drip … drip* of another person's sweat onto my mat, where my face will soon be plastered to in child's pose? I glance around the room. Faces are studious and stoic, bearing no acknowledgement of the germ fest. The hairball next to me doesn't notice the anxiety he's causing. He's breathing in, deeply. Wetly. His gold chain, from which a cross dangles, jiggles with the force of his exhale. The instructor walks right past us in his careful meandering way, avoiding eye contact with the pupils desperate to be singled out with correction or praise. He avoids my frantic glances. I watch another droplet gather momentum and plummet toward the earth from the hairy man's arm. I imagine I can hear it screaming, this discarded drip of water, ammonia, urea, salt, and sugar. I want to scream with it. I imagine drowning in this man's sweat—unnoticed by the instructor, who is smoothing down the shoulders of a woman wearing fluorescent yellow, the lovely skin of her back exposed.

In desperation, I step off my mat, scrunch it away from the stranger, and stand on the floor as far away from the man as I can, so close to the wall that the outside of my bicep grazes it. I look in the mirror. My eyes are round with irritation, and my cheeks pink with exertion and heat. The air thickens further with moisture and oxygen gets stuck in my throat as I try to inhale. As I struggle to breath, my reflection quivers. My horrified face looks back at me in the mirror as my skin vanishes— followed by the layers of thick red muscle. Bones are left, stacked neatly and precariously in a human shape. Then, there is an empty spot where I once stood, legs spread, arms up. I blink and rub my eyes, still able to feel the heat of my skin and the soft texture of my eyelashes.

But the spot next to the hairy man is empty. No crumpled mat, no angry reflection. I wave my hands around and there is no corresponding hand wave in the glass. I bounce up and down as I flick the man's arm, which is still extended into my space, with my finger. He doesn't even flinch. His eyes are closed and he wobbles on his warrior legs. His skin is solid and damp under my fingertips. This time, I howl into the silence of the crowded, unresponsive room. I stare at nothing in the mirror until my body reappears in reverse: bones, muscles, skin, my horrified expression, all slowly sharpening back into place.

Kailey is waiting for me just outside the door of the reeking room once the class ends. The hallway is twenty degrees cooler and one hundred times fresher. I inhale, hard, as sweat chills on my skin and leaves behind goosebumps.

"Sorry I was late. Couldn't find my mat," Kailey says, looking genuinely contrite. "Borrowed one from the front desk."

"I thought your mat was glued to your body."

"Hilarious. Saw the sweaty guy. Should have warned you about him. He's a regular. Loves the back corner. I'm not sure if he purposefully drips on people or not, but he just looks at you blankly if you say anything." She herds me toward the change room.

"But you saw me?"

"Of course." She looks at me strangely. "You looked like you wanted to beat that man to death with your mat when he started dripping on you. I would have been okay with that, but the studio frowns on violence and controversy of any kind."

Samantha Gaston

Bitches Love Brunch

The monthly catch-up brunch with Maggie, Amanda, Chelsea, and Sabrina is at one of those chain restaurants with menus that include innocuous pan-Asian rice bowls and cocktail slushees. A gas fireplace in the newly renovated "lounge" section. After the girls' last few outings waiting in absurdly long lines at crisp-pork-belly-with-salsa-verde places that didn't take reservations, they decided to surrender to a restaurant whose main draw was convenience, which they self-consciously comment on while flipping through the menu. Sabrina has ordered a pitcher of mimosas for the table and graciously pours the round for everyone before Maggie thinks to object.

Maggie rubs the stem of her champagne glass between her thumb and forefinger. She knows she needs to tell Andrew first. But if the four of them were still in their teens or early twenties, when it was less obvious what she should do and when the girls still moved as a pack borne out of inexperience and vulnerability, she would have told them right away. Maybe even revelled in the drama. She considers if she tells them now—at the very least—the news would be a welcome change from dutifully whining about her HR job at an engineering firm where the central heating is always broken. But at this stage in their lives, her friends will assume congratulations are in order, and the decision will be made for her. ("Thirty five?" Maggie's doctor asked at her last visit. "If you're thinking about having kids, I'd get on that if I were you." He sucked some air through his teeth for emphasis. She had made the appointment for a sinus infection.)

The others are married with kids, and she doesn't know how to articulate this feeling of hesitance without offending them or being seen as immature, foolish. It's the same feeling she gets when she laughs off Andrew's suggestions that they finally get married: that in every decision made, the sense of possibility that once fuelled her younger years feels increasingly vague and out of reach. A feeling that an ending is nearing rather than a beginning.

The night before, she had watched the shadows from their TV falling on Andrew's face. She wanted to tell him how she sat on the toilet earlier that day staring at the two pink stripes on the plastic stick. They didn't seem real, those stripes.

They made her recall one particular Saturday morning when she was five. She could still hear the cartoons in the background, taste the milk sweetened with cereal. She had been kneeling at the coffee table in the family room, lost in her colouring book. Without a discernible shift, she was hovering close to the ceiling, watching herself. From above, she was a chunk of pallid flesh, grotesque and vulnerable. A silver strand connected her to the child colouring below. The moment lasted for a few seconds before she returned to kneeling on the beige carpeting. She remembers being newly uncomfortable with her skin, the hairs on her arms. The effort of breathing.

Maggie said nothing to Andrew about the stripes, her disconnection to this new reality, and announced halfway through a cop drama she wasn't actually watching that she should probably get some sleep. She had yoga Sunday morning and was meeting the girls for brunch afterwards. Andrew snickered to himself.

"What?" Maggie turned to him.

"'Brunch.' Girls love that shit. You get to pretend you're on *Sex and the City* for a couple hours," Andrew teased.

Maggie smacked his shoulder, then gave it a kiss. "Bitches love brunch, what can I say?"

She wishes they still playacted their own *Sex and the City* scenes over pancakes. Chelsea trying to figure out if that guy who was absolutely not interested in her was interested in her. Sabrina describing a one-night stand's gargantuan, curiously-shaped penis looking like "an unbaked loaf of bread." Now it seems they mostly talk about Instant Pot recipes and the cost of daycare.

"Maggie, are you not having your drink?" Amanda asks. Maggie stiffens. This had been the giveaway with the others' pregnancies. A drink refusal eventually followed by the big news.

Sabrina mercifully interrupts."Oh, Chels, before I forget! I brought the sleep sack."

"What's a sleep sack?" Maggie asks before she can stop herself.

Sabrina pulls a small, cocoon-like blanket out of her giant leather purse. "It's so babies don't pull their blankets over their faces and suffocate. It keeps them wrapped up but they can still move their arms around. And it reminds them of being in the womb. McKenzie doesn't need it anymore."

"I should cut arm holes out of a sleeping bag and make an adult-sized one," Maggie jokes. She envisions Andrew coming home to her curled up on their couch in her homemade sleep sack. Like a giant caterpillar.

Chelsea ignores her. "Thanks. Jaxon totally needs another, he defiled most of his. We're gonna try cutting dairy from his diet."

"That was Acacia's problem, we just started adding it back this month...."

Over the years, Maggie finds herself checking out of these conversations more and more, letting her mind wander. She suspects it's not out of boredom, necessarily, but a denial of sorts. Today she imagines a deluge of water destroying the restaurant's back wall and flooding the dining room. The diners around her go on eating their Baja breakfast hashes, laughing politely with each other as water spills into their laps. She lets the cold seep through her blouse and closes her eyes at the feeling of buoyancy. The group continues chattering underwater, their hair floating around their heads and mingling with pieces of bacon. She's reminded of a game she used to play as a kid in her grandparents' swimming pool. Two people go underwater and try to guess what word the other is saying.

"Unfortunately his daycare is a nut-free environment so I'm trying to find really good seed butter."

"And she doesn't even bring a pair of indoor shoes for her kid, I'm ready to say something."

"McKenzie came out sunny side up."

"Explain to Maggie what that means."

"Oh. They're supposed to come out facing your butthole."

"We're thinking instead of a birthday party registry we'll ask people to donate to Oxfam."

"Like, if she thinks Ritalin would help I'm not judging her? I'm just concerned."

Maggie thinks about the last time she was in her grandparents' pool. She was fifteen. It was early September and the air was beginning to get that autumn bite to it. Her grandpa had died in August. They'd be covering up the pool that week and the house would be put on the market soon after. Throughout their childhood, Maggie and her sister were at their grandparents' house almost every day in the summer to swim in that pool. Their house overlooked the ocean and had a huge backyard bordered by her grandma's flowerbeds. The pool sat in the middle of it all, robin's egg blue and gleaming. She stayed in the water that last day until she was shivering, floating on her back from end to end and watching an overcast sky. She dove to the bottom and felt the pale blue cement with outstretched palms, crossed her legs and looked up from the pool's floor. Her grandma appeared beside the pool in her floral-print bathing suit and white bucket hat. A cute, elderly splotch. The splotch waved at her and did what appeared to be a few little vaudeville-type dance steps. Maggie's little sister joined her grandma and they both waved at her to swim up.

"Maggie, if you're not drinking that, I'm ready for a second," Sabrina gives her friend a mischievous grin, the one Maggie's watched her hone over the years at parties and bars, her thin lips spread against her wide set of teeth.

Maggie has already looked it up: "Drinking a small amount of alcohol in the first half of the first trimester carries minimal risk." Still, she knows she wouldn't drink if she was certain she wanted to keep it. She could pretend they're still the same singular unit, tell the girls everything, plead with them. Just tell me what I should want. Or, for once, she could make a decision, regardless of what beginning or ending it may offer.

"No way, lady, this one's all mine," Maggie assures her. The girls give little cheers as she reaches for her drink and takes a long swig of the overly sweet orange juice and champagne. Setting the empty glass back on the table, she remembers how she watched her grandma and sister from the bottom of the pool. How they continued to call at her to surface, and how she held her breath for as long as she could.

Jenn Ashton
The Loving Gift

*An excerpt from "Letters to June: A Diary," a novel about
a teen mother who writes diary entries to her role model,
June Carter Cash, while she traverses 1980s Canada
discovering the joys and pitfalls of puberty with a baby in tow*

October 1980, Tofino, B.C.

Dear June,

I can't believe twelve months have passed since Melody was born, my own, and I don't believe what they say about wanting more and forgetting the pain. I haven't forgotten at all, plus I have so many stretch marks on me it's so ugly. I can't imagine doing that all over again. I do want a big family though, maybe I'll just adopt some orphans.

Ode to a Day. I bid you farewell, my precious sun, the night will return when you are done. May you find happiness where you will go, and someone like me, to return your glow.

☺

December 1980, Victoria, B.C.

Dear June,

For my seventeenth birthday, everybody gave something to the baby. I guess that's okay because we don't have much, but I was a bit sad that maybe everybody is forgetting about me.

We're in Victoria right now spending Christmas with my dad. I told him I wanted to be a writer. I think everybody knew that for a long time anyway, but my spelling is so bad. He says that if I want to be a writer I have to read a lot more books and that can help with my spelling. I already read so much, I don't know when I can have more time, but when we get back home I am going to join a writer's club and see if that can help me with my stories.

Happy New Year to you and Johnny Cash. I wish you were my Aunty so I could say, Dear Aunty June.

⌒

January 1981, Tofino, B.C.

Dear June,

I have made some New Year Resolutions! This year, I am going to be a perfect parent, do the dishes after supper instead of the next morning, and start to be a good writer. So far I did what I said I was going to do and my husband, George, said he will watch the baby so I can go to my writing group. I can walk there, I won't go through the ravine at night, but I can go around and it's not that much farther. I wrote a small play that I am going to read if I am allowed to and I'll see what they say.

And last week I had to have a root canal! My tooth really hurt and they gave me pills for pain that didn't work so I have been at the dentist a lot. But it's finished now and I have a gold tooth! My dad told me to keep my mouth closed when I travel in case somebody sees it and pulls it out of my mouth while I'm asleep. I think he was joking.

⌒

January 1981, Tofino, B.C.

Dear June,

The writer's club loved my play! The only trouble is, two things. One: they wanted to read it out loud, so they did, but they didn't know how to pronounce the words correctly. I used ye olde English and I didn't know if I should stop and tell them or not, but I didn't and I just sat on my hands. Two: I am the youngest there by, like, 50 years and I think they didn't know how that would work because they were all drinking wine.

In the end, they said I could go back, but it wasn't very interesting and after they read my play nobody really talked to me. I don't think I'll go back. Besides, when I leave George with the baby he just smokes pot and reads Louis L'Amour. Once he blew smoke into her face like he used to do to the cat. He didn't think I saw him, but I did. I didn't say anything though, I think he felt bad enough already when he realized what he had done. I don't think he should even be smoking in the house at all.

George says this year will be a good one and we're going to go help his uncle build a new barn in the summer when the mill shuts down. They'll even pay us. I am going to visit my friend Mona at her place in Montreal as well, I can't wait! She was surprised when I said I was coming out with the baby, but she always said I could go there any time, so it will be a lot of fun.

Do you want to hear something funny? We had a sunny day here and George was sitting outside playing his guitar when I woke up. When I went outside I saw that the jeep was gone and I said, "Where's the jeep?" and he didn't even know it was gone! I guess that's what you get when you smoke pot for breakfast. He called the police and they found it just down at the bottom of the hill, they think kids just rolled it down there.

Also, the SPCA brought Ti back again. He's not supposed to be outside without his dog tags, but we never got him a collar, so they bring him back and tell us again and again. But today, the SPCA guy was smiling and he said he saw Ti clear a four-foot fence and it was amazing! He didn't say anything about the license this time. We let Ti run beside the jeep when we go up the logging roads, so he's in really good shape.

❧

February 1981, Tofino, B.C.

Dear June,

I wanted to make friends with the people downstairs because I am alone a lot and so I moved the big dresser away from in front of the stairway door and opened it. A man was there and his wife offered me some sort of food and I took it, but afterwards, when I told George he got mad and called them pakis and moved the dresser back. He wouldn't try any of the food, but it was really good and I liked it a lot.

We got a high chair for Mel and we're going to try to have a real "suppertime" and eat at the table properly and everything. I think we have to start being more like a family now that she is older. I got the *Fanny Farmer Cookbook* and it has some recipes in it that I'm going to learn and I'm going to get my mom and Gramma to write some recipe cards for me so I can have my own recipe box too. The baby eats regular people food now, not just baby mush. She has loads of teeth.

⌒

March 1981, Tofino, B.C.

Dear June,

I had the TV on this morning and I was watching the news and I saw your President Reagan get shot. My heart stopped, it just stopped. First, I looked to make sure the baby hadn't seen, but she was playing with the dog. Then I just sat and cried. I've never seen anybody get shot before. Who could be so mean? I think they got the man, Hinkley. They even called it an assassination attempt, just like what happened with Kennedy, but this time it didn't work out. Thank goodness he is okay, I like Ronald Reagan. I still have a choking feeling in my throat when I think about it.

⌒

April 1981, Tofino, B.C.

Dear June,

The drive-in opened and was showing saw *Alien* and *The Rose*. We didn't stay for *The Rose* because I was so scared watching *Alien* that I had my hands in front of my eyes. The baby was in the back seat asleep and George called me a baby because I wouldn't look at the scary part. I don't like scary movies ever since we saw *Amityville Horror* when I was pregnant, it gave me nightmares.

Do you guys go to the drive-in? Probably not, because everyone would want your autograph, but I bet Johnny Cash wouldn't call you a sucky baby.

I don't really like being married. I have to practice my writing because I want to have all my poems published. Then, I can be somebody and get out of here. All I need is a little bit of money.

My dad gave me an old electric typewriter. It's green and huge and pretty noisy, but I'm going to try it out. Maybe it will help me. I have a book that says you can only send typewritten pages to publishers and my typing isn't very good yet. I'm trying to read more like my dad said, but I don't see how that can help me with my spelling. I have a new book called, *Mr. God This is Anna* by a writer called Fynn. I got it because I like his name and the picture on the cover. It's yellow with a black drawing of the girl, Anna. I wonder what my book cover will be like? I want to call my book of poetry "A Passing Fancy."

⌒

May 1981, Vancouver, B.C.

Dear June,

I went to visit my grandma because I had to get away from George for a bit. While I was there, my other grandma died, my mom's mom. My mom called me to tell me and asked if I wanted to go over because the body was still there. When I picked up the phone, I was washing my hair in the sink. I was dripping with shampoo and so I said, "Well, I'm washing my hair right now." She got mad. But I didn't mean I didn't want to go, I was just telling her what I was doing. I didn't mean for her to get mad. I should think before I speak. That was dumb.

Varsha Tiwary

Labours of Women

SHORT FICTION

"But my due date is next week," the woman wails. She has read too many what-to-expect books. She believes in nobility, spirituality of birth. Her labour will be beautiful despite its trial. She will be a brave, strong, wild mother.

"It's not about you," the doctor cuts her off. "It's about the baby. Your water is drying up."

"Drying? How is it drying? I feel fine—the heartbeat is strong, the ultrasound is fine and the book says invasive procedures...." she pleads.

But the doctor rolls her eyes and the husband squeezes her arm, restraining her words.

"We will induce," the doctor says. The husband is already filling out forms. The pressure is on her to do the best for the baby. Questioning the doctor is a hallmark of a bad mother, the very air seems to tell her. That instant hurls her into thing-hood. She is just a womb, a means to perpetuate the species. Pain? Dignity? Self-determination? Narrative agency? These might be exotic notions applicable to creatures from another world. Around her, she sees swollen women, all with The Look. Meek, obedient, worn out, acting their parts. Her pet cats and dogs, the meekest of them, had turned fierce and powerful when about to litter. Evolution, it seems, is not always for the better.

The stark fluorescent preparation room—the paper sheeted steel bed, the hirsute nurse.

"Remove pants and lie down," the nurse says without looking at her.

Shivering, half naked on the steel bed, she stares at a splotch low on the tiled wall. Dirt? Vomit? A 200-watt bulb hangs right above her vagina.

The nurse unsheathes the razor with her gloved hand, clacks her scissors loudly over the dark purse of her pubes. The sweat and coconut oil odour of her contempt fills the tiny space. A blanched look of terror, it seems, is a prerequisite for the nurse to proceed. She begins shearing with a snort. Snip, snip, scrape, scrape. The woman fidgets, and the half lit, bent head of scanty white hair, a river of angry orange vermillion running through, shoots up.

"Do you want to be cut down there?" the nurse asks in a hard, grainy voice.

Done, she swabs alcohol over the exposed prickly mound until the woman winces. The nurse tells her to turn over so she can insert a saltwater tube, to clean her bowels. "To get you in shipshape for the doctor," the nurse, having established her indignity, turns friendlier now. She calls the woman a *kabootri*—a clipped pigeon—and cackles, watching her rush to the washroom.

"Clean up. Don't leave your fat-pigeon squirts behind," the nurse calls out in a merry, sing-song voice.

Why had she expected something nicer? Maybe because of the pictures of cuddly babies and smiling mothers in the doctor's front office. The ward, when she enters, is just two long rows of beds groaning with women, interspersed with bristling machinery—EKG machines, upside down bottles of Pitocin drips on wheeled stands, fetal heartbeat monitors. Speculums and forceps glint at them from a rack on the far wall. The room heaves with contractions and dilations. A churn of anxiety and horror; a terrible hurting—as if in a battlefield—floats in the air.

Her contractions are to be summoned. A nurse fingers her veins. Drip on the right wrist and Pitocin on the left. Spread-eagled, she registers that the women around her are all naked from the waist down. Like her. Their green gowns are frequently turned up and attendants seem to forget to pull them down or draw up a sheet. What, after all, is the point of modesty here? Everyone is on drips and drugs, existing in another dimension. Shame, too, needs context to exist.

The bare walls of the ward are painted a strange rust colour until shoulder level. In the whiteness above hangs a framed picture of Jesus, garlanded in alternate pink and yellow plastic flowers. Next to it is a calendar with a picture of the turbaned minister, Manmohan Singh. Two grand men presiding over all the genitals below, she thinks in the Pitocin-induced delirium, inhaling the ripe smell of blood and bodily excretions smothered in phenyl and Lysol.

From the bed, she can see the shaved kiwi fruits of women across the hall, nestling between thighs—mountainous, plump, painfully skinny. Legs—hairy, smooth; dark like molasses, white like churned butter. Knees raised and held apart, as interns come and plunge a cold, hard speculum inside. The screams of women—the scolding chides that follow—are normal everyday business here. Anyone can locate the ward full of heaving, trembling, groaning, women—oozing bodily fluids— just by following those screams. She is no cowering ninny, but this does not feel like bravery. She alternates between nausea and helpless anger. A kvetchy woman is left on stirrups, her swollen red lips open, a lesson for all. Or, it could just be that the intern got busy fixing a lunchtime appointment at Curry Palace before the examination could be completed.

In the dazed, deep breathing spells between the induced, extra-intense contractions, she sees a woman attendant come in to swab the floor. Clothed and walking, she seems all powerful—full of magical agency. The attendant scrunches her nose, curses and mutters. Poop on the bed, a puddle of broken water. Blood and piss-soaked bedsheets all around. The overflowing bedpans. It is good no one can hear her grumbles. Or if they do, shame flickers in their eyes for a moment, before pain takes over.

At dusk, the trumpet tones of scolding nurses hang in the drugged air. "Stop moaning and groaning," they direct. "Shut up and bear it." "Did you think childbirth was a game?"

They play cards, drink tea, eat fried samosas. They discuss starlets—

is Priyanka prettier than Deepika?—looking like Cruella's cousins themselves.

Every time her turn for an internal exam comes—"Bed six up now"—she resolves not to cry out. She concentrates hard on the red nail paint on the supervising doctor's hand on her knee, her *nakshatra* locket, as the doctor tells the invisible intern scrabbling inside her to go all the way down, feel the mouth of the cervix.

Her womb is a training school for adolescent student doctors. She prays. She tries not to listen to them—by trying to guess the doctor's hair dye colour, counting the slats of the window blinds, feeling the salty taste of blood on her chapped and bitten lips.

The world of husbands, parents, in-laws, and siblings sitting outside the ward—wrapped in caffeinated concern, believing something momentous, noble, and heroic is happening inside. The Birth—a proof of womanhood. Fulfillment; completion. But there is nothing noble or godly about their indignities. If women didn't believe all this fluff about fulfillment and fertility, they would have bolted from this pen—the labour ward.

She remembers the women in the doctor's front office—proud, coy, smug about impending motherhood. She had been one of them.

Oh, if they could have seen this, she thinks, as another rising wail of multiple contractions swells from bed to bed in the labour ward.

Every time a woman is wheeled out they all worry. When would their turn come? They beg, they cry like babies. They whine for their mothers—they who are about to be mothers themselves. They are ready to do anything to escape this misery. They plead with anyone, everyone—the woman who swabs the floors, the barely adolescent intern with a sprout of a moustache, the fat nurses, who have all the power to keep them heaving and pushing on drips or to let them pass out with some nitrous oxide or an epidural.

They all just pray to be permitted to pass out. To be delivered.

Tracey Hirsch

Dinner Party Conversation

AN EXCERPT

Sidney watched his wife's casket sink into the ground. When Helen hit the bottom of the grave, the funeral attendants removed the straps and frame and handed out shovels. Sidney's was the first load of dirt to start burying her. He flinched at the sharp sound of a thousand little rocks pelting down on the pine box as Helen lay inside. It was the sound that signaled she no longer mattered. His breathing got shallower as the dirt and rocks piled up. How can she breathe with so much debris on top of her? Then he remembered, she can't. The funeral, the burial, and the gathering at his mother's home, Shiva, were so guided by tradition that Sidney didn't need to do much thinking or deciding. He stood where told. Nodded when appropriate. Accepted hugs and handshakes. Familiar prayers floated in and out. Words of kindness and sadness congealed into a low moaning white noise that followed him around for weeks.

Sidney and Helen had been high school sweethearts and married the week after graduating university. However, baby never made three. Years of trying and then fertility treatments ended in disappointment. They decided instead to adopt. They considered their options, researched different agencies, sat for multiple interviews, and filled out endless forms. After much time and effort they received news. Helen had stage four ovarian cancer. She was dead within six months, just shy of her 31st birthday.

Sidney's life shifted instantly from babies to Helen over those last few months, and all his time, energy, and emotions were devoted solely to her care. When the end came, Sidney simply disappeared inside himself. His grief was all-consuming, singular, and devastating. He rebuffed all attempts at help or even company. He was alone, in all possible ways.

Two years later, Sidney appeared at a small dinner party hosted by his friend, Nadim. While Nadim was a great host and an excellent cook, even Sidney was surprised at himself that he decided to attend. For months after Helen's death, Sidney was so confounded by his grief he barely left his house. Attending social functions was as likely as becoming a trapeze artist. But after that first year, and the ritual unveiling of Helen's head stone, Sidney's world opened up a sliver. He could carry on conversations—limited, but they qualified. He went back to work after an extended leave of absence. He even laughed occasionally. Invitations for lunch or dinner, after work drinks, even parties started coming his way. He usually declined, occasionally said yes, but almost never showed up, offering some excuse no one believed but everyone accepted.

With Sidney's arrival, Nadim had to shift chairs and people to make room for one more around the table. When Sidney realized Nadim hadn't expected him to show up, his embarrassment painted itself bright red. But now that he was there, he had no choice but to stay. Sidney's seat at the table put him beside Leah who had been watching it all, almost laughing at the fuss.

Leah had lived down the street from Nadim ever since she left her first husband, Luke, a few years earlier. She'd come to label the marriage, *The Time of the Great Transition*. From single to married. From Calgary to Vancouver. From dependent to independent. From fledgling grown up to fully formed adult. From naive to painfully aware. She'd met Luke during the Calgary Stampede while line dancing at a cowboy bar. The attraction was instant and instantly intense. They danced and drank and, before she knew it, Luke had do-si-doed her all the way to the West Coast. He was sexy and magnetic and Leah felt alive with possibilities just being around him.

When the music stopped playing after just a few years, Leah found herself in her late twenties living in Vancouver with a guy she no longer loved in a city where she didn't know anyone beyond his circle. But Leah's love for Vancouver was real and lasting so she stayed.

She rented the main floor apartment in an old craftsman-style home in the funky Commercial Drive neighbourhood and finagled primary use of the back garden in exchange for doing the upkeep. A little weeding and mowing was a small price to pay for her personal haven in the city. She was happy with the life she'd carved out for herself in the aftermath of a marriage where only one party made most of the decisions. Having found her voice enough to leave, Leah had no intention of handing over control again.

While Sidney had worn his grief like an overcoat since Helen's death, that's not what Leah saw when this unexpected guest joined the dinner party. She put him at about six feet, maybe a bit taller. He had a thick head of dark brown hair, mostly short but longer on top, that swept across his forehead. He absentmindedly ran his fingers through it every five minutes or so. He reminded her of one of those old-time movie stars her mother used to swoon over. Classically handsome. Strong without being aggressive. There was a slight stoop in his posture. Leah imagined the stoop was a sign he didn't want to lord over people with his height and handsome face.

In truth the stoop came from grief. Sidney had reached his full height of six foot two when he was eighteen. That unmistakable swagger owned by young men started diminishing with each new attempt he and Helen made to have a baby. He had dropped to six foot one by the time Helen was in palliative care. Two years after her death he was down to an even six feet.

Leah was unlike any woman Sidney had ever met. She was wrapped in jewel tones. A slim emerald green skirt was overlaid with a long flowing blouse of blue and purple swirls that kept slipping off one shoulder. Her hair was piled on her head in a loose bun with strands of natural brown and less natural blond periodically escaping. She wore large earrings of woven wire that reminded Sidney of peacock feathers. Each arm was adorned with multiple silver bracelets that clanged and chimed when she moved. She had presence. Light seemed to radiate from her, at least that's what Sidney saw. Her eyes were intensely blue and rimmed with thick eyeliner. Sidney guessed correctly that the deepness of the blue was from coloured contact lenses, but he didn't care. The sparkle in her eyes couldn't be faked.

"Sidney Bauer, I'd like to introduce the world's greatest neighbour, Leah Prince," said Nadim while pulling out Sidney's chair.

Leah thrust her hand toward Sidney. "Well, hello!"

As Nadim began to explain who this new guest was, Leah stopped him. "Don't say another word Nadim. I'm going to spend all dinner finding out about Mr. Sidney Bauer. If you tell me who he is now you'll ruin my fun." She patted her hand lightly on the seat. "Now sit yourself down and start from the beginning."

Sidney was too shocked to do anything but follow orders. A few months ago he would have been offended that someone, even a stranger, didn't *somehow* know he was in deep mourning. Tonight he felt differently. Lighter. He liked that this woman didn't know anything about him. Didn't know he once had a wife or that she was dead or that it left him broken for the past two years. She seemed to see him as just any other guy. He'd forgotten what that felt like.

"Ms. Prince, it would be my pleasure." He tried to slide into his seat with something resembling flair and ended up knocking over his chair instead. The fact he didn't tumble with it was the only saving grace. That and the jolt he felt when Leah grabbed his arm to keep him from toppling.

After Sidney managed to get himself properly seated their conversation flowed like warm honey. They became so wrapped up in each other they barely spoke to anyone else around the table all night. As the party was breaking up, Sidney thought about asking Leah for her number but shied away from the idea. Yet when he and Nadim walked to the front door to say goodbye, Leah joined them.

Sidney shook Nadim's hand. "Thank you for a really delicious dinner. Glad I decided to show up."

Nadim gave Sidney a gentle squeeze of the shoulder and took a step back.

Sidney turned and extended his hand to Leah. He was rewarded by a warm, firm handshake and a little extra squeeze. "Thank you, Leah. It was really fun chatting."

She looked at him with curiosity and amusement. She pulled him in for a brief hug and whispered in his ear, "Something tells me I haven't seen the last of you."

Sidney gave a brief, self-conscious nod, turned and walked down the path. He felt her watching him—or certainly hoped she was. He never found out. As much as he wanted to know, he resisted the strong urge to turn around, too afraid of how embarrassed he'd be if all he saw was the closed front door.

Japhy Ryder

The German Financier's Daughter

An excerpt from "Glitterball"

The voice of the lecturer begins to fade away (this is a skill I wish I'd have learned decades ago, long decades ago), until it's just me alone with the paper. Me and just a white sheet. *Die weisses Blatt* of my memory ...

... the English Boy has just come inside me. I mean, the waves are lapping around my naked ass, and the first thing he says to me is:

"You know, you do have a choice."

What the hell is that? Back home, Dieter doesn't give me that kind of shit. Instead, he says: "Baby, I love you," then slobbers over my nipples until he goes soft and slips out of me. Then he falls asleep. In my experience, which is fairly substantial, German boys are all like that, one way or the other. But not these English ones. And this one says he wants me to leave Dieter for him. Some chance.

"I'll come to Frankfurt," he says. I have my legs wrapped tightly around his narrow waist. This would not, in any case, be a good place for him to fall asleep. I know some have claimed to walk on the surface of this particular sea, but I don't believe now is the right time for either of us to try it.

"Fuck you," I say, and as soon as I say it he slips out. I'm pretty sure this was his first time.

The palm trees lining the shore of the Kinneret wave at us against a darkening sky. The gentle current of the River Jordan pulls the remains of our love downstream toward the Dead Sea. As if it weren't salty enough already.

⌒

Later, we're fucking in my little cabin. We'll take the day off work to-morrow, you can only prune dates for so long. He talks a lot of shit, this English Boy, but he does like to fuck.

"Ma'agan, oh Ma'agan. To escape this tempest's spell, and return to the outer world's real hell," he says between soft kisses around the arches of my eyebrows. His rhythm is slow and gentle. He likes to pretend po-etry comes to him while we're making love, but I have his number on this one, it's just a piece of graffiti. I saw it scribbled on the wall in the toilet next to the tractor shed. I decide to say nothing. We do have choices, even if sometimes they appear to be of small consequence.

"Mmmmmm," I moan softly instead. I've decided to encourage him when he's doing something I like. Which, I must confess, is quite a lot of the time.

"So, did you decide?" he asks. Oh God, not this again. Yet as he looks down on me, the candle lighting up his face, I find I'm truly touched by his eager fondness.

"I'm flying out of Ben Gurion day after," I tell him. "Dieter's picking me up from FRA."

"We do have choices," he says, but I can tell his heart's not in it. His rhythm slows, then stops. After a brief pause, he rolls over by my side. It's quite likely he's going to continue talking.

But a girl has her ways. I reach down and stroke him gently, and he responds as he always does. We're back on solid ground again. At least for a while. At least for a little while.

⌒

The English Boy arrived here from Jericho just a couple weeks back. Some settler camp on the edge of the Dead Sea, not my speed at all. Pretty much solid desert down there. Not much water around. Not fresh, anyhow.

At first I thought he was just a dreamer.

"You know, I believe we are primarily spiritual beings before we are creatures of this world," was the first thing he said to me. Then later: "My mind is like a palace, there's tall guards with sharp swords on either side of the gateway."

The eagerness with which he tried (without any success, as far as I could see) to fuck the two American girls, led me to suspect there might be a way to sneak in past the guards. Right there, right then, I figured if I played my cards right, I had just about enough time to take him for a quick spin before school started again.

☙

The English Boy has found my birth control pills. Might have known he would. What did he imagine, that I was going to carry his baby? I don't think so.

He's toying with them on the bed. We've thrown the sheet off. "You got these so you can fuck Dieter without …" His voice trails off, but I know what he's thinking. That there's some kind of balance going on here. That, sure, these clinical little pills remind him in the most clinical of ways that his girlfriend has a boyfriend, but also that he gets to—He cuts off my thought. Or rather, me thinking his thought.

"Honey, I love you," he says, placing his arm around my still-sweaty waist.

"Let's…."

☙

Looking back on it, it's incredible how much talking we did in bed. In fact, I can hardly remember talking anywhere else the whole time. Except that first time in the sea. Or was it the river? Whatever. All that Heiligen Land stuff is a million miles away now.

"Why did you sign up for this if you're neither willing nor able to put me high enough on your list of priorities that you can actually—" the English Boy said.

"I have my own world," I cut in coldly, looking him square in the eye. Like I said, this boy could talk a criminal down from a cross if you let him. This was toward the end. "When we let go of what we have, then we have nothing. Then, we're really fucked. Hazaar fucked," I added for good measure.

Considering what we'd spent the morning doing, I wonder now if that might not have been the best choice of words.

"So ..." he said slowly. "What exactly are you saying here?" God he was cute, especially when he got a little more angry, which he did quite often. "Where's the agency in this? When do I get to understand your choices? Like, your choice to fuck me halfway 'round the Sea of Galilee, then run off back to your boyfriend? Is that a choice you made yourself, or do you have no choice at all, you're just trying to navigate out of a tough spot?"

I realized later that was probably the moment I most loved him, his passion, his vulnerability. Probably around about then I decided I wasn't going to tell Dieter about him after all.

"Listen, beautiful," I said. I could feel my bitch-self rising inside as I said it. "How many English boys get to lose their virginity in the River Jordan to a real-life Jewish princess?" I asked. "One whose all four grandparents came billowing out of the smokestacks at Auschwitz, probably settling like magic dust over the backs of peasants labouring in your fair fields of Hertfordshire?" I don't know why I had to add that last bit. Perhaps because he's the first person I ever told I'm Jewish. Perhaps because my mother only ever told one person, who she was never able to speak to again for the rest of her life. Perhaps because I know that I'm not going to be able to tell Dieter after all. And that because of this, this whole trip has been for nothing. A complete waste of time.

The English Boy was silent, and I didn't wait for an answer.

"Think of it as your baptism," I said, twisting the knife further, knowing at the same time I was hiding further behind my own bullshit.

I had to cut this boy out of my life. A girl's got to find a way to exercise her agency in this world …

… and then the voice of the lecturer grows louder and I'm pulled back into the classroom again. In front of me the white page, *Die weisses Blatt*, is covered with dense scrawlings:

לע הכילה ושי לילגה לע הכילה ושי לילגה לע הכילה לע הכילה ושי לילגה לע הכילה ושי
הכילה ושי לילגה לע הכילה ושי לילגה לע הכילה ושי לילגה לע הכילה ושי לילגה
ושי לילגה לע הכילה ושי לילגה לע הכילה ושי לילגה לע הכילה ושי לילגה לע
ושי לילגה לע הכילה ושי לילגה לע הכילה ושי לילגה לע הכילה
הכילה ושי לילגה לע הכילה

ושי לילגה לע הכילה ושי לילגה לע הכילה ושי לילגה לע הכילה ושי לילגה לע
לילגה לע הכילה ושי לילגה לע הכילה ושי לילגה לע הכילה ושי לילגה לע הכילה
לע הכילה ושי לילגה לע הכילה ושי לילגה לע הכילה ושי לילגה לע הכילה ושי
הכילה ושי לילגה לע הכילה ושי לילגה לע הכילה ושי לילגה לע הכילה ושי לילגה
ושי לילגה לע הכילה ושי לילגה לע הכילה לילגה לע הכילה לע הכילה ושי לילגה לע
לילגה לע הכילה ושי לילגה לע הכילה ושי לילגה לע הכילה ושי לילגה לע הכילה
לילגה לע הכילה ושיגה לע הכילה ושי לילגה לע הכילה ושי לילגה לע הכילה ושי
לע הכילה ושי לילגה לע הכילה ושי לילגה לע הכילה ושי לילגה לע הכילה ושי
לע הכילה ושי לילגה לע הכילה ושי לילגה לע הכילה לילגה לע הכילה ושי לילגה
לה ושי לילגה לע הכילה ושי לילגה

Elizabeth Toman

Red Dress

I take a deep breath as I enter the exam room. All is in place: the small desk with computer; the exam table with blue faux leather upholstery and gleaming metal stirrups tucked underneath; the patient, looking uncomfortable and out of place. I shake Mr. G's hand and log into the computer to view his record. My previous notes are lengthy.

"How's everything?" I say, trying to sound cheerful but inwardly bracing because Mr. G is not a happy person. Nothing I say or do seems to make a difference and his list of complaints and ailments keeps growing.

This is when she slips into the room. The door is firmly closed, but she seeps under it, a red blur in my peripheral vision that solidifies slowly, all her pixels coalescing into one sharp image.

"Yes, how *are* we today?" she breathes into the back of my head. I pretend to ignore her.

"I'm not good," Mr. G replies. His voice is robotic, his face immobile. "I'm a lot worse."

My brows furrow into a concerned look. I try to maintain eye contact as Mr. G recites his litany of complaints. He is aching. He is tired all the time.

"Who isn't?" she asks, blowing smoke from her cigarette. No, she is vaping this time. How considerate.

Mr. G continues: Nothing is right. His back hurts and the pain pills aren't working. Physical therapy makes it hurt more. He can't do it.

"God forbid you actually do anything to make your back better," she comments, seated behind me with a clipboard, posture perfect, taking shorthand.

She is in her usual dress, the red one with the tightly-fitted bodice and flared skirt, seated like a 1950s secretary. Her fingernails, long and pointed, are the same shade as her dress. Her shoes are open-toed with three inch heels. She does not let patient comfort or hospital policy get in the way of fashion. This is her usual getup, although the details vary from visit to visit. Some days she accessorizes.

I shake my head and try to focus on Mr. G. "But that's not any different," he says, "that's not why I came in."

She sighs audibly and makes an exaggerated show of dumping the clipboard into the trash bin. "Please," she says, "keep going. I'm dying to hear more."

His voice drones on: He cannot sleep. His breathing is short. His feet feel like they are on fire. The insulin shots make him feel worse. I type quickly, converting to bullet points, nodding as he speaks. He has no appetite. His joints ache. I glance back and she is filing her nails. So stereotypical.

"Really?" she asks. Suddenly there is a buzzing and she has sprouted a hairy foot with thick fungal nails. One is propped up on the sink and she is going at it with a nail sanding machine, the kind they use upstairs in podiatry.

"Is this better?" she wants to know as a dark cloud of spore-filled nail dust fills the room.

"Gross," I say, out loud.

Mr. G looks up from his monologue—which may have moved on to gastrointestinal complaints—and says, "Well, it was only the one time."

"No, I'm sorry, not you. I mean, I have something in my throat. Excuse me," I say, pretending to cough and grabbing a tissue. I think of stepping out for just a minute, but I don't want to leave him alone with her, so I step over to the sink and wash my hands, displacing her.

He starts again. There is coughing most nights. Did he mention he was short of breath? His head throbs. His chest hurts.

Here I stop him. "Chest pain?" I ask, scanning my previous notes.

"We did some testing for that last year, I think. Is this the same pain, or a new pain?"

"The same pain?" she asks. "Dream on, sister. This pain will be quite different. This pain will merit many new tests, all of which will need follow up phone calls, long explanations, although they will ultimately reveal nothing."

She takes a long puff of her cigarette, no longer vaping, and says, "No pain is ever the same."

Indeed, it is not the same pain and Mr. G is afraid it might be his heart. I ask the usual questions and the answers are vague and long-winded, clarifying nothing. She swings her crossed leg back and forth and pretends to nod off, her head jerking awake every few seconds. I decide to do a cardiogram and I stand up to get the nurse, but this is when he pulls a paper from his chest pocket, a square of yellow legal paper that he carefully unfolds.

"I've got a few things to go over," he says as though we have not been talking for twenty minutes already.

She makes a face of mock horror. "That's not ... please tell me it's not ... a list? Please God, don't let it be a list."

But it is a list. Mr. G starts reading, evading my attempts to get him to hand it over so that I can scan it more quickly. Apparently the back pain and chest pain were just a preamble. The list holds his real concerns. He needs new diabetic shoes, he begins. Can I help him get those? He has questions about his medications. Can I write the prescriptions for a new pharmacy? He has heard of a new medicine on television. It sounds better than what he is taking. He's got a mole on his back he wants me to check. Let's see, his blood pressure readings look a little funny to him, they're all over the place. Could I look them over?

He pulls out another paper and starts to unfold it. She has backed up against the wall and cries out, "No. I can't take any more." She makes a pretend gun with her hand and holds it to her head. "Please, make it stop," she whimpers. Suddenly it is a gun—a real gun—and she pulls the trigger, splattering her head and red dress all over the wall in cartoon splotches of colour. But she reappears, almost as quickly, dusting off her dress. It's just a gimmick.

"Let's see," Mr. G says, reading on. "My back. My chest. Oh yes, this is, well, a little embarrassing...."

"Pray, do tell," she says in a husky voice, leaning in.

"I've got a lump," he says, "in my ... you know ... my testicle. It's been there for a while but I think it's getting bigger."

"Oh delightful," she says. "A lump in the testicle. We'll have to examine it. Just the thing."

She is right, I do have to examine it and do so, trying to block her view and give him some privacy.

"I think it's a hydrocoele," I say. "Nothing to worry about."

"But how can you be sure it's not cancer?" he asks.

"Doctor," she says, and she's donned a suit now, pretending to be an attorney. "Why did you feel so certain it wasn't cancer? Did you do any tests? Any tests at all?" She has even brought in a court stenographer who sits, typing in the corner.

I sigh and suggest getting an ultrasound, just to be sure.

"Wouldn't a CT scan be better?" he asks.

The attorney pipes up. "Doctor, would a CT scan have given you better, more accurate information?"

"No," I say, a little too forcefully. "The ultrasound is the best test. We'll get that."

Finally, we are wrapping up and I scan the chart again for anything I might have forgotten. I see notes from the previous visit, three months ago. Wife. Dementia. Nursing home. Did I already ask about her?

"And the wife?" I ask. I've turned off the monitor and am standing to leave. "The same?"

For a second he says nothing but his face, so stolid throughout his monologue, begins to collapse. He takes a deep breath and shakes his head from side to side.

"Gone," he says. "Last month." He covers his face with his hands and for a moment his shoulders heave. "I should never have let them put her in that place." His voice is muffled, his breath shudders like an infant's. He wipes his face and reaches for my hand and I let him, turning around to glare at her, daring her to mock this. But she has vanished completely, for the first time in months, leaving us alone in the exam room.

I would like to start over.

How are we today?

Heige S. Boehm

Black Earth

AN EXCERPT

I reached down into my baby's crib. His arms outstretched, he looked up at me. He smiled, revealing his first two tiny, perfect white teeth. He wasn't an ugly baby. Everyone said that he was beautiful. He had a mop of curly white-blonde hair that bounced about his head like bedsprings, stretching and recoiling. His eyes were liquid silver blue. Maybe if he had been born a girl, I could feel the love they say a mama feels when holding her baby. But I had none of that in me. My baby didn't even look like me. Sure, I too had blue eyes, but they were a stormy, sad blue, and my mousy limp brown hair hung straight. I wore it in two braids on either side of my head.

But today was my day, my choice, and just maybe, I could be like a normal sixteen-year-old girl. I walked down the stairs holding Walde-mar, with his head close to my nose. He smelled like sweet butter. I stood in the kitchen doorway, watching Mama busy herself. She always took to cooking or cleaning whenever she felt upset. She didn't want me to go.

Mama smiled. "Oh, give him here." She took the baby and showered him with kisses. His little pudgy legs wriggled, and his laughter could be heard throughout the house, as Mama did what mamas do so well: love.

The morning rays streamed through the kitchen window, and the warmth of the sun on my back calmed my fear. A glimmer of happiness rose in me. *It's good I'm going*, I thought. I leaned up against the sink, stared at my sun-distorted shadow on the floor.

"Would you like a cup of coffee, Paula?" Mama asked.

She handed me a plain white coffee cup. Holding it, I realized I too was like the cup—plain.

"Are you all packed, Paula?" Mama placed Waldemar in a high chair beside my little sister, Annalisa.

Waldemar dropped his spoon. I picked it up and placed it in front of him, nodded at my mama. As I stepped outside, I slipped off my shoes and walked over the grass, sensing the pulsing of the earth beneath my feet. My mind drifted to my early school years, to the freedom and laughter of childhood. But almost overnight I had found myself walking alone to school. Even my sister Suse avoided me most days, and so did my four brothers.

My younger brother, Michael's, friend, Wolfie, unlatched the back gate and walked towards me. "Hello, Paula."

I bent down and picked a dandelion and twirled it between my fingers. "Hello, Wolfie."

Wolfie smiled revealing his dimples. I knew he had been watching for me. He did that often. I didn't mind.

"I came to say goodbye."

He stood tall, his shoulders square and back. He wore his *Hitlerjugend* uniform with pride.

I handed him the yellow flower.

He took it and put it in his shirt pocket. "I'll miss you."

"I won't miss this place," I said.

"It's not that bad here."

"You want out as bad as I do. Don't pretend otherwise."

"*Ja*. When will you come home?"

"Hopefully never. There is nothing here for me."

Wolfie cocked his head and under his breath said, "Nothing?" His red curly hair flopped over his green eyes.

"You know what I mean."

"I get it, Paula, but remember there are some good things here, too."

⁓

The train that morning smelled of wet newspaper, dust, and smoke. I placed my one bag beside me on the wooden bench for the one-hour train ride and turned to stare out the window at my family waving me off. The train began moving. I glanced back at what I knew, but I couldn't be more relieved to be starting over. I felt a small tug at my heart, but quickly buried that feeling. A sign mounted on the red brick wall read, "Schadesdorf." I closed my eyes and began to think about my travelling arrangements. Once in Dresden I'd have to transfer onto the Berlin train—I would be on that train for two days heading to the Ukraine. I didn't relish that thought—what would I do? I opened my eyes and rummaged through my bag, searching for my blue note book. "Ah, here it is," I muttered. I placed it on the bench beside me and noticed the little going-away gift Mama had snuck into my bag.

All she had said was, "I know you have dreams."

I gently held the present that she had wrapped in newspaper and used twine to secure it. I pulled at the string and watched as the bow came undone. The paper fell to the side, revealing a box with the word "Pelikan" written on the top. Gently I lifted the lid and gasped at seeing the red fountain pen, the one that had been in the *Tante Emma Laden* window. Mama had watched me eyeing it. She must have saved for a long time to buy it. Papa controlled all the money. I opened the notebook, and as I felt the crispness of the blank pages, excitement gripped me. I held my breath and thought, *Adventures will grace the pages.* Gently I took the cap off of my new pen and gave it a quick shake to push the ink into the writing tip.

May 10, 1942
I have to believe that the shadows of yesterday will give way to the light of the sun today.

On my way to the station this morning I wanted to run, I don't know why. Maybe because I hate the war and Hitler most of all. I know I can get into a lot of trouble for writing that, but so be it. I don't want to think about anything anymore. But I worry about Michael and Wolfie. They think they're all grown up, but they're not.

And I know Papa will force Michael to volunteer for the SS. Mama will be left without her boys. She loves Wolfie like she loves Michael. I hope that the two will be okay. I guess I love Wolfie too. But I will never tell him. Papa is excited about the war, he believes it's a good thing for our country. Two days ago I overheard two old men at the post office talking about how our allies, the Japanese, had invaded some place called Burma, and captured Lashio. I asked Mama about that place and she said that Chinese and Burmese people built a long road. In fact, that it was called the Burma Road. She didn't know much more, only that people in Lashio believe in a Buddha. I don't know anything about Buddha.

Paula

☙

The train whistle blew, I glanced up from my notebook, the early afternoon sun spilled brilliantly onto the station platform as we pulled into the Dresden *Hauptbahnhof*. I tucked my pen and notebook back into my bag, stood and pulled on my coat, readying myself to transfer onto the Berlin train.

☙

"Is this seat taken?"

The soft voice made me open my eyes. A girl about my age with freckles that were softly sprinkled on her nose and over her cheeks stood at the bench I sat on.

The girl took a deep breath and shyly asked again, "May I sit here?"

"Oh, I'm sorry." I sat up straight and pulled at my skirt. "Please do." I leaned over and reached out my hand. "I'm Paula."

She sat down across from me. "Gertrud. But you can call me Gertie."

I smiled, "Are you travelling by yourself?" I noticed a soft green scarf she wore. "Pretty scarf." It matched her eyes.

"*Danke.*"

Gertie pulled out a cigarette, her hands slightly shaking. "Would you like one?"

I recognized her uneasiness. Mama's hands always shook too. "*Nein danke.* I don't smoke." I had never taken to smoking, even though it seemed the thing to do. All my brothers smoked. Papa had caught me smoking and with disdain in his voice he said, "Good girls don't smoke– dirty *schlampens* do."

I reached for a cigarette. "I'll have one."

Gertie shrugged and passed one to me.

"*Danke.*" I took a puff and coughed a little.

She held her cigarette between her lips as she reached up for her hat-pin, pulled it out and took her hat off. She ran her fingers through her lovely golden-red blonde hair. "That's better. Where are you going?"

"The Ukraine. You?"

Shams Budhwani

The Ghusl

AN EXCERPT

It was five in the morning when Rohail's father, Deputy General Malik Naeem, knocked on his bedroom door.

"Rohail, you're coming with me for the Ghusl," Malik said.

"What's Ghusl?" asked Rohail.

"The washing ritual; as Bilal's older brother, it is your duty to help wash him before he is buried."

The thought of having to wash his dead brother's body registered slowly with Rohail. He trembled as he stood up from his bed, his feet numb.

"Can't you do it, Dad?"

"No, it must be you. It must be the older brother."

Malik's assertiveness hit Rohail like a bullet. He worked up the courage to walk slowly toward his bathroom door. He turned on the lights and the sink faucet as he looked up at himself in the mirror. His eyes watered. He rinsed his face with cold water. He shivered as he picked up the lathery soap to wash his face. He began breathing heavily, as he grabbed a towel to dry his face.

He changed into a plain white shirt Bilal had gotten him when he visited Vancouver last year, and went down the stairs where he waited for his father.

Malik showed up a few minutes later dressed in his khaki military uniform. His shirt was well pressed and all his service medals were neatly placed on the right side close to his arm.

"Why are you wearing a uniform?" Rohail asked.

"Because my son was just martyred."

"Martyred? In a war he didn't know he was fighting?"

"We are all fighting this war, whether you like it or not," Malik replied.

They buckled up as Malik turned on the ignition and drove out of their gated community.

"Did you know they would attack the school, Dad?"

"No, of course not."

"The news anchor on TV claims that the army saw it coming."

"News in general is full of shit, Rohail. It's just hate-mongering and propaganda. If we saw it coming, why would we let those barbarians kill our children, our families?"

Malik parked the car outside a large courtyard near the community mosque. He quickly walked through the narrow alley next to the mosque and approached a small doorway that led downstairs. Rohail followed him down the stairs into a small room. It looked like a surgical ward. The ceiling lights were painfully bright accentuating the cleanliness of the chamber. The room had a strong smell of bleach and alcohol.

Rohail saw Bilal lying peacefully on a silver metal table, naked. A large white cotton sheet wrapped underneath Bilal and covered his private parts.

Jamal Saheb, the middle-aged man who owned and operated the Ghusl room, approached Rohail and offered him a pair of gloves, a gown, a mask, and a piece of plain white cloth.

Jamal was a dear friend of Malik; they both grew up together and went to the same school where Bilal was shot dead.

"*Inna lillahi wa inna ilayhi raji'un,*" said Jamal. We belong to Allah and to Allah we shall return.

"Shall we begin?" he asked Malik.

Malik offered a quick nod as he took a step back from the ritual. Rohail stepped forward as he pulled up the transparent latex gloves in his hands. He strapped on the medical mask that covered half his face and tied the gown around his waist. His hands shook as he picked up the plain white cloth and immersed it in the freezing cold water. His heart raced and stomach churned. He felt nauseous.

His eyes turned red and he began to take deep breaths as he held on to his tears.

Jamal began the ritual by raising Bilal's body into a reclining position. He instructed Rohail to press gently on Bilal's abdomen. Rohail shivered as he grabbed on to the plain white cloth and pressed his fingers against Bilal's stomach. He carefully massaged and press downwards until it compressed. Jamal washed Bilal's back with water three times, then plugged Bilal's nose and ears with round pieces of cotton.

Rohail observed the four bullet wounds on Bilal's body again. They appeared even bigger than when he saw them at the hospital during identification. Bilal's eyes remained closed, resting peacefully. Rohail grabbed the cloth again and soaked it in the container of bleach and water placed next to the metal table. He pressed it gently against Bilal's pale, discoloured skin. His skin felt hard against the tip of Rohail's fingers. Rohail rubbed the cloth around Bilal's neck that now appeared greenish-black. He dabbed his face and eyelids, ears and mouth. He pressed the cloth against his right and left arms and then his right and left feet. He avoided the bullet wounds shaped like an ever-expanding irregular ring.

Jamal turned Bilal's body toward himself, instructing Rohail to wash the right side. Rohail looked up Bilal's back as he soaked the cloth in the water. His brother's back had three more bullet wounds: two in each of his arms and one in the centre of his back. They were exit wounds. The bullets had passed right through Bilal's body piercing every tissue, bone, and organ in the way. Rohail took a deep breath as he dabbed Bilal's pierced flesh.

He turned Bilal's body to the right so it directly faced him. He held Bilal's arm as Jamal washed the body's left side repeating the same steps as Rohail.

After washing, Jamal tore up a plastic pack containing three plain cotton white sheets. He lay them flat on another table beside Bilal. Rohail and Jamal lifted Bilal's body and lay him on top of the sheets. Malik continued observing the ritual from a distance; he stayed still and did not offer any help.

Jamal wrapped Bilal's body with all three sheets until fully covered. He fastened the sheets with four knots: one above the head, another under the feet, and two around the body.

Rohail looked at his dead brother's body one last time. Tears ran down his face. It was time to say goodbye.

Rohail stepped outside the room and climbed up the dark alley quickly. He grabbed on to a small empty bucket placed right outside the stairway and threw up.

Malik thanked Jamal as he exited the Ghusl room. They both agreed to meet again after funeral prayers and he approached his car.

"Why didn't you help me wash Bilal's body?" Rohail asked as he sat inside the car.

"I'm in uniform, Rohail."

"Didn't you wish to see your son one last time before he is buried?"

"I have to respect the uniform," said Malik.

Stephanie Berryman

What Remains on the Wind

AN EXCERPT

I stood outside of the seniors home at the edge of my small city and looked out into the endless sea of golden prairie stretched before me. A warm wind wrapped itself around me.

"You look like somebody died," my mother said, astute even in the fog of her forgetting. I felt a child's urge to run into her knowing arms. But when I turned to face her, her eyes were vacant. I gave her a sad smile, took her hand and we walked slowly to the park nearby.

She was right, it felt like she had died. Except for these little moments—like shards of a mirror catching the light and reminding me of who she once was—the ghost of her walked with me every day.

When we first got the diagnosis, I asked her what she was most afraid of. "Forgetting my own name," she had said.

It was also what I feared. The time when she would forget my name. We all want to be remembered, hunger not to be lost, to ourselves or to another. And now? Now we are both lost to her but for these glimpses, the briefest, bright flashes in a dark night when the woman she was lights up like a firefly and then is gone.

We walked in silence. She hardly spoke at all these days. All of her words had run out. When we arrived at the park, she stopped to look at a tree. Her head tilted up, taking in the light shining down through the fluttering green leaves, her eyes filled with a childlike wonder. She turned to me. "I think I must have hit my head. Did I hit my head?"

Heartbreaking as it was, her confusion was better than those first few weeks after I put her in the home when she would call me in tears and ask, in a voice breaking with anger, "How could you do this to me?"

As if I was responsible, not only for putting her in a home but for the Alzheimer's itself.

"No Mom, you didn't hit your head. You're just—well—you're sick, so sometimes everything feels fuzzy. But it's okay, I'm here."

She smiled sweetly at me. "That's nice. And who are you?"

The first time she asked me that a year ago, I said in a voice swollen with tears, "It's me, Mom, it's Elaine." She'd looked at me blankly.

Now, whenever she asked, I'd say, "It's Elaine, Mom. I'm your daughter and I love you very much."

"Well, isn't that nice?" she'd say, in the same tone she used to use when someone gave her an unexpected gift.

I forced myself to focus not on what was missing but on what was still there—her soft hands, the kindness in her voice, her awe at the beauty of the gentle light filtering through the fluttering green leaves.

We began to walk back toward the seniors home. My mother, who had once been a long-distance runner, now shuffled more than walked. She wore a loose grey sweatsuit with no buttons and no zippers, and beige orthopaedic shoes with Velcro straps instead of laces.

A memory leapt to my mind of the two of us jogging side by side, then running hard toward home. We ran together for years. When I was in my early teens, she would slow her pace for me. By the time I was part of the university track team, I was the one slowing down for her.

That was a different life for both of us. I hadn't run since the weight of pregnancy, young children, and an aging mother had slowed me to a walk.

She used to be so fast and strong, her long brown hair streaming out behind her. Now she walked by my side, her eyes narrowed, mouth set in a line of concentration as she focused on each slow step. Soon she would forget how to walk.

As we arrived at the home, I took in the scent of laundry. It was a comforting smell, but the fragrance was wrong. Not our detergent. It unsettled me every time—she no longer smelled like herself. I used to spray her perfume on her when I visited. Then I stopped. It was easier not to. The dissonance was too much for my heart to handle.

We walked to her room, past Anna, a petite Polish woman with short grey hair who worked in the kitchen. Without taking her hands out of a bowl of ground beef she was prepping for dinner she smiled and said hello.

We passed through the living room, nodding and smiling at the four other residents—two plump, elderly women with permed white hair, one tall, thin woman in her eighties with long grey hair, and a bald, elderly man with vacant brown eyes. All of them were sunk into couches, hypnotized by the flickering TV. My mother was the youngest resident by nearly two decades.

We were lucky to get her into this place. It was a private home in a bungalow and there was nothing institutional about it. It was the best luck we'd had since the diagnosis nearly five years ago.

When we got to my mother's room, she sat in the soft brown armchair and her eyes searched the space as if looking for something familiar. They flitted over her single bed and the multi-coloured afghan her mother had made her when she was a child, before racing along to a photo sitting on top of a small wooden dresser. It was of the two of us with my girls taken during a beach vacation seven years ago. Even a few weeks ago there was a flicker of recognition when she looked at the photo, but now her eyes were blank as they rested on the image of our laughing, sun-kissed faces.

I pulled the afghan off the bed and draped it over her legs. She'd lost a lot of weight in the past few months and chilled easily.

"I'll see you tomorrow, Mom." I tucked the blanket around her.

She smiled and patted my hand, nodding her assent, her blue eyes warm but tired. It was unsettling, these gestures that were so her, but so empty of her.

Once I was outside I grabbed a pack of cigarettes from my purse and slunk around the corner as furtive as a teenager. Six months ago, I'd never smoked a cigarette in my life. Now it was a comforting ritual, a strange reward for surviving these daily visits.

I savoured the inhale and the long, slow exhale, watching the smoke mingle with the air and disappear. I didn't let myself think that it was poison I was breathing in. It was my secret, all mine. Stolen time. My five minutes where I wasn't working, or with my mother, or with my husband, or taking care of the kids. Five minutes when all I had to do was inhale the smoke, let it fill my lungs, feel the lifting of everything that was weighing me down and then let go.

I stared out at the fields turning to burnished gold in the setting sun. The wheat was ripe and would be harvested soon. I always loved this season, the fullness of the fields, the warmth of late August all the more cherished, knowing the chill of September was lurking.

Where had she gone? As parts of her faded away, I wondered if they flew from her to rejoin the previously disappeared pieces. When she takes her final breath, will the last part of her fly up and make her whole again? Or perhaps her soul was already lingering, just above the home, waiting patiently for that final piece?

My deepest fear was that she was trapped in there. That behind all the layers of cloudy confusion, my mother was buried deep. Like a woman buried alive, suffocating slowly. There was too much dirt between her and the world for her to claw her way up to us. I had to hope my love reached her down there.

It bothered me, not knowing where she was.

I'd dreamt of her last night. In my dream, I went to visit her in the home. She sat on her single bed in her flannel nightgown—the white one with the flowers. I sat next to her and started to cry, whispering, "I miss you so much."

She wept the way she'd never wept in life. Through her tears, she said, "I miss you too."

In the dream, we clung to one another, crying and crying. Her small bony frame shuddering in my arms, the softness of her skin, the wetness of her tears, the way she clutched me to her. It was so vivid. More than a dream. It was a visitation.

I woke knowing she was still with me. Her spirit was lingering somewhere in the cloudy confusion of the present and the past. And I knew too, she would be with me always. Even when that last piece of her flew up and away, my mother's love would remain on the wind, wrapping itself around me.

Janet Southcott

Interruption

An excerpt from the first chapter of "Interruption," a mystery novel

11:32 AM

"You need more evidence. We cannot make a case out of this." The barrister, Paul Gentry, locked eyes with his client in a stare that said conversation over.

Nigel Selkirk winced. "That study, the one I told you about. They're educated people. That has to stand for something." He saw the barrister glance at his watch.

"I'll take another look, Mr. Selkirk, but right now I have a client waiting for me at my office. Good day."

"Will you call me when you've read it?"

The question hung in the high-ceilinged courthouse corridor as the barrister strode away.

Selkirk extracted his cell phone from his jacket pocket and texted: "Go ahead as planned," then perched on a stone window ledge and looked around. The building was unfamiliar and uncomfortable for him. Individuals in expensive suits and carrying briefcases hurried by. The righteous Gentry was one of them. He'd been a suggestion from a friend of a friend. There was a lot riding on his cooperation, but so far he was proving to be the wrong recommendation.

A ping from his phone interrupted his thoughts. Selkirk smiled as he read the message: "Got him. Following."

11:35 AM

A midnight-blue panel van pulled out of its parking space and slowly drove north along Lloyd Avenue. The occupant in the front passenger seat peered out his side window. He was watching one suit weave in and out of the pedestrians.

"Slow down, will ya, you're catching him up," he said in a low voice, as though the person they were following could hear.

The van slowed. "Look at them jackasses panicking behind us," said the driver, sounding stressed. "We'll get some idiot blasting a horn and that'll blow the game away."

"Okay, go with the traffic. We can always come around again. He's not going anywhere we can't find him."

⁂

11:42 AM

Gentry was lost in thought as he made his way to the hotel. He had lied to get away from Selkirk. But the little sketchbook-skinned weasel deserved it. The man's decorations, from the etchings of God-awful creatures climbing up and down Selkirk's neck and, as he knew from previous meetings, extending to his wrists, together with the grossly enlarged earring hole plugged with a black circle, had made Gentry feel queasy from the first time the guy had walked into his office. It had been an instant reaction to not support his case. How could a guy be so stupid, to think they had a chance against Royston?

He'd come up against Royston once before. The pressure in the courtroom had been immense. He had felt the eyes of Royston's lawyer bearing into him. There were many lives negatively affected by the actions of the agricultural giant, and he was damned if his was going to be one of them.

Now he just needed Anna to soothe him in ways that made his body react like a teenager, a feeling he never seemed to reach with his wife. Right now, Anna'd be perched on the bed at the hotel waiting for him.

If he had been paying attention as he continued along the sidewalk, instead of getting hot on his thoughts, he'd have questioned why two men wearing blackout sunglasses and matching grey coveralls were not getting out of his way. He brushed into one of them before realizing, as he came back to the present, that his path was blocked.

⌒

II:44 AM

Nigel Selkirk's phone pinged. "Package received. Delivery as agreed." His heartbeat accelerated. He fingered the plug in his left earlobe, a habit he had when nervous, feeling the smooth, hard rim of wood against his warm, supple flap of skin.

He rose from the window ledge and headed toward the courthouse steps. His soft-soled Toms made little sound as he descended the steps to street level on Lloyd Avenue.

His car was two blocks away, south down Lloyd. As he walked, he forced himself to keep alert to his surroundings, a strength that had never let him down. This was not a bad area, but the elation he was feeling over Gentry could not cloud his trained judgement. People walked by with hands clasped to briefcases—mostly black leather, the odd brown. A duffle bag slung over a shoulder caught his eye and he briefly studied the middle-aged man attached to it. He had a soft face, smiling eyes as he spoke into a cell phone. The people carried their handbags slung tight over shoulders, some slung first over heads then shoulders, some all of the above, plus a white-knuckled hand attached to the bag itself. Differing degrees of comfort on the urban pedestrian street, he thought.

Lloyd Avenue was home to the main civic buildings like the court-house and the downtown cop shop, and nearby to the banking district; on both sides of the avenue, cafés spilled out onto the sidewalk. But it was also near the light rail station. Stations had a reputation for attract-ing thieves and violence. From Lloyd, the station was down one block, on Muir Avenue. The connecting street, Centurian, was sketchy, and he did not blame people for holding onto their valuables. He would too, if he had any on him.

All he had in his pockets was a little change for the parking meter, his car keys, and his driver's licence. He held his keys in his right hand, with the blades of each key between each finger. This was another of his habits. Approaching his vehicle was always a worry. He stopped a few vehicles before his car, in front of an antique shop, and turned to face the large store window. The window reflected the street scene behind him and he watched it intently. He paid no attention to the display of antiques actually inside the store. Instead, he watched for movement or lack of movement: anything odd occurring across the street.

There was a young couple chatting outside a coffee shop. She leaned against a bicycle stand and he stood a little closer than friends would. Somebody, sitting behind them on one of the coffee shop outdoor seats, was holding up a newspaper and Nigel could not see whether the reader was male or female. A man stood looking in a window, just like he was. His store had books in it. As Nigel watched, the man slowly moved over to the door and went into the shop. He heard the faint ring of a cell phone. A woman, wearing a white blouse, stopped and fished the phone from her bag, answered it, then looked directly at his reflection.

He moved from the window and walked past his car. He took the side street west toward Muir and headed for the light-rail station. The woman had made him uneasy. He could pick up his car later.

A cool wind funnelled down Centurian between islands of high-rise office towers. A group of five young people walked on the other side, heading east. Nigel heard male voices and female giggles. None of them carried anything, not one bag between them. He shifted his attention to the sidewalk in front of him and the crossing of an alleyway. Halfway across, his attention was drawn to a buzzing sound.

A fast-moving electric car approached Centurian along the alleyway. A soft impact, and the target was thrown to the right, like a cue ball on a pool table. Something small and metallic flew through the air, skidding along the pavement upon impact. The driver reversed then re-aimed the vehicle and, with a bump and a swift turn to complete the job, disappeared into the throngs of busy traffic around the light rail station.

⌒

11:51 AM
The youths, showing no signs of having seen anything unusual, continued walking east and blended among Lloyd pedestrians.

On the deserted street, the tire-marked body of Nigel Selkirk took its last breath. A few metres away, a ping sounded and the shattered screen of a cell phone showed a new text had arrived.

Rupa Wood

Life After Yamileth

I should tell you, my neighbour has lost her cat. It felt like something you should know, which is why I'm writing this down on paper that I'll throw into the fireplace after dinner.

You may or may not remember me. We met in the summer of 1999 when I was working at Simon Fraser University as a research assistant. My employer was Professor Lakshay Das who taught a course called Altered States of Consciousness.

You appeared at the door to my office in strange clothes not suited to the hot weather and introduced yourself. Hovering by the doorway you asked me if I had any Tampax. I rummaged through my desk drawer to see what I could find.

"My friends refuse to invite me camping because it seems to them I'm always menstruating heavily and would attract bears." You said in a serious way, taking a hairpin out of the pocket of your wool jacket and tying up your thick black hair into something less wild.

"Unless they're polar bears you should be ok," I said, handing over a box. You held it up, examining the label and appeared to conclude them insufficient.

You must be five years younger than me though your name is remarkably similar to mine, save a syllable. My name, Rupa, comes from the Buddhist concept of material form. Your name, Rupam, has its root in Tamil, meaning, to appear.

I had meant for you to take what you needed but you lifted up your creased shirt and folded the half-full box of tampons into the waistband of the long skirt you wore and fled down the corridor.

At the professor's recommendation, I was reading Aldous Huxley's philosophical essay, *The Doors of Perception*. I picked up the book while I waited:

"What is the Dharma-Body of the Buddha?" ("the Dharma-Body of the Buddha" is another way of saying Mind, Suchness, the Void, the Godhead.) The question is asked in a Zen monastery by an earnest and bewildered novice. And with the prompt irrelevance of one of the Marx Brothers, the Master answers, "The hedge at the bottom of the garden."

I was unsure what the passage meant and felt like Huxley's contemplations were going over my head.

When you came back from the bathroom we sat at either end of a desk. I shuffled Zener cards and set the deck face down on the table, ready for the experiment. Zener cards are used to conduct trials investigating extra sensory perception or clairvoyance. Each card has a different symbol: a yellow circle, a red cross, three blue wavy lines, a black square, or a green star. There are 25 cards in a deck containing a total of five of each symbol. I held up the first card between us with its back to you.

I'd completed an undergraduate degree in psychology at the University of Brighton in England, and had come to Canada to study for my masters. At SFU, Altered States of Consciousness was considered a controversial course, although institutions such as the University of Edinburgh and Princeton were involved in research into the paranormal. The teachings of Dr. Das involved the psychology of the unconscious, dissecting evidence for and against extra sensory perception as well as experiments in telesthesia and psychokinesis.

The research position was arranged for me through my professor at Brighton. I was surprised to find myself involved in investigative work generally not accepted in academia, but wanting to honour my commitment, I simply decided not to tell anyone what I was doing.

You were a friend of the professor's daughter and I knew you must have claimed to have psychic ability to end up here as a research subject.

To determine the symbol on the card that was hidden to you and visible to me, you looked deep into my eyes to connect with the image I held in my mind. Your eyes were black like mine, but encircled by thick kohl. Staring at each other so intently caused a strange sort of intimacy, usually reserved for lovers. There was something in your gaze, ethereal and dispassionate, that addressed my naked soul. I tried to hide how uneasy it made me feel.

The initial assessment provided little support for any psychic ability: you guessed eight out of the 25 cards correctly, results which correlated with random guesswork. As I made entries into the computer you asked me how I felt about the work I was doing. I hadn't intended to appear skeptical and, not wanting to offend, I mumbled something about inconsistent results.

"You won't find what you're looking for through consistency," you said.

You didn't think you had ESP. But during a conversation over dinner at the Das's, you revealed that, when you thought about a friend, they would likely call on the phone or you'd encounter them somehow later that day. Similarly, whenever you rang your mother she would exclaim in surprise that she was just thinking of you.

"But I can't summon it artificially," you said, chewing on a blue pen. "It just happens, when I'm not aware I'm creating the thoughts. It's not really much of a psychic power, but Dr. Das wanted me to come in anyway."

I asked you what you did for a living and you told me you were a writer, working on your second novel. I gave you a business card with the contact details of my department at the university and we put a date in the calendar for your next assessment. I bought a new dress to wear to work that day but you never came again.

A few weeks later, I happened upon a copy of your novel at Macleod's Books on Pender. I doubt I would have noticed it in the display but, as I say, our names are unusual in Canada and yours is so similar to my own.

327

The Temple of The Golden Flower was the first book you'd published and I was surprised by how deeply uncomfortable I felt reading it:

The protagonist, Yamileth, living in an unnamed city on the Pacific Rim becomes obsessed with a building called the Golden Flower. Throughout her youth she is told by her mother that it is the most beautiful structure in all the world. Yamileth is tortured by her thoughts of aesthetic and spiritual beauty and disturbed by its permanence amongst a world of decay and renewal. The writing is fraught with a sense of urgency and desperation. In Yamileth's desire to possess its beauty she believes that her only course of action is to destroy the Golden Flower.

I don't know what I was expecting but the work was so intimate and impassioned I found it unsettling. It seemed almost a betrayal to discover your thoughts through your book.

I kept the novel in the bottom drawer of the desk in my home office. As time passed, however, my recollection of you faded enough that I was able to read your stories as they were, without feeling as though I was intruding. I referenced the book every six months or so, turning to the parts of the story I liked best, or rereading it from the beginning.

As a result of my excellent references, the department of cognitive science took me on as a teaching assistant. I published work in the Canadian Journal of Experimental Psychology and graduated with a doctoral degree in clinical psychology from SFU in 2005. Around this time I bought a house on a leafy street in Point Grey where there were a number of other East Indian families. On moving day, as I was carrying the drawer to my desk into the house, a woman who lived across the street came over and introduced herself.

She handed me a shallow Tupperware container of besan laddu and I set down the drawer to accept the gift. Seeing your Sanskrit name on the cover amongst my papers, she asked me about your book. I felt instantly protective over it as I sensed my fondness of the book would say more about me than I intended to reveal to a stranger. But as I described it, my love of the story proved infectious and she requested to borrow my copy.

Around a month later, the book was returned to me. She had been moved by the story of Yamileth. It was hard to hear the interpretation of your characters coming out of someone else's mouth, hearing the names of places I had only ever heard in my head. Knowing that we once had met she asked me if I could arrange a meeting with the author. I told her that the university wasn't allowed to give out such information—but I already knew your publisher couldn't reach you.

Leaving to visit the post-office one afternoon, I met the same neighbour's family getting out of their car. "Mom named her Yamileth," her daughter exclaimed, holding out the most exquisite grey kitten. The woman was obviously still taken by the name.

Recently, their cat went missing.

I couldn't stop thinking about the cat. I took it from the street when no one was around. I keep it in my bedroom at the back of the house. The little grey cat's favourite thing to do was lie in the dark, at the bottom of my wardrobe.

Every day at dusk, when the first of the green stars appear in the sky, I hear my neighbour or one of her children calling out "Yamileth ... Yamileth ... Yamileth ..." by the hedge at the bottom of the garden.

Kally Groat

Observations Between Turbulence and Order

When he woke in the morning, the candle on his bedside flickered as he rushed past it to dress his eighteen-year-old body in riding gear: pants, boots, and long sleeved jersey, which matched the Banshee—his green racing ATV. His friends were waiting outside. He moved quietly between rooms of the house—it was a silence he filled in the space between these walls—and shut the door behind him.

The train tracks vibrate as if the capillary is made up of beetles, a shimmery glint under the sunlight, hissing with the tremors of a distant train. Of the four boys riding today, two in the lead touch tires on the other side of the tracks, park in the grassy ditch and face the rails intersected with the back road.

The two boys glance up the gravel bend: they expect their friends to round the corner, but a blind spot of pines blocks their vision. They kill the ignition on their bikes and wait. These are the moments in which they surrender themselves to their environment.

The two boys relax as they wipe sweat from under their helmets and wait for the breeze that rustles through the parched grass. The sky is stark blue and seems to stretch for infinity. Thoughts are broken by noisy cricket legs. Idle daydreams rise into the weighted air, letting the heat hang heavy around them like a hammock, sluggish and motionless. In the distance, the train horn blows long and casually, almost lazy in its routine.

The tracks aren't visible until they face them head on but this road connects them to the sand dunes and some of the best riding paths around. It's either cross here or traverse the railroad for a couple of clicks at a sketchy incline. They always choose this. They've come here so many times that the trails are etched in their minds like palm lines.

The boys' earliest memory on their bikes was to find the biggest, busiest ant hills to flatten with their tires, as if they were treading on the metropolis of the bug world. It was a universe they were bigger than. They would watch the inhabitants spill out like dotty ink in the dirt, and one after another, the worker ants would send out Morse code as an instinctive message to collectively gather fragments that had gone astray. Dirt, pebbles, pine needles. All to recreate their unified entity. The boys did this mostly because they were young and didn't know any better. But they did understand one rule: what seems like chaos is actually the laws of nature at work.

The two boys hear one bellow of the horn, twice, three times—a fair warning when approaching a crossing. Heat trapped in their riding gear is uncomfortable and they begin to get restless. It's summer and the sun is high. One of the boys standing directly in the sun unclips the toolbox on the back of his bike and lights a cigarette. Smoking passes the time.

Minutes later, the third bike cuts the corner and makes it through with time to spare. A plume of gravel dust trails him, a sure sign he heard the horn and raced it. There's no sign of the last rider as the nose of the train becomes visible, so they share a collective sigh of relief that he stopped and waited. The last boy, no doubt, is lagging not because of speed, but because it's his nature to show off.

The scrape of machinery pulsates the tracks, friction enough to stir up the swelling air. On top of the train's incoming racket is another sound: steady, buzzing, and gaining intensity. The boys can feel it pass through the ground, up to their riding boots. It's familiar, comforting in a way, until the noises seem to compete for the finish line and someone mutters, fuck, so the rest stare ahead: in a spray of gravel and green, the last rider whips around the corner and straightens out right before the tracks, leaning forward with the throttle pinned only a couple metres from metal.

The train guns its horn in one wavering shout, urgent now, and as the rider reaches the tracks, a wide-mouthed, toothy smile stretches across his face, triumphant in his recklessness. The Banshee was made for this—beating time—and the front wheels crunch gravel on the safe side of the tracks. A breath of victory.

But in one more gasp, the horn assaults all senses during its final blow—a wail that hasn't stopped. They can't hear the impact of the train as it clips the back of his quad. They can do nothing but take cover and watch his trajectory as he is whiplashed and tossed through the air like a ragdoll.

They run to him fifteen feet from the collision, his body tangled in his own limbs. He's face up yet not breathing. At first the scene is just noise: the train over their voices echoing back and forth, and they're just adding layers to the mess, running and unsettled and lost at what to do until someone assigns jobs. As one boy calls an ambulance, the other two exhale for their friend; they pump his chest and count and breathe, and want to curse his bravery or stupidity, but there's no time for that. They swallow the fact they're out of town away from vehicle roads.

The boys do what they can not to count down the seconds but to stay in each one. The air is dry and hot and still—there are moments of floating silence where the world still exists outside of them, in dandelion cotton and dry grass, in flayed dust. And, in that pocketed stillness, they could lift themselves up out of the situation, as if they were just kids watching a frantic ant colony methodically putting its hill back together. They could use their magnifying glass to get a closer look, to understand the scene at its finest detail. But time—as it would be for an insect under heated plate glass—is too valuable for mere observation. The rushing of the train pulls them back into gravity. They pulse, breathe, exhale, shout.

An ambulance does make it. When the boy is being rushed away, his friends have nothing to do but relive the moment when he's still flying through the air, as if he never came down. They let him stay there in their minds, floating in the space between fire and the sky.

Though no one can stay there, nothing can live in the place between turbulence and order; they have to go up or down. His body stayed on the ground—moved to its place on earth. That night when they visited the house he had left, the candle on his bedside was burnt out completely.

Karen Poirier

One Thousand Days

AN EXCERPT

Lloyd's boots crunched the gravel. He was alive. Alive, but still in shock, his mind refusing to focus on anything but his steps forward and his trembling breath. He was aware of the men marching in front of him, their quiet despair hung like a sorrowful shroud in air heavy with tension, dirty sweat, and disappointment. He walked in a long column of prisoners ignoring the vague pain shooting up from his right leg. His shoulders ached, gripped by fatigue, and he wished he could drop his hands held up behind his head. The line of prisoners grew longer as they marched along the roadway from Pourville to Dieppe. Heartbroken, they were still united, bound by a collective melancholy. Their ordeal was written on their blackened faces, their torn and dirty uniforms, and their tired, humble steps. This wasn't the quick victory they'd hoped for.

The soldier in front of him teetered and hesitated as his bare feet settled on small rocks lining the roadway. From behind him, Lloyd slowed his pace and his arm dropped to offer support.

"Marz!" yelled a German guard, and both Lloyd and his fellow prisoner straightened and continued in step with the long line of captives.

As he marched forward, Lloyd noticed a white sheet of paper, trampled on and muddy, on the side of the road. He recognized it as one of the many flyers, dropped by British airmen early this morning, informing the French population of the attempt to liberate them.

What good did it all do? he thought. What did we gain by it?

"Halten!"

Lloyd nearly tripped into the soldier in front of him when he stopped walking, then looked up. Another group of battered and captured soldiers were sitting on the side of the road. They were told to stand and the guard motioned to them to file up beside Lloyd's column.

"Handes runter."

The prisoners that understood German lowered their arms and Lloyd followed their lead. The prisoner next to Lloyd limped badly. Lloyd offered his arm and the prisoner gratefully put his own arm around Lloyd's neck for support. Some of the men had bandages around their heads, their helmets hung on their backs by the chin straps that settled around their necks. One man had a bandage completely around his eyes and needed the guidance of another prisoner to show him the way. Lloyd searched the faces of the prisoners, looking for someone familiar to him. There must be some survivors. Some Camerons. Maybe further on, he thought.

A German guard paced back and forth with crisp steps beside the long line of prisoners. He brushed up against Lloyd's uniform and Lloyd felt the guard's gun bump against him and smelled his foul breath heavy with garlic. He heard the guard suck up and spit a gob. Lloyd looked down to see the spittle settle and slide down a rock by his feet. The guard looked unruffled in his grey-green uniform. He was wearing a leather shoulder strap and, attached to his waist, was a leather gun case holding his revolver. The red swastika on the front of his helmet caught Lloyd's attention when the guard looked straight at him. Noticing the look of recognition reflected in Lloyd's eyes, the guard stopped and poked at Lloyd's bare and bandaged leg with his gun. Through a greasy grin and tobacco-stained teeth, the guard said in English, "Did you think we didn't know you were coming?"

Lloyd didn't answer him, instead he looked away.

"Marz!"

The sad line-up of prisoners began walking again. Lloyd took sideways glances at the countryside around them. Pourville, a quiet resort village, lay straddling the beach and, behind them, green fields shone like

335

velvet in the sunshine, dotted with bales of hay and intermittent trees. The occasional villager appeared, nonchalant and seeming unperturbed, continued on with his daily tasks. It occurred to Lloyd that it was strange that nothing had changed. Their struggle hadn't altered a single thing. He wasn't sure what he expected but the sun was shining on rooftops, people were going about their business, the sky once cracked and glazed with smoke and a distant red, had cleared, and the German army was still in control.

They walked two miles through the countryside to Dieppe. The bells sounded louder and clearer as they neared the town. Lloyd glanced down at the bandage on his leg. He began to notice that pain was shooting up and through him with every step he took, jarring his memory of the battle. Why is my pant leg missing? Lloyd continued walking, the weight of a lifetime on his tired shoulders.

The tall houses of Dieppe that seemed to carelessly blend into the sea, rose up in the distance. Lloyd knew they weren't too far away and, as they approached the outskirts of the town, church bells continued to sound. The smoke was beginning to clear and the smell of gunpowder was swept out to the channel by a cooling sea breeze.

When they arrived at the outskirts of Dieppe, Lloyd looked up, then quickly looked away and shut his eyes. When he finally looked again he saw bodies lined up like cordwood alongside the road against a wire fence, one corpse almost on top of the other. German soldiers were carrying make-shift stretchers made out of doors and pieces of plywood with dead soldiers heaped on them. The reality of war rained down, pressed in on his insides and forced back emotional tears stinging at the corners of his eyes. These were his comrades, the young men who would never return home.

They marched through the main street of the town, a sleepy fishing village. Time-worn houses lined the cobblestone streets with outdoor stairways, potted plants, and pale-complexioned exteriors. Cawing seagulls blending with church bells grew louder, marking their way while French citizens with plastic faces walked quickly to work and to the shops. The fragrance of fresh coffee, freshly baked bread, and salty air filled Lloyd's senses. His mouth was so dry it felt swollen and he wondered if he could even speak. He was aware of an intense thirst and an accompanying light-headedness and thought about how much he would love even a sip of coffee. The aroma almost drove him mad in his need for water.

In a small sidewalk café, a group of French men, sitting at a small round metal table, stared at the captive soldiers as they walked by them. Lloyd saw they were very thin and looked to be what was left of an older population, the younger ones either in prison or fighting for the Resistance. One man wearing a cap and a patched wool jacket gave Lloyd a quiet nod as he passed and, another man, frail and elderly, lifted a glass of wine in a subtle salute.

At the end of the street a grey stone church stood, its steeple reaching high toward the heavens and its bell tolling its remembrance of a bloody sacrifice. The red wooden door opened up and wedding guests spilled into the street, followed by the bride and groom. They hesitated upon seeing the ragged group of prisoners. The groom, holding the bride's hand under a shower of rice, continued walking toward the long file of Canadian prisoners.

When they met, the bride and groom showed no emotion, youth erased from their faces. The groom, small in stature, wore a tired-looking suit and the petite bride wore a short, simply styled dress. She carried a bouquet of daisies in her free hand and her dark hair was pinned back with two of the flowers. When the bride and groom passed the barefooted soldier in front of Lloyd, the groom stopped. Without saying a word, he bent over, untied his shoes, and handed them to the soldier with bare feet. At that moment, Lloyd knew. He knew their sacrifice mattered and in spite of the terrible defeat they suffered, the Canadians would not be forgotten.

The tolling bells followed them all the way to the train station, telling a story the local people were too frightened to tell. They tolled for the dead and they tolled for the wounded. They resounded over the hills, the fields, the rocky beaches, and the sea, and they tolled for the heartbreak the defeated army felt.

Jo Dawyd

Beatrix in London

AN EXCERPT

Beatrix knocked on the door and waited. She tucked her cold hands back into her cloak and pulled its hood closer around her neck against the drizzle. Footsteps sounded inside the house, then the door creaked open. A pair of eyes squinted at her for a moment, overshadowed by bushy grey eyebrows.

"Yes?" The door opened a little wider. "Can I help you, miss?" The eyes and croaking voice belonged to a man wearing clothing that had once been elegant, but now with frayed hems and faded colours looked as if it dated from his prime.

Beatrix found her voice. "I—I'm here to answer an advertisement for a governess position. It said to apply at this address to Mr. and Mrs. Webster?"

He didn't answer, just stood with his hand on the doorknob squinting at her and quietly clearing his throat every three seconds like clockwork. Finally he stood aside, sweeping his hand with a flourish to invite Beatrix in. The tattered lace cuffs he wore nearly covered his gnarled fingers and his hand shook a little as he closed the door against the weak morning light. "Wait here."

Standing alone in the centre of the dimly-lit room, Beatrix looked around. The walls were dark with age, the peeling paper showing brighter rectangles where old portraits must have once hung. The low-timbered ceiling showed the age of the building, and the slate floor tiles wobbled a little under her feet. The house was silent. A grandfather clock stood with its pendulum stilled in the corner, and Beatrix felt she had stepped into a place without time.

She took a deep breath and let it out slowly. What am I doing here? She had spent her few remaining weeks in London visiting the lawyer and overseeing the sale of her parent's London possessions. The most difficult thing had been the sale of her father's horses. Those animals had been a constant in Bea's life for the past ten years since her father had purchased the pair of colts. He'd had a gentleness and love for the animals and trained them well.

Muffled footsteps signalled the return of the old man. He appeared and beckoned for Beatrix to follow. "Come."

He showed her into a parlour that was every bit as tattered and sparse as the foyer. At least this room had some daylight streaming through the windows, and a crackling fire in the grate. A woman sat on a chair near the window, her sewing in her lap. Her fingers moved rhythmically, never slowing even as she looked up over the top of her spectacles with vibrant, sky-blue eyes. Iron-grey hair was pulled so severely back it barely showed under the black mobcap she wore. Her pale face was covered in such fine wrinkles it appeared to be made of crepe, and her lips puckered in permanent disapproval.

"Come in, dear." Her voice clipped each word efficiently. "Sit down."

Beatrix perched on a shabby chair across from her host. "Thank you, ma'am."

"I am Mrs. Webster. I placed the advertisement. What is your name?"

"Beatrix Collins."

"Well, Miss Collins, thank you for coming. I never saw myself to ever be in need of hiring a governess, having no children of my own, but I have lately come to be in possession of my great-niece. She is ten years old and in want of a firm hand. I find I am not equal to the task myself, at my age. So, tell me about your education."

"Oh, well, I had all my schooling at home with my own governess. She taught me arithmetic, reading, literature, music, drawing, and needlework. My father taught me Latin and theology, and my mother taught me botany."

Mrs. Webster laid down her sewing, leaned forward, and peered over her spectacles at Beatrix as if she were a specimen pinned onto felt and labelled. After a minute, she spoke. "That is an impressive list of subjects. But tell me, are you any *good* at all of those?"

Beatrix hesitated. "Well, I am not a rare talent in most of these areas, but I can certainly teach each one until such a time as a specialized tutor would be needed. Latin and botany are my personal favourites of the subjects I studied."

"I see." Mrs. Webster picked up her sewing again and her stitches resumed their rhythm, the needle flashing in and out of the linen in a mesmerising fashion.

The silence stretched between them, and Beatrix searched her thoughts for something to say. She hoped it wasn't obvious she was only applying for this position out of dire necessity rather than any desire to teach children. Her latest visit with her father's lawyer had mostly been over her head, but she had come away with the beginnings of a realization of how much money was owed to her father's creditors. Along with the grief of losing her parents and the burden of the monetary debt, Beatrix suffocated under her own sense of guilt in contributing to her father's debts by letting him indulge her silly, childish whims. Yet how could she have known? She was certain her mother hadn't known of the debts either, as she wasn't the type of woman who would insist on a London season and new dresses if it would have been detrimental to their position.

Unless—Unless it was all a ploy to snare a wealthy husband for Beatrix to solve all their problems? No! Her parents were not so mercenary. They had seemed thrilled that a titled and reputedly wealthy heir was showing preference for Beatrix, but wasn't that in support of Beatrix's feelings? Not for any monetary troubles?

"Miss Collins—"

Beatrix felt heat rise to her cheeks as Mrs. Webster's voice broke into her distracted thoughts. "Yes?"

"Do you have anyone who can vouch for your ability to teach?"

"Well, no. You may write to my own governess; she is best able to tell you about my skills and even limitations. She has a new situation in Hampstead. I'm sure I can send you her address."

Behind Beatrix, the door swung open and banged against the wall. She turned in surprise.

"Missus. Webster ... I must have a word with you!" A large man leaned against the doorframe running a hand roughly over dishevelled hair, his words slurring together slightly. He was well-dressed enough—or had been whenever he had originally dressed—but he looked decidedly not sober for eleven o'clock in the morning.

Beatrix glanced back at Mrs. Webster. The lady had become—if it were possible—even more prim and collected than she already was. When she spoke she was quiet, but her voice held an edge of steel. "Miss Collins, permit me to introduce to you Mr. Webster, my husband."

Mr. Webster squinted toward Beatrix. "Oh, I beg your pardon, ladies! I didn't realise you had a visitor, Mrs. Webster. He stood straighter, then gave a gallant—if wobbly—bow. "Pleasure to meet you, Miss Collins."

Beatrix nodded.

"Miss Collins," Mrs. Webster spoke again before Beatrix could think of a greeting, "is applying for the governess position."

Mr. Webster looked back at Beatrix. "This child?" He stared until she felt the need to squirm. "No." He finally said. "No, she is far, far too young. No."

Beatrix waited for Mrs. Webster to overrule him. As far as she had seen, the lady of the house was decided in her opinions, and surely would have her way in this matter. She had seemed inclined to at least give Beatrix a try as governess until her husband had walked in.

Mrs. Webster still looked as steely and disapproving as before, but her words acquiesced. "Very well, Mr. Webster. I find I do agree with you. We need someone much more experienced to teach our niece. Miss Collins, I thank you for your time." She gestured with a pale, elegant hand toward the door.

Beatrix stayed seated and looked from one Webster to the other. Was that it? One objection from a man at least half in his cups, and she wasn't even given a chance? She turned back to Mrs. Webster. "I assure you I am qualified to teach in spite of my youth. Perhaps if I met your niece, you could decide after seeing how we suit each other?"

Mr. Webster shook his shaggy head. "No, young lady, it won't do. It would be like a child teaching a child. Her dear mother would turn in her grave. I'm sorry, but you will have to look elsewhere for a position."

"Quite right," Mrs. Webster spoke again. "I should have realized as soon as you walked in, Miss Collins. It just won't do."

"Very well." Beatrix stood and walked toward the door. She paused, since Mr. Webster still blocked the doorway. After an awkward moment, he moved aside.

"Begging your pardon, Miss."

Beatrix looked back toward Mrs. Webster. "I do thank you for your time." She turned toward the waiting butler and left the room.

When she found herself again outside in the drizzly rain, she breathed a sigh of both disappointment and relief.

Jeff Pitcher

Private Mitchell
and the Rat

An excerpt from a novel set in World War I

Mitchy stretched out on the floor of the small dugout as best he could. He watched the eerie shadows flickering on the earthen roof as his mind raced through all he had seen that day.

He felt an army of lice gnawing just below his scrotum and reached down to scratch furiously. He turned onto his side, trying to focus on anything other than lice, exhaustion, the dead, and the dying. His thoughts raced to Lieutenant Thomas, Second Lieutenant Anderson, and the view of No Man's Land during the attack. Stop, he told himself. Stop thinking. He forced his thoughts up to the clouds. It's what he always did when he was a boy trying to sleep.

There was a rustling at the arse of his trousers. He knew it was a rat nosing around but was too exhausted to move. The rat probably thought he was another dead soldier and was going after his balls.

"For fuck's sake!" he yelled and pushed himself into a sitting position as the rat scurried out into the trench. He reached into his tunic and pulled out a cigarette, lit it and inhaled deeply. The smoke filled his lungs with a momentary sense of something familiar. There would be nothing familiar anymore, he thought. Ever.

What would his grandfather think if he could see all this? A tear spilled down Mitchy's cheek and it shocked him. His mind raced, flashed like a tidal wave to the Café Anglaise: Corporal Bugden at the bar telling him about a new job, about Lieutenant Thomas.

He began to blubber. Where the fuck was the Lieutenant? There's no way Lieutenant Thomas could be dead!

He dashed his cigarette into the dirt, sparks and embers flying. What happened today? Over 800 men. Faces flashed and flowed through his brain. He sobbed, finding it hard to catch his breath and, as he sucked in air, his snot blocked his nostrils making him heave for breath, choking him, drool spilling from his lips onto his tunic. His mind sped through the million pictures he had stored up since arriving in these trenches last night. The flares and shells in the night sky revealing hundreds of bodies strewn over No Man's Land, the deafening roar of bombs from both sides that left his ears ringing, the smell of burning flesh and bone as he traveled through shattered trenches ... and Lieutenant Thomas. Where in the hell was Lieutenant Thomas?

He opened his eyes and, between his legs, the rat sat on its haunches, its black beady eyes moving rapidly from side to side and its nose and whiskers twitching.

"Fuck off," Mitchy muttered. The rat made no move. "I said, fuck off!" But the rat stayed, its whiskers moved quickly back and forth as it sniffed and bobbed its head from side to side. Mitchy stared. The rat stiffened and its eyes focused on Mitchy. It was a stand-off. Slowly, he lifted his hand and moved it down toward the rat, anticipating the rat would dart away—but it didn't. It stood on its haunches and stared him in the eye without even a glance at Mitchy's approaching hand.

Mitchy's breathing slowed. Was this thing not even scared of him? The fucker had probably dined on a dead man and was now too stuffed to move. His fingers neared the the rat's nose and its whiskers began moving in circles, its nose twitching, its breathe inflating and deflating its belly and rib cage.

Why isn't it moving? Mitchy's finger touched the rat's nose and still the rat didn't move. I could fucking kill you with one swipe, thought Mitchy. Or, I could let you live.

They watched each other. Mitchy reached down with his other hand and picked the rat up, raising it until they were looking each other directly in the eyes. He could feel its heart beating under his thumb. It wasn't a large rat, not like some he'd seen in these trenches that were the size of cats. This one fit comfortably in the palms of his hands.

Mitchy whispered, "You're not scared of me, are you? Or, are you more scared of what's out there?" One of the candles sizzled out. He leaned back against the wall, letting his hands, holding the rat, rest on his stomach. He leaned over, blowing out the other candle, leaving them in complete darkness.

He let himself slide sideways down to the floor and, as he settled on his side, he brought the rat closer to his chest, over his heart. The animal smelled of wet earth and its fur was short and soft. He lifted the rat until it was against the skin of his neck and he could feel its heat and even its breath on his skin.

He closed his eyes and drifted off to sleep.

Contributors

FOREWORD

Chelene Knight is the author of the poetry collection *Braided Skin* and the memoir *Dear Current Occupant*, winner of the 2018 Vancouver Book Award, and long-listed for the George Ryga Award for Social Awareness in Literature. Her essays have appeared in multiple Canadian and American literary journals, plus the *Globe and Mail*, the *Toronto Star*, and the *Walrus*. Her work is anthologized in *Making Room*, *Love Me True*, *Sustenance*, *The Summer Book*, and *Black Writers Matter*.

The *Toronto Star* called Knight, "one of the storytellers we need most right now." Knight was the previous managing editor at *Room* (2016 – June 2019), and programming director for the Growing Room Festival (2018, 2019), and now CEO of #LearnWritingEssentials and Breathing Space Creative. She often gives talks about home, belonging and belief, inclusivity, and community building through authentic storytelling.

Knight is currently working on "Junie," a novel set in Vancouver's Hogan's Alley, forthcoming in 2020. She was selected as a 2019 Writers' Trust Rising Star by David Chariandy.

AUTHORS

Alaa Al-Musalli believes that words have souls. She treats her words as living, breathing entities and is very aware of the energies they carry. Her first project, a non-fiction novel that has been brewing in her head and in fragmented chapters since 2011, is a tribute to mothers in war zones. She's both intrigued and petrified by what she's writing, and loving every moment of it.

Adriana Añon is a teacher and a writer. She is originally from Uruguay but has since lived in Japan, Canada, Brazil and the U.S., which has given her an early and ongoing awareness and appreciation of different cultures. Her stories are invariably sparked by personal experience and often revolve around life observations; she likes to take a personal story and get to the essence of what it says about our humanity. Her work has been published in *Teachers and Writers Magazine*, *Chicken Soup for the Soul: Step Outside Your Comfort Zone*, the *Globe and Mail*, and *Reader's Digest Canada*.

Elizabeth Armerding is a writer living in Vancouver, B.C. She was short-listed for *Pulp Literature*'s 2016 Magpie Award for Poetry, leading to her debut publication and a cherished $25 cheque. For further money, Elizabeth works as a film liaison in old buildings where the walls can speak. For sport she can be found drinking at Ikea on an international level.

Jenn Ashton is a writer and full-time visual artist. Born in Vancouver and raised in North Vancouver, she currently resides in Lynn Valley. She has a long publishing history and has recently won a number of awards, including the Muriel's Journey Poetry Prize, the Jericho Writer's Flash Prize, and the 2019 Friends of the British Columbia Archives Aboriginal Research Grant, for work on her upcoming book "Talking with Grandmothers." She has recently discovered her family's rich First Nations history and writes from a decolonized, feminist perspective.

Purnima Bala is a writer, marketer, and artist whose work is influenced by her cross-cultural background and feminist ideologies. Some of her short fiction and poetry can be found on her Wordpress site, *The Dabbling Zone*. She is currently at work on her first novel and looks forward to pursuing her master's degree in Canada next year.

Tene Barber is a non-fiction writer residing in Burnaby, British Columbia. She has enjoyed a twenty-year academic career in the field of design and administrative leadership. She has published *The Online Crit: The Community of Inquiry Meets Design Education* and a variety of travel blogs while enjoying solo adventures.

Stephanie Berryman has been writing since the age of eight, and her writing has helped her come through many challenging times, including the death of her younger brother and her mother. Writing has been Stephanie's way to feel more deeply, to heal, and to bring forth the stories that come from a full and fortunate life. Stephanie writes non-fiction, fiction, and poetry. She is currently at work on her third novel. Stephanie has been published in *Grain Magazine*, *Medium*, *The Ascent* and on *Thrive Global*. As well as a mother of two young children, she is a writer, leadership coach, and consultant.

Heige S. Boehm is the author of *Secrets in the Shadows* a young adult crossover novel. Her writing is influenced by the stories of her parents, who grew up in Nazi Germany and who, at the end of the war, found themselves in East Germany. They escaped with their first two children to West Berlin in 1961, and Heige was born in West Germany in 1964. Ten years later, she and her family immigrated to Canada. Heige studied creative writing at Simon Fraser University. She currently lives on the Sunshine Coast of British Columbia. *heigeboehm.ca*

Tara Borin is a poet and bartender living in traditional Tr'ondëk Hwëch'in territory, in Dawson City, Yukon. Tara was a finalist for Quattro Books' inaugural Best New Poets in Canada contest, and their work appears in an anthology of the same name. Their poetry has also been published in the *Northern Review*, the *Maynard*, and *Prairie Fire*, and in the anthology *Resistance*, edited by Sue Goyette (Coteau Books). Tara is currently at work on a book-length collection of poems about a sub-arctic dive bar, addiction, and community. They can be found online at *taraborinwrites.com*.

Lindsay and **John Borrows** have many things in common. They both write, are lawyers, enjoy spending time in nature, currently live on Vancouver Island, are members of the Chippewas of Nawash First Nation, and share many ancestors. Together they have deepened their love for story and are collaborating on a collection of letters they wrote back and forth to each other from 2010 to 2012 while Lindsay lived in Phoenix.

Danielle Boyd grew up in Kingston, Ontario, and lives in Vancouver, B.C., where the ocean and mountains are her inspiration. Danielle competed for Canada in the sport of sailing at the Rio 2016 Olympics. Life, for her, has always been about pursuing dreams, inspiring others, and doing what you love. Danielle encourages girls to stay active as an ambassador for Fast and Female, and she fights to protect the oceans she loves. She earned a BA in English and psychology from Dalhousie University. In storytelling, she hopes to continue inspiring girls with strong and diverse female heroines.

Shams Budhwani was born in Pakistan and moved to Vancouver, Canada, at age seventeen. As a writer exploring multiple genres, he mainly pursues topics relating to race, identity, culture, and religion in the wider Canadian context.

Barbara Carter lives on the White Rock hillside overlooking Semiah-moo Bay. She chose White Rock because of its thriving arts community. Born in Toronto, she has lived across Canada, from Nova Scotia through Quebec and Ontario, finally finding a home on the West Coast. She is a part of the extensive network of writers on the Semiahmoo Peninsula, and in addition to continuing to create poetry, she is presently collaborating on projects fusing poetry with the visual arts and jazz. Barbara is an arts advocate and educator. A mother, musician, lover of all things creative, and coddler of two little white dogs, she rises every day with anticipation and curiosity. She is never disappointed.

J. G. Chayko is a writer, actress, and international arthritis advocate. She started writing as a child, crafting poems for her great-grandmother, who always said she would be a writer. She has published poetry, fiction, and creative non-fiction and is the author of a popular blog called *The Old Lady in My Bones*, based on her experience living with rheumatoid arthritis. Her story and work have been featured in *Arthritis Digest* UK, *Health Central*, and *Pain Free Living Magazine*. She is a contributing writer to the book *Real Life Diaries: Living with Rheumatic Disease*. She is currently working on a novel.

Carly Daelli has been a writer since she received honourable mention in her hometown newspaper's writing contest in seventh grade. Since then, she has reported for numerous local newspapers around the U.S. She has also written for an international roller derby magazine under her derby name, Feist E. One. A high school swim coach, she loves working with young people from all backgrounds, which has led her to writing middle grade and young adult stories (when she's not writing swim practices). Born in Wisconsin and a Midwesterner at heart, Carly lives in Colorado with her husband and two daughters.

Jo Dawyd has been imagining love stories all her life. Everything from a stack of construction paper to her dad's fancy chess set to her sister's marbles—taken without asking!—became tools to play out the epic dramas of her invention. She began using words to form her stories and hasn't looked back. Her short story "Miss Gardiner's Birthday" was published in *Hot Apple Cider With Cinnamon: Stories of Finding Love in Unexpected Places* in 2015, and she has also had non-fiction articles published in *FellowScript*. She is currently writing her first novel.

Elisabeth de Grandpré is a writer and a youth-services library clerk. She lives in Montreal with her partner and cat. She has a BFA in theatre and a BA in liberal arts from Concordia University. Fangirling, she learned dialogue from repeated rewatches of shows by Joss Whedon and Amy Sherman-Palladino. When not writing, she is often reading widely, from Regency romances to young adult novels. She identifies as an introvert Slytherin with a Ravenclaw rising.

Maggie Derrick is a writer, artist, true-crime aficionado, and professional dog friend. She has published three novels on the platform Wattpad. The first of these, *The Star and the Ocean*, was one of fifty Watty Award winners in 2017 (out of over 280,000 entries worldwide). Writing predominantly works of fantasy, Maggie likes to tell stories about queer characters and magic. Her current project is a rewrite of "The Witch's Patron," a novel she originally drafted as part of NaNoWriMo in 2016. Maggie lives in Vancouver with her spouse, cat, and very bitey puppy.

James A. Duncan is Vancouver born and island raised, and didn't think any of his work was any good, let alone publishable. Mentored by Carrie Mac, James is now receiving the feedback he needs to further his great career. When he is not writing, he finds himself cycling, swimming, or watching something on Netflix. He wishes to thank P.D. JDS HS and his cohorts for their support and feedback.

Emelia Symington Fedy is the co-artistic director of The Chop, a theatre company based in the Coast Salish territories that tours its new works nationally and internationally to critical acclaim. Emelia also works for CBC Radio and is a guest lecturer at UBC in the new media studies program. She curates the popular website *Trying to Be Good* and facilitates workshops and retreats for womxn about the necessity of creativity. She is working on her first book, a memoir for teenage girls.

Lindsay Foran is an Ottawa-based writer, mother (to human and canine children), runner, and reader whose short fiction and poetry has been published in a number of journals. She keeps busy writing, mothering, and proving that work-life balance is a hoax meant to make mothers feel either permanently exhausted or eternally guilty. She is currently seeking representation for her debut novel, "Because of You."

Kerry Furukawa is a Jamaican who works as a teacher in Japan. She finds writing fiction exceedingly challenging but is currently working on her first collection of short stories. She blogs occasionally at *furukawakerry.com* for fun.

Melissa Garcia lives in Quesnel, B.C., where she spends her time writing from her small family-run farm. She was first published in 2018 in *The Old Veranda Swing*, an anthology of creative writing. "Liliana" will be her first published novel.

Samantha Gaston is a diligent cubicle dweller by day and an anguished writer by night. She has spent her time with the Writer's Studio working on her short stories and the elusive (some would say maddening) beginnings of a novel. Sam procrastinates writing by baking labour-intensive cakes or standing at the edge of seaside cliffs with a stoic expression on her face. She lives in her hometown of North Vancouver with her husband.

Kally Groat was born and raised in Hinton, Alberta, a place where—for better or worse—some would say she's never left, and some would say she's always leaving. She earned a BFA in creative writing at the University of Victoria and spent some years contemplating doing the work. Her first publication placed in Historica Canada's Indigenous Arts and Stories Contest; you can also find her writing in *SAD Mag*. Most of her stories centre around home and small towns and her Métis heritage, and almost always feature some sort of animal. If we're being honest, she would rather be fishing.

Robert Jay Groves is a second-generation Vancouverite and a proud father of two adult children. He holds a bachelor's degree in honours chemistry from UBC, and in 2015 he retired from a thirty-year career in the RCMP forensic laboratory. Rob is a first-time novelist who, with the help of TWS, is attempting to combine his knowledge of solving real-world crimes, his love of trivia and nostalgia, and his passion for reading mysteries into a publishable manuscript.

Cecil Hershler was born in South Africa and immigrated to Canada in 1974. He has told stories and acted in plays that explore the conflicts and tensions of that troubled yet beautiful African land, and his passion and support of the arts come out of this journey. In recent years, he has started writing poems and essays. One essay was made into a CBC Radio Outfront documentary and a second published by the *International Association for Near-Death Studies in Vital Signs* in 2014. He lives in Vancouver with his wife. They have four children and six grandchildren.

Tracey Hirsch spent 25 years in the corporate communications field, working in the energy, banking, technology, and telecommunication sectors before closing the book on that career in 2018. She joined the Writer's Studio at Simon Fraser University as the first step toward a new focus on creative writing. Could she do it? That was always her question. Born in Ottawa and raised in Calgary, Tracey moved to Vancouver in 1994, where she found her forever home on the West Coast. She has one husband, three sons, and one dog and is working on her first novel.

K Ho is a queer writer and feminist photographer living on unceded Coast Salish territories (Vancouver, B.C.). In their work, K explores issues of race, power, sexuality, repression, and guilt. They are currently writing a novel of literary fiction that examines the reverberations of a homophobic event in the lives of four Chinese Canadian protagonists. K's photography, found at *photosbykho.com*, centres the visibility of queer and trans BIPOC (Black/Indigenous/people of colour). At parties, you can find K hiding in the bathroom in a moderate way.

R. D. Hughes. Englishman. Newly minted Canadian. Self-proclaimed author. A fiction writer dabbling in fantasy, science fiction, young adult, horror, and many more. Inspired by the heroic epics of many authors, combined with his talent of world-building. R. D. Hughes aims to create vivid and exciting worlds for the current and future generations to come.

Ashley Hynd is a poet with mixed ancestry who lives on the Haldimand Tract and respects the Attawandaron, Anishnawbe, and Haudenosaunee relationships with the land. As it is for many people with mixed heritage, the knowledge of her history is unclear. Her writing grapples with the erasure of her history and is as much an act of reclamation as it is a call for accountability for what has been lost. Ashley was longlisted for the CBC Poetry Prize, shortlisted for *Arc* Poem of the Year, and won the Pacific Spirit Poetry Prize.

Kim June Johnson is a singer-songwriter and writer living on Hornby Island, where she runs a small-batch granola stand, teaches yoga, and shares a drafty old house with her two darling daughters, two self-important cats, and one angelic Bernese mountain dog. As a performer, her live shows often combine songs with storytelling and read-aloud poetry. Her writing has appeared in print in *Room* and *Contemporary Verse 2* and online at *Literary Mama*. She is currently working on a young adult novel and a memoir about leaving her fundamentalist Christian faith.

Yong Nan Kim left her native Korea for Paraguay and later Brazil at age ten. She has worked as an interpreter/translator and taught linguistics, translation, and interpretation in the U.S. and Vancouver, B.C. She's currently writing a coming-of-age memoir, "My Year Without Books." Her stories and poems are about a Korean child's immigrant experiences in Paraguay and Brazil in the 1970s and 1980s. She also writes children's stories, folktales, and ghost stories for her daughter and seven nieces and nephews. When not reading while walking, Yong likes snowshoeing, hiking, and learning new dance moves.

Madeleine Lamphier has spent the past eighteen years as a firefighter, thirteen of those as a mother, and has recently taken a position as a training officer, where she molds unwitting young men into feminists. She enjoys meditating, dancing, and most forms of escapism. Madeleine lives in Tsawwassen with her husband, two daughters, and their handsome but fantastically stupid dog.

Tamara Lee is a writer and editor from Vancouver, B.C. She enjoys writing in a variety of genres, especially fiction and creative non-fiction. Her short stories have been published online and anthologized in several small-press publications, including *Where's My Tiara?* (Ideate, 2017). Her non-fiction has appeared in the *Globe and Mail*, the *Montreal Review*, and *The Establishment*. Currently completing a novel-length manuscript entitled "Scaling the Levels," she is also working on a collection of short stories. "This Close" is part of that collection.

Jessica Lemes da Silva lives with her wife and daughter on the unceded territories of the Musqueam, Squamish, and Tsleil-Waututh First Nations (Vancouver, B.C.). She is originally from Miami, Florida, raised by Brazilian and Portuguese immigrants. Growing up with a grandmother more Catholic than the pope, her writing explores themes of belonging, living truths, families (chosen and otherwise), and bridging the worlds of queerness and religion. Jessica has worked in sound design at Skywalker Sound and now teaches elementary music in Vancouver's public schools. When she's not teaching, you can find her writing at the local coffee shop.

Catherine Lewis is a Chinese Canadian writer born in Hong Kong and raised in Scarborough, Ontario, and in North Vancouver, B.C. After completing a UBC BSc in genetics and a postgraduate diploma in IT, she has worked as a software engineer ever since. In recent years, she has revived her dormant love for writing, finally enrolling at the Writer's Studio to develop her craft and to turn her musings into literature. As a writer of non-fiction, in prose and poetic form, Catherine is working on memoir projects and a poetry collection. In her spare time, she enjoys attending dance class.

S. Sloan MacLeod is—allegedly—a Vancouver-based multidisciplinary artist, but she aspires to one day transcend time and space to become a metaphysical being. She enjoys piña coladas, getting caught in the rain, and writing obtuse bios.

Kelly-Anne Maddox is a creative non-fiction writer living in Ottawa. Her essays have appeared in *Blank Spaces* and *Cleaning Up Glitter: A Literary Journal*. She has contributed to the *Local Tourist Ottawa* blog and previously wrote a monthly satire column for *Off-Centre Magazine*. She holds a PhD in French literature and is currently working on a memoir about the year in which she grew a new life as her mother's came to an end.

Jacqueline Mastin is originally from Edmonton, Alberta, where she completed a BA in creative writing and Spanish literature. She relocated to the West Coast in 2009 to pursue a career in animal welfare, and later went on to study English literature and editing. "Bone & Earth" is the opening story in a collection she has had the opportunity to put together in the Writer's Studio Online. "Telling Lives," another story she workshopped this year, received an honourable mention in *The Fiddlehead*'s 28th annual literary contest and was published in the spring 2019 issue. Jacqueline lives, reads, and writes in Vancouver.

Michael Aaron Mayes was born and raised in Calgary, Alberta. After graduating from McGill University with a business degree and an inexplicable love of writing, he began his career as an advertising writer. Since then, he worked as a writer and creative director at various advertising agencies before going rogue as a freelancer to spend more time writing longer stories. Michael currently lives just outside Vancouver in Squamish, B.C., where the mountains are nearby and the snow is only occasional.

Karen McCall lives in Toronto and is a part-time facilitator for creative writing workshops at Anishnawbe Health. She is a member of the Toronto Writers Collective. Karen recently graduated from Ryerson University with a degree in journalism after more than 25 years in corporate communications. She was a copy editor at the *Ryerson Review of Journalism* in 2017, where she also published several features and docupoetry. The Writer's Studio is Karen's first venture in writing creative non-fiction. She is working on a coming-of-age memoir about growing up in Toronto as a hippie in the 1960s.

Rowan McCandless is a storyteller, thrift-store enthusiast, and chai-tea lover, writing from Manitoba's Treaty 1 territory. Longlisted for the *Journey Prize Stories 30*, her fiction and creative non-fiction have won awards, most recently the 2018 Constance Rooke Creative Nonfiction Prize. Her work has appeared in literary journals such as *The Fiddlehead*, the *Malahat Review*, *Prairie Fire*, *Room*, and *Skin Deep: Race and Culture Magazine* (Great Britain), and in the anthology *Black Writers Matter*. She is currently completing a short story collection and a hybrid memoir-in-essay. Discover more at *rowanmccandless.com*. Follow her on Twitter @rowanmccandless.

Isobel McDonald lives in the unceded territory of the K'ómoks First Nation on wild, magical Vancouver Island. Many years ago at Hollyhock, she was anointed as a Green Witch by the famous herbalist Susun Weed. Her Green Ally is Salmonberry. When not writing stories featuring witches, she works on crime fiction and is an enthusiastic member of Sisters in Crime, Western Canada.

Sam Milbrath is an author and copywriter living in Vancouver, B.C. She studied science, nature, and art history at the University of Victoria and blends her love of these topics in her writing. Sam is writing a young-adult fantasy trilogy in which her heroine, Luna, goes on an epic adventure of self-discovery in the watery depths of a climate-change-stricken Pacific Ocean. "The Tail of the Lake Monster" is a spin-off of her work-in-progress prologue of book two in her trilogy.

Brynn Morgan is a young writer living in Maple Ridge, B.C. She is currently working on her first novel, a young adult fantasy, which has been at the back of her mind for years. If she isn't writing, she's either sketching out her characters or playing with her two dogs.

Isabella Mori writes poetry, novels, short stories, and non-fiction and has published two books of and about poetry, *A bagful of haiku—87 imperfections* and *isabella mori's teatable book*. She has published and blogged over a thousand articles online, has won the 2018 Cecilia Lamont First Prize in poetry, and is the founder of Muriel's Journey Poetry Prize. She grew up in Germany in an artists' household and has lived in South America. A contributor to and editor of *Family Connections*, a newsletter on mental health and addiction, Isabella has a master's degree in education and works in the mental health/addiction field.

Emma Murphy is a versatile writer, concocting anything from search-engine-optimized blog articles to song lyrics, but she has a passion for crafting speculative fiction narratives. It all started when she was too small to reach the keyboard and relied on dictation to type out her first "proper" story at the age of five. She loves exposing herself to different story mediums, such as video games and music, and thinking critically and creatively about the material. A Surrey native, she works as a freelance story consultant for several online productions and has connections all over the globe.

Zofia Rose Musiej is a Polish–Carrier First Nations interdisciplinary artist who lives and performs music and poetry in the unceded territories of the Musqueam, Squamish, and Tsleil-Waututh nations. She is a slave to the muse, loves to busk in East Van, and is currently working on two manuscripts (poetry and creative non-fiction) and an EP.

B. D. Neufeld is a Canadian writer and visual artist, born and raised on the prairies of Manitoba. She previously studied poetry under Dr. Scott Thurston and Dr. Harriet Tarlo at the Ted Hughes Arvon Centre, Lumb Bank. Her photography was previously published in *Meat for Tea: The Valley Review*.

Ingrid Olauson is the author of the poetry chapbook *Pragmatics*. Her criticism and poetry has appeared in *Charcuterie*, the *Bartleby Review*, and *Issue Magazine*, and her catalogue essay for the exhibition *What's Her Problem*, on L.A.-based video artist Michele O'Marah, was published by Art Speak in September 2017. In 2015, she wrote and directed the play *Fort Eff*, which was performed at Deep Blue in Vancouver. Ingrid attended Emily Carr University of Art and Design from 2010 to 2015 and lives in Vancouver, B.C. with her fiancé and two dogs.

df parizeau is a multi-disciplinary writer who ties his shoes "bunny-ears" style and still has all of his wisdom teeth. Experimenting with several different forms and praxes, you are more likely to find him eavesdropping than working on his craft. Despite his aptitude for procrastination, df's work has been featured online and in print by publications such as *Sea to Sky Review*, *Lyre Magazine*, *w49 Magazine*, and *Thin Air Magazine*, the latter of which earned him a Pushcart Prize nomination for poetry in 2018.

Jeff Pitcher is the artistic director of Theatre Newfoundland Labrador and the author of over fifteen professionally produced plays, including the *Ed & Ed Trilogy*, *The Known Soldier*, *Elvis & Mavis*, and *17 Men*, along with adaptations of *A Christmas Carol*, *Peter Pan*, and *Robin Hood*. He currently splits his time between writing in Vancouver and working with Theatre Newfoundland Labrador.

Karen Poirier, author of "One Thousand Days," has been writing for ten years. Although a work of fiction, it was inspired by stories about her father, who was captured in the Dieppe raid then imprisoned in a POW camp in 1942. Her writing credits include two books, *Across a Prairie Sky* and *Ronald and Donald*. She lives with her husband in the Alberni Valley. She is an elected member of the Society of Canadian Artists and an associate signature member of the Federation of Canadian Artists.

Kathryn Robbins-Pierce is a first-generation Canadian of British ancestry, born and raised in Manitoba in three diverse settings: Fort Churchill Military Base on Hudson Bay in the Interlake district, a farm near Teulon, and Winnipeg. She has had a varied career, including teaching ESL and family counselling at Vancouver Community College and clinical social work in mental health with Fraser Health, as well as private practice. She has resided in the Lower Mainland since 1977. She is a past editor of the *Barnacle*, the newsletter of the Barnet Sailing Co-op. She aspires to write a self-help memoir.

Montana Rogers is a writer and ESL educator from the United States. In 2014, she was awarded a Fulbright ETA Grant that took her to the beautiful country of Bulgaria to teach English for two years. She has contributed articles to *NewEngland* and other online publications. Her fiction has appeared in *gravel: A Literary Journal* and *The Sea Letter*. She is currently at work on her first novel.

Hailey Rollheiser is a writer in Vancouver, B.C. She completed a BA in English literature at the University of British Columbia in 2017. Her work is forthcoming or has appeared in *The Rumpus*, *SAD Mag*, and *Daily Hive*. She writes non-fiction as well as young adult fiction, and her work often explores themes of feminism, sexuality, and power dynamics. She also works as a special-needs assistant and is originally from Chilliwack, B.C.

Japhy Ryder comes to creative writing from a journalism background and is now working on his second novel, "Glitterball." Inspired by sources as diverse as Ovid, David Bowie, and Patanjali's Yoga Sutras, the book follows the author on a journey of recovery from addiction and bi-polar disorder. Japhy also exhibits hallucinogenic photo-based artworks that capture the emotional states accompanying his explorations of the B.C. interior, and performs his own sassy brand of rock-and-roll with the Vancouver-based band Kings of Kavorka.

Jane Shi is a queer Chinese settler living on the unceded, traditional, and ancestral territories of the Musqueam, Squamish, and Tsleil-Wau-tuth First Nations. Her essays and poems have appeared in *GUTS*, *Loose-Leaf*, *Poetry is Dead*, *PRISM*, *Room*, and *Thirteen: New Collected Poems from LGBTQI2S Writers in Canada*, among others. She wants to live in a world where love is not a limited resource, land is not mined, hearts are not filched, and bodies are not violated. Her dumplings can be found on Twitter @pipagaopoetry.

Kadee Wirick Smedley is a lifelong storyteller who weaves faith and humour into her true-life tales. Now recovering from a decade of pastoral ministry, Kadee is a regular contributor at the *Wisdom Daily*, an online Jewish magazine. When she isn't writing, Kadee officiates weddings; troops about with her large, loud family; and drinks in the written word like water. She lives in Vancouver, B.C., with her husband, four kids, and their remarkable cat.

Jordan Smith lives a sometimes tortured existence on a small, mythical island in Alt'kitsem. He is known as the local placemaker. Mr. Smith can often be found swearing and shaking his fist at the sky. He is learning to speak again, one word at a time.

Janet Southcott enjoys writing about curious characters and dubious situations. Living on the west coast of Canada, her imagination runs wild. Writing groups, workshopping, and critiquing have played a role in strengthening her eye for details, helping with her latest endeavour, a 95,000-word thriller, "Interruption." She has edited short stories, journalistic articles, and websites and written reports, newsletters, and opinion pieces. But her love is fiction, where boundaries of length and topic are endless and her characters grow with every word.

Born and raised in Manila, **Steffi Tad-y** lives in Vancouver.

Terri Taylor is a Vancouver-based creative non-fiction writer who can often be found in a cozy corner of her favourite café completing her spiritual memoir, "Transcending Forgiveness: Healing Beyond Betrayal." She teaches Archetypes and Sacred Contracts and has studied intensively with many teachers such as Deepak Chopra and Caroline Myss. She has also completed a two-year Art of Spiritual Guidance program with Atum O'Kane and continues to study advanced spiritual guidance classes. A regular host of mediation groups, Terri also hosts two metaphysical book clubs. You can find her online at *optimistical.wordpress.com*.

Varsha Tiwary considers writing an essential tool to authentic and engaged life. She had always written, but without understanding the craft of it. She is grateful that over the last year she had opportunity to learn the craft and be a part of a vibrant, generous community. She dreads a returning to her day job, lest she lose her writing. Varsha's short stories, memoirs, and essays have appeared in *DNA-Out of Print* (short fiction shortlist, 2017), *Kitaab, Basil O'Flaherty, Muse India, Jaggery-lit, Manifest-station,* and *Spark, Usawa, Café Dissensus,* and *Kaani.* Her pieces are forthcoming in *Gargoyle* magazine and *Shenandoah.*

Elizabeth Toman writes short fiction and essays. She lives and practises medicine near Albuquerque, New Mexico.

Alli Vail is a writer living in Vancouver. She has been a fashion blogger, a copy editor for a New York–based graffiti magazine, and an award-winning journalist and editor. She is working on several fiction and non-fiction projects.

Deborah Vieyra has been trying to quit writing for years. Whether the Writer's Studio will be her treatment centre or her drug supplier remains to be seen. She holds a BA in theatre and performance from the University of Cape Town and an MA in applied theatre arts from the University of Southern California, the latter of which was made possible by the good people that administer Fulbright scholarships. Deborah has also published bits and pieces here and there and, if unable to stop giving in to her unmanageable compulsions, might hope to do more of this.

Melanie L. Walker writes creative non-fiction and plays and is currently working on short memoir pieces. She works as an administrator in the performing arts in Vancouver. Growing up in the suburbs and in rural coastal British Columbia, she's lived as both a blonde settler and an inheritor of mental illness and trauma. Melanie believes in the power of pollinators and hopes to die in a field of sunflowers.

Janna Walsh writes poetry and creative non-fiction, both influenced by her travels to more than three dozen countries. She is particularly fascinated by places that offer an experience of two worlds connecting in a profoundly spiritual way. She has been writing since childhood and was first published in a poetry anthology at Indiana University at age sixteen. She has since published educational reports, newspaper editorials, and in anthologies, most recently in *Write On Downtown* and *Our Community*, journals of Arizona State University. Janna is currently working on a chapbook, *Thin Places*, poems capturing a look at places where travel may soften our boundaries.

Martha Warren is a writer and poet. Her subjects have ranged from fairy stories to aspects of law. Born in Vancouver, she returned from Europe twenty years ago to raise her two children, and lives on the North Shore. What she enjoys most about TWS is the sense of community, and the momentum the program gives her to keep writing.

Jacqueline Willcocks is a writer and a poet originally from Calgary, Alberta. After a particularly nasty flu in 2018, she decided to do the thing that has been scribbled in journals for over a decade: go back to school and be a writer. After gallivanting as a dancer, mother, and yoga teacher for almost two decades, she plucked up the courage to nurture the nagging desire that has been with her since she read "Old MacDonald Had a Farm" to the class in kindergarten. To tell her story, in her own words, from her true voice. She is incredibly grateful to have landed in the Writer's Studio with artists and teachers who deeply inspire her.

Rupa Wood grew up in London, England, with a garden full of rabbits. Her writing explores the philosophy of commonplace magic.

Production Credits

Publisher
Andrew Chesham

Managing Editor
Emily Stringer

Production Coordinator
Laura Farina

Section Editors
Sylvia Symons – Poetry and Lyric
  Prose
Rebecca A. Coates – Speculative
  and Young Adult Fiction
Christina Myers – Non-fiction
Alessia Yaworsky – Fiction

Production Team
Reese Kim Carrozzini –
  Production Editor
Maggie Derrick
Kiran Dhanoa
Samantha Gaston
Tamara Lee

Copy Editors
Elizabeth Armerding
James A. Duncan
Catherine Lewis
Kally Groat
S. Sloan MacLeod
Sam Milbrath
Zofia Rose Musiej
Kathryn Robbins-Pierce
Kadee Wirick Smedley
Jordan Smith

Acknowledgments

The students of the Writer's Studio would like to thank their mentors for the guidance and insight they have provided. We would also like to extend special thanks to the mentor apprentices for their support throughout the year.

We extend our gratitude to Hood 29 (4770 Main Street) for graciously hosting our monthly reading series.

Thanks to Yosef Wosk for his generous support, which helps us bring alumni and students together for the production of this anthology, strengthening our community.

Thanks to John Whatley and SFU Publications. We're grateful for their support, guidance, and continued belief in the importance of *emerge* and the writing it publishes.

Joanne Betzler and Grant Smith's continued support of our program and the anthology has allowed us to make the *emerge* book launch a fun and lively event.

We would all like to thank Vancouver's local independent bookstores for selling *emerge*. We urge our readers to support the booksellers that support local writers.

Artist's statement

Karen Poirier

FEATHERS

Recently I've collected various feathers. Why? As an artist, always searching for inspiration in the language of lines, shapes, and patterns in nature, I am struck by the beauty of something so organically ordinary. As in a good painting, the feathers are perfectly balanced: delicate and strong. Both are necessary for flight.

I've always thought that an image should suggest a story or emotion, as well as satisfy the elements of good composition. In this drawing, even the shadows play a role. This particular piece was created with charcoal, a medium that can portray both softness and dramatic darks. It has been my great pleasure to be a part of the TWS program this year and I'm honoured my work was selected for the cover of *emerge 19*.

Elzevir A*a* Q*q* R*r*

The interior of *emerge* is set in DTL Elzevir. Originally created in the 1660s, Elzevir is a baroque typeface, cut by Christoffel van Dijck in Amsterdam. As noted in Robert Bringhurst's *The Elements of Typographic Style*, baroque typography thrived in the seventeenth century and is known for its axis variations from one letter to the next. During this time, typographers started mixing roman and *italic on the same line*. The Dutch Type Library created a digital version in 1993 called DTL Elzevir. It retains some of the weight that Monotype Van Dijck, an earlier digital version, possessed in metal but had lost in its digital translation.

The interior of *emerge* is printed on Rolland paper, produced by Rolland Inc, Canada. The cover for *emerge* uses Kalima CIS paper, made by Tembec Inc, Canada. Both papers are Forestry Stewardship Council (FSC) and Sustainable Forestry Initiative (SFI) Certified, and are acid free/elemental chlorine free.